# BLOOD NINJA II

Also by Nick Lake

# BLOOD NINJA

# Blood Ninja II

## The Revenge of Lord Oda

### NICK LAKE

SIMON & SCHUSTER BFYR

New York   London   Toronto   Sydney

SIMON & SCHUSTER BFYR

An imprint of Simon & Schuster Children's Publishing Division

1230 Avenue of the Americas, New York, New York 10020

SIMON & SCHUSTER BFYR is a trademark of Simon & Schuster, Inc.

For information about special discounts for bulk purchases, please contact Simon
& Schuster Special Sales at 1-866-506-1949 or business@simonandschuster.com.

The Simon & Schuster Speakers Bureau can bring authors to your live event. For more
information or to book an event, contact the Simon & Schuster Speakers Bureau at
1-866-248-3049 or visit our website at www.simonspeakers.com.

Book design by Krista Vossen

The text for this book is set in ITC Esprit.

Manufactured in the United States of America

10 9 8 7 6 5 4 3 2 1

Library of Congress Cataloging-in-Publication Data

Lake, Nick.

Blood ninja II : the revenge of Lord Oda / Nick Lake. — 1st ed.

p. cm.

Summary: In sixteenth-century Japan, Taro, a vampire like all ninja warriors, tries to
protect his mother and defeat the power-hungry Lord Oda, who he believed was dead.

ISBN 978-1-4169-8629-4 (hardcover)

[1. Ninja—Fiction. 2. Vampires—Fiction. 3. Japan—History—Period of civil wars, 1480–
1603—Fiction.] I. Title. II. Title: Blood ninja two.

III. Title: Revenge of Lord Oda.

PZ7.L15857Bm 2010

[Fic]—dc22

2010010110

ISBN 978-1-4424-1185-2 (eBook)

FIRST
EDITION

For my mother.
Thank you for teaching me to read at such an early age.

# BLOOD NINJA II

THE PORTUGUESE PORT TOWN OF NAGASAKI, JAPAN,

1566

*It was night.*

*It always had to be night.*

*The blind man traced his fingertips along the wooden wall of the warehouse, inching his way toward the door. He could smell the sea now, a sharp tang of seaweed and brine everywhere around him, as if the ocean were extending its fiefdom into the very air. It was raining heavily—the blind man could hear the drops pattering on the water, to his left.*

*The warehouse was longer than he had expected. It seemed he had been walking its length all evening. But then it had to be large. This was where the* nanban—*the barbarians from the south—stored the goods they brought over from China in their enormous, fat-bellied ships: silk, silver, china tableware.*

*And guns.*

*"What do you see?" he asked the boy, Jun, who was walking before him.*

*"There is a barbarian ship at anchor. The lamp on the tallest mast is lit, but I can't see any sailors."*

"Good. And the warehouse door?"

"Ahead, I think. There's a patch of darker shadow."

The blind man nodded. "Lead me."

Jun took his hand—the blind man felt him shiver at the contact with the scarred, rough flesh—and the boy pulled him gently forward. They walked quietly, cloth slippers on their feet. The shadows concealed them from sight, and the pattering of the rain deadened the soft sound of their passing.

A perfect night for their work.

Jun stopped, and the blind man reached out in front of him, running his hands over the door, its hinges, its metal handle in the barbarian style. Then he frowned. Where the door should have met the jamb, there was a narrow space—a vertical fissure running parallel to the wall.

The door was open.

The blind man held his breath, while motioning for Jun to stay still. Between himself and the boy, they had set up everything— learning when the sailors would be drinking belowdecks, bribing the guard to meet them here at the side entrance to the warehouse. Then the blind man would knock him unconscious, and take the guns before they could be smuggled up-country and into the possession of one of the wrong lords.

"Open the door very slowly," he whispered to Jun. "Tell me what you see."

There was a light creaking sound. "A table," said Jun, under his breath. "There's a kind of red meat on a plate, half-eaten. And a glass of blood."

"Beef and wine," said the blind man. "Not blood." He knew that the barbarians ate cow, which they called waca, after the Portuguese name for that gentle animal, and that they drank a red alcohol made from grapes. He'd also heard that they drank this wine in their churches, saying that it was the blood of their god, though he was not sure whether this was only one of the more hysterical rumors about the worshippers of kirishta.

"Anything else?" he whispered.

"Next to the table is a long case on the ground. It has been smashed open."

"Is there anything inside?"

"No. It's empty. And there's—" An intake of breath. "There's something on the ground. It could be wine, or . . ."

Blood.

He heard Jun stoop and pick something up from the floor. Then a heavy, cold object was placed in his hands. He turned it over, seeing it with his touch. A long bar, with two prongs jutting from either side.

A cross.

The blind man had seen these things, before his eyes were burned out. The kirishitan barbarians worshipped the symbol, saying that it was on such a cross that their god was nailed to die. The blind man thought it was strange to kneel down before the thing that killed your god—but he supposed that if you could eat the flesh of the cow, which the Buddha had declared holy, and you could drink blood in your churches, then celebrating your god's death was nothing.

Not that he could reproach them, of course, when it came to drinking blood.

The blind man slipped the cross into a pocket sewed inside his kimono. There was a chain attached to the upper end of it, and he supposed that it had until recently hung around someone's neck. The guard's, perhaps. Something had happened here, and now the guns were almost certainly gone.

He cursed quietly. "We should go," he whispered to Jun. Someone else had heard about the guns, it seemed. Someone had come and killed the guard, or taken him away, and then they had stolen the precious merchandise.

He was irritated, but not surprised. As soon as he himself had heard the rumor, he had made his way south. The Portuguese had brought a new kind of gun in their latest shipment, it was said—one that used a spark created by a wheel of metal to ignite the powder, not a fuse, and could consequently be fired reliably in the rain. The blind man knew that many of the daimyo already had guns—Lord Oda was said to have constructed thousands of them on the original Portuguese model, and even trained regiments of his samurai to use them in battle. But they were long as spears, unwieldy, and made useless if the weather was wet.

The blind man had fought battles before and was familiar with the violent simplicity of the art of war. To possess weapons that could be disabled by the weather was not a good strategy. But to be the only one with weapons unaffected by the elements? That was worth killing for.

As he followed Jun back the way they had come, his fingertips stroking the wooden wall, he wondered who could have done it, who could have gotten there before him. Oda was dead—killed in his own tower. It could have been Sumitada, perhaps, who had converted to the kirishitan religion and called himself Bartoromeo now. It was Sumitada who had given Nagasaki to the barbarians, receiving in return the first choice of silk, which had not been seen in Japan since the Chinese stopped sending it direct, protesting against the Japanese wako pirates who preyed on their ships.

But the blind man had some experience with the missionaries who ran the Portuguese port, and he knew they were not fools. They needed Sumitada for their port, but they knew he was not important to the country's future—he was little more than a leaf, floating on a pool, and the ripples that moved that leaf were the powerful lords like Tokugawa.

Besides, Sumitada was a coward, not a strategist. He had become a laughingstock among the samurai for his conversion, and was hated by the peasants in his dominion. The blind man had even heard that once, Sumitada-Bartoromeo was walking in the countryside, when he came upon a shrine to a local cockerel spirit, adorned with a statue. He had smashed the statue, screaming blasphemous imprecations against the Shinto gods, talking madly of idols, and if he had been any less than a daimyo he would have been cut down where he stood for his disrespect.

Daimyo or not, the blind man didn't think Sumitada would make it through another year.

There was a change in the sound of the rainfall, and the blind man realized that Jun had stopped. He heard footsteps, coming toward them from behind.

Many footsteps, moving fast.

"Who is it?" he said, as the footsteps surrounded them.

"Barbarians," said Jun. His voice was quavering, nervous. "They have tattoos on their arms, and they are carrying daggers."

"Sailors?" the blind man asked.

"I don't know. They are tall and white and have green and blue eyes, like cats."

Portuguese, *thought the blind man.*

The blind man heard one of the men—he was just in front, to the right—say, in heavily accented Japanese, "Stop, thieves."

The blind man held up his empty hands. "We have stolen nothing."

The man—the blind man guessed he was the leader, perhaps even the captain of the ship—took a step forward. "Our guard is gone. Our guns are gone. And you are here."

The blind man backed up against the wall. "We can settle this like—"

"No. We settle this with your deaths." There was the sound of weapons being raised, and Jun screamed as the men closed in on them.

The blind man was not yet old, and he feared death. But he was here of his own will—the boy was here because he was paid. He gripped Jun's arms and pulled him against the wall, turning his own body to cover him. Then—and in the same heartbeat—he formed his hand into the karana *mudra for expelling demons, the index and little fingers extended, which was a weapon disguised as a tool for meditation. He struck at the boy's neck with his hardened fingers, finding the pressure point that would put him out for an incense stick, at least. The boy slumped to the ground. Good. Better that he lie there, unharmed.*

The blind man felt the souls of all the men he had killed crowding around him, as if they had returned as hungry ghosts from the realm of annoyo *to weigh him down, to cling to him like pale parasites. He had lived a long time, and in the last month he had promised himself that soon he would retire from the world, enter a monastery, and kill no more men.*

*But not just yet.*

*Yes, the blind man feared death. He had made so much of it, sent so many men to Amida Buddha, that if he was lucky he would be reincarnated on four legs, and if he was not, he would spend his next lifetime being boiled in a pot, the souls of his victims feeding insatiably on his being, for the dead are always hungry.*

*And now he would be forced to make more.*

*As if he were holding a magnifying glass to a scroll, he brought the world into focus, centering his qi. He could hear every raindrop, and he knew where they hit the ground, and where they were prevented from doing so by the bodies of men. Then there was the smell of them. A blend of sweat, sea salt, and rum—and underneath all that, the iron scent of blood. The blind man had heard that when Lord Oda lost the use of his right arm, he learned to wield his sword in his left, compensating for his loss. Something similar had happened to the blind man, his sense of smell becoming so acute that he could almost see these barbarian sailors, glowing in the dark around him like skeletal assemblages of red tubing, pulsing, pulsing with fresh blood.*

*He felt the first man move toward him, swinging something in his hand—he could hear the* whum, whum, whum *it made as it rotated. It could have been a sword, or it could have been a rope.*

*It didn't matter.*

*He heard the man sidestep to hit him with the thing that sang in the air, and he felt pity. These men were corpses, and they didn't even know it. The blind man ducked, turned, struck out with his heel. The barbarian dropped to one knee—it made a* crack *sound against the stone—and cried out, but the sound was cut off as the blind man drew his concealed blade and let it leap for the man's throat.*

*Another one approached him from behind, the rain pattering on his head as loud as temple bells, and the blind man threw his left hand back while his sword impaled another man before him. The fingers of his rear hand struck the same spot he had aimed for on the boy, though this time he did it harder. The man behind fell, as the one in* front screamed, trying to pull himself off the blind man's sword. With a twitch of his wrist, the blind man withdrew the blade, thrusting it up and to the side in the same movement, cutting another's throat.

The other men had a better idea of what they were dealing with now, and two of them came at him from either side, throwing out their arms to try to contain him. But they would sooner catch one of the raindrops that gave them away; they would more easily spear the very wind. He moved back, so quick it made the attackers' movements seem exaggerated, as if they were moving through a different medium—they were creatures of liquid, and he was a creature of the air.

They were still bringing their arms together, still believing he was there, when he gutted them. Now three men attacked him at once, and he was forced to adapt his tactics. He brought his foot up, hard, between the first man's legs, while striking behind him with his sword, and simultaneously driving his left palm up to smash the middle sailor's nose. Fighting fair might be the best way to accumulate good karma, but as far as this realm of samsara went, it was also the best way to get yourself killed. Without pausing, he followed his punch with a dose of steel to the gut, then stepped forward. The man he had kicked in the groin was still doubled over, and it was the work of a child to behead him.

The blind man heard curses, presumably Portuguese. He was no longer thinking now, but was lost in a type of Zen meditation, where the question of what belonged to his body and what was outside of it became meaningless. He was the rain, and the wind, and the stone below his feet.

A very faint voice at the back of his mind told him this fight was unfair, but he knew that there was no fairness in fighting—only the dead, and the living.

He was living. Everyone else was dead.

He avoided a blow from an irrelevant weapon, dimly hearing the whap as it sliced the air where he had been standing a moment before, and then he brought his sword up to eviscerate the barbarian. The man screamed, shocked, as if this were not to be expected. The blind man sighed inwardly. As soon as these men had stepped onto the quay, they had been dead. Better that they accept it—otherwise they would not believe they were in *annoyo, and their reincarnation would be hard on them.*

Amida Buddha, *he called out silently, as he leaped toward the last of them.* I call on you and on all good karma to assist these souls in their journey. *With hands of iron, he snapped the man's wrist, hearing his dagger clang on the stone. Then he gripped the man's head and angled his mouth to bite his neck, feeling the blood flow into him, making him stronger.*

*He drank deep.*

*Breathing hard, letting the body of the barbarian fall to the ground, the blind man slowly sheathed his sword—it slid into a scabbard that lay snug against his side, under his robe. He was turning to the boy when there came a metallic scraping sound from toward the sea. He froze. From the other side, by the warehouse wall, came another. Then another, from the left. And the right.*

*Slowly he turned full circle, listening to the rain. A dozen men, at least, were encircling him, keeping a safe distance. He concentrated. Each of them held something out in front of him—something long and hard.*

*Guns.*

"It's raining," *he said, conversationally.* "If your guns don't fire, you will have to engage me hand to hand. And then you will die." *He said this with resignation, not pride.*

"No," *said one of the men, his accent that of the samurai class. These men were Japanese.* "These guns are new."

"They fire—," *began another of the men.*

"With a spark," *said the blind man, nodding.* Of course. Perhaps it was finally time to face the afterlife, and see what torments awaited him there.

"Father Valignano said there was a ninja in town," *said another voice, and it was a voice the blind man knew well. Oh, so very well.* "He didn't say you were blind. Before we kill you, I would like you to tell me what you know about these guns. Where did you hear of them? Do you know of my plans for them?"

The blind man didn't answer, only lowered his hands to his sides. "My lord," he said, kneeling on the cold, wet stone.

There was a grunt of surprise from the darkness that was all he would ever see. "You know me?" said Lord Tokugawa Ieyasu.

"Of course," said the blind man. "I have served you long enough."

Lord Tokugawa took a step forward—the blind man could hear, from the pattern of the rain's pattering, that he wore his full samurai regalia, the horned helmet included. The blind man wondered, in a distant corner of his mind, why Sumitada had allowed Lord Tokugawa to come here. He must have thrown in his lot with the most powerful daimyo, the blind man supposed, now that Oda was dead.

"Shusaku?" said Lord Tokugawa.

THE NINJA MOUNTAIN, SOMEWHERE ON NORTHERN

HONSHU ISLAND, THE SAME DAY

*Watashi wa . . . hiragana o . . . yomu koto ga dekimas . . .*

Taro traced his finger along the line of symbols, speaking the sounds out loud. "I . . . can read . . . hiragana."

"You can," said Hana, smiling.

Taro grinned. For now, it was only the hiragana that he had mastered—the simplified form of writing that was used mainly by women. But now that he had learned these forms, he would be able to progress to the kanji, and eventually be able to read and write the language of the nobles. Hana had already showed him the character for the word "field," and he could see how it showed a field from above, subdivided into sections, and he marveled at how the Chinese had created tiny, perfect pictures of the things around them, to make them into words.

"Now," said Hana, "you owe me some sword practice." The previous autumn, Taro had fought against Hana's father, Lord Oda, a sword saint whose skill with the blade was feared and admired throughout the land. Taro had held his own—and in the end the cruel Lord Oda had died, falling down the stairs of his own castle. Since then, Taro's mastery of the sword had only increased, to the point that even here, at the mountain stronghold of the ninjas, there was no one who could teach him anything new.

"Well, if you want to be beaten again . . ." From beside the writing table, Taro pulled out his *katana*. It had been given to him on his return to the mountain, a gift to celebrate his victory over Lord Oda. As a ninja, he would use a short-sword called a *wakizashi* for most missions, but there was nothing to compare to fighting with the full-length sword.

That was if he remained a ninja, of course. Taro was no longer sure what he should do, now that his mentor Shusaku was dead. It had been Shusaku who had always known what to do, Shusaku who had saved Taro's life and then led him and his best friend Hiro through every subsequent trial. Taro knew that he couldn't stay here on this mountain forever, pretending that the world outside no longer existed. But what could he do? He didn't know if he could go to Lord Tokugawa and present himself as the daimyo's long-lost son—Shusaku had said that the lord would be horrified to have a vampire for a child. Of course, Lord Tokugawa's other sons were dead now, so perhaps he would welcome Taro, no matter what had happened to him—but it was an enormous risk to take.

Neither could he go and look for his mother, though he was desperate to do so. On the night when he and Shusaku left his home village of Shirahama, Shusaku had given her a pigeon, telling her to set it free with a message when she was safe. But the pigeon had still not arrived at the ninja mountain—it had been the first thing Taro asked when he returned here from Lord Oda's castle. So he was trapped at the mountain. He couldn't leave, because if he did he might miss her message when it came. At the same time he was conscious that all the time he waited here, she was somewhere out there, alone. He wanted so much to see her again and run into her arms—he was a ninja now and he had killed men, but he still needed his mother.

And then there was Hana. The girl was the daughter of a daimyo—she had spent her life being groomed for marriage to another lord. Taro wasn't sure that, deep down, she could really want to settle for him, a peasant and a ninja. It was true that his real father was Lord Tokugawa, but blood wasn't everything. There was also training, etiquette, an appreciation of the arts. He was only just learning to read. For most of his life he had done little but fish and hunt for rabbits. Even if Hana *did* want him now, would she feel that way in ten years' time, when she realized that he couldn't offer her gardens, and tea ceremonies, and serving girls, and beauty?

Yet he knew, too, that he could not give her up. The selfless thing to do would be to release her, to send her away, to live the life she'd been meant to live. Only where would he send her? She could not return to her father now that Taro had killed him. And besides, Taro was not selfless. Every time he looked into her deep brown eyes he knew that he would keep her if he could.

He had not spoken to her of this—had not even told her his feelings—but his deep desire was to one day marry her. The problem was that he could not condemn the daughter of a lord to the life of a ninja's wife, and so he would have to make more of himself, somehow. If he could not do it by claiming his birthright as a Tokugawa, then he would have to do it some other way. Learn to read. Learn to write. Learn the sword, and how to make music, whether with a koto or with steel. Then perhaps one day he could become a samurai in Lord Tokugawa's guard, never revealing his true identity—perhaps, if enough time had passed, Lord Tokugawa would not recognize Hana.

One day. But right now, Hana turned as she walked down the stone corridor, and gave him a dazzling smile, and Taro shook the thoughts of the future away, like summer gnats. For just a little longer, he would stay here in the mountain, where everything was simple, and he could pretend that the bad things had never happened—his adopted father's death, Shusaku's sacrifice at Lord Oda's castle. As long as he was here, he could imagine, even, that

Shusaku still lived, and that one day he would see the ninja step out from some hidden alcove and take up his training again.

Leaving the cave, Taro and Hana followed the long tunnel that led to the main hall, which was the crater of the volcanic mountain, cut off from daylight by an enormous sheet, painted with stars. When they stepped into the wide, twilit space, they saw Hiro, practicing alone. His sword in his hand, he went through the kata, a sequence of formalized movements the ninja student was expected to master completely, so that they could be called up in a fight without thinking.

Taro had learned them but didn't use them for practice or for fighting—he didn't need to, he was so fast that he could invent his own moves, reading the movement of his enemy's sword by keeping his eyes locked on theirs.

"Hiro," said Taro. "Would you like to spar with us?"

Hiro turned to him and smiled, though his eyes no longer contained his old joy. "No, that's all right. I'll continue with these moves." He held his sword out straight, knees bent, and leaped into a feint-strike. His mind and muscles had been hardened by the events at Lord Oda's castle. He wasn't Taro's fat, jolly friend anymore—he was something more serious, more considered, more angry. Their betrayal by Yukiko, a ninja girl who had taken Lord Oda's side against them, had shocked him deeply, as had the death of Shusaku, the guide and mentor who had looked after them ever since the father who had raised Taro was killed by ninjas in Lord Oda's employ, and his mother sent away into hiding who knew where.

Taro watched Hiro move, and wished that he could see him grin instead, and tell stupid jokes. But who could blame him? Taro felt the pain of Shusaku's death too, every day—and it was worse here in the ninja redoubt, which Shusaku had shown them for the first time. He was hurt by Yukiko's defection, too—though not as much as Hiro was. Taro had never been close to the girl. In fact, she had always seemed wary of him, jealous of how quickly he had been made a real ninja. It hadn't surprised him all that much when she turned on them, if he was honest. He had always detected a steel core in her, sharp edges, as if she were a sword made flesh. And he had always known that she was envious of him, for being turned into a vampire so young, so quickly.

When Taro's father was killed, Shusaku had rescued him after Taro had been wounded by one of the many attackers. But the only way he could save Taro's life was to bite him, to change him into a vampire, and at that moment Taro had become something Yukiko had craved for years—something that ordinarily was achieved only after many years of training at the ninja mountain. He had become a *kyuuketsuki*—a blood-sucking spirit-man.

Strong. Fast. Powerful.

Then, when Yukiko's beloved sister had been killed defending Taro, she had found all the excuse she needed to turn against him and his friends—it had been Yukiko who had alerted Lord Oda to their presence in his tower, nearly killing them all.

"Taro," said Hana, interrupting his thoughts. "Would you like to leave it for another time?"

He shook his head and took up his sword, settling into the *ku* stance of emptiness. As she tried for a strike, he parried and counterattacked, his mind half on the flashing movement of the swords and half on the future. What was he to do now? Last year Shusaku had revealed something even more shocking than the secret of the ninjas: He had also told Taro that the man killed in the beach hut in Shirahama had not been his real father. Taro's true father was Lord Tokugawa, one of the most powerful daimyo in the country, and the man who many thought would one day be shogun. As if that wasn't enough, a fortune-teller—Yukiko's foster mother—had told Taro that he himself would be shogun one day.

But these were abstracts. There were two things that were concrete, two things that pulled Taro in opposite directions, like twin poles, and it was these two things that he pictured as he flicked Hana's sword aside and touched her neck with his blade.

She cursed in a very unladylike manner and bit her lip as she steadied her sword into her opening stance.

One of the things—one of the poles of Taro's existence—was the Buddha ball. Before he died, Lord Oda had spoken of it, as had the fortune-teller, when she spoke to Taro of his destiny. It was a ball, made for the last Buddha, that gave its bearer dominion over the world and everything in it, because it *was* the world in miniature. Taro had thought it a tall tale, but he now had reason to believe that it was in Shirahama, hidden by his mother at the bottom of the bay.

The second thing was his mother. She was meant, as soon as she was safe, to send the pigeon Shusaku had given her; that pigeon was ever-present in Taro's thoughts. Taro could no longer exactly remember what his father had looked like—the man he had always thought of as his father, anyway—but his mother's face was fresh and clear in his mind, and was constantly appearing before him when he closed his eyes to sleep.

It was a moment before Taro realized that his sword was no longer moving. Hana stood before him, arms folded, her *katana* leaning against her leg. "You're thinking of the ball?"

"Hmm? Oh, yes." Taro shrugged apologetically. Even frowning, like this, Hana was beautiful, and he felt a pang of guilt that instead of enjoying this time with her, safe from all enemies in the mountain, he was worrying about the ball and his mother, and how he could secure them both. Lord Oda was dead, but his second-in-command, Kenji Kira, was still abroad in the country, looking for Taro. He, or someone else, could find the ball and use it to cause untold damage. But what if Taro went looking for it, went to Shirahama, and his mother meanwhile was hurt, or killed? Or worse, what if she sent word of her location, and he wasn't there to learn of it? What if the information fell into someone else's hands, someone less than scrupulous? Someone like that weasel Kawabata, who had already betrayed Taro once . . .

Of course, his mother might already have been killed, and when Taro thought of that possibility a thick snake would squirm in his belly and he would find himself unable to sleep, the images of his mother and the ball rotating in his head, like the Sanskrit symbols on a prayer wheel.

"I'll come with you," said Hana, "if you want to go and look for it. You have only to say."

Taro nodded. He knew she would. She would go anywhere with him—she had shown him that already. She'd seen him kill her father, and she'd still walked by his side out of the castle and come to the ninja mountain. Foolish of her, really. Couldn't she see that he was nothing but a peasant, no matter what blood flowed in his veins? Couldn't she see that everyone who was close to him died or disappeared—his foster father, Shusaku, his mother? But of course he couldn't bring himself to send her away—she was so beautiful, so kind, so intelligent, and so skilled with a sword. She was like no girl he'd ever met.

There was something else, too. He thought Hana liked him— he was sure he could see it, in the cast of her eyes sometimes, and in the way she teased him. But he wasn't sure. Her father was a monster—perhaps she would have left his castle with anyone who came along and saved her; perhaps Taro had only been in the right place at the right time. If he tried to send her away, he sensed, he would learn whether she felt for him as he did for her, and he wasn't sure he was ready to learn that yet.

"I shouldn't be fighting," he said, looking down at the sword in his hand as if he wasn't quite sure how it had gotten there. "I'm too distracted."

"Don't worry," said Hana, smiling. "I wouldn't take advantage and hurt you."

"That wasn't what I meant. If I don't concentrate, I could kill you." He lowered his sword, stepping back.

Her smile disappeared. "Oh."

"Later, we'll eat together. Well, you can eat—I'll . . ." He would have some blood, from one of the pigs kept in the caves.

"Yes, that would be good." She gave him a hurt look, then turned and walked away. Taro wondered if everyone he loved would do that eventually—either die or leave him, or become changed, like Hiro. Perhaps it was what he deserved.

As if to underline his own thoughts, Kawabata Senior chose

that moment to step out of a hidden panel in the rock, which was made of stone fixed to a wooden door. Even from close up, it looked identical to the rock wall, and Taro had still not gotten used to the way that people would sometimes emerge from this secret passageway, using it as a shortcut to the main hall.

Kawabata stopped when he saw Taro. Scowling, he turned on his heel and vanished again into the darkness. Taro sighed. Kawabata had tried to get Taro killed, along with his companions—sending a ninja to Lord Oda to warn him that they were coming to his castle. Luckily, his son, Little Kawabata, had managed to prevent the messenger from reaching his destination.

When Taro had returned to the mountain, unharmed, he had been welcomed as a hero by the people here. All except for Kawabata, who had trembled when he saw Taro entering the cave system, Little Kawabata by his side. The son had denounced the father, and Kawabata, on seeing the contempt in the faces of his fellow ninjas, had asked for permission to commit seppuku.

Taro had refused. He had seen enough death at that time, and he didn't wish to watch Kawabata cutting open his own stomach in front of him. Besides, if there were people who gathered rice and people who gathered fish, then Taro was a person who gathered death. He had seen so many people around him die—he could not see another. But of course he had done the worst possible thing, as always. Kawabata might have forgiven him for living—especially as his great enemy Shusaku was dead as he had intended—but he could not forgive the slight on his honor that Taro had inadvertently given. Even one who had committed a great sin could cleanse himself through seppuku, yet it was in the power of the sinned-against to grant this redemption to the sinner, and Taro had not done so.

He had denied Kawabata his purity, and Kawabata would not forget it. Taro knew that he would have to kill the man one day, or change his mind about the seppuku—otherwise Kawabata would be sure to try once again to destroy him. But he kept putting it off. Since his father, too many people had died on his account.

He threw his sword aside, and Hiro looked up, startled, as it skidded across the sandy floor. Taro made a vague gesture to his friend, a wave of his hand that said something like, *Forget it.*

He was entering the tunnel that led to the sleeping quarters when one of the younger women—Taro thought her name was something like Aoki—came running out of it and nearly barreled into him. Breathless, she held out an object toward him with both hands, nodding furiously at him to take it.

The object cocked its head and said, *Coo.*

Taro stared at the pigeon. He was dimly aware of Hiro, coming up beside him and putting his hand on his shoulder. He was pleased his friend was with him.

He reached out and took the bird, gently holding its wings so that it could not fly away. Its eyes darted from side to side, and it made a stream of gurgling sounds that could have been complaint or pleasure.

Tied around the pigeon's leg was a very small scroll. Taro gripped the bird with one hand while he loosened the string holding the message with the other. He unfurled the parchment.

His lips moved as he deciphered the hiragana, and he was filled with joy that his mother had found someone to write on her behalf, and that he could read it.

*My dear Taro,* said the note. *I am at the Tendai monastery on Mount Hiei. I am safe, but I would give anything to see you again. With affection, your mother.*

Taro leaned against the wooden wall of the hut that led into the mountain, its floor concealing a tunnel to the mountain of the ninjas. A spring sun blazed in the sky above him, bathing the countryside in a light that was almost granular, so fine and shimmering was its appearance.

This was a peaceful spot. It was for that reason that he had chosen it as his brother's last resting place, and he was conscious as he sat in the sunlight that his younger brother's ashes were part of the earth beneath his feet. It was another constant reminder of Lord Oda's cruelty—for it had been Lord Oda who had imprisoned the youngest Tokugawa boy, along with Lord Tokugawa's wife, and starved them to death. But before dying, Lady Tokugawa had begged Taro to take her son's body with him, and he had been unable to refuse.

He closed his eyes, enjoying the warmth. The blood in his eyelids dyed the darkness of his consciousness red, and he thought that fitting. Blood was part of his being now, something he required in order to survive. The sun was only showing him the truth.

He sighed, the warmth and the coming of spring ruined by his thoughts. He wished he could simply enjoy being a vampire—but how could he enjoy a condition that required him to hurt others? He could survive on pig's blood, yes, but it didn't give him the strength and power he needed to go to his mother, to protect her from men like Kenji Kira. He felt, without knowing quite why, that he would be called on again to fight, even to kill.

And to do that, he would need human blood. He would need the strength of two men coursing through his veins—his own, and that of his victim's.

He heard something so faint a human wouldn't notice it—a sound like breath, which was made by the stirring of the air as someone far away moved quickly through it. He shielded his eyes with his hand, seeing the dark figure flitting up through the field. It was the vampire he was waiting for. The only other vampire who could move in daylight, because it was Taro who had turned him, giving him his own blood to drink.

The figure, growing larger by the moment, was the only person he could see, though from here he could see for many *ri*. The hut was high—higher than the clouds sometimes—and it was half a day of walking downhill before you came to the nearest village. Anyway, the people who lived down there never strayed near the mountain, if they could help it. They knew that unpleasant fates awaited those who did. Taro was glad no one from outside had come upon him since he had returned here—he was not as pragmatic or hard-hearted as the other ninjas, and killing a peasant just for being in the wrong place seemed cruel. On the other hand, he understood the need for secrecy, and realized that if the people of the area knew what was really hidden in the mountain, they would not rest till the vampires were destroyed.

It would be an unpleasant dilemma, and he was pleased not to have faced it.

*I wish I could be more like him, more fearless and thoughtless,* thought Taro, as Little Kawabata came more clearly into view, slowing as he spotted Taro by the hut. Taro would be leaving as soon as he could, with Hana and Hiro—tonight, if possible. He wanted Little Kawabata to know. Once the two boys had been enemies, but a grudging respect had formed between them—even if, as now, Taro was frequently irritated by Little Kawabata's blithe acceptance of his status as a dark spirit, his unwillingness to scrutinize more closely his actions. Little Kawabata was impulsive, instinctive. This trait was an irritation, but it could also be useful—as when Little Kawabata had taken it upon himself to warn Taro of his father's treachery, and so had saved all their lives.

"You've been hunting," Taro said, as Little Kawabata stood before him. The boy's face was flushed, his movements strong and lithe.

"Yes."

"Which prey?"

"Which do you think? Vampires are meant to feed on human blood. You might be satisfied with pigs, but I am not."

Taro sighed. "You risk the whole mountain, if we're discovered."

Little Kawabata raised his eyebrows. "I don't think that's likely."

"You don't think it's likely? You've been feeding on human blood."

"Oh, come on," said Little Kawabata, flopping down against the wall, raising his face to the sun and closing his eyes, stretching his arms languorously. "People don't expect *kyuuketsuki* in the daylight—that's why I went out when the sun was shining."

"They don't expect to be attacked at any time of day. It'll put them on their guard."

"I thought of that. I knocked the man out first. Came at him from behind with a thick branch. Then I bit his ankle, drew the blood from there. He'll think it was a snake."

"Well," said Taro, "as long as you don't do it again." He had to admit, though, the thing with the snakebite was clever. "Especially not after tonight." He held up the note. "I'm going to find my mother."

Little Kawabata didn't read, so Taro explained the message. The other vampire frowned. "You don't think it strange that the pigeon took so long?"

Taro *did* think it strange—though he was so pleased to finally hear from his mother that he had tried not to think about it. "Perhaps. You think it's a trap?"

"I think it's suspicious. When did you leave Shirahama? In the autumn? It's spring now. The cherry blossom has nearly reached us already, even this far north. No pigeon takes two seasons to fly from Mount Hiei."

"I know," said Taro, frowning.

"Someone could have caught her, made her tell them about the pigeon. Or someone could have intercepted her pigeon, and worked out what it meant. It has your name on it, after all. It would be easy, then, to send a fake message—lure you to a place where they could kill you. Lord Oda is dead, but Kenji Kira is still seeking you. A prophetess told you that you'd be shogun—that's a good reason for any number of lords to take your life."

"I know," said Taro. "I've thought of all these things. I'm not stupid."

"I didn't say you were," said Little Kawabata, with a smile. "I'm only saying . . . that you should be cautious."

Taro snorted with laughter. "*You're* telling me to be cautious?" He could see a smear of blood on the other boy's chin, where he had fed on a peasant, risking the very secrecy of the ninja mountain.

"Yes, well. I might rush into things, but it doesn't mean you have to."

"But if it was you, wouldn't you go? Wouldn't you want to see your mother again, even if it turned out to be a trap?"

Little Kawabata paused, then nodded. "Yes."

"I thought so. Anyway, Hiro and Hana will come with me— we'll all three of us have swords. If it starts to look dangerous, we'll turn back. But the way to Mount Hiei is simple—there's a road that runs direct to the mountain, for pilgrims. And many inns along the way where no one will look askance at a group of travelers."

"And I'm supposed to just stay here, am I?" said Little Kawabata.

"I thought you were worried it was a trap."

"I am. It sounds exciting."

Taro rolled his eyes. "We need someone to look after the mountain. Do you think you can handle your father in my absence? He must not know where I'm going—just in case."

"Of course," said Little Kawabata, slightly grumpily. "Everything will be fine, don't worry."

"And you'll stick to pig's blood from now on?"

"Yes," said Little Kawabata, with a long-suffering sigh. "Whatever you say, *Lord* Taro. The mountain will be perfectly safe while you're gone, you'll see. It will be as if you had never been away."

"Good," said Taro. He cleared his throat. "I was right, you know. To save your life."

Little Kawabata averted his gaze. "If you're going to get emotional," he said, "I might be sick. Just go and find your mother. I'll watch over things here."

Hana thought it would take the best part of a week to reach Mount Hiei. She had walked some of the pilgrim trail herself, with her father. At one time, she said, Lord Oda had spent a lot of time on Mount Hiei, with the monks, trying to win them over to his cause, which was the unification of Japan. The monks had been unfailingly polite, yet had ultimately resisted his offers. They were a warrior order, well armed, and they did not need to kneel to any of the daimyo. They were themselves one of the great powers in the country.

Taro hoped this was still the case. If the monks of the mountain retained their independence, then they couldn't be part of a trap involving his mother. They couldn't be working with Kenji Kira to destroy him. Of course, it was possible that the *monks* wanted his death. Perhaps they had heard of the prophecy—that he would be shogun—and they wished to end his life before he could threaten their power.

Well, it was a risk he was going to have to take.

They traveled by day, for the most part. It was known to only some that Taro could withstand daylight, and so most people looking for a young vampire would not expect to find him walking the road in the middle of the day. On the third day, they passed close to Shirahama—Taro could even see the bay, gleaming to the west in the late afternoon sunlight, a silver dish against the mossy green of the land. He wondered, still, what secrets that bay held in the embrace of its rocky promontories. His mother had dived on the day his foster father—the man he had always believed *was* his father, until Shusaku revealed his true identity—was killed.

What had she been doing? That she had been diving was not so unusual: She was an ama, one of the women divers who made a living harvesting abalone and oysters from the seabed. But she had difficulty with her ears; the pressure hurt her, and more and more in those months Taro had seen her pale and bleeding. She had promised him she would not dive so often, or so deep, as she once had. And besides, she had been diving that day near the wreck, a place that every man and woman in Shirahama knew was cursed, and potentially lethal. And was it a coincidence that she had gone there on the very day that they were attacked? Taro had wondered about it ever since. Earlier on that terrible day, he and Hiro had heard a rumor of *kyuuketsuki* farther down the coast. Could Taro's mother have heard the same rumor, and believed that the bloodsuckers were coming for her? Taro already suspected that the Buddha ball had been passed to the amas for safekeeping—what if *that* had been the reason for the dive? It had occurred to Taro too that the Buddha ball might have been passed down to his mother— and that she might have hidden it in the waters by the wreck, in the place from which it had originally come. It was a dizzying thought—that down there, beyond the misty haze of the sea-fog, through the leaves of the cedar trees, the ball might be shining under the water of the bay. . . .

He shook his head. If it *was* there, then it wasn't going to move—he had all the time in the world to find it, once he had found his mother. For now, he had to concentrate on the most important thing—getting to Mount Hiei, seeing her again.

Hiro inclined his head toward Shirahama. "We could go and visit," he said. "It's so close." Neither of the boys had returned to their home village since being forced to leave, six months before.

Taro shook his head. "Too dangerous. This is the Kanto—we're better off on the pilgrims' road." The Kanto belonged to Lord Oda, but all the daimyo respected the right of pilgrims to approach Mount Hiei in safety. It was only by sticking to the road, with its cobbled path, shade-giving trees, and frequent inns, that they would be able to reach the sacred mountain safely.

As they spoke, Taro felt a raindrop splash on his neck. Dark clouds were massing above. He led Hana and Hiro back to the road, and as they walked, the rain fell heavier and heavier. Soon the three of them were soaked to the skin, rain drumming a constant rhythm on their heads, seeping into their clothes and running down their ankles into their clogs. They plodded on miserably.

In this way, they walked for half a day, the light dimming steadily. When Taro saw the light of an inn ahead, he knew they would have to stop, even though it wasn't yet night.

"Oh, good," said Hana. "Maybe they'll have a fire. I feel like I'll turn into a fish."

As they neared, Taro could see that the inn was a crude place—just an assemblage of wooden planks. There were no windows. From outside, he could see a smoky interior, thickset men sitting on the ground and drinking from simple cups.

"It's a tavern," he said. "I'm not sure it's a place for a lady."

Hana smiled. "Well, if I was a lady, I wouldn't go in." She opened the door and sloshed inside, dripping on the floor. Hiro shrugged and followed her.

Taro blinked when he entered, his eyes smarting. Most of the men were smoking pipes—a habit they'd acquired from the Portuguese and Dutch. There was also a hibachi in the middle of the room, and because the inn had no chimney, the smoke from the charcoal brazier simply hung in the air, a gray cloud that hovered at head height. Hana led the way to a table near the fire. Several men looked up at them curiously, but their gazes didn't linger for long. No doubt they took the three companions for ordinary travelers, bedraggled by the rain.

Then, as they passed one of the other tables, Hana gasped and stopped.

"Hayao?" she said.

There were three people at the table: a woman and two men. One of the men was in the garb of a Taoist priest, the other a samurai, to look at him. The woman stood between them, her hand on the samurai's shoulder. It was the samurai who had drawn Hana's attention. He was a gaunt man, though Taro could tell he had once been handsome. He looked up at Hana, a confused expression on his face. His eyes blinked slowly, once, twice. With a pained, deliberate motion, he brushed the woman's hand so that it fell away from his shoulder.

"H-Hana?" he said softly.

Hana stepped closer. "Gods, Hayao, are you unwell?"

Taro thought he must be. The man was painfully thin, his skin sallow and sick-looking. The woman, too, seemed unwell. She was desperately pale, like an origami person, a person made out of white paper. The samurai didn't answer Hana—the woman at his side was caressing his cheek, and he closed his eyes as if in bliss. Something about the situation struck Taro as very odd. He wondered if the man was drunk.

The priest stood. His manner was grave, oddly formal. "My lady," he said. "You know this man?"

Hana gave a bemused smile. "Of course! This is Hayao. He is one of—I mean, he is one of Lord Oda's retainers. He taught me . . ." She lowered her voice so that the men on the other tables would not hear. "He taught me to ride and to fight. What happened to him?" The samurai's eyes were still closed, and he was murmuring something through his thin, gray lips. The pallid woman at his side stroked and stroked his skin.

"He is . . . suffering," said the priest. "I'm taking him to Mount Hiei."

Hana clasped her hands together. "That is where we are going," she said.

The priest nodded. "I thought this could not be a chance encounter," he said. "Perhaps we should go somewhere more private, and I can tell you more about our friend here. Hayao is known to you—it's not impossible that you could help. I myself have known him only since . . . his illness."

"If I can help, I will," said Hana.

The priest edged past the thin samurai, coming round the table to stand in front of Hana. Taro stumbled backward, a strangled cry on his lips. He held out his hand for something, anything, to steady him—and found himself holding on to Hiro's shoulder.

"What's wrong with you?" said Hiro. "You look like you just saw a ghost."

"You don't see her?" said Taro.

"See who?" said Hana. Both she and Hiro were looking at him oddly. The priest didn't seem to know what was wrong either.

Taro was staring at the woman standing beside the samurai, Hayao. She had not stopped her stroking, and it seemed to Taro that she was also whispering something, something only Hayao could hear. She had not once looked at Taro—or his companions or the priest, for that matter. It was as if she had eyes only for the samurai. She was in love, it was plain to see. But that wasn't what had shocked Taro.

It was the fact that the priest had just walked right through her, as if she wasn't even there—and even now he stood such that part of his body overlapped with hers, revealing her to be no person at all but an insubstantial thing, made of smoke or mist.

A ghost.

## THE PORTUGUESE PORT TOWN OF NAGASAKI

*Shusaku gripped the rail, feeling his way up the ramp onto the ship. When he stood on the deck, he felt the incessant rocking of the sea, moving the wooden boat gently from side to side, as if to remind its occupants of its power. Shusaku had never felt comfortable on the water. But at least he was able to swim. The same was not true of the sailors—it was better to die quickly, they reasoned, if the boat went down, than to waste time and energy on a false hope of survival.*

*Shusaku couldn't understand men so resigned to the mortal danger of their profession. True, his own profession was lethal enough— but he was different. He armed himself. What these men did—sailing without knowing how to swim—it was like going into a battle without a sword. He felt Jun's hand, gentle, on his back, pushing him forward. Curse the boy. Shusaku did not like ships.*

*"There's a step in front," said Jun. "Two paces."*

*Shusaku nodded, grateful. It would be humiliating if he tripped. It was bad enough that the sailors and samurai could no doubt detect his fear, his nervousness of the sea. Shusaku had insisted that Jun come with him—the boy was his eyes, and he needed him. To his surprise, Lord Tokugawa had accepted.*

"There!" said a rough voice, as a hand held Shusaku's arm, helping him up onto the deck. "Thought we'd never get you on board."

"Thank you," said Shusaku.

He heard a gasp from the man. "Your eyes . . . and your skin . . . gods. Who did that to you?"

Shusaku smiled at the directness of the question, which no noble would have spoken. He could smell the sea on this man, its salt penetrating deep into his pores and his hair. This wasn't a samurai. Behind the man, he could smell others, too—men who were not the gun-carriers from the quay but rougher, sea-soaked characters. Their blood pumped thickly in their limbs, made strong and warm by hard work and sea air.

"No one did this," said Shusaku. "There was . . . a fire. I was burned."

He felt and heard Lord Tokugawa moving up beside the sailor, or whatever he was. "Shusaku, I apologize for this man's brusqueness. Say the word, and he is dead."

The man took in a sharp breath.

"No," said Shusaku. "He was only surprised. But . . . who are these men?"

"Wako," said Lord Tokugawa.

Shusaku's mouth dropped open. Pirates? *What was Lord Tokugawa doing on a pirate ship?*

Lord Tokugawa took a step forward and put his hand on Shusaku's shoulder. "Come belowdecks. I'll explain." He turned. "You others—stay up here. Draw up the anchor. I want to be in Kyoto by nightfall tomorrow." To Shusaku he said, "Your boy can stay up here. I'll help you with the steps."

As they descended into the ship, Shusaku heard one of the men whisper to another. "That's the great ninja Shusaku," he said. "They say he could sneak into the shogun's bedroom, if he wanted to. I heard he's killed so many people while they slept, that once he woke one of his victims and gave him a sword, just to make it more interesting."

*Shusaku smiled. Actually, it had been a loaded arquebus. He had been curious as to whether the man could get off a shot before he killed him.*

*He couldn't.*

*Below, in the cabin, Lord Tokugawa indicated to Shusaku where there was a cushion on the floor, then sat down facing him. He pressed a cup into Shusaku's hand.*

"*O-sake,*" *he said.*

*Shusaku bowed, grateful. He had never been served rice wine by a lord before, even when he was a lord himself, albeit of a lower stature, and fighting as a banner-carrying samurai by Tokugawa's side.*

"*Pirates?*" *said Shusaku.*

"*Of course. It allows me to travel secretly. And*"—*the lord lowered his voice*—"*it gives me a scapegoat.*"

"*The pirates stole the guns,*" *said Shusaku slowly.*

"*Yes. That is what the Portuguese will believe. Not for nothing are you a ninja.*"

"*But . . . you need the guns yourself. No?*"

"*Only one, with which to make copies. The others will be left with the* wako, *as my gift for their services.*"

"*Left with them? This is their ship, then?*" *Shusaku had been on Lord Tokugawa's private vessel, in another lifetime, it seemed, another wheel of* dharma, *and it had seemed much larger and taller than this one.*

"*It is. They will take us to my own ship, under cover of night. We should be there in one or two incense sticks.*"

"*And then . . . you will betray them.*"

*Lord Tokugawa laughed. "Not at all. I will simply present them with the guns—all but one of them. They will use them, to carry out their dark work. And why not? They are impressive guns. They are also well suited to piracy. The* wako *up till now have been unable to use firearms—the spray from the sea puts out the fuses.*"

*Shusaku nodded. "Clever." But of course it was—Lord Tokugawa was not known for rash action, or clumsy thought.*

"*No, no, not at all,*" *said Lord Tokugawa, refusing the compliment as was customary.* "Anyway, it won't take long for word of the wako with the special guns to get back to the missionaries, and to Oda."

"Oda?" said Shusaku, surprised.

"Indeed. He bought the guns, you see. They were to be smuggled to him tonight."

"But Oda is dead."

Shusaku felt the shift in the air as Lord Tokugawa leaned back swiftly. "What? When?"

"Last autumn. The b—that is to say, I—I killed him."

Lord Tokugawa let out his breath. "That would very much surprise me—because I saw him only last week. We inspected our troops together."

Shusaku blinked uselessly. All was darkness around him still, and becoming blacker by the moment. Lord Oda was alive? When Shusaku had escaped from Lord Oda's castle, blind and staggering, he had distinctly heard a passing servant say that the daimyo was dead, broken by a fall down the winding staircase of which he was so proud.

And Lord Tokugawa—why was he still treating with him? The two daimyo had an official alliance, Shusaku knew, but surely the events at Oda's castle would have changed all that? Surely now their hidden enmity must be known by all, spoken of openly?

Until one of the lords was shogun, and the other dead, there would be no true peace between them. He stammered, "I must . . . have been mistaken."

"Clearly," said Lord Tokugawa. "Otherwise I would be shogun."

Shusaku had not thought of that. "Ah . . . yes."

"The other person who is rather conspicuously not dead," said Lord Tokugawa, a dangerous tone creeping into his voice, "is Lord Oda's daughter, Hana. You received instructions to kill the girl in the tower, didn't you?"

Shusaku sat back on his cushion. The tower. Of course. He must have misread the message, or it had been ambiguously worded. It had never been about Lord Oda—to attack him was unthinkable, would unbalance the whole teetering structure Oda and Tokugawa had created, the creaking complication of manners and protocol and open *declarations of trust that kept all-out war from breaking out and engulfing the land. Nevertheless Oda had sent ninjas against Lord Tokugawa's son—his secret son, Taro, hidden in a fishing village. Of course Lord Tokugawa would want revenge. A daughter for a son.*

His son, *thought Shusaku. Oh, gods. Suddenly he felt more vulnerable, more open to the harsh elements, than if he was standing on the deck in the sea spray, feeling the first gentle breeze that announced a* taifun. *He was in greater danger here, and Lord Tokugawa's anger was a greater storm.*

*He sat very still, thinking.*

*Lord Tokugawa cleared his throat. "And what of my son?" he asked. "Is that another mission you did not accomplish?"*

*Shusaku felt himself tremble a little. He was disarmed—literally and figuratively. The samurai had taken his sword, and now he was sitting belowdecks on a pirate ship, blind, facing the most powerful daimyo in the land, while a small detachment of samurai paced the deck above, accompanied by vicious, murdering* wako.

*It almost made him feel alive.*

*"I failed you," said Shusaku, feeling the lie as a weight in his chest. "Your son is dead. That is why I never reported back."*

*Lord Tokugawa said nothing.*

*"I . . . was outnumbered. The other ninjas were too many. And then . . . later . . . I was hurt. The sun, you see."*

*He heard Lord Tokugawa shift on his cushion, waited for him to say something. Finally the lord spoke. "I see. Tell me, how did my son die?"*

*"A sword," said Shusaku. "In the stomach." It was true—and not true. What he did not say was that after Taro was stabbed, he had bitten the boy, made him a vampire like himself. But one didn't make a lord's son a vampire, especially when that lord was in the process of making himself shogun.*

*To do so would be to make oneself dead.*

*Shusaku did wonder about Taro, of course. When he'd come to in the courtyard of Lord Oda's castle, he'd heard people running and shouting, saying that Lord Oda was dead. He had heard no one men-*

tion Taro, and he had been eager to escape. Feeling his way up the wall, he had made it to the top before the pain seized up his muscles, and he fell the height of six men to the moat below. The impact had driven the breath from his body and the spirit from his mind, and he had come to consciousness later, mercifully lying upward-facing in the shallows, among the reeds. He had stayed there for some days, covering himself in mud, living inside his pain.

And then, when he had known that he was truly blind—that his vision was not coming back—he had begun to make his way out of Lord Oda's town, pretending to be little more than a pitiful beggar. He hoped Taro would return to the ninja mountain—he'd be safe there, or safer than anywhere else. He himself could not return. Kawabata would seize on just this chance to take over, to overthrow him. And besides, he was a freak now, a monster. Taro would have to fend for himself, much as Shusaku missed the boy.

"And the marks?" said Lord Tokugawa, startling him back into the present. "The scars, on your skin?"

Shusaku's tattoos had been untouched by the fire, and now they stood proud of the skin, blacker and more pronounced than ever. Around them, surrounding them, interweaving them, was a mass of blistered red scar tissue, where Shusaku's flesh had been burned almost to the bone.

"They were protection," he said. "To help me against the other ninjas."

"Like Hoichi," said Lord Tokugawa. It was the thing that came to everyone's mind—the story of the haunted man who was painted with the Heart Sutra by an abbot, in order to hide him from the sight of his ghosts. Specifically, the part of the Heart Sutra that said, Form is emptiness and emptiness is form. Form is not different from emptiness, and emptiness is not different from form. This incantation, etched upon the body, prevented spirits from seeing a person, reminding them—for even spirits are Buddha's creatures—of the essential unreality of the phenomenal world.

"Yes, like Hoichi," said Shusaku. "And like Hoichi, I was punished." In the story, the abbot had forgotten to paint Hoichi's ears, and so the *ghosts had torn them off, in their anger, for ghosts are always hungry. He pointed to his eyes. "My eyes gave me away. The man I was fighting cut them out with his sword."*

*"And the burns?"*

*Shusaku had not seen them, but Jun had described them to him— and others had too—so he knew what the lord meant. "The sun. I lay in full sunlight for an hour, or more, before I came to my senses."*

*Lord Tokugawa gasped. "And you didn't die? I thought that was what happened with . . . your kind."*

*"No. I believe that the sutra saved me. The sun is a god, is she not?"* In the Shinto religion that had held sway in Japan before the coming of the Buddha's teachings, and that had now been assimilated into Buddhist faith, the sun was called Amaterasu, and as a god she could no more ignore the Heart Sutra's command than a vampire could.

The sun, Shusaku believed, had not seen him completely—only the parts of him uncovered by tattoos. It had burned him to the quick, but only to a pattern, leaving the tattoos untouched.

*"Remarkable,"* said Lord Tokugawa. He sucked his teeth. *"But I have an idea,"* he said, *"of how you can redeem yourself for your failure."* He stood, and Shusaku heard him moving across the room. There was a shifting sound as of hard objects being moved, their friction against one another.

Shusaku bowed his head, waiting for the sound of the blade being drawn, then the whisper of its edge against the air, cutting the very atoms through which it moved—the last thing he would hear.

Instead something was placed in his hands. Something long and cold, mostly wooden, with a lever at one end, and decorated all over in metal, chased with flowers and thorns.

A gun.

*"Hold on to that,"* said Lord Tokugawa. *"You'll be needing it."*

"She is a *gaki*," said the priest. He had taken a room at the inn, and Taro, Hana, and Hiro had joined him there. The samurai sat cross-legged on the floor, ignorant of their presence, staring into the eyes of the woman who sat before him. "A hungry ghost."

Taro murmured a silent prayer to Buddha. A ghost? But those things didn't exist, couldn't exist, *shouldn't* exist. He knew that only he, of all the people in the room, seemed to be able to see the woman, but there must be some rational explanation.

*But then*, he reminded himself, *vampires don't exist either*. . . .

"It's all right," said the priest. "She won't hurt you. She has eyes only for him." He nodded to the samurai.

"Yes," said Taro. "He is all she looks at."

"Can you describe her?" said the priest.

Taro looked at her, though he didn't like doing so. There was something unsettling about the woman, about the way that he could just—if he looked from the right angle—see the grain of the wooden floor through her. He had noticed her pallor before, the paper-whiteness of her skin. He hadn't noticed the black eyes—not black irises, but the whole eye black, as if ink had been dripped into her eye sockets, as if they were the inkwells for the white paper of her body. He shivered uncontrollably.

"Her eyes . . . her eyes are wrong. Black. Her hair is long and braided behind her head, in a single braid." He forced himself to be more specific. "She has a beauty spot on her left cheek."

The priest nodded. "She is as she was described to me, by one who knew her in life."

"Why don't *we* see her?" asked Hiro. He was adjusting the angle of his head, trying to perceive the woman in front of the samurai.

"I don't know," said the priest. "I can't even see her myself— I know she is there only because of the man's condition, and the way that sometimes he murmurs to someone who isn't present. And I have spent many years specializing in the exorcism of spirits. I once cured Lord Tokugawa, when he was sick in the mountains." He peered at Taro. "There's something special about you," he said.

Taro sighed. He was sick of people telling him that.

"Did you hear that?" said Hiro, punching Taro's shoulder. "You're *special*. Perhaps I should erect a shrine to you, and people can come pray to your goodness."

Taro pushed Hiro and the two grappled, briefly, before they were distracted by a mumbling from the haunted samurai. Taro and the others turned to him, but he did not seem to see them—his eyes looked through them, as if it were they who were the ghosts. Since he had spoken Hana's name, he had said nothing more.

"He was so strong," Hana said, a little distantly. She was looking at the samurai, Hayao. Taro felt a pang of jealousy. He wondered, suddenly, whether Hana had harbored feelings for the man when he was training her, when he'd been handsome and powerful. He dug his nails into his palms.

"I believe you," said the priest. "I was called in by his family when he was already sick. But he was a *hatamoto*, was he not?"

Hana nodded. "He was the best horseman in Lord Oda's army."

"And what about you? You were part of the household?"

"I was . . . a serving girl. Lord Oda dismissed me when I failed to brew his tea properly."

Taro didn't think the priest believed that, but the man nodded after a moment. "What seems certain to me is that fate has intervened in this meeting. You know this man, and your friend can see the ghost that is haunting him. I've never *heard* of a person who could see the hungry ghosts feeding on others. That I happened to meet you here, in this inn . . . I don't think it can be chance. I propose that we travel to Mount Hiei together."

Taro considered for a moment. This could be part of some elaborate trap, he supposed, but it seemed too coincidental—if it hadn't been raining, they would not have stopped at this inn, but would have continued onward until full dark. Besides, five people would be safer than three. Or six, he thought with a shiver, if you included the ghost.

"Very well," he said. "Tomorrow we will take the road together."

The priest smiled. "Wonderful." He bowed. "My name is Oshi."

Taro, Hana, and Hiro bowed and introduced themselves.

"What is happening to Hayao?" asked Hana. "Is the ghost . . . feeding on him?" She glanced at Taro as she said this, a troubled expression on her face, and Taro felt a spasm in his stomach. *I'm a vampire*, he reminded himself. *I'm a monster. She will never love me.*

"Yes," said Oshi. "She is hungry. She is feeding on his *qi*. Ghosts can consume no other food."

Hana's eyes widened with horror. She glanced at Taro again, and he knew the same thing was going through her head: *The ghost is not unlike me.*

"Why him?" asked Hiro.

"Mostly," said Oshi, "a ghost will attach itself to a person for no reason, other than bad luck. The ghost of a man who drowned might seize another swimmer, in the same place, and cause that swimmer to drown too. It's said that if a drowned ghost kills another in the same manner, they are freed. Or a group of ghosts will take a liking to a person, because of a skill that person possesses, or a mere accident of his appearance."

"Like Hoichi," said Taro. Heiko—Yukiko's sister—had told him the story of the blind musician who was haunted by the ghosts of the noble Heike family, so much did they love it when he played the *biwa* and sang to them the song of their clan's tragic destruction. Taro still couldn't help shivering when he thought of the blind man, surrounded by terrible figures whose presence he could not even apprehend, such was the darkness in which he moved.

"Like Hoichi," said Oshi, nodding. "Indeed, most of those who are haunted are like Hoichi. They don't know about it, because they don't see the *gaki* feeding on them. There is more than one kind of blindness. They may think they are ill, perhaps, but they don't suspect the truth."

"So what happens to them?" said Taro.

"They die. A ghost is always hungry. It feeds on the life force until the victim dies."

"He'll die?" said Hana, horrified.

"I'm afraid so. Unless the Tendai monks on Mount Hiei can help. I have exhausted my own abilities—nothing I have done has rid him of her. But the monks on Mount Hiei possess other secrets. Sutras, and the like, that were written by the Buddha himself. It is the last chance. That is why I am walking to the mountain."

"So the person being haunted doesn't even know they are dying?" said Taro. "They don't see the ghost?"

Oshi spread his hands. "In most cases. But that is where priests like myself come in. We are consulted, usually by a family member, and if we arrive in time, we are often able to help. We give charms, prayers, *shiryo-yoke* to hang in the windows. These things help to keep the spirits away."

"Like Hoichi's writing."

"Exactly like that."

Taro thought of Shusaku's tattoos. Would they have made him immune to ghosts, then, too? Of course, Shusaku was dead himself now, and Taro felt it as a stab in the stomach, as he always did when he remembered it. He wondered if the ninja master would be wandering the Pure Land alone, unseen by the other souls there, because of his protective marks.

That would be appalling. Unless, of course, Shusaku was in one of the hell realms. Then it would be a mercy.

"But," said Oshi, gesturing to the painfully thin samurai sitting on the wooden floor, "sometimes, as in this case, it is worse."

"Worse?"

"Yes. A person is sometimes haunted by a ghost that is more . . . connected to them. Usually it is a karma connection—perhaps someone with whom they were in love, in another lifetime, or in this one. These people see their ghosts—usually, they believe that the person is still living, because the ghost appears to them as a healthy human being. That is what happened to Hayao. The girl was his lover."

Was it Taro's imagination, or did Hana blanch at that? He must be imagining it. She couldn't have had feelings for this man Hayao. She'd come with him, hadn't she, when he'd walked out of Lord Oda's castle? Taro glanced at the samurai, sitting gazing into the eyes of the ghost that only he could see, perceiving her as a living woman. He shivered. "What happened?" he asked. He felt a desperate desire to know how the samurai had ended up with that thing of blood-drained skin, as well as a frisson of terror at the idea of being told. It was as if his skin was trying to go in two directions at once.

"Yes," said Hana. "Where did this ghost come from? When I left . . . Lord Oda's castle, he was fit and healthy. He was teaching me the bow."

"These things can happen quickly," said Oshi. "But it's a long story. I will explain everything to you on the road, as we travel. As much as I can, anyway—I don't know the whole thing, because it was only once he was already haunted that I was called on to help. For now, I suggest we get some sleep. It's still a long walk to Mount Hiei."

The five of them divided the floor space as best they could. Taro contrived to place himself as far as possible from Hayao. He couldn't bear the sight of those wasted, once handsome features, nor could he stand to be near the pale woman no one else could see. The woman never once looked at him—he didn't think she was aware of anyone but Hayao. But her very impossible presence was awful.

He noticed, though, that Hana curled up to sleep closest to Hayao, and that rat inside him started to chew again, and he clenched his fists. *You're being crazy*, he told himself. *The man's sick—she's just concerned for him.*

All the same, he found it impossible to sleep.

THE MOUNTAINS NEAR MOUNT FUJI,
THREE MONTHS EARLIER

*Yukiko pulled the cloak tighter around her, shivering. She didn't like these high places, with their thin, cold air. There was something mean about them, something cruel and remorseless, that reminded her of swords, arrows, bullets—those pitiless instruments of death, those sharpened pieces of cold metal.*

*Yukiko was an instrument of death too, but she did not think of herself as cruel—she was passionate, rather, fueled by fury and revenge. She was a living thing, hot-blooded, a hawk, not a blade. She belonged down in the warm, striving, fighting. Not in this inhuman coldness. She felt that the cold wanted nothing more than to creep into her veins and still them, and she cursed Kira for leading her here.*

*Trudging up the path, she rounded a corner and saw smoke ahead, coming from a hut. She was glad—for the warmth it promised, and for what it meant. Months now she'd been tracking Kenji Kira. Then, finally, the breakthrough—he'd written to Lord Oda, saying that Taro's mother was at a monastery on Mount Fuji, Taro no doubt with her, and that he was riding there without delay to kill them. This despite the fact that Mount Fuji was over the border, in Lord Tokugawa's province.*

*Impetuous fool.*

*Yukiko knew Taro was not at Mount Fuji, knew also that Kira would kill Taro's mother without thinking through the consequences. She had set out for Mount Fuji herself, hoping to stay his hand. Yet when she arrived—or rather, when she drew near, for the samurai massed in the region prevented her from getting too close— she found that the monastery had already been destroyed by Lord Tokugawa's army. The rumor was that the monks had defied him one too many times.*

*She knew that Kira would have turned back, would not have risked capture by Lord Tokugawa's troops. And so she had hunted for him, chasing gossip and horse-trails farther and farther into the mountains.*

*And finally, here she was, at this little hut. The question was— what was Kira doing here? There could be no strategic value in holing up in the high places like this. She ducked behind a tree, as a samurai wearing the Oda mon stepped out from the hut, stretching in the pale light.*

*Well, she was about to find out.*

*She stepped out, keeping her hood up as she approached the man.*

*"I'm looking for Kenji Kira," she said as he looked up, startled.*

*"What?"*

*"I'm looking for Kenji Kira." She could be patient. It was something she'd learned about herself, these past months.*

*The samurai grabbed her arm, peered at her face. "What are you doing all the way up here?" he asked. "Pretty girl like you."*

*Yukiko sighed. "I'm looking for Kenji Kira."*

*"So you say," said the man. "He isn't here, as it happens." He kicked the door open with his heel and dragged her inside. She let herself be dragged—there was no point giving herself away. But she could feel the steel against her side where her sword was strapped.*

*Inside the hut, three other samurai turned to look at her. They were rough men, with uncut beards, missing teeth, and scarred faces.*

*Battle-hardened men, violent men, used to doing Kira's dark bidding.*

*She took a deep breath.*

*"Little girl's looking for Kenji Kira, she says," the first one said.*

*The fattest of the men stood up. He stepped toward her. "What for?"*

*"I can't say," she replied. "Not to you. I need to speak to Kenji Kira himself." This was wasting her time. Where was Kira? She'd been sure he'd be here, and now it seemed like he had vanished into the thin, cold air.*

*The fat man backhanded her; light exploded in her eyes as her neck snapped round. She raised a hand to her cheek, felt blood trickle on her fingers. The man was wearing heavy rings; one of them had broken her skin. "She's a spy, I reckon," he said. "We should kill her."*

*"But first," said another—he had a missing eye, she noticed with disinterest—"we may as well have some fun with her."*

*The samurai who had dragged her in tore her cloak from her, and even with the fire going in the back of the hut she felt her skin rise up instantly in goose bumps, felt the cold prying at her with its icy fingers.*

*Then the thick fingers of the samurai were pulling at her too, fumbling at her clothes. She let him—she was looking over his shoulder, fixing the positions of each man, the places in the room and on the earth in which each would die.*

*Suddenly, the samurai backed away. He was staring down at Yukiko's waist, at the sword pommel there.*

*"That's . . ."*

*Yukiko glanced down at the petals carved into the hilt. "Lord Oda's mon. Yes." She drew the katana. It was perfect—no, more than perfect. It was in its imperfections that it showed its beauty, its craftsmanship. The silver wave that ran down its length was not completely even, yet it shone in the light of the fire like a river of moonlight, the colors of the different steels used in its manufacture clear to see. The edge was so sharp it sang even as she drew it, cutting the very fabric of the air.*

*"I've seen that sword before," said the samurai with the missing eye. "It belongs to Lord Oda. It was made by Masamune."*

*Yukiko nodded. "Yes. A sword of violence. One of the few remaining." It was said that Masamune swords were built to kill, where others might be made to protect. They liked the taste of blood, it was said. Yukiko appreciated that. She liked the idea that her sword was no cold and remorseless instrument, devoid of intent. She liked the idea that her sword wanted revenge as much as she did.*

*Inside her, in the darkness of her mind, she pictured her sister, lying dead after Kenji Kira killed her.*

*"How . . . did you . . ."*

*"How did I get it? Lord Oda gave it to me. After he asked me to find Kenji Kira, and deliver him a message."*

*The samurai closest to her, the one who had taken her cloak, backed away. "We meant no harm, little girl," he said. "We apologize. Kenji Kira is . . . not well disposed. But we will take you to him."*

*"Where is he?" she asked.*

*The samurai pointed to the ceiling. "Up the mountain, just half a* ri *or so. He won't come inside anymore. We're not sure, actually, what—"*

*Yukiko wasn't listening anymore. Her sword leaped, and the man was open from throat to belly. He fell to the ground, spraying blood that pattered on her skin, warming it.*

*"He said sorry!" said the fat man.*

*"I know," she said. "But this is a Masamune sword. I didn't have to draw it, but now I have, it must taste blood. You should know that."*

*She danced forward. The fat samurai, to give him his due, managed to get his sword into his hand, but she smacked it aside with her blade and took him on the point. The sword—so sharp it seemed it could cut through the world itself—came out of him like he was made of butter, then snaked round behind her almost of its own accord and removed the top of one-eye's head.*

*She turned. There was one samurai left, and he was armed. He held his sword before him like a talisman that might protect him. She noticed that his arms were trembling. She slid her sword back into its scabbard.*

*"You," she said. "Take me to Kenji Kira." The man was young—*

*he hadn't spoken the whole time, and his beard had barely grown in. He had light brown eyes that reminded her of her sister's.*

*She was a hawk, not a blade, and she had hot blood inside her and was capable of pity.*

*The man ran at her, screaming. She sighed, then sidestepped, tripped him as he went past. His head hit the wooden wall of the hut with a dull thud; she knelt to drop the tip of her sword—it took no more force than that—into his back and through his heart.*

*The walk from the blood-filled hut took only moments, it seemed, and then she was in the highest of high places; she could see the peaks of the other mountains all around her. Kenji Kira was lying among broken rocks in a gully that led to the summit. A trickle of water ran down the rocks, perhaps to widen into a stream lower down. As Yukiko approached, he was licking this water from the stone. There was no moss here, even—it was too high. Only cold stone, the bones of the mountain.*

Gods, *she thought. She had heard that Kenji Kira had once been trapped on a battlefield, watching tiny creatures feed on his dead comrades, and ever after he had been obsessed with the idea of avoiding the state of decay, of making his body proof against putrefaction. It was even said that his loyalty to Lord Oda derived from a promise Oda had made—that if and when Kira died in his service, he would have him embalmed, or frozen in ice—the stories differed on that point.*

*Now it seemed he was attempting this process for himself.*

*He looked up. "Who . . . are . . . you?"*

*"My name is Yukiko. I come from Lord Oda." She held out the sword, showed him the mon.*

*He nodded wearily. "Kill me then," he said. "Just . . . leave my body here. I should like to be cold. To be stone. I should like . . . not to rot."*

*She stared at him. "I'm not here to kill you," she said.*

*Now it was his turn to stare. "No? But I failed. I did not find Taro. I do not know where to look."*

*"You found his mother's message. You went to the place she was."*

*"Yes. And it was destroyed. Lord Tokugawa did it. For all I know he has Taro now. He has his son. He has his heir."*

*She smiled. It took an effort—every atom of her being was telling her to kill this man, to avenge her sister Heiko's death at his hands. But that could wait. It would be sweeter if she waited. She was patient. It was something she'd learned.*

*"Taro was not at Mount Fuji," she said.*

*He peered at her. She saw how thin he was, how the skin stretched tight over his bones. It was true, everything she'd heard about him—it was as if he was turning already to stone, to something hard and cold. She couldn't understand how he could want this. How he could want to be something other than human. "You're . . . sure?" he asked.*

*"I'm sure. Taro is at the ninja mountain. Now—did it not occur to you that, having intercepted his mother's message, you could simply substitute a different one? Send him a false message?"*

*"You mean . . . trap him?"*

*She nodded.*

*"But . . ." Kira stammered. "I would not be capable of getting a message to the ninja mountain. I don't know where it is."*

*Yukiko forced herself to smile again. "No. But I do." She reached down and held him under one armpit, helped him to his feet. It seemed a travesty, to be assisting the man who had killed her sister—she had the impression that she would be bringing him down from this high cold place into life again, that she was leading him out of death itself, and that felt wrong.*

*Still, she reminded herself—over and over, like a mantra—that she would kill him one day, when the time was right, and make him suffer as she had suffered. If he died here he would have what he wanted; his body would grow cold and still and would lie here among the rocks without rotting. For now, she needed him to believe he could make everything right, that he could capture Taro for Lord Oda, and return to the daimyo's good graces. She needed him to be happy when she killed him.*

*He was shivering, his skeletal body wracked by spasms as they descended the path. When they passed the hut he raised a twitching hand to point it out. "My men are in there," he said.*

*"No, they're not," she replied.*

He glanced down at the blood on her clothes, and said nothing.

As they continued downward, the air began to warm, and he shivered less. She had some dried meat in her cloak—she tried to get him to eat, but he would let nothing but water and herbs pass his lips, and the occasional acorn he found on the ground. At one point she saw him chewing on a stick.

Strange man, *she thought. He seemed to think he was already becoming rock, that his body would never decay—she heard him mumble about stones in his entrails, about the contamination of the flesh. It was nonsense, of course. Yukiko meant to make sure that he putrified and boiled with maggots, like a dog.*

But at least for now he was growing stronger, seeming to regard with pleasure what lay ahead, the prospect of trapping and killing Taro. That was good. She wanted him strong and she wanted him pleased. She wanted him coursing with blood, his heart pumping his life force, his whole body singing the joy of its existence when she killed him.

She was a creature of passion, after all, not a pitiless instrument. She was not of the high, cold places; she was of the forest and the field, a fierce hunter, not a stealthy assassin—a hawk, not a blade.

She would wait until Kira was on the verge of achieving all he hoped, until his heart was hammering in his chest, filling him with the pleasure of being in the world, and then she would cut it out with her sword and he would bleed out all his blood, all over the indifferent ground.

Oshi was not a big man—he was shorter than Taro, with the sunken chest of one who had spent his time with books, not swords. But he must have had deep reserves of strength, because he had been traveling with Hayao for some days now, he told them, pulling the samurai in a small, two-wheeled cart. Taro was impressed. The priest was evidently dedicated, to drag his patient all the way to Mount Hiei.

But Oshi wasn't on his own anymore, and so Hiro took the cart for the first part of the walk that day. It had stopped raining, but the stone of the path shone with moisture, and the moss on the trees was greener than green, as if the whole world had been washed clean.

As they walked, Oshi told the friends about what had happened to Hayao. It seemed that the samurai had fallen in love, on a return visit to his mother's home in the mountains of the north. The girl had been as beautiful as her name, which was Tsuyu, for she was named after the plum rain. And now this girl was the ghost that traveled with them, and that Taro had to avoid looking at, because of the way that it floated along beside Hayao, some of its body in and some of it out of the cart.

"But how did she die?" said Hana.

"I'm getting to that," said the priest. "There's no rush, is there? Mount Hiei is still a long way away."

"Tell me about it," said Hiro, panting as he pulled the cart.

Oshi smiled. "Very well, since you ask." He took a breath and stretched his back, as if thinking where to start. "This Tsuyu, she did not get on with her stepmother, when her father remarried. So her father built her a small house in the hills. Her only visitor was a local monk, who had undertaken to teach Tsuyu the women's characters her father wished her to learn—but not, of course, the Chinese characters a man of similar rank would be taught."

Taro looked down, embarrassed. He, too, knew only the hiragana.

Oshi didn't seem to notice. "One day the monk brought with him a friend—Hayao here. It goes without saying that he was handsome, his carriage and bearing fitting for a samurai of his rank."

Taro glanced at Hayao, slumped in the cart, trying to imagine the man strong and vigorous. It was difficult.

"When he and Tsuyu saw each other," continued Oshi, "they fell in love immediately—and though the monk kept a careful eye on them, they contrived to declare this love to each other. As Hayao left, Tsuyu whispered to him that if he did not return she would surely die.

"Hayao was only too glad to return, but sadly etiquette would not allow him to visit the small house alone. He waited and waited for the monk to invite him again—but the latter, having seen hints of the developing romance as clearly as an astrologer might read a fortune in the stars, avoided the young man scrupulously. He knew that Tsuyu's father would have him killed if he besmirched—or caused to be besmirched—the honor of the lady of the plum rain."

Hana snorted at this. "Men," she said.

Taro looked at her. What did she mean by that?

Oshi just shrugged. "Fathers must look out for their daughters," he said. At this Hana did blush—and Taro knew she was thinking of how her own father had ordered her to commit seppuku, when he knew of her treason.

If Oshi noticed her discomfort, he didn't say anything. They were walking through a long, broad valley of rice paddies, and as the sun rose higher and higher in the sky, he continued his story.

"Not realizing the true reason for her love's neglect, Tsuyu wasted away in the little house on the mountainside, and very soon died of a broken heart. She was buried in a nearby cemetery among the plum trees.

"Hayao, of course, knew nothing of this death, since his only channel for news of the girl was the monk, who had taken to ignoring him. But one day the monk unexpectedly arrived on his doorstep. 'Forgive me for keeping my distance for so long, friend,' the monk said. Hayao forgave him instantly—his only preoccupation was with seeing Tsuyu again, and he knew that the monk was the one who could arrange it. 'I forgive you, of course,' he replied, 'but only if you will take me once more to see Tsuyu, my plum blossom rain, my cool dew on a hot day.'

"The monk's face fell. 'I am sorry to tell you, Hayao, but the girl is dead. I am afraid that when you saw her last, the meeting, though brief, was long enough for her to fall in love with you. But I was afraid to take you to her again, in case her father got wind of it and had me killed. When I heard that she had died, it was clear to me that she had suffered a broken heart.'

"Hayao could not believe his friend's words. 'But I love her, too!' he cried. 'Surely I could have convinced her father of my honorable intentions?'

"The monk smiled. 'Oh, Hayao, how hard it must be to be so handsome that girls will die for love of you! But come, let us not keep talking of the dead. All we can do now is open a bottle of sake and repeat the *nenbutsu*.'

"But Hayao could not move on—he remained frozen with grief for many months. Every night he repeated the *nenbutsu*, and the name of Tsuyu was never absent from his thoughts, and nei-ther was the memory of her lithe figure and almond face absent from his imagination."

Oshi paused. "That part of the story I had from the monk—he was the first person I talked to, when Hayao's mother asked me to help. He felt awful. Had he known, he said, how badly Hayao would take the news of the girl's death, he wouldn't have spo-ken so flippantly. But he was a product of his Buddhist training. I believe he couldn't help but think of a girl who would die of love as being . . . silly, frivolous perhaps. He didn't treat the matter with the due respect, and it may yet prove the death of this fine young samurai."

"You don't really think he'll die, do you?" asked Hana, looking stricken by the thought.

Oshi shrugged and gave a heavy sigh. "Perhaps not. But things are bad. I was surprised when he spoke yesterday—it has been days since I heard his voice. It must have been because he recog-nized you. Were you two close?"

Hana looked at Taro, then down. "We spent much time together," she said.

Taro bit his tongue.

"But since then," said Oshi, "it doesn't even seem that he sees us." They all glanced at Hayao, who was lying in the cart and crooning.

"Does it get worse with time, then?" said Hiro.

"Yes. With every day that the ghost spends at his side, he loses more of his strength. He becomes less and less himself, and more like a husk with no flesh inside. Eventually he will be . . . scooped out. Empty."

There were tears on Hana's cheeks, Taro noticed.

"The rest of the story," said Oshi, "I had directly from Hayao—in part at least. I also had to speak to his neighbor, to piece together what had happened. But I did speak to Hayao at length. This was when he was still able to talk of it, when he had moments of lucid thought—though for the most part he thought that Tsuyu was real, and alive. He believed, I think, that I was trying to take away his happiness—that I was part of some conspiracy designed to remove Tsuyu from him, because of her low birth, perhaps. That was how it started—and over time, it grew worse and worse. Now he is as you see him now. She's the *only* thing that's real for him."

"How did she find him?" asked Taro. "You said she died apart from him. "

"Yes," said Oshi. "From talking to Hayao and his neighbor, I believe she was able to locate him during *obon*, when the spirits of the dead are drawn to those with whom they share karmic connections. I know, because Hayao told me, that when the festival drew near, he loaded his *shoryodana* shelf with rice and water for his family ghosts. In particular, though, he dedicated all his offerings to Tsuyu. On the night of the first day of the festival, he lit his lamp and repeated the *nenbutsu* once more. Then, it being a hot and oppressive night, he went out to the veranda in search of cool air. He sat there dreaming of Tsuyu—getting up only once, to fetch incense sticks, which he arranged around him to drive away the mosquitoes.

"All of a sudden, he was disturbed by the clopping sound of a woman's *geta* clogs passing in front of his house. He looked over the hedge that surrounded the garden and saw a woman walking past, holding a beautiful decorated lamp.

"As he looked, the woman turned to face him, and he was surprised to see Tsuyu.

"'Hayao!' she cried out, rushing toward him. 'I thought you were dead.'

"'And I thought *you* were dead!' replied Hayao. Tripping over his feet, he ran out into the street and invited the woman inside. Once seated, Hayao gave his side of the story and Tsuyu explained hers.

"'You see, Hayao,' she said, 'this monk who taught me was so afraid of causing me dishonor, and so losing either his position or his head, that he tricked you into believing I was dead! And he told me *you* were dead, hoping no doubt that we would forget each other.'"

"She was cunning," said Hana.

Oshi smiled sadly. "The dead always are." He gestured to the samurai in the cart. "Hayao was overjoyed, of course. He cursed the name of the monk who had contrived to separate them, but he was glad to find that Tsuyu was still alive. He told her how much her loved her. 'And as for me,' replied Tsuyu, 'I would gladly disobey my father to be with you, even if it should mean that he responds with a *shichi-sho made no mando*, a disinheritance for seven lifetimes. Come, will you not allow me to stay tonight?'

"Hayao hesitated. Not only was it highly improper to have an unattached girl to stay, but also he was worried that the nosy local gossip might notice. 'The thing is,' he said, 'I have an annoying neighbor called Yusai, who is a *ninsomi* and tells people's fortunes by looking at the shapes of their faces. It happens that this is not the only way in which he likes to scrutinize other people, however—he also rejoices in learning the business of all his neighbors, and then telling it to his *other* neighbors, as if to spread the bounty of gossip evenly around the neighborhood. If you stay, I fear he may discover us.'

"Hayao asked the girl if he could visit her at home, but she said no, he couldn't. Her father had fallen in the world, it seemed, and she had been forced to move to a peasant house among the plum trees. She was embarrassed to receive him there.

"'Very well, then,' said Hayao. 'But because of this busybody Yusai, you must leave before daybreak, and quietly.'"

Hiro had started to sweat, as the day warmed, and Oshi motioned for him to put down the cart. He lifted it himself and began to pull it along the path—slower than Hiro, but steadily. "That's as much as I could draw out of Hayao," he said. "When I spoke to him, he seemed to think that I had been sent by the monk, his erstwhile friend, to convince him his true love was dead. He was quite unpleasant to me, I must say. He was paranoid—thought everyone was conspiring with the girl's father to deny their happiness."

"Poor man," said Hana.

"Yes. All the time she really was dead, of course—it was she who was lying to him. The rest of the story is from Hayao's neighbor, Yusai. A man who, I must say, was just as bad a gossip as Hayao said. Still, it made him a useful source of information. One night Yusai the fortune-teller was unable to sleep, and wandering in his garden, he happened to hear a voice through his neighbor Hayao's paper window. He peered in, by the light of his night-lantern. Inside, under the shade of a mosquito net, Hayao was talking intently to someone. The strange thing was that Yusai couldn't see who he was talking to. He did hear what Hayao was saying, though.

"'And if your father should indeed disinherit you for seven lifetimes, you will come and live with me forever. And if he comes to claim you back, I will fight him. My sword has not tasted blood for many months.'

"There was a pause, then Hayao said. 'Ah, my dear. I am so happy that you are not dead. I love you.'

"All of a sudden, the moon came out from behind a cloud and lit up the scene inside, so that for Yusai it was as if a lighthouse's beam had swung around and illuminated the room. What he saw made him fall backward, into the cruel thorns of a rosebush. For just a moment, in the light of the moon, he thought he saw the pale shape of a woman—though afterward he convinced himself he had imagined it—and then it was gone, and he realized Hayao was speaking to nothing."

"Ugh," said Hiro, shivering.

"It was Yusai who alerted the monk, Hayao's friend, to what was going on. He thought Hayao might have gone mad, but of course the monk knew immediately that he was being haunted, and he called for me."

"What did you do?" said Taro.

"I told him that if the woman was truly a ghost, he would start to see a change in his neighbor's face—the signs of death would appear upon it. It was possible, you see, that the man was possessed by a living spirit—such as that of a girl who was obsessively in love with him. But those cases are rarely fatal. In the case of a ghost, though, the effect is much worse. A man whose lover was a *gaki* would not live long. For the spirit of the living is *yoki*, and pure; the spirit of the dead is *inki*, and unclean."

"And she was a ghost, of course," said Taro.

"Yes. Yusai returned to me a week later. His neighbor's hair had grayed, he had lost weight. He rarely left the house."

"What did you do?"

"I told Hayao that he was consorting with a ghost. He laughed at me—he said he had found his love again, and I wanted to take her away. He accused me of collaborating with the monk who had cheated him. I asked him to at least come with me to the cemetery where Tsuyu was buried, to clear up the matter."

"Hayao was angry, but he came with me and the monk to the cemetery, which was planted all around with plum trees. It was not long before we found a relatively new tomb, one befitting a noble. On the tomb, no proper name was written—only the *kaimyo* name that is given after death. I stopped a monk who happened to be walking by, and asked who the tomb belonged to.

"He said it belonged to a young woman named Tsuyu, as I had known he would. He mentioned what a tragedy it was, that she had died so young of a broken heart. At that, Hayao became very pale. He told us what she had said, about moving to a small house among the plum trees. I took him aside. I told him that the karma that bound him to the girl was not a negative one, and that she was not feeding on him for revenge, but only because she needed him by her side. I told him it seemed likely to me they had been lovers in a previous life; I told him I accused him of no weakness. And I asked him to allow me to help."

"Did he?" asked Hiro.

"Yes. I lent him a powerful *mamoni*. It is a pure gold image of the Buddha—a *shiryo-yoke* that protects the living from the dead. I told him to wear it in his belt. And I gave him a scroll with a holy sutra, the Ubo-Darani-Kyo, the Treasure-Raining Sutra, which he was to read aloud every night. Also, a package of *o-fuda* charms, written on paper, which he was to paste to every window and door of his house. They are meant to prevent the dead from entering."

"But it didn't work," said Hana.

"No. The next week Yusai came to me again. It seemed that he had looked through the window every night, and every night Hayao had been speaking to his invisible lover. She had attached herself to him so firmly that even those measures would not work against her. Hayao, meanwhile, was so ill as to be lost. We tried to speak to him, but he didn't even see us. He could see only Tsuyu. And the weaker he became, the stronger she grew. Soon she was with him constantly, not just at night."

"Couldn't you paint him?" said Taro. "Or tattoo him? I mean, put the Heart Sutra on him so she wouldn't see him."

"Thinking of Hoichi again," said the priest approvingly. "But no. It wouldn't work. That only prevents an unconnected spirit from seeing you—it doesn't protect against one with which you have a karma connection. The girl knew him, probably had known him in more than one lifetime. There was no hiding him from her."

"But how did she get past the *o-fuda* in the windows? The scroll?"

"That," said the priest, "is what I don't know. I intend to ask the monks on Mount Hiei—if anyone can help, it is them."

After that, Oshi fell silent. He was breathing a little heavily now, the cart weighing on him, and Taro offered to take over. He was not a big man either, and so he was careful to draw the cart slowly, so as not to reveal his unnatural strength. Oshi was a Taoist priest, a man who dedicated himself to the exorcism of evil spirits. Taro wasn't about to let on that he himself was a *kyuuketsuki*.

They walked on in this way for several incense sticks, not speaking much. Hana seemed deep in thought, and Taro saw her glance many times at Hayao, concern written clearly on her features. He knew it was ludicrous to be envious of such a man—a man being slowly killed by his dead lover. But he was—he was envious of those looks; wished Hana would look at him that way.

She didn't, though. In fact, it seemed she'd barely looked at him since they left the ninja mountain. He found that a small part of him hoped Hayao would not recover, so that nothing would change. He hated that part of him.

And then they turned a corner on the broad flank of a hill and saw Mount Hiei before them. Taro had never seen the sacred mountain before, but he knew instantly what it was—it was so huge and so perfectly shaped that it couldn't be anything else.

"Nearly there," said Oshi.

Hana grinned. "It is just as I remembered it," she said.

The conical mountain rose above the very clouds, so that its peak was beyond the rain, as if too elevated and rarefied to be sullied by such earthly things. Before them, the path ran straight, until it climbed into the foothills in looping swathes and steps.

Just in front of them, though, was a small wood in a natural dip—perhaps a holy wood dedicated to a local *kami*. Indeed it seemed that the peasants of this region had cultivated their paddy fields around it, leaving the grove of trees untouched. It gave Taro a slightly queasy feeling, as they crossed from the light into the dappled place under the leaves. He was just thinking that this would be a perfect place to lie in wait for pilgrims, to ambush them just as they neared the mountain and lowered their guard—when a man dropped from a branch ahead of him, a sword in his hand.

*Shusaku wished he could see Lord Tokugawa's eyes, to perceive if his employer was serious.*

*"You want me to smuggle the gun into Hongan-ji? Alone?"*

*"Yes."*

*"The fortified lair of the Ikko-ikki rebel monks? The most fiercely guarded castle in all of Japan?"*

*"Yes."*

*Shusaku's head spun. The Ikko-ikki were based only a few ri from Mount Hiei, on a hill above Osaka, and their reputation was if anything even more ferocious than that of the Tendai monks from Hiei. Geographically, then, they were close, but philosophically, the Ikko-ikki were as far from the Tendai sect as could be. Where the monks of Mount Hiei participated in the great readings from the Lotus Sutra, believing that the path to enlightenment was gained through careful study of its every word, the Ikko-ikki rejected the idea that enlightenment was something to be learned—claiming that anyone, even a humble peasant, could accede to karmic liberation. They did not use written texts of* any kind. They called themselves the Pure Land Sect, after the heaven of Amida Buddha, which they said even an illiterate peasant could reach.

The samurai, of course, hated them. All the lords and nobles followed the Tendai sect. It appealed to them, for it said that holiness was to be found through dedication, money for ceremonies, and the ability to read. To them, dharma was contained in a book of ancient scriptures that it cost money to reproduce, and that they could therefore control.

For the Pure Land believers of the Ikko-ikki, dharma, and the potential for total perspective, was contained in every leaf of every tree, and in every droplet of rain. Any man could access it—he had only to look. The karma accumulated through a person's past lives—or through the generations of their family's dominion—was meaningless. A person could choose, at any moment, to seek the light of understanding, no matter whether their ancestors were lords, their karma as clean as their robes, or tanners who had spent their lives elbow deep in animal piss.

Needless to say, the Ikko-ikki were exceptionally popular with the untouchable eta, whose role it was to carry out the filthy tasks, like tanning, and who were barred by traditional Buddhism from paradise, their status on a plane slightly higher than that of a pig, or a murderer.

Nor was their philosophy the most dangerous thing about the Ikko-ikki. Unlike the Tendai monks, they believed that aggression, not defense, was the best path to survival. In the years since the Portuguese had arrived, the Ikko-ikki had armed themselves with thousands of guns, even setting up a forge on the top of their mountain lair to construct their own. They recruited peasants to their cause, especially those disgruntled with the high levies of the crueler lords, like Oda.

Any intruder—anyone seeking to infiltrate their castle—would simply be shot.

Shusaku swallowed. "You realize I'm blind?"

"Yes."

Clearly this was to be Lord Tokugawa's response to everything.

"I'll need the boy, Jun. He is my eyes—without him I don't stand a chance. With him, I might just be able to get up to the monastery. . . ."

"Good, then it's settled."

"But—but," Shusaku stammered, "getting there is one thing. Surviving is quite another. The Ikko-ikki hate ninjas just as much as they hate samurai. They'll kill me."

"No. They are expecting you. Have you not seen it yet—my plan?"

Shusaku wondered if the daimyo's words were chosen deliberately, to remind him of everything he would never see. This was the way with Lord Tokugawa—it was always difficult to tell exactly what he meant—whether he meant to kill you, hurt you, or only offer you a cup of tea. That was what made him so dangerous, and so successful.

Still, Shusaku tried to think like the other man. Why would Lord Tokugawa give one of these new guns to the Ikko-ikki? There could be only one explanation.

"You wish them to copy it? To make more?"

Lord Tokugawa clapped softly. "Well done. Why?"

"To arm your men."

"No. To arm the Ikko-ikki."

Shusaku blew out air. "But they detest the samurai!"

"They are men. They may detest whom they wish, but they love power, like anyone else. I have promised them their own province."

Shusaku spread his hands. "Very well. So they will not kill me. All that is required is that I make my way to the castle, without being able to see, without anyone to help me, and deliver to them a gun that every daimyo in the land—not to mention the Portuguese—is desperate to lay their hands on."

"Well," said Lord Tokugawa, "that's mostly it. There is a small complication, though."

"Really?" said Shusaku sarcastically. "What would that be?"

"You'll have to get past my army first."

Shusaku put his face in his hands. "You'll have to explain, I'm afraid."

"It's very simple," said Lord Tokugawa. "Lord Oda is my ally. He wishes to eliminate the Ikko-ikki. So, to show my support for him,

*I have sent one of my divisions of samurai to help his cause. Right now, the combined armies of Oda and Tokugawa are laying siege to Hongan-ji monastery, determined to crush the rebels and seize their mountain."*

Shusaku's head was beginning to hurt, and he remembered why he had always been glad to leave Lord Tokugawa's side and set off on dangerous missions, where all he had to worry about was people being very anxious to kill him, rather than someone snarling up his thoughts with twisted logic. "You are laying siege to the castle. You are helping Oda to destroy it. Yet you also want to send this gun there, so that the Ikko-ikki can use it to stand by your side when you take the shogunate."

Lord Tokugawa clapped a hand on his shoulder. "See?" he said. "I told you it was simple."

*This is it,* thought Taro. *It was all a plot, ever since the pigeon, to bring us to this place to die.*

Another man dropped to the ground behind them, and then more stepped out from the trees. Taro registered the peculiar detail that they all appeared to be wearing the loose robes of monks.

He backed against Hiro, and felt Hiro do the same—both of them covering their rears. Hana closed in with them. All three unsheathed their swords, Taro's of course in his hand long before his friends had drawn theirs. Oshi was opening and closing his mouth like a fish.

From the shadows of the trees ahead of them stepped an old man. He, too, appeared to be a monk. He was ancient, his head shaved and his eyebrows bushy, as if growing longer to compensate for his bald pate. His face was lined with deep wrinkles, and in one hand he held a staff. He seemed to be leaning on it as he moved, yet something about the heaviness of it made Taro think it might be a weapon, as well as an aid to locomotion.

The monk spat on the ground at Taro's feet.

"We have been aware of your coming for some time," he said. "We smelled the stink of corruption."

Taro stared. "What?" He'd been expecting . . . he didn't know what he'd been expecting. Perhaps gloating at how easily he had been duped, how simple it had been to forge the message from his mother and so bring him here to die. He hadn't been expecting this.

"This is a holy place," said the monk. "We do not allow the tainted here."

Oshi spread his hands. "It is not the samurai's fault," he said, indicating Hayao in his cart. "He's haunted—we only brought him here to see if you could help. . . ."

"Not him," said the monk. "Him." He pointed to Taro. "We don't allow the spirits of night in this place."

"It's daytime," said Hana. "Spirits of night don't go about in daytime."

At this the monk frowned. "That is strange, certainly. But we are not mistaken. This one is a *kyuuketsuki*."

Oshi gasped and took a step away from Taro, and at that moment the monks attacked. The old man, suddenly lithe and nimble, was in front of Taro in a flash. Taro brought his sword up just in time— and caught the staff as it hushed down through the air toward his temple. His arms ringing with the blow, he staggered back, aware of Hana and Hiro fighting too, their swords darting and circling.

Taro attempted to center his *qi*, got himself into a better stance. He focused on the old man's eyes, reading his movements. His sword snapped left, blocked a strike—counter-struck at the man's arm. But the monk was quick, and he was never where Taro thought he would be. Clash. Block, parry—strike. The sword and the staff seemed locked in a complicated sequence of pre-planned movements, so impossible was it to gain any advantage. He was aware of Hiro, behind him, struggling too—he could hear his friend panting for breath, and that made him afraid because he knew how strong, how hard his friend had become.

He heard a small gasp from Hana and turned to see that

she'd been disarmed—she stood quite still, composing herself, as the monk she'd been fighting stepped forward and picked up her sword.

*No,* he thought. *No, we can't die here, just when the mountain is in sight....*

Then a burst of pain in his head, flashing—just for an instant the forest scene before him transformed into a nighttime sky, a constellation of bright stars in blackness.

He put one hand to his head, felt blood. With the other he jerked his sword, blade biting into the staff just as it was about to sweep his legs out from under him. He heard Hiro swear angrily.

There was an intent, serene expression on the monk's face. Taro had never seen anything like it. This man must be four times his age, and yet he was holding Taro—a trained ninja—at bay with seemingly no effort at all. The monk gazed back, his expression neutral. He met Taro's next strike easily, then seemed to lose patience for a moment. He flicked the staff and Taro's sword went flying, landing among moss and leaves to his left.

Taro took a deep breath. He glanced behind him and saw that Hiro, too, had lost his sword. The three of them, Taro and his two friends, stood in a tight circle, surrounded by armed monks. Oshi stood over to the side, an expression of pure confusion on his face.

"Now, vampire," said the monk. "Explain yourself. Why do you come to our mountain?"

Taro opened his mouth, but he was winded—no words came out. He was still stunned that the monks had so readily identified him.

"What about these others?" said the monk, gesturing to Hana and Hiro. "The girl is of high birth, I hear it in her voice." He turned to Hana. "Did he hurt you? Did he bite you? How did he make you follow him?"

Hana gave a shocked laugh. "Did he— What? No. He's our friend."

"He's a bloodsucker."

"No. I mean, yes. But he doesn't kill. He didn't choose this.

It— He was just a peasant boy, and then the ninjas—"

Taro glared at her, and she stopped talking.

The monk swung his staff in the air, as if unsure what to do.

"What are you waiting for?" asked one of the others—a fat man with a red face. "Kill him. He is a spirit of night. He is evil."

But still the old monk hesitated. "I will allow him to explain himself before he dies," he said. He turned to Taro. "Talk," he said. "Tell me why I should not destroy you for the corrupt spirit you so certainly are."

"If I still had my sword," said Hiro, "I'd gut you for that."

The monk smiled. "It is well that we beat you, then," he said. "Not that it was difficult."

Hiro scowled. Taro gave his friend a wan smile. He could always rely on Hiro.

He cast his eyes toward his sword. It was too far—he would never reach it. And anyway, the monk was too fast. He wouldn't stand a chance. Tears welled up, threatened to spill over. He could feel the earth below his feet, the cool breeze on his face. He could smell pine needles, and his own sweat.

"I'm a vampire," he said, trembling. "It's true. But I'm not evil, I swear it. I know that most vampires kill, but I was taught not to. I was . . . made like this by a good man. His name was Shusaku, and he died trying to protect me. When he saw that I could stand the sunlight, he said . . . he thought . . . he believed that there was something different about me." He stopped, breathing hard. "I learned from him to feed on the blood of animals when possible, never to kill if I could help it. I'm just trying to find my mother; I haven't seen her for so long. . . ."

Gradually he realized that there was a very strange expression on the monk's face. He trailed off.

*"Shusaku?"* said the monk. "Endo no Shusaku?"

Taro nodded.

"And he's dead?" The monk put a hand to his chest.

"Yes. He died in Lord Oda's castle. We were— Well, we were there."

The monk rubbed his forehead with his hand. He took a long, deep breath. "I'm sorry to hear that," he said. "More sorry than you can know. Still, if Shusaku thought you were special, perhaps . . ."

To Taro's surprise, Oshi came to stand nearby. "The boy can see ghosts," said the priest. He pointed to Hayao again, curled up in the cart, for all the world like he was sleeping. "I brought this samurai to seek your help with the *gaki* that is haunting him. The boy can see her. He near keeled over dead with fright the first time we met. I've never met anyone who could see them before—save for the haunted party, of course. I should say that makes him special."

Taro stared dumbly at Oshi, grateful beyond words.

The monk continued to run his hand over his brow. "I know why *you're* here, then," he said to Oshi eventually. "But what about the boy? What's a vampire doing approaching the holy mountain—even a vampire turned by Shusaku?" He turned to Taro and inclined his head, waiting.

Taro fumbled for the message in the sleeve of his cloak. "I had—I came—I wanted to—"

"Taro is looking for his mother," said Hana. "She sent him a message, saying she was at the monastery on Mount Hiei. We thought perhaps it was a trap, but—"

The monk had gone pale. *"Taro?"* he said. "You're Taro?"

"Y-yes."

"Well, why didn't you say?" The old man stooped and picked up Taro's sword, returning it to his hand. "We have been waiting for you for so long," he said. "Your mother had quite given up hope."

*The thing about being blind was that he perceived all the people around him as blood and shadows, not seeing the individual contours of their faces or the secrets in their eyes, and so to him they were nothing more than ghosts—or prey.*

*It tormented him, and it made him a monster at the same time.*

*It tormented him because he had enough ghosts already; they gathered around him, dragged at him, trying to pull him down. He had killed far, far too many men, and this evil was a cloak that he wore always.*

*And it made him a monster because the people he was aware of, those close to him, were not people in the true sense, they were just branching, treelike structures of blood, pulsing red in the darkness. Even Jun was nothing but blood to him, the sound of a heartbeat, the smell and whisper of veins and arteries.*

*He sensed Jun's hesitation.*

*"Someone?" he whispered.*

*"Yes," said Jun. "Ahead. A patrol, I think."*

*They were close to the cliffs that led to the temple of the Ikko-ikki. They had crept through the camp on the Tokugawa side, Jun acting as the eyes and Shusaku the ears of their composite person, Shusaku perceiving the camp as a conglomeration of sleeping bodies, their bloodskeletons pulsing in the blackness that was his entire world. No one had woken, and no one had been abroad—save for one guard, whom Jun had wanted to kill, and whom Shusaku had insisted on skirting, so that they were forced to travel farther.*

*Now they had reached the cliff, and this was where the guards would be most thickly distributed. It wasn't unfeasible that the Ikkoikki might send raiding parties at night—strong young monks to climb down the cliffs and enter the enemy's camp, sowing death and disruption. This, Shusaku reflected, was where the spilling of blood would become unavoidable.*

*Jun led him slowly forward, and at length he became aware of the men. They were gathered at the foot of the cliff, and Shusaku could feel the heat—and smell the smoke—of the fire they had built. They almost deserved to die, he thought. Certainly their commanding officer would kill them, if he saw them. A fire was an idiocy, pure and simple. What did they think, that the Ikko-ikki would be courteous enough to come to their hearth and introduce themselves—that they would be drawn to the warmth as a moth to a flame? All the soldiers were doing was telegraphing their position.*

*He sighed. None of this made it better, of course. He would like to think that these men were requesting their own deaths, that their stupidity made them deserve it—but really he was just going to send more people to the Pure Lands or to hell, depending on their karma, just to further Lord Tokugawa's ambitions.*

Lord Tokugawa saved you, *he reminded himself.* He took you in when you were made a vampire, when anyone else of his class would have disowned you.

*He took Jun's wrist, made him stop.* "Sneak round to the other side of them. When I snap a branch, that's my signal. Go to them and ask if they've seen an old, blind man. Say you've lost your grandfather. Or something. It doesn't matter."

"Right," said Jun. He flowed into the night, taking his blood with him, its ceaseless whistle and whisper.

Shusaku waited. He had a wakizashi in his hand—the gun, his precious cargo, was strapped to his back. He edged closer and closer to the fire, his slipper-clad feet silent on the pine needles. He was conscious of trees to his right and rock to his left—the air sounded different as it passed over each of them.

Soon the men resolved into three branches of beating blood, arranged around the heat and nostril-clogging scent of the fire. He heard Jun address them.

"Excuse me . . ."

He didn't listen to the rest. He moved forward, hobbling a little, deliberately. He let the sword hang behind his back.

"That him?" he heard one of the men ask. "Gods, boy. What are you and the old cripple doing here, anyway? Don't you know there's a siege going on?"

"He wanders off sometimes," said Jun. "He's blind, and his mind isn't right either."

"Be a kindness to finish him off, sounds like," said one of the men, and another guffawed.

Shusaku shuffled closer. He could hear the heartbeats of the men and they were calm, relaxed—the slow rhythms of men who don't know they're already dead. He took off the first's head even as he was laughing, and the laughter continued for a moment as the head was severed from the body, the lips still moving. Shusaku stuck out his tongue, felt the blood patter on it, like snow when he had held out his tongue to it as a child.

He spun, and nailed the second man to the ground with his sword, the blade slipping between the ribs and sticking the body fast to the cold earth. At the end of his motion, he heard the head of the first man hit the ground, a dull sound like a bruise made audible.

He sensed the body he had just pinned with his sword twitching, could hear every pulse of every muscle, the horrible mumbling from the mouth.

The last one, and he paused.

61

He could have retrieved his sword, but he didn't bend. Maybe, when it came down to it, good karma was about giving people a fair chance—maybe he was haunted because his profession called on him to kill people without giving them an opportunity for defense. He stood still, aware of the flicker in Jun's heartbeat that bespoke confusion.

"Master . . . ," began Jun.

Shusaku raised a hand to silence him. He told himself that what he was doing was lunacy—that if the soldier was sensible, and screamed for help instead of trying to fight, everything would be over. But would that be so bad? Soldiers would come running, many of them. It would be an honorable way to die, or if not honorable, then fitting at least. He could finally meet those ghosts that clamored at him, let them haul his soul down to hell.

But the soldier didn't scream—he was a brave one; an idiot. He had something in his hand—Shusaku couldn't tell because it was still. Then there was a thwup, and Shusaku was aware of something spinning toward him through the night, something that hissed as it parted the air.

Crossbow, he thought. Well, at least that's a challenge.

He waited until the last possible moment and then he ducked, reached out casually, and plucked the bolt from the air—it heated from the abrupt stop, burning his hand, but he registered the feeling as sensation, not pain, and was glad for it. He was already moving, flipping the bolt in his hand, and as he did so he heard another thwup, and two paces later a jolt of pain lanced into his shoulder.

This one's fast, he thought. It really will be a shame to kill him.

Fast as the soldier was, though, there was no way he could string a third bolt in time. Shusaku leaped the fire nimbly and came down just in front of the soldier—though he didn't stop his forward momentum, just rolled when he hit the ground and came up bolt in hand; stuck it through the soldier's heart and felt it burst out the other side.

Whoosh-boom . . . and then nothing. The heart stopped.

He stood, pulling the barbed bolt from his shoulder and wincing at the pain. He liked the pain—it reminded him that these men would have killed him, if they'd had the chance. It didn't make their deaths excusable—but it made them inevitable, and that was something he appreciated.

He knelt and put his lips to the throat of the most recently killed man; he liked fresh blood, if he could get it. There was that always pleasurable moment of tension, as when you touched water in a small vessel and felt the resistance of the surface—and then his teeth burst through the skin and he felt blood splash into his mouth. He sucked it down greedily. He could feel the warmth spreading through his limbs.

"What are you doing?" hissed Jun. "Do you want to get yourself killed?"

Shusaku stood, then shrugged.

He gestured to where he could hear the air on the cliff. "Can you find a way up it?" he asked. He knew Jun was resourceful—it was why he'd chosen the boy.

Jun paused. "I think so," he said finally, though he didn't sound sure. That was good. Shusaku didn't like people who promised what they couldn't deliver. He followed Jun to the rock face.

What felt like days later, they reached the wall at the top of the cliff. It was a moonless night—Shusaku and Lord Tokugawa had chosen it for that very reason. Shusaku and Jun had been quiet, but not silent. It wasn't possible to be silent when climbing a cliff, which was littered with stones and earth that could slip and fall.

As such, Shusaku was not surprised when a hand gripped his arm as he reached the top of the wall and a blade touched his neck, cold and sharp.

"Show me your face," said a voice. A torch was thrust toward him; he could feel its heat.

"Ah," said the voice. There was a pull on Shusaku's arm, and he tumbled gracelessly to the ground below the wall. He had tired himself with the climbing. A moment later he heard Jun drop beside him. He concentrated—there were several men in front of them, in a fan. He suspected that guns were trained on them, fuses ready.

"We were expecting you, Shusaku," said another voice, a deeper one. It came from a man whose blood beat strongly in his veins—a fighter, though not young. The voice, a deep baritone, was full of authority. "Lord Tokugawa sent a pigeon. He told us you would be bringing a gift."

Shusaku unstrapped the gun from his back, held it out. He felt someone step forward and take it from him. Then there was a low commotion as the Ikko-ikki gathered around the weapon. Shusaku heard one of them give an admiring gasp, another cluck his tongue against his palate.

"Ingenious," said the deep voice—the leader, Shusaku guessed. "This part—here—twists back. And when it is released, it strikes the flint—here. The power is ignited by the spark. No need for a fuse."

"It fires in the rain, I gather," said Shusaku. "Though the gods know why Lord Tokugawa thinks that's so important."

"I suppose," said the deep voice, "it very much depends on whether it's raining at the time." He turned—Shusaku heard the rustle of his vestments. "Can we copy it?"

Another man—his voice was older, had more of a tremble to it— made an equivocal sound, a sort of humming. "I should think so," he said eventually. "We will need time, though."

"You won't have much," said the leader. "Lord Tokugawa says the guns will be needed soon."

"For what?" said Shusaku.

"Lord Tokugawa didn't say. He never does. And yet he's rarely wrong, is he?"

Shusaku sighed. No, he wasn't, at that. He was never wrong, in Shusaku's experience. So the guns were significant, but for now he just couldn't grasp why. Yes, they fired in the rain—but what if you faced your enemy on a sunny day? Lord Oda's troops, massed at the bottom of this mountain, were armed to the teeth with traditional fuse-fired guns. If they attacked on a blazing summer day, the Ikko-ikki would be decimated, newfangled guns or not. The only way Lord Tokugawa's plan would work was if there was some way of controlling the weather. . . .

He jerked back into the scene, realizing that someone had just spoken. "Sorry?" he asked.

*"We asked if you would like to stay for a while. You look like some-one in need of . . . peace. You are hurt, I see."*

*Shusaku bristled. "My burns have healed."*

*"I wasn't referring to your wounds," said the leader. "I was refer-ring to your soul. I sense a weight on it. I sense . . . guilt."*

*"All evil done clings to the body," murmured Shusaku.*

*"Truer words were never spoken. But we have something special, here on the mountain. You could have a room. Time to meditate. To think on the things you have done, maybe to atone."*

*"Maybe one day," said Shusaku regretfully. "For now I must return to Lord Tokugawa. He has not finished with me. When he has, I may return." He turned to where he could hear Jun's distinctive breathing.*

*"My assistant will stay, if you don't mind," he said. "I nearly dragged him down with me tonight. If I got him killed, I could never forgive myself."*

*"Of course," said the Ikko-ikki leader.*

*"No! Master! I will come with you, I will—"*

*Shusaku waved a hand. "I have spoken. You will stay here until I return. I don't know what Lord Tokugawa is planning, but there will be blood. There's always blood. And if I can help it, I'd like yours to stay in your veins."*

*"Very well," said Jun heavily.*

*"Look after that gun," said Shusaku to the Ikko-ikki. "I had to kill men to get it here, and I wouldn't want their deaths to be totally in vain."*

*"No deaths are in vain," said the leader. "I promise you that."*

*At this, a sharp pain shot through Shusaku's heart, and he let out a ragged breath. He hoped it was true, wished it was true, but feared it wasn't.*

*"Till the next time," he said. Then he vaulted over the wall, and his hands found purchase on the rock.*

*Blindly he climbed downward, toward the sea.*

The old monk—it transpired that he was the abbot of the monastery atop Mount Hiei—led the way. His sprightliness surprised Taro. Most of his monks followed just behind, though two of them had stayed with the companions to help carry Hayao's cart up the steep hill. The abbot had examined Hayao and said that he was in a desperate state, but that with effort, and luck, they might be able to save him.

Then he had looked intently at Taro. "I don't believe in accidents," he said cryptically.

At the top of a particularly steep section, Taro stopped, not to get his breath but to admire the view laid out behind them—a patchwork of rice paddies, the trees of the grove in which they had been ambushed only twigs from up here. He turned to look up the hillside. He could barely believe that his mother was there, waiting for him. The abbot said she had been living at the monastery since the winter, when she had arrived barefoot, her feet bleeding.

Hiro came up behind him, breathing hard. "Are we . . . nearly there . . . yet?" he asked. He was leaner now than he had been before, but he was still heavy, and the climb had been hard on him.

"Yes," said Hana. She turned and faced up the mountainside, pointing to a curving roof, just visible beyond a row of *ume* plum trees. "That's the Hokke-do." The building she referred to was a graceful temple, its roof curved like a dragon's, scaled with red tiles. And as Taro looked, he realized that from one end of the roof a dragon's head sprang, while from the other curled a tail. Below the red roof were clean white columns.

The blossom season was here, with the first warmth of spring, and the trees were covered in a pink froth that fell from the branches when they were moved by the breeze. The tiny flowers lay on the mossy ground and swirled in the air around them, living up to their name of *Tsuyu*—plum rain. Taro found that he couldn't look at the beautiful flowers without thinking of the horrific ghost that was draining Hayao's life energy, killing him slowly with love.

"Is that where the readings take place?" said Taro.

Hana nodded. She had explained about the Hokke-do, and how it was there that the Tendai monks of the monastery would hold readings of the Lotus Sutra. The monks carrying Hayao had nodded in approval at her knowledge. She had drawn closer to Taro and Hiro to whisper the next part—that her father had sponsored these readings on occasion, usually to honor a dead family member, and so Hana had spent some time on the mountain. They had decided to keep Hana's identity a secret for as long as they could. None of the monks seemed to recognize her—she had been a girl the last time she visited the mountain, not a young woman—and it seemed judicious not to tell anyone that she was the daughter of a powerful daimyo, and not only that but one who had developed an enmity with the monks.

Hana had told Taro and Hiro that there was tension between Lord Oda and the abbot. They were not far from Oda's province here, and the power of the monks disturbed him, more with every passing year. It had been a long time since she or anyone of the Oda household had visited the monks.

In the time of the last emperor, the Tendai monastery on Mount Hiei had been closed to any outside authorities, and as a result had been swamped with criminals seeking to evade capture. The monks had been forced to learn to fight, and now they were custodians of a great martial tradition, and keepers of many a secret technique. That they were also ten thousand strong in number explained Oda's nervousness—the monks, in fact, were the greatest power in the land, after the lords.

Hana was sure that her father wished to destroy the Mount Hiei monastery, and all the monks who lived there. He could not tolerate this challenge to his strength. But, as ever with these things, there had to be a pretext for attack—Oda could not simply lay waste to a revered and ancient institution, without some good reason. So the monastery still stood, on top of this mountain, guarded by warrior monks. And now Oda was dead, killed by Taro's own hand. There could be no better place for Taro's mother to hide.

They passed under the plum trees, the blossoms catching in their hair. At the end of the row, they came to the Hokke-do— a square temple with a graceful, curving dragon-roof suspended over white columns. Surrounding it, casting long shadows over it, were tall cedar trees, their tops high above. The large building was empty, its columned sides open to the elements, giving it the appearance of a cave, or a mouth with long teeth. Taro paused for a moment to give Hiro a chance to catch up.

"Oh, great," said his friend, looking upward.

"I thought you might say that," said Taro.

Above them extended a continuous path of steps, rising in twists and turns to crest a brow, where it disappeared for a moment, before reappearing much higher up. All along the side of the cracked, mossy stone steps were regularly spaced prayer wheels, creaking in the wind. Taro followed them with his eyes. Thousands. A person climbing, if they spun every wheel, would let fly into the heart of the universe an extraordinary number of prayers to Kannon, the bodhisattva of compassion.

But Hana didn't want to continue the climb just yet. She grabbed Taro's hand and pulled him toward the Hokke-do. "Come on," she said. "This is where the scrolls are kept. You have to see them." She glanced down the mountainside. The monks carrying Hayao were far behind, deep in conversation with Oshi.

"Scrolls?" said Taro.

"The Lotus Sutra that Saido copied, when he first came to the mountain. It's the oldest Japanese copy of the Indian sutras."

"My mother is up there," said Taro. "Perhaps we'll look at them later. . . ."

"Yes," said Hana. "Yes, of course. We'll carry on."

But her eyes were so bright with enthusiasm as she glanced at the Hokke-do, her passion so beautiful, that he smiled and said, "Let's have a look first. It won't take long. I last saw my mother in the autumn. I can wait a little longer."

She smiled at him then, the most unselfconscious and lovely smile he had seen since they'd met Hayao and a heaviness seemed to have come over her heart. Her hand was warm in his, and he wondered if she could feel how her touch sped his heart rate. And now that he was thinking about his hand, he felt it begin to feel strange and foreign at the end of his arm, as if it belonged to someone else, and then he felt his face flush with heat. He pulled his hand from hers and ran past her, as if he were in a hurry to see the sutras.

Stepping into the cool gloom of the temple, he was struck by its simplicity. Soaring above, the roof was unornamented, just a graceful assemblage of beams. The room was empty, apart from a number of cushions propped against the columns—ready, Taro presumed, for a reading of the sutras. He couldn't imagine sitting still for eight days, listening to a monk reading from a scroll, but then he supposed that a lot of things the nobles did were strange.

"Not much to see," said Hiro, stepping up beside him.

"Shh," said Hana. "Have some respect."

Hiro rolled his eyes. Hana stood in the center of the room, looking at a small dais, on which stood eight scrolls. At least, Taro assumed they were scrolls—what he saw was in fact the gold tubes, carved at the top with dragons, in which the scrolls were kept.

"No guards?" said Hiro.

"No need," said Hana. "The whole monastery is the guard. There are ten thousand monks here, and they all know how to fight. There are lookouts posted all around—I'm sure they already know we're inside. You'd have to be mad to try to steal the scrolls."

"But they must be valuable, no?" said Taro.

"Extremely. They are very old."

"It still seems strange, then, that they're not hidden away."

"Why? They are holy. To the Tendai, the scrolls are not just the word of Buddha. They are . . . everything. The world. *Dharma.* It is as if the scrolls don't just contain the secret of the universe— they actually *are* the universe. Do you understand?"

"No," said Hiro simply.

"Well, it would be unimaginable for anyone to take them. Trust me. They won't come to harm." She reached out a hand to touch one of the gold tubes, then withdrew it. She stood for a moment contemplating them.

Hiro picked his nose.

"I can *see* you," said Hana.

Hiro stopped. Cleared his throat.

"This is a special place, you know," Hana said, though her voice was more amused than irritated. "We're standing in *history.* And not just the scrolls—this very hall is where Genji paid for a reading of the sutras, on the forty-ninth day after Yugao's death. It lasted eight days, one for every book of the Lotus Sutra."

"Sounds boring," said Hiro.

"Who's Genji?" said Taro.

Hana looked at both of them with a sad expression. "You don't know *Genji no Monogatari*? It's a great work of literature. Maybe the greatest."

"Oh," said Hiro. "What happens?"

"Well, there's this man who's the son of one of the emperor's courtesans, and he has several love affairs, and then at one point he's exiled to the seaside, and then he comes back, and has another love affair, and then the woman he's seeing dies and—"

"That sounds even more boring than the eight days thing," said Hiro.

Hana sighed, exasperated. "Then you'll have to try reading it one day. Actually, *you* could, Taro. It's written entirely in hiragana, because the author was a woman."

"Great," said Hiro. "Maybe Taro can read it, and then tell me what happens. Very briefly."

Just then one of the monks who had been carrying Hayao peered into the gloom, through the pillars. He frowned at them. "What are you doing in there?" he said.

"I was just showing these boys the scrolls," said Hana. "They were both very eager to see them."

"Women aren't supposed to come in here," said the man sullenly. "Except on special occasions."

Hana looked down—not at all the confident, fearless girl Taro was used to. Taro sensed she was biting her tongue. As Lord Oda's daughter, she had spent much of her life being made to learn calligraphy and flower arrangement, instead of the riding and fighting she loved. After the freedom of the ninja life, this restriction on account of her sex must gall her. All she said, though, was, "I didn't know. I apologize."

"Very well," said the monk. "Now come. The abbot will be waiting for us."

Hana gave a last lingering look at the scrolls, bowed to them, and then walked toward the door. "Let's go," she said to Taro—as if they hadn't just been told to leave anyway. "I'm looking forward to the climb. When he's panting for breath, Hiro hardly says anything at all."

Hiro made a face at her back.

Outside, Taro joined his friends at the bottom of the steps lined with prayer wheels. Sighing, he stepped up, gripped the first wheel, and set it spinning. Each wheel said the same prayer, when spun—*om mane padme hum*, the characters writing the words on

the air as they revolved, the mysterious Sanskrit letters an incantation to the bodhisattva of compassion. A person didn't need to say
anything, just spin the wheel. All the same, to the prayer encap-
sulated in the symbols carved on it, he added his own silent one.

*Please, keep my mother safe forever,* he thought. He looked up
at the peak, so close now. All these months he had been separated
from his mother, and now only a set of steps lay between him and
her. He felt light as air, as though he could fly up them, though he
could see from Hiro's expression that his friend didn't share his
excitement.

Hiro spun the wheel on the other side of the path. "One
down," he said grimly.

C
H
A
P
T
E
R

1
2

Even Taro was panting when they reached the top of the path, the wheels behind him hissing as they spun on their axes. He stepped forward onto the grassy summit. When he turned around, he gasped. Hills lay in gentle folds below him, like kimonos that had been discarded on the floor. Far away to the east lay the sea, glittering in the late-day sunlight. The town of Kyoto, capital of Japan, was spread out before it. This was the town where the boy shogun lived, the child who technically ruled the country, and who every daimyo secretly wanted to replace—none more so than Taro's own real father, Lord Tokugawa.

"Beautiful, isn't it?" said Hana.

Taro nodded. He could understand why the monks would have found this a good place to come, and meditate.

"It's just as abbot Jien said," she went on.

"I'm sorry?" said Taro.

Hana was always forgetting that he was only a peasant by nature. She recited:

*"From the monastery
On Mount Hiei I look out
On this world of tears,
And though I am unworthy,
I protect it with my black sleeves."*

Hana swept her hand over the distant hills.

"He meant that when he looked at this view, he felt a desire to shield the world, and the people in it, from harm. Even though it was useless."

Taro looked at the tiny pillars of smoke rising from houses, the trees like bonsai, the rivers gleaming in the light. Yes. He could understand what the poet meant.

Hiro came slogging up the steps to stand next to them. He glanced at the view. "This is it?" he said.

Taro looked at Hana and smiled.

Just below them, on a plateau below the peak, was a large structure similar to the Hokke-do, its roof a sweeping upturned parabola, dragons leaping from either end. From this building came the abbot.

"*Irasshaimase,*" he said, giving Taro a little bow. "Welcome to the monastery."

"Thank you," said Taro. He was looking around the monk, trying to see if his mother was there.

The abbot smiled. "Of course. Come with me." He led the way down a path that ran past the building.

They descended through a rockery, the stones planted with many beautiful flowers and interspersed with many circles of carefully combed sand. At one point they turned, startled, as a muffled *bang* echoed from somewhere over to the west, followed by another.

"Thunder?" said Hana.

"No," said the abbot. "Only our unruly neighbors, the Ikko-ikki." He pointed to another mountain, closer to the sea—on the other side to the direction from which the friends had approached.

It was a tall, dark mountain, topped by a cliff. And perched on the cliff was a building like a castle.

"Ikko-ikki?" said Taro.

"They call themselves monks," said the abbot dismissively. He set off again, apparently not in the mood to explain further. Behind his back, Hana shrugged at Taro.

The abbot indicated the vast hall that lay before them, its four open sides surrounded by a grassy space filled with *ume* trees. "Our residence," he said.

Before the residence hall the lawn extended to cliffs, presided over by a wooden framework containing a single enormous bell. Monks were gathered here and there on the grass, talking quietly. A few sat alone, cross-legged, contemplating the view, while others sat with their heads down, contemplating only something that lay within.

Taro was looking around with wonder, stunned by the beauty of this place. Then, as if by some sixth sense, his head snapped around; perhaps he had heard a familiar footstep, something just below the level of his consciousness, that told him everything was about to change.

A woman stepped from the shadow of the hall and onto the grass, and Taro would know that step anywhere, that slight turning of the heel, that way of walking so carefully, as if the ground might at any moment rear up to bite her.

He broke away from the abbot, and then he was running, ignoring the monks as they looked up at him with irritation. She was turning then, and her mouth fell open, and then she was moving too, heedless of the ground and the imaginary dangers it might pose, just rushing toward her son.

He flung his arms out as she did, and they swung each other around in their embrace, laughing.

"Taro!" she said. "My son! You came. I was so worried, when I left Mount Fuji, that you would not know where I had gone. . . ."

When the world was no longer spinning, Taro pulled away to look at her, to see her face. There were a few more wrinkles, perhaps, around her eyes, but otherwise she was unchanged, and he could hardly believe that the last time he'd seen her was that night in Shirahama, in their hut, when his father had just been murdered.

But then her words penetrated his consciousness.

"What do you mean, Mount Fuji?" he said.

"Isn't that where you've come from?" his mother asked.

Taro frowned. "No. We came from . . . somewhere else." He wasn't ready to talk about the ninja mountain, not yet. "From where Shusaku—he's the one who saved us—used to live. Your note said Mount Hiei."

She shook her head. "No, it didn't. It said Mount Fuji, because that was where I was. Then I had to leave—the monks heard that Lord Tokugawa was going to destroy the monastery. It was in his province, and he was ridding himself of all enemies, so—"

"Wait," said Taro. "You sent me a note saying you were at Mount Fuji? When was this?"

"Nearly a year ago," said his mother. "As soon as I arrived there."

Taro was experiencing an unpleasant sinking feeling. "Oh, no," he said.

"When I left," his mother continued, not realizing the danger yet, "a monk accompanied me. They felt Mount Hiei would be safe—there are ten thousand monks here, all well armed, and the daimyo are concerned with the Ikko-ikki, on the other mountain. But I left word for you—I thought that was how you came to me."

"No," said Taro. "I came because someone sent me a note saying you were here." He dug in the folds of his cloak, handed his mother the note. "Is this what you sent?" he asked, though he already knew the answer.

"No," said his mother.

Taro stared at her. "But that—it doesn't—" He puzzled over it. "Did you send another one? Could one of the monks have sent it?"

"No," said his mother.

He shivered. Clearly it was a trap. Someone had intercepted

her message, killed the pigeon, and sent another one much later, giving his mother's new location. But who? And for what reason? He looked around him. As his mother said, there were ten thousand monks here, and they would all fight to the death to protect the monastery. His mother was a valued guest here; so was he, it seemed. And the abbot had possessed ample opportunity to kill him back there in the woods, where they'd been ambushed.

He couldn't work it out.

It didn't make sense, but he didn't have long to worry about it. Hana and Hiro had come up behind him. Hiro pulled Taro's mother off the ground and spun her around. "It's good to see you!" he boomed. Taro's mother giggled as she twirled through the air.

"You too, Hiro," she said. When he finally put her down, she looked him up and down appraisingly. "You look different," she said. "Stronger."

"A lot has happened since we left Shirahama," said Taro. "I'll tell you all about it, I promise." He thought about this for a moment. No, perhaps not *all*. He could tell her he was a vampire, maybe—but to tell her that he had killed Lord Oda? Perhaps not. And then there was the question of his true parentage. He had some difficult questions to ask of her. Right now, though, she was standing in front of him, smiling, and he could think of nothing but the fact that he had found his mother again, after all this time.

The abbot walked over. "I am pleased you have been reunited with your son," he said to Taro's mother. He turned to Taro. "I have heard so much about you, these last few months. Of course, you're not quite . . . what I expected."

"Why is that?" asked Taro's mother.

The abbot spread his hands. "I am sure Taro can explain later," he said. He gave Taro a sharp look, one that seemed to say, *I hope you can, anyway*. Taro nodded at him. He knew he was here on the abbot's forbearance, to some extent. He was a vampire, and this was a holy place. He had known, from the moment the abbot recognized his name in the grove, that he would have some explaining to do.

"For now, though," said the abbot, "let us rejoice that a mother and son have found each other again." He turned to Hana and Hiro. "I imagine you are hungry, no?"

Hiro grinned. "Ravenous," he said.

"Well," said Taro's mother, "some things never change, at least."

That night the monks honored their new guests with a feast. Taro could not eat the food, of course, but he was touched and surprised when the abbot led him to the back of the dining hall and showed a squealing pig. Taro drank enough to sustain him, without doing the pig any lasting harm. Then he returned to the hall and laughed with the others as Hiro imitated the surprise on Taro's face when the monks dropped from the trees. There was little chance to talk to his mother, to find out what had happened to her since they last met, but for then Taro was satisfied to be close to her, after so long.

Midway through the feast, Taro took the abbot aside. He didn't explain anything about the ninja mountain, but he told the elderly monk about the note, and how he suspected this might be some kind of trap.

"But what trap?" said the abbot. "We will not harm you here. If I wanted you dead, you would be dead."

"Yes," said Taro. "I thought of that myself."

"It's a mystery," said the abbot. "But who is to say the note was not sent by a kind spirit? That it was not the action of some bodhisattva, of some *kami*, of the turning of the wheel of *dharma*?"

"Er . . . ," said Taro. "Yes, perhaps." But he was not convinced. He was nervous, and he couldn't stop looking around the hall, and startling whenever anyone moved their hands too quickly to their robes.

*There's danger here,* he thought. *I know it.* His instincts had not let him down before, and so he remained always tense and on guard, though smiling at his mother and Hiro to help them to relax.

The next day Taro sat with his mother and Hiro under an ancient plum tree. Hana had gone off with the abbot to look at the scrolls—he had promised to take one out of its gold casing and show her the actual text written so many centuries before by the monastery's founder, Seido. Taro had suggested to Hiro that he accompany her, so that he could sit alone with his mother, but Hiro had looked at him as if he was mad.

"I'm just worried," said Taro, "that it might be a trap." He didn't like the fact that the pigeon had taken so many months to reach him, and that the message had changed. And yet there didn't seem to be any threat here. His mother was safe, and the mountain was crawling with well-armed monks.

"The monks at Mount Fuji might have sent it," said his mother. "It's just strange that it took so long."

Taro sighed. "Perhaps. Except your first bird never reached the ninja mountain, so why did this one?" He'd told his mother about his training at the mountain, as if he'd gone straight there from Shirahama, and from there to Mount Hiei. Anything to do with Lord Oda, or his castle, he had left out. He and Hiro and Hana had left it to be understood that Hana, too, came from the ninja mountain.

His mother put her hand on his. "It doesn't matter. I'm just glad you're here at last."

Taro smiled at her. He was glad to be here too. He could sit and hold her hand forever, he thought. She had developed more lines, yes, but she also seemed healthier, now that she was not diving anymore. But the work was hard, and the sea claimed its price too. It got into the ears of the ama, salting them up, turning them slowly into coral, as if the sea were invading—bit by bit—their bodies. And their eyes were always bloodshot, their skin always wrinkled by the water.

Now, though, Taro's mother's eyes were a clear, light brown, like the leaves of the maples and cedars that still lay on the ground, and her skin was plumper, firmer. A vein throbbed, healthily, in her neck.

Taro looked away. He was better at controlling his urges, but the thirst still grabbed him sometimes like a ferocious wind that wanted to strip away his identity and leave a beast in his stead, desperate only for blood.

"—girl," said his mother, and Taro realized he had missed something.

"Sorry?" he said.

"The girl, Hanako. Do you love her?"

It took Taro a moment to think who his mother meant. Then he realized she was speaking of Hana. They had changed her name, just slightly—they didn't want anyone knowing she was Lord Oda's daughter. Taro looked down again, out of embarrassment this time, not the controlling of his blood-thirst. "I—ah—"

"Yes," said Hiro. "He does. He moons over her all the time. He's always looking at her, then going red."

Taro hit his friend's arm. "I—," he began. "That is to say . . . I felt, when I met her, that I knew her. "

His mother nodded, a faraway look in her eye. "
"That is the way it is." Taro wished he could kno
of his father—the father who raised him—or Lord '
could see no way of asking.

"Tell me about this place," he asked instead. '
here."

His mother touched the trunk of the tree. "Whe
hama, I didn't know where I was going. But then I h
on the road mention the Fuji monastery, and how th
of the daimyo were still being frustrated by the wai
thought it would be a safer place than any, so I made
But then we heard Lord Tokugawa was about to at
moved here, as I told you. I expected it to be a refug
arrived . . . I found something I hadn't quite foreseer

"Really?"

"Yes. I was looking for safety. But what I found v
I suppose." She smiled, embarrassed, and looked do
som that had fallen into the palm of her hand. "It wz
I arrived, and the spirits of the dead were loose in tl
husband had just been killed. It could have been a c
but the monks helped me. They taught me meditation
me to see that this world of tears is only temporary ai
like the reflection of the moon on the surface of the v

Taro raised his eyebrows. "And to think you were
ama once . . . ," he said playfully.

She laughed, getting to her feet. "Come," she sai
you around." She led Taro and Hiro through the ha
the giant bell to the grassy meditation area. Heading d
showed them the various buildings: the initiation ha
and the watchtowers. Taro feigned interest, his mind
tery of the slow pigeon—and Hana's face—while Hi
constant chatter.

As they walked, though, Taro felt himself relaxing
distraction. He was in the company of his mother, long
best friend. He should enjoy it while it lasted. Slowly he

some of the harder things—things he had not wanted to bring up ıightaway. They spoke at length about Taro's father, conjuring man from the air before them, seeing him together, remember- his strength and kindness. And Taro told his mother everything ıt had happened to him—or almost everything, anyway.

It was enough, though, to walk with her, through the shade the pine trees, and watch the many-clouded sky above, always ›ving and always the same. Finally they returned to the medita- n area, where Taro's mother led them to another *ume* tree, even ›re gnarled and ancient than the one they'd been sitting under. ıe sun was low, and its light filtered through the pink blossoms, ›ating the impression that they stood within a canopy of intricate ticework, designed to refract and color the light. A builder of ınples could not have emulated it.

"The monks sit by this tree all day sometimes," Taro's mother ıd. "They say that watching the plum rain is a kind of meditation."

"Huh," said Hiro. "Sounds like a nice way to spend your life."

"They say not. They call it *mono no aware*. What they are trying do is to understand, completely, that nothing in the world lasts. ıat everything is . . . transient. They say that the plum rain is a mbol of the unreality of the world. It always falls, you see. And ›en there is only the bare branch. They say that if they can only asp this idea firmly in their minds, the world will for them take ı its essential lack of form, and they will be only light. That is ›eration."

Taro nodded. "I see." He didn't, really, but his mother had a ır-off look in her eye, as if what the monks had told her accorded ith some secret intuition of her own. "You would like to stay ›re," he said. It was more a statement than a question.

His mother looked at him, surprised. "I—that is to say—yes, ›rhaps I would. There is something . . . peaceful here. I find what ıe monks say interesting."

From the west came a *bang*—like the one Taro had heard on ıs arrival. It did not sound especially peaceful to him. He raised ıs eyebrows.

His mother rolled her eyes. "Yes, the Ikko-ikki do their best to distract us with their guns."

"They fire them often?"

"Oh, yes. Lord Oda and Lord Tokugawa are laying siege to their mountain. It has been going on for months. It is said that the Hongan-ji, the Ikko-ikki's fortress, is impenetrable, but the daimyo will not give up. They hate the Ikko-ikki, and it appears that the feeling is mutual."

"But I—I heard that Lord Oda was dead," said Taro.

His mother frowned. "Really? I'd have thought the monks would know, if that was the case."

Taro pursed his lips. This was odd. Come to think of it, no one they had met on the walk had mentioned Lord Oda's death. Oshi had never spoken of it. Wasn't that strange? One would think that the news of a daimyo's murder would spread quickly over the country. Was the Oda camp keeping it secret, somehow?

Well, it was something to think about. Right now, there was an odd expression on his mother's face, and he realized that if she wanted to stay here, he was going to have to get some answers quickly. Kenji Kira was still looking for him; the daimyo were just awaiting an excuse to attack the monastery. "Mother . . . ," he began. "The night Father was killed. Why did you dive over the old wreck?"

Her eyes sharpened. "I needed to hide something."

Taro took a breath. "The ball."

She went pale. "You . . . how do you know about that?"

"Someone mentioned it."

His mother seemed to be thinking, weighing things up in her mind. "I was hiding the ball, yes," she said finally. "When I heard the talk of *kyuuketsuki*, I knew that something evil must be coming for it."

Taro flinched at that. Was that how his mother would see him? As something evil?

"But you must promise me to leave it where it is," continued his mother. "Do you understand? That thing is dangerous. There are people who would kill for it."

Taro knew that all too well. But he took his mother's hand and said, "I promise." What did the ball matter, when he had his mother back?

Taro's mother cleared her throat. "Hiro—do you think you could find me a drink of water?" she asked.

Hiro nodded slowly. "Yes, of course," he said. With a glance at Taro he walked away, toward the main temple building.

Taro's mother held on to his hand. "Ninjas killed your father," she said eventually. She was not meeting his eyes, he noticed. "One of them saved you. You said he took you to his mountain, trained you. Do you know why your father was killed? Why you were saved?"

Taro swallowed. He didn't know how much his mother knew, but one thing was for certain: If her husband was not his father, she must know it. He remembered the strange, faraway look that had come into her eyes when she saw the *mon* on his bow, back in their peasant hut before everything changed. "I . . . Shusaku thought it was me the ninjas wanted to kill." He weighed up what to say next. "He believed Lord Oda sent them."

His mother sighed. "Yes, I thought as much." There was a tear on her cheek—though she made no move to brush it away. "Taro," she said softly, "there is something I need to say to you, something about your father. . . ."

Taro squeezed her hand. "I know," he said. "Lord Tokugawa is my father, isn't he?"

His mother closed her eyes for a moment. "Who told you?" she asked.

"It was the *mon* on my bow," Taro said. "Shusaku recognized it."

She shook her head. "Stupid of him to leave that with you. He always was arrogant." But the way she said it was fond, gentle.

"Were you . . . did you love him?"

His mother smiled. "In a way," she said. "I was . . . attracted to him. You will learn that there are different kinds of love. The love I felt for your father—for the man you knew as your father—was different. Deeper. You must believe that neither of us meant to hurt you. He was a kind man, a good man. When he saw how I had been abandoned, with an infant son . . . he married me, and he never cared what people said about it."

Taro smiled. "He loved us," he said. He was thinking of the way his father had carried him up from the beach, the day he was bitten by the shark.

"Yes. And I loved him. You know that, don't you?"

"Yes, Mother. I know it."

"Good. Lord Tokugawa, though . . . I was very young, you must understand that. And he was the heir to a lordship—he came to take the waters, like the prince in the first story of the Buddha ball. Actually, he was always fascinated by that story." She paused. "Shirahama was Oda territory then too, of course, but his father— the Tokugawa daimyo at the time—had a good relationship with Lord Oda's father. That alliance was forged a long time ago. So Ieyasu—I mean, Lord Tokugawa—would recline in the *onsen* springs and recite poetry. He would train at swords with his men. I had never encountered such . . . cultivation. It was quite over- whelming.

"I don't know what I expected—maybe that he would take me to his castle and marry me. He didn't. He did leave me with some money, and the bow for you."

"He wanted an heir," said Taro. "Someone he could hide from Lord Oda, or anyone else who might harm him."

"Perhaps," said his mother. "And as a strategy it is not alto- gether foolish. His other two sons are dead, are they not?"

A frisson passed through Taro, as he thought of the younger half brother he had buried on the ninja mountain. "Yes," he said.

"But I don't think it was just that," said his mother.

Taro frowned. "Then what?"

His mother spoke almost as if thinking out loud. "He really was obsessed with that old story," she said. "The Buddha ball, and the ama woman, and the curse on the line of emperors. You know the whole thing?"

"Yes. A prophetess told me."

His mother nodded, as if this confirmed some terrible suspicion.

"But why didn't you tell me the story?" said Taro. "Why didn't I hear it in Shirahama?"

"The Buddha ball is dangerous," said his mother. "The people who want it are dangerous. I sensed that even at the time, though I was too infatuated with Ieya— with Lord Tokugawa to care. I believe he knew I was the guardian of the ball, the ama who had been chosen to keep it safe. He never asked me for it; he's too subtle for that. But I wonder . . . No, perhaps it is too far-fetched."

"What?"

"I wonder, I suppose . . . whether he didn't just want an heir his enemies wouldn't know about. He *knew* the story, Taro. He knew that the prince's son returned the ball to the ghost of his mother, and he believed she gave it to the amas for safekeeping. He believed the ball was real. He knew, too, that the same ama had cursed the line of emperors, saying that one day the son of an ama would rule the entire land. He knew and he . . ."

The ground suddenly felt unstable under Taro's feet. "And he got himself a son with an ama," he said, completing his mother's thought.

"Yes. Not just any ama—a beautiful young woman who had been entrusted with the care of the ball." She smiled, embarrassed. "I really was beautiful, you know," she said. "Everyone said so."

"Of course," said Taro. "You're beautiful now."

His mother squeezed his hand. "I may be imagining things," she said. "All this may be nothing. But I've always thought . . . and when the ninjas came it seemed to me to confirm it . . . I've always thought that Lord Tokugawa chose me deliberately. That he came to Shirahama with a single goal in mind—that he came to make a son. A son who would inherit the Buddha ball, and the country, too, and rule Japan in the name of Tokugawa."

For several days Taro passed the time pleasantly—talking to his mother, sparring with Hiro, enjoying the stunning views and serenity of the mountain. His only sadness was that he saw little of Hana. She seemed always to be with the monks, discussing fine points of Buddhist lore, or sitting with Oshi and Hayao, trying to draw the ever-weaker samurai out, to get him to respond to her voice. Still, that rat of jealousy gnawed at Taro's guts.

On the third or fourth day, Taro was sitting with his mother under the ancient plum tree when the abbot appeared and asked if he would take a walk with him. He began to excuse himself from his mother, but she waved him away with a smile. "Go," she said. "You can't spend every day talking to an old woman like me."

"But you've a very interesting old woman," he said.

"Be off with you," she said.

When Taro and the abbot were alone, the abbot turned to him. "You've told her you're a vampire? I presume you weren't when you last saw each other. She would have mentioned it, I'm sure."

Taro coughed, embarrassed. "No," he said. "I don't know how to." He'd spoken at length with his mother about his true parentage, and about his journey to the ninja mountain, but he had still found no way to tell her what he had become, or how he had killed Lord Oda.

"Good," said the abbot. "In fact, I think it's better if you don't. Your mother has achieved a certain . . . serenity here. It would only disturb her. But you can talk to me about it, if you like."

Taro told the abbot what had happened to him since he left Shirahama—leaving out anything to do with the prophecy, or Lord Oda. He didn't want anyone knowing he was Lord Tokugawa's son. He thought these monks were good people, but who could tell what they would do if they knew they had such a valuable pawn in their possession?

The abbot listened carefully, offering considered comment and sympathy at key points in the story. Actually, Taro was impressed. He had expected more judgment from the man. As they rounded the main temple building and neared the central tree once again, Taro felt more easy, less burdened, than he had in weeks. It was almost like being with Shusaku again—though as usual, the mere thought of Shusaku sent a pain like a sword blade through him.

"What would you like to do?" asked the abbot suddenly.

"About what?"

"About everything. Your life. Will you stay here? You would not starve—we have plenty of game on the mountain, if you would appreciate something with a little more life than the pigs."

"I know," said Taro. "I smelled deer. It's just . . . I have things to do." He was thinking of the Buddha ball. If he didn't find it, then someone like Kenji Kira might, and that would be a disaster. He'd promised his mother he'd leave it where it was. But he could find it. Make sure it was safe.

"I could teach you," said the abbot.

Taro smiled. "I don't think meditation is for me."

"I was thinking more of the sword," said the old man.

Taro paused. The abbot had disarmed him with such ease,

down there in the wood. It *would* be good to learn from him, to see if he could increase his own speed. He'd thought, arrogantly, that he must be among the best—but if his fight with the abbot was any indication, he was far from being a sword saint.

"You can teach me what you did down there?" he asked.

"I don't know if I can teach you. I can show you the way. You'll have to teach yourself."

"What does that mean?" asked Taro. But the abbot just smiled enigmatically.

They were walking past a well-tended rockery, enjoying the panoramic view of the lowlands and the sea, when Taro noticed Hayao sitting with the ghost, Tsuyu, deep in conversation. He glanced at the abbot, who was gazing innocently ahead of him, but Taro wasn't convinced. He thought perhaps the old monk had contrived to bring him here.

"He's the other reason I would urge you to stay," said the abbot. "At least for a while." He turned to Taro and stopped. "You see her now?" he asked. "The ghost?"

"Yes. She's sitting beside him. Her head is resting on his shoulder."

"I can't," said the abbot wistfully. "I see the samurai, and I see the empty sky. I see no girl. I can't help but agree with Oshi that there must be a reason you two met. I think perhaps your destiny is tied up with that of this poor man."

Taro bit his lip. He could think of one way in which their destinies might be linked: if Hana were to fall in love with Hayao. But he shook himself, told himself he was being crazy. Right now the man was speaking to a woman who wasn't there.

Taro realized the abbot had been talking. "Sorry?" he said.

"I was saying that you might be able to help him," said the abbot. "I would love to help you with your sword fighting, but I believe you might be able to assist us in our work too."

Taro felt annoyed. "Why do you want to help Hayao so much?" he asked. "He's a *hatamoto* for Lord Oda. Ha— I mean, I heard that Lord Oda was no friend to the monastery."

The abbot nodded slowly, then smiled. "You are right. First, I must tell you that we would help anyone in such dire need. The man is dying. Would you not feel a duty to prevent that, if you could?"

Taro looked down, ashamed. "Yes," he said.

"Good. But as I respect you, I won't lie to you. It does strike me that this could be a good thing, to provide such much-needed assistance to a prominent member of Lord Oda's retinue. If we save his life . . . Well. Perhaps Lord Oda might be persuaded to look more kindly on us."

Taro didn't think Lord Oda would look kindly on anything, since he was dead. But he kept quiet. For some reason the news was not widely known, and he didn't want to get into any long and potentially awkward discussions.

"I understand," was all he said. "What I don't understand is what you think *I* can do about it. I don't know any spells, or sutras, or what have you. I can barely read."

The abbot sat down on the grass and motioned for Taro to do the same. "You don't need to," he said. "Just tell me again what you see."

Taro peered at the samurai and the ghost. "I told you. She's sitting next to him. He has his arm around her, and she is leaning her head on his shoulder. They are talking—whispering, really. I can't tell what she is saying."

"She is speaking in the language of the dead," said the abbot. "If he can understand her, then he must be close to death himself."

"I don't know if he can understand her. He just tells her he loves her."

"Hmm," said the abbot. "The problem for me is that she shouldn't be able to get so close. Between Oshi and I, we have equipped the man with charms and scrolls that should keep even the strongest ghosts at bay. I have sutras here that were old when Buddhism came to Japan, and yet they seem to be useless against the *gaki* that has taken hold of him. I fear that if something isn't done quickly, he will soon die."

Taro sighed. For once Hana was not with Hayao, speaking to him of the old days, of how he trained her to fight when her father feared for her life, but he still resented the pale-faced samurai with the prominent bones. Even so, could he really let the man die, if there was something he could do to help?

"What do you think I can do?" he asked.

"I don't know. Usually the bond of a love connection can be broken, with the right tools. In this case, I believe that her karmic bond with Hayao must be strengthened by something—something that enables her to get past any defenses I can erect."

"But what could that thing be?" said Taro.

"Again, I don't know," said the abbot. "You see her, and I don't. Observe her closely—stay close to him and to her. You are the only one who can see her—I must believe there is a reason for that. Watch for something, anything, that might help us. And then tell me what you see."

Taro sighed. "Yes, very well," he said. "And then you'll teach me your skill with the sword? What is it—a special kata? A unique way of training?"

The abbot smiled. "It is simpler, and infinitely more complicated than that," he said, cryptically. He took a small scroll from his cloak and threw it to Taro. Taro caught it and frowned at it.

"What's this?"

"The secret of the sword is in there," said the abbot. "It's all right," he added, noting Taro's puzzled expression. "It's written in hiragana." Taro cursed Hana—she must have told the abbot about teaching him to read. Suddenly he felt his cheeks heat up with irritation.

"What about sparring?" he said. "Training. Practice. You're telling me the secret of your speed is in this stupid scroll?"

Taro didn't even see anything—one moment the abbot was standing there in front of him with his arms at his sides, and the next there was a dull explosion of pain in Taro's left temple, and then the abbot was holding out a wooden *bokken* sword—one he'd evidently just hit Taro with.

"Did you see that coming?" said the abbot.

"No," said Taro, through gritted teeth.

"Not such a stupid scroll then, is it?" said the abbot. He turned on his heel and began to walk away. "Help that samurai," he said over his shoulder. "It will be good for your karma if you can save his life. And read the scroll. Reading is good for you too."

Taro sat cross-legged on the grass of the plateau, watching Hayao and the ghost-woman as the sun set behind the Ikko-ikki fortress to the west. He had noticed that in the last day or so, the gunfire appeared to have stopped.

He found his attention drifting from the tragic couple to the splashes of color on the horizon, the burning clouds over the sea. He'd thought that once he found his mother again he would achieve some kind of peace, but to his surprise he was as restless as he had ever been. In Shirahama he had thought that he wanted adventure; the noble, violent life of the samurai. Since then he had learned better than anyone that there was little nobility in it—and a lot of violence. Yet even though he had left the village, and fought and traveled and seen things few people would, he still found himself looking to the horizon. Already he was thinking of leaving here, going looking for the Buddha ball.

*This lust for adventure,* he realized for the first time, *is like a curse.*

Although, beside his mother, what was there to keep him here? There was the abbot and his so-called secret, but what a load of nonsense that had turned out to be. He took the scroll from his pocket and turned it idly in his hands. It was just an old story about a man and a harp—he was sure he'd heard it before from his mother. Irritated, he dropped the scroll on the ground.

There was a gentle cough beside him and he turned to see Hana, smiling at him. He was sitting down, but his heart was still able to stumble. He smiled back uncertainly. Hana sat down on the grass.

"The abbot told me you would be here," she said.

Taro shrugged.

"He spoke highly of you. Said you were trying to help Hayao." Her smile was brighter than the sunset.

"Oh. Y-yes, yes I am." He blushed. Then he realized that she was probably only concerned for Hayao, not admiring of his charity, and he looked down at the grass.

"He means a lot to you, doesn't he?" he asked. "Hayao, I mean."

Hana frowned, surprised. "Yes . . . I mean, no. He taught me to fight, when my father decided I was no longer safe. He treated me like . . . like I wasn't a girl. I liked him for it. But this thing with the ghost—it's not him in particular. I just think it's sad. Don't you? This girl, she really loved him, and now she's killing him, even though she probably doesn't even want to. It's tragic."

Taro made a noise that could have been agreement. He was thinking about what Hana had said—that Hayao had treated her like she wasn't a girl. And here he was, mooning over her, blushing at the things she said, gazing at her beauty. He couldn't be less like the thin, pale samurai.

"He's handsome," he said, with false absentness. "I mean, he must have been. Before the ghost."

"I suppose so," said Hana. "Yes."

Taro felt that he would like the cliff to move closer to him, and drop him off the side. He hadn't known what a mistake it would be to come here. Already he barely saw Hana—she was always having discussions with the monks that he couldn't possibly follow, conversations about arcane points of Buddhist law. Either that or she was admiring the temples, or joining the monks in painting birds and drawing kanji characters with perfect, sweeping calligraphy.

Doing all the things that, as a peasant, Taro could never do. He wanted to pick up the abbot's idiotic scroll and tear it up, but he just sat there with his hands folded over his knees.

"So . . . ," said Hana, after a while. "What is it you're doing, exactly?"

Wearily Taro pointed to the couple. "I'm watching them. The abbot said there must be something tying them together. Some object that is making the karmic bond stronger. But I can't see it, if there is one." He sighed.

"Describe her," said Hana.

"Who, the ghost?"

"Yes. Tell me what she looks like."

"I don't know," he said. "She has dark hair. . . ."

"All Japanese women have dark hair."

"Er . . . yes. Her eyes are large. They are black inside—all black. The whites of her eyes are black too. Do you know what I mean? It's like someone poured ink in her eyes."

"Ugh," said Hana.

"It's horrible. And she's very, very pale. White, really. Also, she has a beauty spot on her cheek. She has full lips—I wouldn't have expected that, from a ghost. She is a little older than you, I think. Small ears. What else do you want me to tell you?"

"I don't know," said Hana. "What about her clothes?"

"She's wearing a blue kimono. Clogs."

"What kind of kimono? Silk?"

"Ah . . . I . . ." He peered closer. "I would say no."

"And the clogs. Are they worn? I mean, on the bottom. Can you see, the way she's sitting?"

He could. The girl was sitting cross-legged, like him, and he could see where the wood of the bottom of the *geta* clogs had been scoured by contact with the ground. "Yes, they're worn," he said.

Hana nodded. "She was not rich, then. What about jewelry? Rings?"

He examined the hand that was stroking Hayao's cheek, and the other, laid demurely in her lap. "No."

"Hair?"

"I said she had dark hair."

Hana rolled her eyes and patted his arm. "I was thinking of how it was arranged. Tied up? Down?"

"Um. Tied up. No, pinned up." He stood, to get a better view. Hayao didn't even register their presence. "There's a clip—like a butterfly."

"Made from?"

"The clip? I'd say . . . ivory. And mother-of-pearl."

Hana clapped her hands. "That's it!"

"It is?"

"I have seen such clips. They come from China—the Portuguese bring them by ship to Nagasaki. They are *very* expensive."

Taro looked at her blankly. "And . . . ?"

"And she is not rich. We have established that." Hana stood quickly and grabbed his hand—something like an electric shock went through him at the soft, unexpected touch. He felt as though a wild animal—a doe, maybe—had just, against all reason, put its nose to his hand. She pulled him to his feet and dragged him along.

"Where are we going?" he asked.

"To find the abbot," said Hana.

"Why?"

"Don't you see? Hayao must have given her the hair clip. It is the thing that is binding them."

Suddenly Taro *could* see. No wonder Hana would never be interested in marrying him—he even *thought* like a peasant. He could not reason in the same way, make observations and draw conclusions from them.

Hana stopped and he ran into her, and for one thrilling

moment he had to hold on to her waist, to keep from falling.

"What's that?" said Hana, looking behind them. "Did you forget something?"

"What's what?"

Hana pointed to the scroll, the one the abbot had given him, lying on the ground where Taro had thrown it. He shrugged. "It's nothing," he said.

Two nights later the abbot stood with Taro under the plum tree where Taro's mother spent most of her time. The others had gone to bed, but the abbot had asked Taro to stay awhile, and then had led him out into the courtyard.

"You did well," he said. "Oshi went to the grave. They disinterred the plum rain girl. In her hair they found a clip, in the shape of a butterfly."

"Will Hayao be all right?" asked Taro.

"I believe so, yes. Oshi spoke to the monk who introduced Hayao and Tsuyu—he is distraught by the whole affair, as you can imagine. He confirmed that Tsuyu began wearing the butterfly clip in her hair soon after she met Hayao. He noticed it at the time, but he thought that by keeping them apart he was doing the right thing, and he didn't know how powerful these tokens can be. He believes now that Hayao gave it to her, as a symbol of his love, during their brief meeting. That's just the kind of thing that would bind her to him even more strongly—it contained a part of him, his love for her, and so it allowed her to come to him, even past the *o-fuda* and the golden Buddha, and all the sutras I chanted."

"The clip," said Hayao. "What did you do with it?"

"Destroyed it," said the abbot. Then he gestured to the shadows at the edge of the courtyard. A man stepped forward—Hayao.

Taro's mouth dropped. He'd only ever seen the man peering into the face of the ghost-girl, muttering. Already the samurai's face showed more color. He smiled at Taro. "Thank you," he said. He bowed.

Taro bowed back. "There is no need. I only said what I saw." He paused. "I'm sorry about Tsuyu. You must have loved her very much."

"I did. I do. But she was killing me. I don't remember very much . . . yet the abbot has told me what happened. I am very grateful to you for your help."

"I didn't do much," said Taro. "I just saw her."

Hayao sighed. "So did I, to my cost. She did not mean to hurt me," he said. "I'm sure of that. Anyway, we will see each other again. In the next life."

"I hope so," said Taro.

"For now," said the samurai, "if you ever need my help, you will have it. Ask for Hayao. I am known in these parts."

"Thank you," said Taro. He paused. "Actually, there is something." He turned to the abbot. "Could you give us a moment alone?" he asked.

The abbot bowed, then melted into the darkness.

"There is a girl here," said Taro. "I don't know if you remember her. She was with me when I first met you."

"Hana?" said Hayao. "It seems to me I saw her, but then again it feels as though it could have been a dream." A faraway tone that Taro didn't at all like had crept into the man's voice.

"Yes, Hana. She's here on the mountain. But listen—no one knows who she is, you understand? No one knows she's Lord Oda's daughter, and we need it to stay that way. Please, don't tell anyone. And call her Hanako, if you can."

"Why?" said Hayao. "What is she doing here? Has something happened to Lord Oda?"

"It's a long story," said Taro. "I would rather not speak of it."

Hayao bowed, a little stiffly. "Very well. I cannot hide that I know her—but I will not reveal who she is."

"Thank you," said Taro.


"He would have died," said the abbot conversationally. When Hayao had left, to look at the night sky, he said, the abbot had reappeared at Taro's side, almost as if he had known when to come back, as if he had been listening. But that was paranoid, Taro knew.

"You saw how the ghost was draining his flesh. How his skin was hanging from his cheek. Eventually he would have simply wasted away. Of course, the man is one of Lord Oda's samurai, which complicates matters. But I hope that our . . . intervention might reach the lord's ears. Soften his attitude toward us, perhaps. For the moment the lords besiege only the Ikko-ikki. Their opinions are more controversial than ours. But I expect they will attack our temple, one of these days. There are some who wish to rule Japan all on their own. We are too powerful to let such people sleep soundly."

Taro licked his lips. "Hmmm," he said. He was wondering if *anything* would reach Lord Oda's ears—as far as he knew, the man had died on the stairs of his own tower. But he said nothing.

"Anyway," said the abbot. "For now Hayao is simply a stranger who found comfort here, and healing. He will go out into the world thankful to the monks of Mount Hiei. I am grateful to you. And you should be proud of what you have done."

Taro nodded. He *did* feel proud—for so long he had brought only death to those around him. Now he had saved a man, and it had been simple. He could do it again, he thought.

Something appeared in the abbot's hand,, and he passed it to Taro. "I believe you mislaid this," he said.

Taro looked down at the scroll in his hand. "I—yes. I must have left it somewhere."

"Indeed. Somewhere like the ground?"

"Perhaps I dropped it."

"Indeed."

Taro flushed. "I read it. I didn't understand. It was just a children's story."

"Children's stories are not just anything," said the abbot. "Don't you know that?"

For a horrible moment, Taro wondered if the man was referring to the story of the Buddha ball, the story Shusaku had dismissed as a children's tale, and that had turned out to be utterly, terribly true. But the abbot just smiled. "Read it again," he said.

Taro sighed. "Very well."

The older man touched his arm. "There really is a secret," he said. "I'm not lying to you. The problem is that I can't tell you what it is. You have to come to the understanding yourself. That's why I gave you the scroll. The story . . . helps."

"Right," said Taro, unconvinced. "It seems like it would be a lot quicker if you just told me."

The abbot grinned. He pointed to the scroll in Taro's hand. "This is the secret, then." He waved his hand, and Taro was no longer holding the scroll. Taro stared down at his empty palm. He turned, searching the ground around him. "It's simple," said the abbot. *"There is no sword."*

"I don't understand," said Taro.

The abbot reached into his cloak and drew out a *katana*. He raised his hand; there was an impression of movement. The air fluttered in Taro's hair. The abbot gestured to the ground. Lying there were several tiny pink flowers, each of them cut neatly in half. They had been falling from the cherry tree, he realized. The abbot had cut the blossoms even as they fell.

"That is what you will be able to do," he said, "when you understand that there is no sword. Now, try it." He handed the sword to Taro.

Taro settled into his stance, then struck—hard—at the falling blossoms. The sword slashed uselessly through the air. He cursed, tried again. Failed.

"You were right!" said the abbot, a little more sarcastically than Taro would have liked, for one of his age and wisdom. "I told you the secret, and now here you are—a latter-day Musashi. Your speed defies belief."

Taro grunted, irritated. He gave back the sword. The abbot replaced it in his hand with the scroll.

"Read it again. You never know when enlightenment might strike." With that, the abbot disappeared into the darkness, much as Hayao had done. Taro thought about looking for Hana, to tell her that he had helped Hayao—that the samurai was recovering. But he thought she probably knew already. No doubt they were somewhere in the temple complex, catching up on old times.

Cursing, he stalked off into the night.

He was a vampire, wasn't he? A vampire and a peasant. Well, he should stay outside then.

And hunt.


The deer passed below Taro's branch, nuzzling at the small yellow flowers that grew amid the mossy stones at the edge of the small clearing. Taro judged his moment, then dropped, aiming for the deer's back.

Something, some ancient survival instinct, made the deer look up, and then it was gone, a flash of springing legs.

Taro rolled when he hit the ground, and in the same movement he was up on his feet, following the dappled fawn as it sprang into the shadows, flashing through the trees. A human wouldn't have had a chance at following it on foot, but Taro was quicker and more agile than any ordinary mortal. He barely glanced at the rocks and roots as he leaped over them, switching left and right, avoiding the trees. His arm hit a branch and he spun, winded, but a moment later he was running again, the scent of the deer—musk, scat, and mud—strong in his nostrils.

There was a cliff ahead and the deer paused, before ducking its head down and launching itself to the left—but that momentary halt was enough for Taro to leap, and trace an inexorable trajectory through the air.

He slammed into the deer with all his weight, his hands going to its short antlers. With a sharp twist, he broke its neck—he believed in being merciful.

The deer was dead before it hit the ground.

Taro knelt beside the body, his knee on the rock of the precipice. He bent his head and bit down on the creature's neck, drawing its still-hot blood into himself, feeling his strength growing. It was as if a fire were being lit in his stomach, purging him of his cares and his weakness. He felt invincible.

There was a *bang* and he barely paused, so used had he grown to the gunshots from the Ikko-ikki fortress. But then he stopped feeding. He looked up. That shot had been *close*.

For the first time, he truly took in his surroundings. He was crouched at the top of a cliff—though its height, and the sharp stones at the bottom, did not worry him. What drew his attention was the valley that spread out below, a long inverted V, with its narrow end tapering to a gulley that led almost directly to the top of the mountain Taro was on.

Camped in this valley, crowding to its edges, was an army.

The valley was long—at least two *ri* to its other end, where the fat end of the V spilled out into gradually descending, rolling countryside, as if the valley were a kind of river of emptiness that had run out of violent energy as it broke down from the mountaintop, laying waste to the rock and earth in its path. Where the valley petered out, the facing mountain rose, lower than Mount Hiei but with a craggier top. Here, on the peak, Taro could just make out a castle, smoke rising from the dwellings inside its high, serious-looking walls.

The Hongan-ji; the lair of the Ikko-ikki. Yet the army in the valley below was not facing *that* mountain. Ranks of troops—

thousands of them—were moving slowly up the hillside, in full armor, toward Taro's mountain. Toward the Tendai monastery. At the rear was a small cavalry section, but what drew Taro's horrified, fascinated stare was the front rank—a row of hundreds upon hundreds of men with rifles.

All marching toward *him.*

Above the heads of the troops fluttered flags, hoisted high on poles. On them, black against white, was the *mon* of Lord Oda.

Lord Oda's army was attacking. Taro thought of the pigeon, and the strange delay before it reached the ninja mountain. Kenji Kira. Somehow Taro knew what had happened.

He had been lured to this place to die.

Taro burst into the hall where the monks slept, banging his *katana* against the bell as he ran past it.

"Up! Up!" he shouted. "The samurai are coming!"

He heard confused cries, men asking one another questions, their voices blurry with sleep.

"The samurai!" he shouted. "Get ready to fight!"

The abbot had told him that every monk on the mountain was trained, and every one was armed with a sword. In emergencies, the monks could muster thousands of men in minutes, all deadly efficient fighters.

Taro hoped they had practiced often.

Coming to the other end of the hall, he flew through the doors and into the courtyard. At the other end was the smaller room where his mother slept. He entered without knocking. His mother sat up on her bed, blinking at him.

"Taro?" she said.

"You must go," he replied. "Get out of here. Lord Oda's samurai are coming."

"Why?" she said.

"I killed Lord Oda." As he said it, he felt sick, as if the deer's blood had gone bad inside him, or still retained some essence of the deer's being, and was sloshing around in there to disorient him, and take its revenge. He had provided the pretext. Years, these monks had been here, perfecting their fighting skills, meditating, and assisting the haunted. Now men were coming. Men with guns.

And it was all Taro's fault.

He was looking down, and was surprised when he felt his mother's hand on his chin, lifting his face to look at him.

"These monks have waited for this day for many years," she said.

"They don't have guns," he replied.

His mother nodded. "That is true. Well, we will hope for rain."

He stared. "Rain?"

"Guns use fire. The rain puts them out."

He still stared. "That's it? You're just going to hope for rain?"

His mother sighed. "Listen. I didn't tell you the truth before. If I die, I want you to—"

"No! You're not going to die. You're going to leave."

The door behind them opened, and the abbot entered. "It's too late for that," he said. "They have surrounded us."

Taro looked from his mother to the abbot, then back at her. She was more beautiful than ever. In the doorway, two more silhouettes appeared, then resolved themselves as Hiro and Hana. They both held their swords in their hands.

"We fight?" he said to them, and to the abbot.

All three nodded.

"Side by side," said Hiro.

"Always," said Hana.

"They have guns," said Taro—he felt like he was the only one who understood this, understood what it meant. "Hundreds of men with rifles. I saw them marching up the hill at the head of the army."

"Indeed," said the abbot. "Like the Ikko-ikki, Lord Oda is obsessed with guns. The Portuguese have convinced him that the modern methods of warfare are more effective. That it is easier to kill people from a distance."

Hiro frowned. "They're right, aren't they?"

"They make it easier to kill, perhaps," said the abbot. "But not easier to live with it afterward. Better to look a man in the eyes as you kill him."

"Are you serious?" said Hiro. "This is going to be a slaughter. Do you have any guns at all up here?"

"No," said the abbot.

"So basically we're going to hold off hundreds of gunmen with nothing more than our swords, and our sense of honor?" said Hiro.

"Yes," said the abbot. "But we have years of meditation on our side. Decades in some cases."

"Oh, gods," said Hiro. "We're going to die."

The abbot smiled. "Do not give up hope just yet. Guns are notoriously difficult to use in battle. They take a long time to reload—that gives us many opportunities to make sorties, to cut and slash into the line. They often misfire, and they don't work at all in the rain."

Taro glanced at the night sky, through the open window. It was completely clear.

"Well," said the abbot. "We shall attack them when they are reloading."

"How long have we got?" Taro asked him.

"Not long. They are already on the lower flanks."

Taro went to stand with his friends, and put an arm around Hiro's shoulder. "Are you ready, my old friend?" he asked.

"Oh, yes," said Hiro. "There are samurai with guns coming, but the monks have been meditating, so I feel much better." He touched Taro's blade with his own, and they made a *ting* together. "Still, better to die together, eh?"

Hana moved to Taro's other side. She touched his cheek, then looked into his eyes. Quickly she kissed him on the cheek, and Taro smelled jasmine and roses, and felt that he might faint.

"If we die," she said, "come look for me in our next lives."

*Kenji Kira pressed his spurs into his horse's side, watching the troops advance before him. Excitement and hunger swirled in his stomach. Finally he would take the boy, as Lord Oda had asked so many months before. And then, when Lord Oda was shogun, Kenji would be given a province, a title, a wife befitting his stature. Perhaps even Lord Oda's daughter.*

*He looked up at the peak of Mount Hiei, gray in the moonlight. Yes, Hana would be there, with the boy. He was looking forward to seeing the look on her face when he killed Taro. She had humiliated him, going off like that with the peasant. But Kenji would make her pay. It was all so beautiful. At first, when he found the message from Taro's mother on that hillside, he had ridden hard to Mount Fuji with his men, aiming to kill her right away, to slaughter her and then send her body bit by bit to her son, to draw Taro toward him.*

*And that would have been enjoyable. But then two things had happened. First, he had arrived at Mount Fuji to find that Lord Tokugawa had razed the monastery there, slaughtering all the monks. The place*

was a wasteland, and worse than that, a wasteland controlled by
Tokugawa samurai. Kenji Kira had been forced to turn around long
before he reached it, to regain the safety of strong Oda land.

He had cursed and ground his teeth, knowing that the woman was
beyond him now, was probably dead.

But then Yukiko had come to him. She was just a girl, but she wore the
colors of a hatamoto, and she carried a Masamune sword—a priceless
sword of violence, made by the master of the bloodthirsty weapon. Oda
had given it to her, she said. She was strong and lithe and pretty, and
she bore a sealed scroll that announced her as a protected favorite of the
lord. Yukiko had wanted to know Kenji Kira's plans, and he had told her.
When he did, a smile spread on her smooth, cherry red lips.

"The message," she'd said. "Taro awaits it night and day. Why not
just send it? Only make it Mount Hiei instead. We have thousands of
men, there in the valley below the monastery. They are pointing toward
the Ikko-ikki right now, but you could turn them around. Destroy the
monks of Mount Hiei and capture Taro. Lord Oda would be grateful for
both. So very grateful."

Kenji had stared at her. "I don't understand. His mother was at
Mount Fuji. She isn't at Mount Hiei."

"So?" said Yukiko. "It doesn't matter if she's dead. He doesn't
know that. Tell him she's at Mount Hiei, and he'll come."

"You think so?"

"Oh, yes. He'll come to his mother, like a good boy. And then all
we have to do is wait."

Kenji had seen something in her then, a steeliness, a stoniness,
and he had recognized it. This girl, like himself, had a heart of rock.
She would help him to achieve his destiny—to kill Taro, and to marry
Lady Hana. He had instructed one of his men to write the note immediately, and had consulted Lord Oda's keeper of pigeons, to find a bird
that had been captured from the dead body of one of Lord Tokugawa's
pet ninjas. Kenji had hoped that the bird would fly to where Taro had
gone—but even he could hardly believe it when Yukiko brought word
that she had seen Taro, the fat boy, and Lady Hana in an inn on the
pilgrims' road to Mount Hiei. And just the other day, he had person-

ally watched through a Portuguese spyglass as the three companions climbed the path to the monastery, Lady Hana beautiful even in her rude clothing.

Just thinking of Lady Hana sent a warm glow through his groin, a feeling accentuated by the raw power before him, the army that awaited his command to begin a historic slaughter.

Power.

He turned to where Yukiko sat on a horse beside him. She smiled at him. She was not wearing armor, much as he had recommended it. She simply sat bareback on her horse, the precious sword in her hand. Her skin was the color of snow, as befitted her name, and her lips were the color of blood. He raised his own sword in a salute to her, this magnificent goddess of death. She held up her own, then touched the blade to her lips.

The gods have sent me this girl, *he thought*. She is here to remind me of the value of hardness, to keep me on the right path.

His stomach curled into a cramp, and he took a small pebble from his hand and slipped it into his mouth. He sucked on it, savoring its cool, hard, mineral roundness. Soon he would swallow it, continue the long process of making himself stone.

But not quite yet.

One day, yes, he would turn from corrupt flesh into something more permanent, free of disgusting fluids and waste. The process had already begun in his bladder—the Portuguese doctor to Lord Oda had told Kenji there were stones in there, and had seemed surprised that Kenji was so pleased. Didn't he understand? This meant Kenji would one day be everything he wanted—he would be rock, and stream, and salt. It was all worth it, his diet that included no meat or flesh of any kind, that allowed him to eat only rice and water and stones.

No maggots or flies would ever feast on his flesh, as they had on his companions, when he lay injured on that charnel field after the battle against Yoshimoto. Sometimes, in the night, he still woke screaming, remembering how he had been trapped on that battlefield, injured and helpless, as the low creatures fed on his friends, crawling into their eye sockets and out of their mouths, taking away tiny parcels of their

*beings, spreading those great warriors far and wide, as if they were
untouchable* eta *people, to be buried in mass graves.*

*But this would never happen to Kenji Kira. He had seen one possible end—the horror of decomposition and the indignity of invasion
by insects and vermin. Yet he would not succumb to it. Ever since the
day he was finally rescued, and left that place of rot behind, he had
allowed only rice and water to pass his lips, and the occasional pebble.
Nothing living and nothing that had lived, nothing corrupt.* I will be
stone, *he told himself.* I will not rot like the others. I will grow thinner and thinner until I am just bone.

*Not yet, though. Kenji knew how to draw out his pleasures, and
he knew that patient waiting was part of the enjoyment of the hunt.
Everything depended on planning and care. If he wanted to destroy
the monks of Mount Hiei, he had to command every movement of
these troops. He raised his hand—the one that was not clutching Lord
Oda's banner—and waved the gunners forward. When they reached
the monastery's defenders, as they surely would, on the upper slopes of
the mountain, then the guns would greet them first.*

*No one had used guns in this way before in a battle. They were
too unwieldy, too slow to load, too dependent on the weather. But
tonight the weather was clear, and Kenji Kira had the benefit of Lord
Oda's vision, for the daimyo had seen how the guns could be employed
more effectively, with three lines of gunners ensuring that as the guns
were firing, new ones were continually being loaded and primed. The
monks would meet an endless wave of fire, the bullets mowing them
down like blades of grass before a scythe.*

*Already, such was the brilliance of the idea, Kenji was almost
starting to think he had discovered it himself. At any rate, it would be
a pleasure to see it in action.*

*He swept his eyes over the samurai before and around him. Three
thousand men, a mixture of* hatamoto *and arquebusiers, the specialist gunners who had been recruited from among the lower ranks, then
trained in secret for months to master Lord Oda's firing technique.*

*Three thousand samurai, against ten thousand warrior monks.*

*Ordinarily, it would be a slaughter. And indeed, it still would be.*

*But the guns would ensure that it was the monks, not the samurai, who fell on their precious mountainside and nourished it with their blood.*

*Fire flared, higher up the slope, and Kenji's heart leaped. They have guns too, he thought. But it was only a torch. It was followed by another, and then another, and the ranks of monks began to appear from the gloom, like the ghost of an ancient army—only perhaps half a* ri *from where Kenji Kira stood. They stood firm, in countless ranks, armed with swords that gleamed in the torchlight. They had the advantage of height.*

*Yet Kenji had the advantage of guns. The arquebusiers had lit their fuses, and now there were many hundreds of little red glows ahead of him, bobbing in the air, as if an army of fireflies were leading the attack. Some of Kenji's bolder, and stupider, samurai were rushing up the hill to meet them, and arrows came hissing from the monastery, felling several, knocking them screaming to the ground. Kira had few archers, but there were some purists who had rejected the guns, referring to keep their wooden toys—some of these knelt and loosed arrows of their own back at the monastery. A couple of monks went down, not many at all from the thousands and thousands who stood waiting. No matter—all of them would perish before Kenji Kira's guns. Right now they were swatting at mosquitoes, little realizing that a wolf pack was watching them.*

*He tugged on his horse's reins, bringing it to a halt. "Samurai!" he shouted. "Would you like to live in glory?"*

*"Yes!" echoed the troops.*

*"Would you like to die in glory, and be reborn as lords?"*

*"Yes!"*

*"Then go," he said. "Fight with honor, and if you must die, do so also with honor. Tonight we destroy Mount Hiei. This battle will live forever in history, and you will learn of it in your future lives, when your teachers speak of great conquests. We cannot be defeated. We are the samurai of Lord Oda Nobunaga! If there is fear in your belly, seize it. Make it the fire that drives you. If your hand trembles on your sword, or your gun, it is only because it thirsts for blood. Let*

*your hand strike—let it kill." He lit an incense stick. "When this has burned down, we will stand here once again, and we will be heroes."*

*Kenji Kira had orders not to kill the boy, to bring him alive to Oda for questioning, but he knew that it would be useless to ask the men to spare any boys they found. The monastery was a place of learning—it was crawling with boys. Anyway, Yukiko said that Taro would survive nearly any wound, so long as he was not struck in the heart, or decapitated. Either of those wounds, she said, would definitely kill him.*

*"They would definitely kill anyone," Kenji Kira had replied. "That's why I always cut off heads, if I can." He'd expected her to laugh—she'd shown herself to be a peculiar, bloodthirsty girl.*

*She'd looked at him strangely, though. "Really?" she'd said. "I wonder, have you ever decapitated a woman?"*

*He'd felt her gaze burning into him, and for some reason felt afraid, though he wasn't going to show it to a slip of a girl like her, even if she did have Oda's particular favor. "Yes," he'd said simply.*

*She'd nodded and turned away from him.*

*Sitting on his horse, he sighed. He would never understand women. But soon he'd have Lady Hana, the most refined and beautiful woman in the land—once he was the hero of the assault on Mount Hiei, Lord Oda could not possibly refuse him her hand in marriage.*

*He dismounted, motioning for the others to do the same. From here, the slope became too steep. He planted the incense stick in the ground, and as it smoldered, it filled the air with a scent of sandalwood and jasmine.*

*The girl, Yukiko, clapped softly. "Oh, and one more thing," she said softly. The samurai turned to look at her. "Leave some of them for me." She twirled her sword in her hand.*

*Some of the men laughed, their courage lifted—and only Kenji suspected the girl was not indulging in idle rhetoric, that she would kill ruthlessly if she got the chance. The men turned once again to the field of battle, standing proud in their armor.*

*Kenji Kira beckoned his second-in-command. "Send the three lines forward," he said. "Wait for the monks to move before they fire."*

*They didn't have to wait for long—something else that Oda had seen rightly. The monks were aggressive, made bold by hundreds of years of imperviousness. Without even a cry of battle, or an order, they were suddenly moving down the slope, a deadly wave, impossibly vast. From one end of the slope to the other, all Kenji Kira could see was swords, and shaved heads.*

*Kenji waited. He knew the value of patience.*

*When he could see the monks' eyes, read the furious anger in their expressions, he smiled. "Now," he said, rather quietly. It was not necessary to shout—the order was awaited, and all that was required was for his second-in-command to swing Lord Oda's banner in an arc above his head.*

*The first rank of arquebusiers kneeled—this, alone, was five hundred men. Then they fired as one, the sound deafening, like thunder.*

Taro ducked, nocking another arrow in his bow. The Tendai monks did not believe in guns, but when he'd said that he was a good shot, they had put him with some of the other monks, sheltering behind the pillars of the lower monastery buildings, bows in hand. Below them was the main company of monks, waiting the order to engage. Taro and his fellow bowmen were having to fire over them, aiming high, to rain down arrows on the attackers.

At Taro's feet were two quivers, both full of arrows. Torches had been lit, but none of them near to where the bowmen stood, so that they could fire from the cover of darkness on the front line of the samurai.

*Thwock.* An arrow struck the pillar, burying itself deep in the wood, quivering. Taro whipped around, aimed, drew, and fired—the arrow arced up, graceful, then ended its parabola in the stomach of one of Lord Oda's archers. The man dropped to his knees, then was knocked forward and trampled by the men running up the hill behind him. Taro turned himself back so that the pillar covered him, nocked, drew, turned again, and fired.

Nock, draw, fire, over and over again. Once he and the monk to his left aimed for the same man, and Taro saw two flights sprout from the man's chest. *That's a waste of an arrow,* thought Taro momentarily, then he nocked, drew, and fired once more. The first quiver at his feet was nearly empty, and yet the samurai were still coming, some of them now breaking through the sharp shield of arrows and clashing with the monks before Taro, armed with swords in the Tendai tradition. Yet there were not many of these samurai—Taro almost got the impression that they had broken from the main force of the army through exuberance, or an eagerness to die. Either that or the commanders had sent a small detachment of lunatics forward, to probe at the monastery's defenses, to show where the monks were weak.

*Where are the guns?* thought Taro. He had seen an overwhelming force of fusiliers, when the army was below him in the valley. Now he saw a glimmering mass in the darkness that could have been the body of the army, and these few dozen death-wishers who were running up toward the monks—one less now, for his arrow found its target and sank into a samurai's groin, felling him.

Another arrow from below hissed past him, disappearing into the darkness of the hall. He withdrew his head, picked up another arrow, and readied it. Then he rotated around the pillar, aimed—

—and stopped his hand. The monks below, the ranks and ranks of monks with their shining swords, were moving even as they uttered their loud battle cry, surging down the hill toward Oda's army, the few remaining samurai of the suicidal foreguard swept up by the mass of men as a landslide consumes village huts, vanishing. Taro had nothing to aim at now except the monks, and they were on his own side, and he loosed his hold on the bowstring, let the arrow fall to the ground. An awful feeling dug claws into his chest—he had been wondering why Oda didn't send more men forward, and he sensed he was about to find out.

Then the front ranks of Oda's army, the ones that had held still as their foolhardy, brave companions assaulted the monastery, were kneeling—Taro could see them now in the light of the torches the monks carried, and he cried out, *"Stop, stop!"* to the monks below, but they were too far away now and too many, and they didn't stop. Taro stared, no longer bothering to conceal himself behind his pillar, his breath stopped in his throat—he wouldn't realize it until his vision blackened some moments later, and air rushed into his lungs, hungry to occupy his body.

There was a crashing, rolling, incomprehensibly loud *boom*, like the sound of a thousand thunderclouds, and for a moment the full extent of Oda's army was illuminated, an enormity of armed men, lit by pinpricks of fire in the night.

*Oh, gods*, thought Taro, as the first swathe of monks were torn apart by the wave of bullets, screams filling the night air. *There are too many. It will be a massacre.*

He threw down his bow, and he ran.

*The nearest monks fell, screaming, and Kenji Kira smiled. Even as they bled onto the grass, the second rank of his arquebusiers stepped forward, handing their already loaded guns to the first rank, taking in return the spent ones. Freshly armed, the first rank aimed again, fired. More monks went down—the mountainside was beginning to look like a grave, piled high with corpses.*

*Meanwhile, the second rank passed the spent guns back to the third, who passed forward the third and final preloaded gun. As the second man waited to hand this to the first, the third began to load the original weapon. In this way, as Lord Oda had seen, the guns could be made to fire indefinitely—as long as the bullets did not run out.*

*Kenji Kira felt that tightening in his groin again. It was beautiful, this. The monks, with their training, and their sharp swords and their secrets, were breaking themselves apart on his guns, like futile waves against a rocky beach.*

*Fire. Pass back. Reload. Fire.*

*Kenji moved forward, to get a better view. Already, thousands of the monks lay dead, each of their corpses a rebuff to the* hatamoto *who led the arquebusiers, and who had dared to contradict Kenji's direct orders, saying that he believed it would rain tonight.*

*Rain! As if Kenji Kira could be stopped by something so ephemeral, something so . . . mundane. An army of* kami *might stop him, or demons. Not rain. It would prevent the guns from firing, yes, but there were other ways to kill monks than with guns. He had ordered the* hatamoto *to kill himself, and then he had himself taken on the command of the guns. He looked up at the sky. A few dark clouds, but it was already almost over. If Susanoo, the* kami *of thunder, wished to stop this massacre, he was too late.*

*The monks were almost destroyed. Some had made it as far as the ranks of arquebusiers, but there were traditional samurai in his army too, and these were able to move forward, between the rows of gunners, and engage any survivors hand to hand. Some of them might run, of course—try to escape over the other side of the mountain. But Kenji had a surprise for them.*

*Soon this battle would be over, and he could make his way to the temple. The boy would be there, with his mother.*

*And cowering with him, hoping the boy could protect her, Hana.*

The bullet struck Taro in the left shoulder, knocking him on his backside, among the men who had already fallen. He touched his back—it had gone right through, which was a mercy, because he would not have to dig it out of his flesh. For just a moment he wished he had run away, instead of going to find Hana and Hiro, instead of thinking that he might do something to help.

Screams. The prayers of the dying. The smell of sulfur in the air, as if the mountain had erupted. His sword—he'd dropped his sword. It didn't matter. There were swords everywhere here, and their owners no longer needed them.

He clutched Hana's calf, pulled her down with him into the melee of limbs and weapons, the detritus of the dead. He squeezed her hand.

"You're hurt," she said, and he had to read her lips, because the guns were still firing. How could there be so many, and how could they be always firing? The abbot had assured them that guns took a while to load, and so were impractical for large assaults.

And yet the monks were being annihilated.

Taro pressed his fingers to the wound in his shoulder, wincing at the pain. It would heal, of course, but not as quickly as he would like.

From down the slope, wisps of smoke rose into the air as the guns continued to fire. Monks poured down the mountain, trying to break through, but so many had already fallen that the ground had become a mat of bodies, and the grass was visible only in small patches here and there.

He pulled Hana closer to him, putting his lips close to her ear so she could hear what he was saying over the ceaseless, booming roar of the guns. "Where's Hiro?"

"Oh . . . I don't know," she said, shaken. She began to get up, as if to look for him.

"No," Taro said. "Don't stand." He twisted around, looking back up the slope, scanning the bodies for his friend. Then he saw a large shape, crawling toward him.

"Gods," said Hiro, pulling himself over the body of a monk who had been shot through the eye. "Have they the demons on their side?"

"I don't know," said Taro, relief that Hiro was alive coursing through him like fire. "But I feel like I'm in the hell realm." He reached out to embrace his friend—just as a bullet whined over his arm, sounding like an angry wasp. He dropped lower and crawled forward, holding Hana's hand, until the three of them were huddled together among the bodies. A monk to their side turned to look at them, his eyes glassy. He groaned, then closed his eyes again.

"We have to go back," shouted Hiro. "This is hopeless."

Taro nodded. "All together," he said. "Hana—keep hold of my hand. Hiro—follow close behind." He began to pull himself up the slope, slithering over the bloody remains of the monastery's defenders, trying to keep his skin from being slashed by the dropped swords. But his left arm moved only sluggishly, and pain was shooting through his chest. He stopped, gasping.

"He's hurt," said Hana to Hiro.

Hiro looked at the blood spreading on Taro's shirt. Concern flooded his face. "Oh no . . . Is it bad?" He shuffled forward, touching Taro's arm.

Taro grunted. He was weighing something in his mind—a dilemma he had experienced before. But it didn't take long for him to reach his decision. If he lost his strength now, Hana might die, and so might Hiro. He had to get back to the buildings, see if it was possible to hold out behind the walls, force the shooters to come closer.

Feeling a familiar twinge of nausea, he turned his face from his friends, then lowered it to the man below him—he could see from the open eyes that the monk was dead.

But the blood would be fresh.

The neck was exposed, and he closed his lips over the flesh, then bit down. The heart wasn't pumping. He had to suck to draw the blood out, but it was hot and thick in his mouth, the taste of everything good he had ever eaten. He drank deep, feeling the dead man's power suffusing his muscles. The pain in his shoulder ebbed, as if carried away on a tide of blood.

When he pulled away, the corpse's neck and face were white, drained by his feeding. Such was the vigor pulsing through him, the joyful strength, that he didn't even feel disgust. He gripped Hana's hand, turning to check that she was still there. She met his eyes, then looked down—he didn't know if it was to spare his embarrassment, or because she was revolted by him.

*It doesn't matter, as long as she lives.*

Taro began once more to crawl up the hill, feeling his way slowly along the pile of bodies and the occasional patch of wet grass. Twice, a sword cut him, slicing into his flesh as he hauled himself over the blade. He ignored the pain, concentrating on moving, and on the little movements of the hand he held behind him, which told him that Hana was still alive, still crawling. There was a long, rolling *boom* from somewhere behind him, and he thought at first that it must be an enormous gun, but he realized it was thunder when a drop of water landed on his ear, and then heavy rain began to fall. Soon Taro was soaked, and he didn't know where his shirt was cold with rain, and where it was cold with his blood. He frowned. Something had changed. Yes, that was it. He could no longer hear the guns.

*The rain . . . ,* he thought. *It's stopping them firing.* It was as if some god, some *kami*, had intervened in the battle.

He dared to look up, and found that they had hardly moved on the slope. He cursed, crawling onward. It took so long, and the field of corpses was so endless, that he began to wonder if they *were* in hell. *But if I am in hell,* he thought, *then why has Enma not greeted me?* Looking down the hill, he saw that the awful line of samurai gunmen were lowering their rifles, hesitating. There was an impression of disorder among the ranks. Taro smiled. *Their fuses are going out, and they have no other weapons.* Part of him wanted to pick up a sword, any sword, and run down the hill, over the bodies. Part of him wanted to crash into the line, cutting and slashing, killing as many of the gunmen as he could, making them pay for the cruel, detached deaths they had dealt. But he turned away from them to look up at the main monastery building, and he crawled.

When he slid off the final body and lay on the dew-covered grass near the accommodation hall, it took him a moment to realize it. He was still crawling, muttering to himself, when he saw that what was going by beneath his eyes was only grass—*just* grass. He looked up, then back. Hana crouched behind him, her hair hanging lank and damp over her face. She was panting. Hiro lay flat on his back beside her, and Taro thought he saw tears on the boy's cheeks.

"Come on," he said unnecessarily. He pushed himself to his feet, then leaned back to help Hana up. "Hiro, get some swords."

On his knees, keeping his profile low, Hiro scavenged among the dead. He passed a sword behind him to Hana, then scurried over with another two in his hands. He threw one to Taro, handle first, and Taro hissed with pain when he caught it.

Hana put her palm over his wound, frowning. "Are you all right?" she asked.

"Yes. It is healing already." The human blood was still fresh in him, and it made his flesh quicker than usual to close over.

She let out a long breath, then threw her arms around him. "I thought you would die," she said.

"It takes a lot to kill him," said Hiro, smiling weakly.

Taro nodded. "I think they'll try, anyway." Already he could see samurai with swords pushing past the useless gunners, racing up the hill to confront the monks hand to hand.

Just then Hayao appeared from around the corner. He had a *katana* in his hand, and Taro took a step backward. The man was an Oda samurai—Taro didn't know if he had returned to his old allegiance, now that he was cured of his haunting.

"Wait," said Hayao. "I won't harm you. I—I owe my life to you. I'll fight with you."

Taro turned to the samurai forcing their way up the hill. "Those are Lord Oda's men," he said. "You would be a traitor, in their eyes, if you chose to defend the monastery."

Hayao shrugged, but Taro could see this was no casual decision—there was a sick light of shame in the man's eyes. Taro could see what it cost him to betray his lord. Taro knew to his detriment how closely the samurai held their notions of honor. "Nevertheless," said Hayao.

"You've made the right choice," said Hana, smiling at him with admiration.

Now for the first time Hayao hesitated. "Do you not . . . I mean, do you side with the monks? Hana*ko*?" He stressed the final syllable of her fake name, his meaning clear. She was Lord Oda's daughter, and yet she was siding with the monks.

"I am no longer what I was," said Hana. There didn't seem to be anyone within earshot, but it was well to be careful.

Hayao nodded slowly. "Very well," he said. Together the four of them backed toward the temple buildings. A samurai came charging at them, but Hiro tripped him and Hana opened his belly as he went down, and they kept close together as they moved.

"We need to get out of here," said Taro. "Maybe if we go over the summit, and back the way we climbed . . ." He turned to look up the stone path. Then he frowned. Above the mountaintop, a red glow lit the sky. But it was long past sunset, and many incense sticks would burn down before dawn came.

"What's that?" he said. But the glow was flickering, pulsing, and he thought he knew.

"Fire," said Hiro, his voice empty. "It's fire." Taro didn't know how the fire could be burning so hotly, even in the rain, but he knew that his friend was right. He had seen forest fires before, when he lived by the sea in Shirahama.

"Oh, gods," said Hana. Taro stepped over to comfort her, to reassure her that he would never allow her to be harmed. But then he saw the expression on her face and realized she was not worried for herself. "The scrolls," she said. "The Hokke-do is on that side of the mountain." Without saying anything more, she began hurrying up the steps to the peak. Taro limped after her, one hand over the hole in his shoulder. He could feel the flesh there knitting itself closed, but it still ached when he moved.

"Hana!" he called after her. "They're only scrolls!"

Hayao drew level with Taro, passed him, then caught Hana by the arm. "My lad—I mean, Hanako. We should go back, look for shelter."

She shook him off, her hair streaming in the wind, her face flushed with effort and emotion. Rainwater streamed down her face. "No," she said. She turned to Taro. "They are not *only* anything. They are beyond value." And then she was moving again, taking the steps two at a time. Hayao pressed after her, Taro and Hiro following.

Soon they came to the top of the mountain, and Taro could only stare, speechless, at the violation that had been done to the beautiful view. Below them, fire was sweeping slowly upward, like a vast long beast eating the cedar trees, undeterred by the rain. Great billows of steam rose from where the flame met the falling water. As he watched, one of the trees exploded with a dull *pop*, creating a bright, evanescent glow. The fire was growing at a steady rate, and soon it would begin consuming the *ume* trees below the Hokke-do.

Heading down the hill toward it, already a small, dark figure against the steps, was Hana.

"Hurry," said Taro, but when he set off toward the steps, Hiro grabbed his sleeve, pulling him back. "What?" said Taro.

"Oh, gods," said Hayao. He pointed, back the way they had come. Taro looked. Nearest to them, the training hall stood inviolate. But below it was an appalling sight.

Samurai with swords in their hands were entering the clearing outside the accommodation hall, in clusters of two and three. Taro turned back to Hana's disappearing form, then back again to the samurai. They were moving forward, trying to get to the buildings, and no organized defense stood against them.

*My mother is in there*, thought Taro. He stared at the advancing samurai in horror.

The monks had been scattered by the volleys of bullets, thrown into disarray—those of them that remained, anyway. These dazed survivors were engaging the samurai, but there were not enough of them to staunch the increasing flow of attackers.

*Hana . . . or my mother.*

Taro flicked his gaze from one side of the mountain to the other. He met Hiro's eyes briefly, and for once his friend offered no commentary. He only held up his sword. "Whichever way you go," he said, "I'll follow."

Taro smiled at him. He knew it—knew that Hiro would go to hell and back with him, if he needed—but it wasn't what he needed.

"What is it?" said Hayao, oblivious. "What's wrong?"

"My mother is in that hall," said Taro. He pointed to where the samurai were threatening to overwhelm the temple building.

Hayao put a hand on his arm. "I'm sorry," he said. "You go—I will go after Hana, try to keep her from killing herself."

Taro hesitated. If Hayao saved Hana's life, she'd be grateful; he might lose her to the samurai . . . and yet his mother . . .

He steeled himself, silencing the petty voices inside him. Hayao was a good man, and a trained samurai—and he wasn't injured, whereas Taro was still moving slowly from the ball that had gone through his shoulder. And besides, if they were taken by Oda's men, perhaps Hayao could convince them he was with them.

"Thank you, Hayao," he said hurriedly. "Yes, please, go. I will see you again when this is all over. Hiro—go with him. Protect her. I'll be with you as soon as I can."

"I'll come with you," said Hiro. "I don't—"

"No," said Taro. "Go after Hana. Please."

He closed his eyes for a moment.

*Forgive me, Hana.*

Then he threw himself down the slope toward where his mother was.

*Kenji Kira watched the roiling mass of the arquebusiers, the chaos of their panicked movements as they dropped their weapons. Rain hammered on his helmet and breastplate, like percussion.*

Now this, *he thought,* this is war.

*The monks who had survived the volleys of fire were surging through the disarmed arquebusiers, who scurried, bewildered, with their useless sticks. The monks cut them down where they stood, their* katana *finding in this moment the perfection of their purpose, drinking down blood.*

*A man with a gun ran past Kenji—or nearly, anyway, for there was a protective cordon of armed and armored samurai around Kenji, keeping him at arm's length from the mess of the fighting. Kenji had kept his elite guard back, behind the guns, ready for the hand-to-hand engagement. It was going to come a little quicker than he had planned, of course. But he was looking forward to it. His sword was thirsty.*

*As he ran past, the arquebusier shouted something about Susanoo, the* kami *of storms, and how he was punishing them for their arrogance.*

*Kenji sighed. These men would fight to the death, commit seppuku over
the tiniest offense if you asked them to, but allow for a single moment
the seed of superstition to plant itself among them, and soon a great tree
of fear would surge upward, its expanding branches sending the men
scattering.*

*Now the gunmen were running around in a panic, aimless, their
very movements chaotic—as if they were things that had only entered
human bodies, possessing them, and had little idea of how the joints
were meant to articulate. They were no match for the ruthless, organized monks, who cut them down mercilessly.*

*"Should we help them?" said one of the samurai.*

*"No," said Kenji. "Leave them to die." He felt angry with the gun-
men for failing him. A small voice at the back of his mind told him
that it was he who had ordered the attack when clouds had been gathering, but he ignored it, as he found it was best to do with such troublesome voices. He dismounted from his horse, gesturing for his men to
do the same. The mounts would be hopeless on this treacherous mess
of dead bodies.*

*He looked up the slope. There were not many monks left, any-
way. All the rain was doing was bringing forward the final part
of Oda's battle plan, when the best of the samurai would storm the
mountaintop with swords in hand, raze the buildings, and extermi-
nate the last of the Tendai monks. Already he could see the smoke
from the other side of the rise, where a picked detachment of his men
had set fire to the Hokke-do. Lord Oda had specially ordered that
part of the temple burned to the ground—the scrolls were the heart
of the Tendai order, he said, and without them the monks would
wither and die.*

*And the sweetest part of all—to humiliate the boy before Hana,
maybe even to kill him, if he was forced to it. Lord Oda would simply have to accept that these things happened, in war. Then he would
claim his rewards. Hana, perhaps.*

*Of course, he had hoped that the casualties on his side might be
minimal, so as to increase the glory of his victory. But the guns had
not been his idea in the first place. He was happier here, with his*

samurai, fighting the traditional way. And he knew that his samurai guard—the elite of Lord Oda's army—would respect his wishes if his karma did not hold good, and he died. They would take his body and ensure that it was burned immediately, so that no insects could make it their home. Then they would scatter him among the rocks at the base of the mountain, so that he would be forever stone, impermeable and eternal.

He stalked forward, pushing through the last remnants of the panicking gunners. Suddenly a monk leaped up—apparently he had been feigning death. He had a sword in his hand, and he ran straight at Kenji Kira, screaming.

"Face me like a man!" the monk shouted.

Kenji Kira waved a hand, and two of his samurai stepped forward, pincerlike, and caught the monk on their swords, cutting him in half at the waist. If these monks expected Kenji Kira to fight with honor, then they were greater fools than he had taken them for. Not that he would not kill, if it came to it. In fact, as he fought his way up the hill he met a great deal of resistance, and he had cause to remember Lord Oda's maxim that a man defending his home is worth ten samurai.

The monks were desperate. They fought viciously, with great skill. But they were horribly outnumbered. The rain had stopped the guns, but much too late to do any good—already the bullets had claimed most of the monks, leaving an embattled minority to defend the temple. Kenji Kira glanced to his side and saw Yukiko, cartwheeling elegantly over a startled-looking monk, landing in a graceful crouch on a corpse behind him, and eviscerating him from behind. Kira saluted her, raising his sword.

She didn't respond—and indeed he regretted the gesture a moment later when a monk brought his sword up in a glittering arc, taking advantage of Kenji Kira's exposed flank, nearly opening his chest. He blocked just in time, stumbled on the armor of a dead man at his feet, and had to catch one of his samurai by the shoulder to keep upright. The samurai spun on the monk, but another monk swung at the same time, and his sword met the samurai's throat, ruined it.

Kenji Kira snapped his sword down, to parry another strike—the monk who was attacking him was no older than fifteen, but he fought with hard-eyed conviction, no doubt spurred on by the carpet of his dead friends at his feet. The young monk settled into a strong fighting stance, careful not to slip on the blood and guts below him. His sword rose very gently up and down in his hand, as if it were breathing. Kenji Kira looked up to see more monks flowing down the hill behind him, forming a semicircle he and his few remaining men would have to fight their way through.

Well, so be it.

Kenji Kira let the dagger in his sleeve drop into his left hand, then flicked his wrist. The monk's face twisted into an expression of surprise, as the dagger thwacked into his chest. Kenji Kira didn't even waste movement—he leaped at the other nearest monk, his sword a silver rainbow in the rain, and took off the man's sword arm at the shoulder. The men behind him disappeared, and so did the mountain—there were only the monks, and their swords. This had happened to him only rarely, yet he embraced the battle rage as if it were an old friend. The world shrank to the point and edge of his sword. He was lost in the battle.

Two monks came at him together, swords flashing, but wherever the swords were, it was so easy to be elsewhere. Time seemed to have slowed down—he could see the blades coming long before they moved, and when they did move it was as if they dragged through sap, not air. He almost found it too simple to evade the clumsy hacks and slashes, as he danced with his sword, killing each monk in turn. His vision had gone red—he didn't know if that was a symptom of his battle-rage, or a mist of blood in his eyes.

He turned, and jumped, and cut and thrust, and when he came back to his senses he found himself in a circle of dead men, his sword arm trembling. Some of the dead were samurai, and some small voice inside him said he had probably killed them, too.

Well, so be it.

He looked up and he saw that he had reached the main hall, the accommodation hall where he was sure Hana would be. He turned *to look for Yukiko but could see her nowhere. She would be inside, no doubt. He just hoped she wouldn't get to Taro or Hana before him.*

*He raised his sword for attention. "Kill the remaining monks here," he said, "then move up the hill. If you see a girl of noble appearance, leave her for me."*

Taro moved through the hall like a ghost. He could hear the clash of metal on metal, the screams of men.

There was a samurai ahead of Taro, grappling with a monk. Taro waited till the monk's body was clear, then stabbed the samurai through the gap in his armor, a clean cut through the chest. The man fell forward, blood bubbling from his mouth.

The monk began to thank him, but Taro kept moving, flitting from shadow to shadow. In the courtyard, two monks ran roaring at a samurai with a gun. The samurai fired, his fuse spared from the rain by the leaves and blossom of the plum tree. He hit one of the monks, but the other kept going, his sword arcing up in a classic *ii-aido* move. The samurai's gun hand—and the arm and shoulder attached to it—cleaved off and thudded to the ground.

The monk turned to Taro, his sword still up, ready to attack.

"I'm with you!" said Taro. "I'm looking for my mother."

The monk nodded. "The guests are in there." He pointed to the room where Taro had last seen his mother.

Taro grunted a thanks, then banged on the door. "Mother!" he called. "Let me in!"

The door creaked open, and his mother ran out to embrace him. "You're alive," she said. Then she saw the blood on his shirt, the hole where the bullet had penetrated, and her mouth formed into an O of shock. "You're hurt."

"Yes. No." He touched the already forming scar on his shoulder. "I'll explain later." There was the sound of footsteps behind him, and he whirled, ready to face one of the samurai.

And then Kenji Kira appeared in the doorway of the hall.

Lord Oda's retainer was smiling. In his hand was a sword, which dripped blood—*tap tap tap tap*—on the wooden floor. He had lost even more weight since Taro had last seen him, so that he appeared almost as a *gaki*, a vengeful ghost come to feed on Taro's strength. Against the shadow of the doorway, his skin was almost translucently white, and his eyes bulged out of a horrific visage, a death-mask of hollow cheeks and taut, fleshless lips.

"You must be Taro," he said.

Taro said nothing. He knew that Kenji Kira had never laid eyes on him before, but Taro had seen *him*. He'd watched from his hiding place, on two separate occasions, as Kira had murdered defenseless people. First, he had seen him kill an old peasant man, just for harvesting some honey in Lord Oda's forest. And then he had been present when the revolting man murdered Heiko, the brave older sister of Yukiko. Heiko had sacrificed herself for Taro's sake, distracting Kenji Kira and allowing the others to escape. It was, in part, Heiko's death that had warped Yukiko's mind and led her to turn against Taro.

Taro relaxed into the stance of combat, his sword steady in his hands. This time it was different. This time it would be him facing Kira one-on-one. And he was *far* from defenseless.

His mother held his arm tightly. "Who is that?" she whispered.

Taro cracked his neck. "Kenji Kira," he said, not bothering to lower his voice. "He killed my friend. I swore I'd kill him if I ever met him again."

Kira rolled his eyes. "Yes, yes, I'm sure you did. And now I'm going to take you to Lord Oda, where you'll be tortured and most likely die. There's no need to be theatrical about it." A couple of samurai appeared at his side but he waved them back irritably. "The boy is mine," he said.

"Lord Oda is dead," said Taro.

Kira looked genuinely confused. "I saw him this morning," he said. "He is very much alive."

Taro frowned. "But . . ."

"You thought you *killed* him?" said Kira. He laughed hollowly. "He was injured, the night you stole Hana away. But he did not die. You are a boy—how could you hope to kill a sword saint such as he?"

Taro felt faint. He concentrated on the ground beneath his feet. Well, perhaps Lord Oda was not dead—it did seem strange that no rumors had reached them of his demise. But Taro had defeated him once. He could do it again. He shrugged.

"It doesn't matter," he said, more bravely than he felt. "I will fight you, and I will fight him if he comes for me. I'm not afraid of you. I intend to kill you. So if you want me, you may have to kill me."

"I'm prepared," said Kenji Kira, " for that eventuality."

Taro turned to his mother, put his hands on her shoulders. "Get behind me," he said.

When he turned to face Kenji Kira again, the man was frowning. "Your mother is here," he said. "But where is Hana?"

Taro stared. "I'm sorry?"

"Hana. Lord Oda's daughter. Where is she? I'm . . . concerned about her."

"She's far from here," said Taro, hoping that it was true. The last he had seen of her, she had been running toward the Hokke-do as it burned, driven by a mad desire to save the scrolls.

Rage crossed Kenji Kira's face, like a *taifun* over seawater, and then was gone just as quickly as it had arisen. He slashed his sword through the air experimentally, then nodded to Taro. "Come, then," he said, pointing to Taro's *katana*. "Let's see what you can do with that thing. Either I kill you or I return you to Lord Oda alive. Both outcomes would please me."

Taro closed his eyes for a moment, feeling the few drops of rain that made it past the overhang of the roof and through the branches of the plum tree. He concentrated on the feel of the grass through his thin *tabi* slippers. In his hand, the sword was light, the sword was *nothing*. He let himself become one with it, and then he moved.

Kenji Kira met Taro's first strike with a textbook deflection, using a smooth, classic kata form. He spun, meeting Taro's next strike with a low parry. Then he pressed forward, his sword flashing in the semidarkness. Taro allowed himself to fall back, watching not the moves that Kira made, but the rhythm of his whole body, his attitude, his *style*. He tried a lesser-known attack—a low feint, followed by a tricky reversal into a neck-strike. Kira responded with the perfect kata for the occasion.

But that was the thing, Taro was realizing. The man only had the kata—taught movements and deflections; not the innate instinct for the weapon that had marked Taro out from the start. He held for a moment longer, even letting one of Kira's lunges slash a wide cut in his thigh, which made his mother gasp. He ignored it, and her, keeping his balance while he used a high attack to make Kira back off.

"You're weak," said Kira. "Your dead ninja friend didn't teach you well enough."

Taro bit his lip, forcing himself not to respond. He was concentrating most of all on not killing the man too quickly.

"I was surprised you came," said Kira, dancing to the side as Taro made an obvious play to cut open his stomach, pretending to be less skilled than he truly was. "When we sent that pigeon, we didn't think you would take the bait. Your mother must mean a lot to you."

"Yes," said Taro. "She does."

"Still," said Kira. "You must be either very brave, or very stupid. To walk into a trap like that."

"Well," said Taro through gritted teeth, his sword hand yearning to be freed, "I didn't know for sure it was a trap."

"Ah. Stupid, then." Kira feinted left and then threw his sword forward, trying to run Taro through, but Taro had seen the intended move and was no longer in that spot when the blade transfixed the air. He aimed a low cut at Kira's legs, and was rewarded with a red gash on the man's thigh, to match his own.

"Gah!" said Kira, angry now. He redoubled his efforts, making a series of fast, aggressive strikes, pushing Taro back. Taro looked into the man's eyes and saw only vanity, selfishness, and pride. He was almost disappointed—the man who had murdered his friend was nothing but a bully. He decided he had played long enough with this mouse. He got his blade inside Kira's and turned it aside with a flick of the wrist. Then, in a movement fast as the flash of sunlight on a darting fish's scales, he raked his sword along Kira's, to the hilt, and pushed hard to the side.

Kira's sword fell to the ground, and he looked at Taro, his breath ragged. He was if anything even paler now, a man made of snow. Taro saw blossoms falling, impossibly slowly, and one of the flowers settled on Kira's forehead. He felt the benediction of the moment, and he raised his sword for the kill.

Pain exploded in Taro's stomach, and he looked down to see a dagger hilt protruding from it. Kira's arm was outstretched—he must have thrown the knife, though Taro hadn't seen him move. He stumbled, as Kira—quick as a cat—leaned down and picked up his sword. Taro just got his own blade up in time, as Kira brought his sword round in a viciously fast strike, aimed at Taro's neck. As the swords clashed together, Taro felt a tearing agony in his stomach—he was aware of the dagger falling from it, his blood rushing after it, as if to catch it. The pain was astonishing, staggering. It was a shadow that spread from the wound, enveloping him, and he was a scared child cowering inside that darkness.

He could hear his mother screaming and he blinked, realizing that Kenji Kira was no longer in front of him. Instinctively he raised his sword, two-handed, so that it was behind his head—and he felt the impact when the blow Kira had meant to decapitate him was absorbed by the blade and his jangling wrists.

He somehow turned the older man around, moving just quick enough with his sword to defend against any lethal strikes. Then Kira ducked, spinning round as he kicked, and Taro felt his ankle give way. He crashed heavily to the ground. With an effort, he got his sword up just in time to block the next blow—but his strength was slipping away from him, and the older man's sword carried enough momentum to bite into his shoulder.

Aghast, Taro looked up at the skeletal face of Kenji Kira, contemplating the hideous idea that this might be the last thing he saw.

He was preparing to die when there was a flurry of movement from the doorway, and a flicker as of someone moving very quickly toward Kira from behind, almost flying, and then there was a handspan of steel jutting out from the older man's chest.

Taro and Kira both stared at it, then raised their eyes to each other, their puzzled expressions mirrored for a slow instant. Blood welled in the older man's chest. He raised one hand to touch the sword that had impaled him, as if to check that it was real. He opened his mouth and let out a low groan. It was a sound like emptiness.

"The blade is resting by your heart," said a voice from behind Kenji Kira, and it was a voice Taro knew. "When I twist, you die."

Kira's eyes opened wide, as the face that belonged to that musical voice peered over his shoulder and smiled at Taro.

Yukiko.

Taro stared at her, speechless—the girl who had been his and Hiro's friend, and who had betrayed them to Lord Oda. He felt the ground become less solid beneath him, as unreality seeped into the edges of things. What was she doing here, on this mountain? How did this young girl come to be smiling here, among so much carnage, with her sword through Lord Oda's most trusted agent?

"Why?" said Kenji Kira, his voice full of pain and confusion. "You . . . said . . . you wanted the boy too."

"I do. But I want you first."

"You'll . . . die . . . for this," said Kira.

"No. I have the full support of the samurai," said Yukiko. And indeed, as she said it, a man bearing Lord Oda's *mon* came into the courtyard and leaned against the wooden wall, nodding to her. "They follow my wishes, for my wishes are Lord Oda's."

"I . . . serve . . . Lord Oda."

"Yes. You have been loyal. But loyalty is nothing. You know that better than anyone."

Kenji Kira opened and closed his mouth, like a carp, and with as little effect.

"Do you know what your life cost?" said Yukiko.

"No," said Kira.

"You are looking at the price, right in front of you. I told Lord Oda I would give him Taro, and the other ninjas in Lord Tokugawa's employ, if he gave me your life. He agreed."

Taro was looking into Kenji Kira's eyes, and the horror and disappointment he saw in them made him feel something he never thought he would feel. He felt sorry for the man. "Yukiko," he said. "Wait." He struggled to his feet, but the samurai behind her drew his sword, with a faint *swish*. He moved to face Taro, his stance saying that if Taro tried to help Kira, he would have to deal with the samurai first. Not that Taro would try any such thing— he knew that for Yukiko to kill the man was a matter of a movement of the wrist, something he would be powerless to stop.

"No," said the girl. "He dies now." The shining steel tip that protruded from Kira's chest moved a little as she spoke, and he screamed. "But listen carefully, Kenji Kira. I want you to approach the River of Three Crossings knowing the person who killed you, and why."

"Tell . . . me."

"You killed my sister, Kenji Kira. Her name was Heiko. You beheaded her on a dusty road, next to a cart. And you killed the woman I called mother. She was a prophetess."

"Ah," said Kenji Kira, a measure of resignation in his voice.

"So. When the demons ask who killed you, say that it was a girl named Yukiko. They will have heard my name from other dead lips, I think."

"Yukiko," said Taro. "You don't have to do this."

"Yes, I do," said Yukiko. She moved the blade again, just a fraction, and Kira blanched. "But there's just one more thing, Kenji Kira. Your body. I ought to tell you what I plan to do with it."

The man's eyes twisted from side to side, frantic, and Taro frowned. What was this? Kenji Kira looked more scared now than he had when he saw the blade sticking out of his flesh.

"Know this," said Yukiko. "Your corpse will be taken from here by the samurai and thrown into the river by Lord Oda's castle, where the *eta* rinse the piss from their hides. You will be eaten by fish and snails. Worms will feed on your flesh and then grow wings, and they will fly away with you in all directions, such that none will ever find you."

Kenji Kira opened his mouth wide and uttered a scream that chilled Taro's blood, a long wail like that of a baby, a wordless death poem.

"Enough," said Yukiko, and twisted the blade hard. The scream was cut off instantly. Then she withdrew the sword in a smooth, wet motion, and blood burst forth from Kenji Kira, as he pitched forward to crumple on the ground, dead.

*Shusaku was nearly at the coast again—had nearly reached the safety of Lord Tokugawa's pirate ship—when he heard the blackness around him open up in a chorus of thunder, a sound like the sky tearing apart. He had heard that sound before. It was the sound of guns.*

*He turned, confused. He was sure he was heading east, toward the sea—he had retraced his steps carefully—yet the gunfire did not come from behind him. He was certain it was coming from the north, from the direction of Mount Hiei.*

There is a battle, *he thought.* And it is not the Ikko-ikki who are being attacked.

*He stood for a moment, listening to the guns. There were more than he had ever heard before; an impossible number, the guns firing nonstop. He didn't understand how it was possible. Lord Tokugawa had mentioned nothing about an assault on Mount Hiei, though he knew that, like the Ikko-ikki, the monks of the holy mountain were hated by the daimyo for their power and their influence.*

It must be Lord Oda, *he thought. Certainly Shusaku had encoun-*

tered *fewer samurai guards on his way than he had expected.* He's
attacking Mount Hiei. But why?

*Something about this troubled him. For many years he had relied
on his instincts to keep him alive—and his instincts told him there
was something strange about this battle he could hear. What could
possibly make anyone suddenly attack the Tendai monks? They were
fierce warriors, and there were ten thousand of them. A commander
would have to be very sure of victory, or the prize would have to be
worth the expenditure of many lives.*

*He paused. The prize. It couldn't be—*

*No. He had been on the verge of drawing a ludicrous conclusion—
something he had avoided for as long as he had followed his instincts,
because unjustified conclusions were just as likely to get you killed. He
had been thinking—stupid, he knew—that Taro might be there. That
a boy who would be shogun was a prize worth having, even if it meant
going through the Tendai monks to get to him.*

*But no, it was preposterous. Taro was at the ninja mountain, and
he was safe.*

*He told himself that, again and again, like a mantra.*

*As the guns continued to fire, he shrugged and continued on his
way. Lord Tokugawa had instructed him to return immediately to
the ship—he wished to sail on to Shirahama, he said. That was where
Shusaku had first met Taro, so long ago it seemed now. It was also
where Lord Tokugawa believed the Buddha ball to be—and he had
made it clear that retrieving the ball was his next and most important
goal.* It isn't real, *he'd wanted to say.* It can't be.

*But he had a horrible feeling it was.*

Taro stood, speechless, looking into the smiling face of Yukiko. Pain throbbed in his stomach and his ankle, and blood dripped from his dagger wound to the ground.

Yukiko wiped Kenji Kira's blood from the blade of her sword on the sleeve of her kimono. She put one foot on the dead man's throat, then spat on his corpse.

"When I met him, I thought that I would kill him straightaway," she said. "But then I reminded myself that pleasures can be increased by patience." She moved lightly toward Taro. "What better than to use him to get to you? Then I could kill him, and destroy you."

Taro gripped his sword, holding his ground. "You'd really kill me?"

"I didn't say I was going to kill you," said Yukiko. "I said I was going to destroy you."

"Your sister was my friend. I didn't mean for her to die."

"No. But you let it happen. And you conspired with Oda's daughter. You are a traitor through and through!"

"No!" said Taro, shocked. "It's you who's the traitor."

Yukiko laughed, a delicate sound like a small prayer bell. "I am a traitor, yes. But I know it at least. That makes me less dangerous than you."

Taro trembled. Deep down he had always feared that although he might not wish it, his actions, even his mere existence, seemed to lead to the deaths of others. Ever since Shusaku had rescued him, that night that seemed so long ago, he had done nothing but sow seeds of murder around him, and the deaths that had grown from those seeds had threatened to overwhelm him, cutting off his light. The fortune-teller who had raised Yukiko and her sister Heiko, then Heiko herself, then Shusaku . . .

"See?" said Yukiko. "You know I'm right. You're a poison, Taro." She came at him then, and as she brought her sword round in an arc, she whipped a smaller *wakizashi* from her kimono with her other hand, and then she was attacking furiously, with both blades—no longer a girl but an infernal device, whirling sharp and fast.

Taro raised his sword and darted toward her, working to hold off the girl's attacks. He had never seen anyone fight with two swords before, had been completely unprepared for it. Yukiko was grinning. "I had this idea from Miyamoto Musashi," she said, not even out of breath. She danced away from him for a moment, holding his eyes with hers. "A sword saint defeated long ago by Lord Oda. But he wrote a book, and in that book he said something very interesting."

"What was that?" said Taro, concentrating on centering his breathing, gathering his *qi*. His movements were still slowed by the wound in his stomach, though it was healing already. He could feel the muscle knitting back together, hot needles clicking in his flesh.

"He said that a man could spend his life mastering the blade, but he'd never be as good as the man who spent one day mastering *two* blades."

She pounced, striking high with the *wakizashi*. Taro didn't know if it was a feint or not, but it didn't matter. The whole system of feints and strikes was obliterated by the simple, horrific addition of a second sword. What possible difference did it make whether she intended the strike or not, when she had another blade, which could come at him from anywhere?

His wrist snapped up, without conscious thought on his part, blocking the short-sword. He saw a gleam from the corner of her eye, and his hand came round, but it was too slow—pain seared into the back of his leg, causing the world in front of him to brighten for a moment, and then he went down heavily on one knee.

He tried to stand but hammered down again on the knee, and could only raise his sword to try to fend off the strikes that came faster than ever, and then, suddenly, his hand was twisted painfully, and the sword dropped from it to the grass.

Wearily he opened his robe, exposing his chest. He touched the skin above his heart. "Make it quick," he said.

"All right then," said Yukiko, and she tossed her short-sword into the same hand that held the *katana*, and advanced toward him, her index and pinky fingers out in the mudra for banishing evil. *She's going to kill me with her bare hands*, thought Taro. She bent down, smiled at him, and then struck his neck, hard, with the extended fingertips. Agony exploded at the front of his mind, a constellation bursting into being before his eyes, and he thought, *This is it, now I die*. He knew she had aimed for a pressure point of some kind, imagined that the blood to his head would cease in an instant to flow.

He waited. The stars faded, and the tree and the grass came slowly back into focus. Yukiko still stood in front of him, smiling. She slid her *wakizashi* into her kimono. Taro didn't understand. He wasn't dead. What was she doing? He held his hand out to push himself up from the ground, only his hand wouldn't move.

His legs wouldn't move. Yukiko stepped to the side, and he tried to turn his head to follow her. He couldn't move it.

*She's paralyzed me.*

Yukiko disappeared from view, and Taro strained against the numbness in his nerves, trying to see where she had gone. What seemed an eternity passed, as the blossoms gently fell from the plum tree above.

Finally Yukiko stepped daintily into his field of vision. She made a beckoning motion to her side, where Taro couldn't see.

Two samurai approached, and between them, supported or dragged by them, was Taro's mother.

Yukiko laughed that delicate laugh. "Do you remember," she said, "what you said after my sister died? How you were paralyzed, and could do nothing to help?"

Taro couldn't speak, couldn't nod.

"I'll take that as a yes," said Yukiko. "I never believed you, of course. But I thought this would be fitting."

She weighed her sword in her hand, letting it slash the air. Then she gave a signal to the samurai and they stepped away, leaving Taro's mother lying below the gnarled bough of the tree. Tears were running down her cheeks, but when she turned to Taro, what he saw in her face was not fear so much as urgency.

"Taro, my love," she said quickly. "If you live . . . That thing we were talking about before. It's not—"

Yukiko sighed, stepped forward, and plunged her sword into Taro's mother's heart. She let go of the hilt, and the blade hung there a moment, so perfectly still, before the body holding it horizontal fell backward, and the blade stood shining then from the chest, as if marking the spot where the worst thing of all had happened.

Taro wanted to scream, to cry, to run to her side, but could do nothing.

Yukiko turned to him with a businesslike air. "Best to just get it over with, I thought. I can't stand all that emotional good-bye stuff."

Absentmindedly, Yukiko wiped Taro's mother's blood from her sword so that it mingled with Kira's on her sleeve, and Taro thought that was perhaps the greatest insult of all; *he* would have killed her without hesitation at that moment, woman or not. His mother's body lay still on the ground, blossoms drifting down through the air toward it. He could not speak aloud, but he spoke a mantra in his head.

*Please kill me please kill me please kill me . . .*

But her sword remained in its sheath. She stopped in front of him, still smiling.

"I'm not going to kill you," she said.

Taro stared at her.

"And I'm not taking you with me either." She bent down till her lips almost touched his ear. "Don't tell the samurai this, but I was meant to bring you to Lord Oda." She stroked his hair. "Well. Lord Oda can find you himself. I've had *my* revenge."

She turned to face someone out of Taro's vision—one of the

samurai, presumably—and then pointed to Kenji Kira's corpse. Taro could just see the man's feet, and the pool of blood in which he lay.

"Pick that up," said Yukiko. "We'll find an *eta* grave somewhere and throw it in."

But just then there was a clattering of feet on a wooden floor, and someone burst through the door of the main hall.

"Lady Yukiko!" he shouted. "The monks are rallying! They must have kept men in reserve, hiding in the buildings. We're overrun!"

Yukiko cursed. "Back to the camp," she ordered. "Leave Kira here. He's dead—that's the main thing."

And then she left.

For what seemed a long time, there was just the space in front of him, the corpses, and the rain. His field of vision was limited to the gnarled trunk of the tree—he came to know its every whorl and knot—his mother's dead body, Kenji Kira's motionless feet, and the grass before him.

It was a kind of meditation, but it was the meditation of a demon, not a follower of Buddha—a punishment from the deepest bowels of Enma's hell. He couldn't raise a single finger, or even move his eyes—all he could do was look on his mother's dead body, and see the flowers fall. His tears would not come, but his thoughts raced through his mind, as if in mockery of his body's immobility. He remembered everything: his mother's head breaking the surface of the water, her arm upraised as in triumph, holding a bag of abalone torn from the reef. Her face in firelight, as she prepared rice with fish for himself and her father. The love and terror in her eyes, when he had been wounded by a shark, and his father carried him back to the village, expecting only that he would be able to lay his son's corpse at his wife's feet.

From what seemed a long way away, he could hear the sounds of battle. Screams, music of steel on steel. But it was fading, all the time, and Taro could tell that the fight was all but over.

He thought, *She has taken away what I love, the way she thinks*

*I did to her.* Then another thought came to him, and soon it was repeating itself over and over, till he thought he would go mad. *What if she knows where Hana is? What if she takes her, too?* If that was true, then his only hope was Hiro. But what chance would Hiro have against Yukiko, now that she fought with two swords?

But there was nothing he could do. There was nothing he could do but lie there, with the damp grass pressing into his cheek, and the smell of blood in his nostrils. *I should have stayed at the mountain,* he thought. He'd known it must be a trap, deep down— had realized as soon as the pigeon arrived that it couldn't possibly have taken so long, that he was a fool if he thought he was just going to find his mother, and start his old life again. And now what had he done? He had brought death to his mother's sanctuary. He was a curse. Because of him his father and his mother were dead—Heiko, too.

He cried, but no tears came—he was crying without moving, his whole being and soul were crying, and then the heavens joined him, because rain was falling on him, pricking at his skin.

Gradually, impossibly slowly, the light grew brighter, and the stars above the *ume* tree faded from sight, to be replaced by a reddening that was not fire, only the sun rising. A half-moon still hung in the lightening sky, as if a reminder to the world that even in the light, things of darkness could hold their sway, and death could come at any time. All he wanted to do was sleep, to disappear into blackness, and not to know anything anymore. But he couldn't even close his eyes.

He could hear people running and shouting on the other side of the accommodation hall. He heard no clashes of steel, though, no gunfire—and he supposed that the fighting was over. He couldn't tell who had won. He didn't even care anymore. He supposed that when someone made their way to the courtyard, he would find out.

If it was the samurai, they would kill him.

If it was the monks, they would help him, make him live.

And that would be worse.

With the dawn came another fire, and this one spread from the tips of his fingers to their knuckles, crawling like burning bugs, ever so slowly. This torture inched its way up his forearms, then spread across his chest, and in its wake, he was left with the ability to stretch his fingers, joint by joint, then his arms, and finally his legs and the rest of his body. Gasping at the pain as the blood filled his extremities, he began to pull himself to his feet, and so foreign was the bulk of his body to him that he felt as if he were hauling another person's heavy carcass into the air; his legs were no longer his, but belonged to someone altogether lumpier and more clumsy.

He was staggering toward the door when the abbot stepped through it and—seeing Taro's state—rushed forward to put a hand under his arm, supporting him. Behind him came Hiro, and when he saw Taro he gasped and ran to take his other arm. Hiro's face was blackened with soot, his eyebrows and eyelashes singed. Taro wondered vaguely what had happened to him, could not for the moment remember when he had last seen his friend. Everything seemed very confused.

"Oh, gods," Hiro said. "Taro . . . your mother."

"Yes," said Taro. It was all he could manage.

"Was it . . . Kenji Kira?" Hiro was looking at the man's body on the ground, seeming so weak and emaciated in death that it was hard to imagine what a powerful enemy he had been in life.

"No. Yukiko."

Hiro made a choking sound. "She . . . was here?"

"Yes."

Inside the hall, men lay on all sides, some dead, some wounded. There was a sweet stench of blood, and the air was full of the groans and whimpers of the hurt. Taro looked around blankly. "The samurai?" he asked.

"Gone," said the abbot. "I was leading our strongest fighters. We were hiding among the trees by the meditation area, in case the samurai should breach our first defenses. We were lucky—we escaped the guns. Thousands did not. But then, when the rain came, the guns were made useless. The samurai attacked with swords—and we were waiting for them."

They emerged, finally, from the hall into the light, and Taro could see what the abbot meant: Dead samurai lay everywhere. There were no monks, giving the impression that the samurai had been struck down by some vengeful act of god—the bodies of the defenders having been carried already into the halls, Taro guessed.

A single samurai knelt among the dead, his hands together, and Taro was about to question his survival when he turned, and Taro saw that it was the man who had been haunted. What had his name been? It all seemed a lifetime ago now.

The man nodded to Taro. "I owe allegiance to Lord Oda," he said. "But these monks saved my life. I had to fight by their side." It was a statement, but it carried the inflection of a question, of a plea.

"Yes," said Taro, and the man nodded, a tear in his eye that might have been relief. *Hayao,* he thought. *That's his name.*

Taro was becoming stronger by the moment, and now he turned all around, searching the scene that lay before him. He looked into Hiro's eyes, and his friend glanced down, and in that moment he knew.

"Hiro," he said. "Where's Hana?" The abbot looked at him strangely, and too late he remembered that she wasn't Hana here, she was Hanako. He didn't care.

Hiro still did not look up. "I think you had better come with us," he said in a flat voice.

"No," said Taro, staggering. "No, no."

Hiro's face was twisted with pain. "I'm sorry, Taro," he said.

EARLIER THAT NIGHT

*Hiro and Hayao flew down the steps two at a time, rushing to catch up with Hana. When Hiro could fit it into the rhythm of his running, he struck the prayer wheels, awakening their prayers to the bodhisattva of compassion. He thought compassion was what the mountain needed tonight. The way before him was lit brightly, that was one thing at least.*

*It was the source of the light that was the problem.*

*Below, the Hokke-do's roof blazed fiercely. The trees around it were torches, the whole landscape seemingly transposed from the hell realm, where it was not terrible and unnatural for whole mountainsides to be on fire.*

*Hana was lighter than they were, more graceful. She flitted downward as if the steps were not even there. Hiro, on the other hand, was panting, his bulk getting in his own way, as if his own body were trying to frustrate his aims. Hayao drew ahead of him after only half the steps.*

*When she reached the bottom of the steps, Hana turned and*

*headed straight for the burning Hokke-do. Hiro stopped, drew a deep breath, and shouted out.*

*"Hana! No!"*

*She turned, and paused as she recognized him. Hayao stopped too, the three of them utterly still for one moment. She hesitated, and Hiro began running again—he'd hold her still, if he had to. But then she gave them a little bow. "If anything happens," she called, "tell Taro I'm sorry. Tell him . . ." She shrugged. "Tell him I'll see him in the next life. I'll always see him."*

*She was already moving, too quick to catch, and then she was inside the building, as if swallowed by its toothy mouth, all red columns and darkness. Smoke billowed from inside it, and Hana disappeared into it like a ghost.*

*Hiro ran forward, Hayao beside him. The heat hit him like a massive, physical presence, forcing its fiery fingers into his nostrils, his mouth, his ears. He coughed, feeling the smoke curling itself into his lungs. He tried to move forward, but found that his feet simply would not obey, that they would not take him through that doorway.*

What those scrolls must mean to her . . .

*His eyes streaming with tears, his throat tearing like it was being ripped from his neck, he stumbled back, driven from the door by the force of the flames. He was surprised to see Hayao run into the building, roaring.*

He'll die, *he thought.* But gods, he's brave. *He'd noticed Taro looking at the man with jealousy in his eyes, and now he could understand why.*

*A moment later, though, Hayao came stumbling out, and there was no Hana in his arms. His hair was on fire—he didn't seem to have noticed. Red weals stood out angrily on the flesh of his arms and face. He went past Hiro and collapsed to the ground, and Hiro rolled him in the dewy grass, flapping at his hair with his cloak until the flames went out.*

*"I couldn't . . . I couldn't even see her," said Hayao. Hiro saw that there were tear tracks on his cheeks—where his tears had been burned away, leaving salt on his skin. "I tried," he whispered.*

"I know," said Hiro. "I know."

His eyes were always on the door where Hana had vanished, and as the moments went by he thought he saw her several times, but it was only a trick of the flickering light, and she didn't come.

Sweat prickling his skin, tears drying on his cheeks, he sat down heavily at the bottom of the steps, as the world burned around him. Flames licked at the columns of the Hokke-do, hungry to consume it, as hell is always eager to consume the things of our realm. There was an almighty crash as part of the roof collapsed, sending up showers of red sparks that glittered in the air like jewels. A blast of hot air rushed past Hiro's face, like a departing ghost.

She was not coming out.

He was surprised to note that a small part of his mind—a contemptible part, a base part—wanted him to get up and retreat, carry himself far from this fire that was threatening to kill him.

He ignored it. Only when the remaining beams crashed to the ground, sending up showers of ash and sparks—only when the flames had died down and the ground and air began to cool—did he feel a tugging on his arm, and then Hayao was hauling him to his feet.

"She's dead," said the samurai. "But you don't have to be."

Hiro shrugged. He followed Hayao as the samurai began making his way slowly up the hillside. Behind them, the ruins of the Hokke-do—no longer a temple but a tomb—smoldered quietly in the gradually brightening air.

Taro stood on the mountaintop, and the devastation of the landscape was a mere echo of the devastation inside him.

Looking down the slope, he could see the winding stone steps, lined on either side with prayer wheels. There was a stiff wind, and as it blew the wheels turned, creaking, on their hinges—sending out useless prayers to a bodhisattva of compassion who was evidently not listening. Ash danced in the air, which itself seemed to be shivering—distorted by the heat of the small fires that still burned in the forest—so that it seemed the whole world was shaking with grief.

At the bottom of the steps was a pale gray oblong where the Hokke-do had stood. Taro could see monks moving over it, as small as ticks crawling on the skin of an animal, sifting through the debris to look for the scrolls, or any trace of Hana.

Because Hana was in there, or had been in there. Consumed by the fire. Taro had just left the body of his mother, and now he was expected to accept that Hana was dead too. He felt something tear inside his chest, and thought that thing might have been something he needed, in order to *be* Taro. Guilt opened its leprous, rotten arms and embraced him, covering him with its stink. If he had gone after Hana instead of his mother, then they might both be alive. He could have gone into the flames, and come out with her. He was a vampire—the fire would have hurt him, but he would have healed better than a human. And if he had not been near his mother, then Yukiko might not have killed her to hurt him.

*I made the wrong choice,* he thought. *I made the wrong choice and now this is hell that I'm living in.*

He looked up at the abbot, his gentle old face framed by sunshine—a grotesque light from heaven that Taro would from now on despise, since it did nothing but illuminate things he could not bear.

"Permit me to commit seppuku," he said. What he wanted was to kill Yukiko and every one of Lord Oda's samurai—but he would settle for himself, because in the end it was he who had failed his mother and Hana.

"You are one of Buddha's creatures," said the abbot. "That is not in my power to permit."

Taro cast his sword aside and opened his mouth. The sound that came out of it was the howl of a wild creature, not a human being, but the sound—like everything else apart from the fury of revenge, the decay of guilt—was a thing of no consequence at all.

*Yukiko strolled past the tents. Between them were corridors of air, and in those corridors she could see beyond the tent tops to the mountain beyond, where she had left Taro with the body of his mother. Some of the samurai had died, of course, but there were still thousands. That was the thing about Lord Oda's army—it was like the waves. You could slash at it all you liked, but it would just keep coming.*

*There was still the problem of Lord Tokugawa, of course. His army camped on the other side of the river, tens of thousands of them. Lord Oda had requested their help with the assault on Mount Hiei, but they had declined. They had no quarrel with the Tendai monks, they said. They would continue with the siege of the Ikko-ikki. Damn* them, *thought Yukiko. If they had only joined the battle, the monks would be utterly destroyed now.*

*Well, they would be dealt with later. The time must come when Lord Oda would order war against Lord Tokugawa, and then all those smug samurai would die.*

*She glanced to her left, getting her bearings. About one* ri *away, on the other side of the river, fluttered a pennant bearing Lord Tokugawa's* mon. *The sight disgusted her—Taro was Tokugawa too—but she had learned not to push Lord Oda on the topic. His surface alliance with Tokugawa was still necessary, he said, and so the farce of the two enemies besieging the Ikko-ikki monks continued.*

*She stepped over a large stone and turned right, counting out four tents before she came to one that was like all the others, if anything a little smaller and dirtier. Already she'd killed an assassin sent to the larger, more ostentatious tent at the fork in the river—the one decorated with the Oda* mon *and surrounded by well-armed, if inattentive, samurai.*

*Idiots.*

*She skirted a pile of what looked like horse manure. Really, you had to admire the man. If she were a daimyo, she would make her life all sake and tea and hot baths, when she wasn't hunting down her enemies anyway. She wouldn't live among sweating men and excrement. But Lord Oda was different. He did not mind discomfort. He only minded defeat.*

*Taking a breath to steady her nerves, she pushed aside the fabric covering and entered the tent. Light flooded in from outside, but she wasn't worried about that—Lord Oda might be a vampire, but he had been created from Taro's blood. The sunlight wasn't going to harm him. And when he finally turned her, the same would go for her. She would be vampire, but she would be free, like Taro.*

*Not that Taro would ever be truly free again. He would walk the earth with his mother's ghost behind him, like a shadow. Distractions might give him ease, for moments at a time, as when clouds cover the sun and your shadow disappears. But a shadow is stitched on, as is the most profound grief, and it will always come back.*

*Yukiko knew this intimately. She saw her sister everywhere, still. Even called to her sometimes. But the people who turned around were never her.*

*Lord Oda was conferring with one of his generals, but he waved the man aside when he saw Yukiko, beckoned for her to approach.*

The general subtracted himself ingratiatingly from the tent, walking backward, bowing all the while.

Lord Oda looked up at her, his eyes taking in the blood on her kimono. "My daughter?" he said.

Yukiko was surprised that he would ask about the girl first, not Taro. "I heard she went into the Hokke-do when it was burning, to try to save the sutras. She didn't come out."

"Fool!" said Lord Oda. "You were told to leave her in peace."

"I was on the other side of the mountain. And anyway, she betrayed you. I thought you would be pleased. . . ."

"Then you are a cretin," said Lord Oda. "She was my only child. My heir. How could I want her dead?"

Yukiko edged backward, seeing the fury and disorder in his eyes. She had not expected this. "I—I mean, I thought you ordered her to commit seppuku, that night when Taro attacked the tower."

"I did," said Lord Oda. "But I was angry. I wasn't thinking. Besides, one of my concubines was with child then. But the pregnancy . . . failed. I have sired no other children."

He coughed, then wiped his eye with his sleeve. Yukiko stared at him. He's a weakling! she thought. The great sword saint was shedding actual tears over his daughter.

"She went into the Hokke-do as it burned, you say?" he asked at last.

"Yes."

"So she died bravely. Like a samurai."

"I suppose so, yes," said Yukiko, feeling increasingly uncomfortable.

"That's good," said Lord Oda, almost to himself. "Good." He looked down. "She betrayed me—you're right about that—but she was beautiful, and headstrong and clever." He looked at her as if for confirmation. Pathetic!

"Er . . . yes," said Yukiko.

"And now, of course, I have a loyal girl in you, do I not?"

Yukiko nodded.

"Good. Because if you fail me . . ." He drew his finger over his throat. Then he sat up straight and blinked slowly, as if to close his mind to the topic of Hana and open it again on more important matters. "What about Kira?" he asked.

"Dead."

"With honor?"

"No," said Yukiko. "I killed him from behind. He cried." She stared into the eyes of the daimyo, willing him to blink, to rebuke her. But he only shrugged.

"And Taro?"

"Alive. I killed his mother before his eyes."

Now a hardness came into Lord Oda's expression. "You're sure this will work? I don't like to think that he's up there"—he waved a hand toward the general direction of Mount Hiei—"and I can't just go and make him tell me where it is."

"I explained this," she said patiently. "He would never tell you. However, with his mother dead, he will go to the ball. He must. He is consumed now by thoughts of revenge, gnawing at him like rats. I know the feeling. He will go to what will give him power; to what will enable him to destroy us. He will seek out the ball." She stretched her back, yawning. "Anyway, it's his closest link to his mother. I assume he will start by returning to Shirahama, where he grew up."

"So he will go to Shirahama. Then he will seek the ball and its power."

Yukiko sighed. "It's not the power that interests him, I don't think. He has more honor than that. Real honor, not samurai honor. It's tedious, I can tell you. He's always thinking about the right thing— that's why he's so dangerous. He makes people believe in him, and then they die. The ball is more than a source of power to him. It's an heirloom from his dead mother. That is why he will go to Shirahama."

Lord Oda grinned. "You are a cold one, aren't you?"

"No. It's the dead who are cold." And hungry, she thought. Many times she had sensed her sister's presence—a different thing from seeing her in the backs of strangers—and had felt a draining of her strength. Many times she had woken sweating, and seen Heiko's face pale and drawn in the gleam of her sword, or the clear water of the *well. Yukiko was haunted, she knew it. She only hoped the blood she was spilling would satisfy her dead sister.*

*"You know he'll want to kill you?" the daimyo asked. "You're not concerned about that?"*

*"No. He's weak. All I had to do was draw a second sword, and he became as defenseless as a baby."*

*Lord Oda shrugged. "Very well. The risk is yours to take, anyway. But you had better be as tough as you say."*

*"I am."*

*"Well," said Lord Oda, picking up a brush and dipping it into a pot of ink. "I suppose all we can do is wait, and hope he leads us to it."*

*"He will. And then, when you have it, you will seal our bargain."*

*"Hmm?"*

*"You'll make me a vampire."*

*"Oh, yes," said Lord Oda. He bared his lips, showing his long teeth. Then he bent his head, contemptuously indicating a broken thing that had once been a man, lying in the gloom at the back of the tent, its skin white and shrunken, so forcefully had it been drained of its blood. "If you* are *as tough as you say, I rather look forward to a meal with a bit more fight to it."*

Taro stood swaying in the dawn light, as the many plumes of incense all around him mingled with the mist that rose from the grass. As always, Hiro was beside him—and Hayao was not far off, his face healthier than when Taro had first known him, though there was a sadness about the eyes that had not been there before.

"I'm sorry," said Hayao. "I promised you I would protect her."

"It's not your fault," said Taro.

*It's Yukiko's, and it's the samurais', and they will all die. It's Lord Oda's, and he will die too if he's not already dead; it doesn't matter to me.*

*It's mine, and when my enemies are dead I can die too, and rest.*

He blinked, his eyes sore from the sleepless night, but closing his eyelids was not enough to make the bodies disappear, nor to rebuild the halls of the monastery, which lay in ruins on the mountainside, their remaining beams and struts blackened, so that they seemed the skeletons of fell and enormous beasts. The samurai had so far not returned, but why would they need to? The mon-

astery was destroyed, and only a handful of monks remained. The
dead were assembled in greater numbers than their mourners.

Ahead of Taro, on a raised wooden bier, was his mother, lying
beside Kenji Kira and the monks who had died in battle. Hiro had
said that they should throw the man in a ravine, or give him to
dogs to eat. But Taro had refused. Yukiko had wanted to defile
Kiro's body—and he would do nothing to give Yukiko pleasure.

"We give him his due rites," he had said. "He was a human
being. We will send his soul on correctly. Where it ends up is
another matter entirely."

"I am proud of you," the abbot had told him.

"Really?" he'd replied. "I deserve none of your pride." And
then he had turned and stalked away.

Back in the awful present, Taro gazed at his mother's body.
Like the monks, she was dressed in a clean white kimono, her
head facing north, so that her soul might find its way to the Pure
Land. Hana's body was not here. Although monks still searched
the ruins of the Hokke-do, Taro was sure they would find nothing.
The fire that had killed her had also cremated her, releasing her
from physical attachment and scattering her ashes on the wind.

It was the morning after the battle, yet it felt like years had
passed. Taro had not slept or eaten. All he wanted to do was to
go to Shirahama and recover the ball from the bottom of the bay.
When he had it in his hands, he would use it to draw Yukiko to
him, and then he would kill her, and everyone who had fought
with her.

For now, though, he had to wait. The abbot wished to begin
the funeral ceremonies immediately, for fear that the souls of
the dead might linger on as *gaki*, feeding on the few monks who
remained. There was also the fear of disease, even if the abbot
hadn't expressed it out loud. A month would pass between the
funeral rites and the cremation, while the monks continued to
read the sutras and chant prayers, hoping to speed the souls of the
dead to a glorious rebirth. With so many dead on the mountain,
and the days already warming as spring began to turn to summer,

the abbot could not risk waiting even a single day to begin the obsequies.

Taro viewed the corpses through vision blurred by tears, exhaustion, and incense. All night the monks had been chanting, repeating over and over again the last sutras taught by the Shakyamuni Buddha on the day of his death, hoping that the good karma accumulated by their repetition might cling to the dead. Taro fingered the *tazu* beads looped around his hand, the shining balls of jade seeming the only hard thing in a world that had become smoke, liquid, and the monotonous recitation of men. The words of the Buddha seemed to float through him, occasionally snagging like fish on the hooks of his consciousness.

> O disciples, if there were one who came and
> dismembered you joint by joint, you should not
> hate him but rather include him in your heart. . . .
> If you succumb to thoughts of hatred you block
> your own *dharma* and lose the merit you have
> gathered. Patience is a virtue which cannot be
> equalled even by keeping the Precepts and the
> Austere Practices . . .

Taro almost smiled. It was clear from the sutras he had heard echoing all night that he would never attain nirvana. He could no more include Lord Oda or Yukiko in his heart than he could step off this mountain and walk through the clouds to the sea. He had already made up his mind—as soon as the funeral rites were over he would go to Shirahama to find the Buddha ball.

And he would use it to destroy his enemies.

He closed his eyes, meditating not on nothingness and the abandonment of desires, as the Buddha taught, but on the deaths of those who had taken his friends and family. The ninja who had killed his father. Yukiko. The nameless samurai who had burned the mountain, destroying the Hokke-do and Hana as if they were driftwood to be burned with no consequence. All those responsible would die, and their deaths would be only the beginning of their suffering, such are the torments reserved by hell for the killers of the innocent.

He had caused death before, and he had paid for it in pain and guilt—but this, this was different. This was vengeance.

When he opened his eyes again, the chanting had finally stopped. He saw that the sun had broken free of the mountains and now hung suspended in the eastern sky.

The abbot, who was standing by the bodies, motioned for Taro to come forward with the coins. Taro had six coins in his sleeve for his mother, so that she could pay her fare over the River of Three Crossings, the Sanzu, and thus enter the realm of death to be judged by Enma and be reborn, or wake in the light of the Pure Lands, or suffer forever in hell, as he decreed. *It will be the Pure Lands,* Taro thought. *It must.* Later today, when he left the mountain, he would lay a further six coins on the razed ground of the Hokke-do, in the hope that Hana might find them.

Approaching the bodies, he laid the coins on his mother's lap, his hand for a moment brushing against hers, which was cold as stone and no longer felt human. Taro hoped her journey would be easy. He believed in his heart it would be, for a person's crossing into death was determined by their karma, and who could have led a life of greater compassion than his mother? She had avoided the meat of four-legged creatures, dived the holy waters off Shirahama, and worshipped regularly at the shrine of the Princess of the Hidden Waters, protector of amas. On her way into death she would walk over the bridge inlaid with pearls and gold, while the sinners waded through rivers of snakes.

The abbot held a razor in his hand, and now he inclined his head to Taro, an unspoken question. Taro nodded. The day before, the abbot had asked Taro's permission to grant his mother the status of a monk, in recognition of her sacrifice for the monastery's sake, and so her funeral was also her ordainment, and it was necessary that the abbot shave her hair.

Taro marveled at the abbot's composure as he made a gesture

to his fellow monks, then approached the bodies. All night the abbot had chanted the sutras, yet his eyes were clear and sharp, his movements flowing. Taro felt that were it not for Hiro's hand under his arm, he would simply collapse to the ground, and never get up again.

The abbot touched the razor to Taro's mother's forehead, and bowed his head. "Throughout the round of rebirth in the three realms, the bonds of love cannot be severed. To cast off human obligations and enter into the unconditioned is the true repayment of blessings." He repeated the verse three times, then held out the razor to one of the monks, who held a stick of incense beneath it so that the scented smoke wreathed around the blade. Then he made the respectful mudra of *gassho*, the razor still held in his hands, before carefully shaving her hair.

"In shaving off hair," he said, "we pray that all living beings should be free from mental afflictions and in the end achieve nirvana."

Holding Taro's eyes with his own, the abbot then placed a hand on the body and began to speak in a low voice. He had warned Taro, earlier, that the ceremony was the same, whether the person about to be inducted into the Tendai ranks was living or dead, and so Taro knew that the abbot would speak to his mother as if she was alive.

All the same, he was not prepared for how much it hurt.

"Oh laywoman who has recently returned to the source," said the abbot, "if you wish to take refuge in the precepts, you must first make repentance. Repeat after me: I entirely repent the evil actions I have committed in the past, arising from beginningless greed, anger, and delusion, and manifested through body, speech, and mind. . . ."

Taro stared at his mother's serene face, and for a moment felt that she must be on the point of answering, that she would simply sit up and say the words back to the abbot, but she did not. She only lay there, unmoving.

Taro felt a tearing sensation in his throat, and his eyes welled up with tears, and he knew that if he didn't exert control on himself, he would break apart and be carried away by his own body, his mind fragmenting into the sound of wailing and the water running down his cheeks. He knew the monks meditated to find their place in the *dharma*; he meditated only so as not to break apart.

Absently he heard the monk's words again, though these had been flowing all the time, low and unobtrusive. "You have attained great purification. . . . Next you must reverently take refuge in the three treasures: Buddha, *dharma*, and *sangha*."

Taking a dish of water from a monk who had come close, the abbot sprinkled it on the dead woman. He took a bell from his robe and rang it, once, then began to chant, the other monks joining in.

"*Hail refuge in Buddha,*
*Hail refuge in dharma,*
*Hail refuge in sangha.*
*I take refuge in Buddha, honored as highest,*
*I take refuge in dharma, honored as stainless,*
*I take refuge in sangha, honored as harmonious . . .*"

*You may,* thought Taro, *but I do not. I take refuge in nothing. I will not rest until these deaths are avenged.* Some part of him was aware that he wanted to deal death to others only to distract him from his guilt, but he didn't care. Once he had taken his vengeance, he would die himself. He was sure the Buddha ball could arrange that.

The chant finally over, the abbot again began talking, this time listing the ten precepts, which after the first—*Do not kill*—Taro ignored, for they did not and could not apply to him. He was empty inside, and the only thing that would fill him up was the deaths of those who had hollowed him out.

Finally the initiation was over, and the abbot stepped away from the bodies. He breathed in deeply, then addressed the gathered mourners. "We are painfully aware that birth and death give way to each other, that cold and heat cannot exist together. They come like lightning flashing in a vast sky; they go like waves calming on a great sea. Today that is the case with these people you see before you, who have returned to the source. Understanding the impermanence of all things, they take nirvana as ease. I respectfully request the pure assembly to repeat after me the name of Amida Buddha . . ."

"*Namu Amida Butsu,*" said Taro, with everyone else, but the words were empty as unstruck bells.

The abbot held out the torch. "We humbly pray that their spirits might cross over into the Pure Land; that their karmic afflictions might fade away; that the lotus will open its highest grade of blossom, and that Buddha will grant a rebirth."

And, because all rituals, no matter how elaborate, must always end abruptly with that which has been feared and awaited for so long, he touched his hand to Taro's mother's forehead, then turned and walked away, the other monks following.

Taro let out a long sigh. It was over.

Shrugging off Hiro's consoling arm, ignoring Hayao's sympathetic gaze, he turned and walked quickly from the others, wanting to be off this mountain and far away. With Hiro behind him—he could hear his friend's breathing, his heavy footsteps, but Hiro knew him well enough not to speak or intrude—he wandered down the mountain slope away from the surviving temple buildings and the surviving people, touching his hands to the trees and staring sightlessly at the stones and moss.

At first he heard only shouting from a long distance away, back on the other side of the mountain, where the stone steps led down to the world beyond the monastery. It intruded into his consciousness only as much as the harsh cawing of the crows above him, in their precariously high nests.

But then the shouting grew louder, and finally there was a monk running toward them through the trees, babbling something incomprehensible. The man stopped before Taro and Hiro, his hands on his knees, gasping for breath. Taro's hand went to his swords, thinking that the samurai had come again.

"Another attack?" he said.

The monk looked up, his face burning red with his exertion, and shook his head. "No . . . not that," he said, through tearing rasps of breath.

"Then what is it?"

"The . . . girl . . . in the Hokke-do . . ."

"Yes?" said Taro. *Gods, they've found her body,* he thought. *I don't know if I have the strength to see it. . . .* "How . . . bad is it?"

The monk took a deep breath. "You don't understand," he said. "She is not dead."

Her skin was smooth, her hair glossy and black. The fire seemed not to have touched her at all, as if she were precious to it. Beside her lay a skull—presumably that of a monk who had been caught in the Hokke-do when it burned. The remains of the hall were all around her. A blackened beam, two hand-spans wide, had been snapped by the falling roof, as if it were a twig, and lying under it were ashes that Taro hoped had come from the burning walls. Charred remnants of pillars stuck up from the ground like the stumps of burned trees, warped shapes of melted glass glinted in the light, and everything stank of charcoal.

Even as Taro looked down on her, monks were going about on their knees in the fine ash, picking up the larger fragments of the monk's bones with chopsticks, making sure to place them in the urn in order from toe to top of the head, for otherwise the dead man would lie unquietly, upside down.

Taro touched Hana's face—it was warm. He kneeled and put his ear to her mouth. To his shock he found that she was breathing, very slowly but steadily. Her chest rose and fell, and yet she did not wake. He pinched her arm—nothing. He could not understand it. Even the floor of the building was burned away, so that she was lying on a bed of soft ash. "It's impossible," he said. "The heat alone . . ."

Her eyelashes, as delicate as threads of silk, were not even singed.

"It is a miracle," said the abbot. He gestured to a pair of large charred beams, lying crosswise a few paces away. They were blackened by the heat, with great cracks running along their length from the intensity of the fire. "Those were on top of her. When the monks lifted them—and it took four men to move each one—she was lying underneath."

Taro, still kneeling, spoke in her ear. *"Hana."*

"She won't wake," said the abbot. "We've tried. She just lies there, sleeping."

Hana's arms were folded over each other, and she lay on her side, her whole body curled and wrapped around the golden scrolls. Taro could see that she had held them close to her, then huddled around them, protecting them from the fire with her own flesh. He was in awe at the extent of her sacrifice—she had been willing to *die* for these sutras. And yet she wasn't dead. She was lying here, breathing gently, still clutching the precious treasure of the monastery.

Taro saw where her hand was gripping one of the golden tubes and tried to uncurl her fingers. He grunted, surprised. They were unyielding as china, or stone.

"We tried that, too," said the abbot. "It is impossible to remove them."

Taro looked at her with wonder. A rosy blush was on her cheeks, the shadow of a smile on her lips. He half expected

*hoped*

that she would simply stand, brush off her kimono, and none of this would be real. The only hint that things were otherwise was that her eyes were closed.

"How did this happen?" he asked the abbot.

The abbot shook his head. "I've never seen anything like it before. But there is one thing—" He broke off, as if unsure of what he was about to say.

"Yes?" said Taro.

"When the founder of the Tendai monastery copied those scrolls, it is said he received help. From Kannon, the bodhisattva of compassion. She gave him insights not contained in the original Sanskrit. That is why these particular sutras are so special—they are the only ones to contain the words of Kannon herself."

Taro glanced behind him at the path that led to the summit. Though the wind had died down, the prayer wheels—dedicated to Kannon—continued to creak on their axles, reading out their endless prayers to the air. It was an eerie sound, he realized suddenly.

"You think Kannon did this?" he said.

The abbot shrugged. "It's possible. When Kannon died, she could have melted into oneness with everything, because she had achieved enlightenment. But she turned her back on that bliss and returned to earth to help humanity. Those scrolls contained the very distillation of her wisdom, and your friend was ready to give her life to save them. I believe Kannon would understand that, and respect it. Perhaps she used her power to keep the flames from the girl."

Hiro frowned. "If Kannon saved her, why doesn't she wake?"

Again the abbot made a gesture of resigned ignorance. "Even bodhisattvas are not all-powerful, for there is a flow in the world that even enlightenment cannot allow us to dam, or divert. Kannon may have saved her body, in gratitude for her sacrifice. But perhaps she could not save her soul from making the journey into death. That is a voyage that cannot be reversed. At least, not since—"

"No!" said Taro. "She's not dead." He felt as if he had been struck in the stomach. He touched Hana's mouth—something he had never done when she was awake. "She's *breathing*," he said.

"I've seen men continue breathing, after they have been dealt blows to the head," said the abbot. "And yet their souls have left them. They do not speak or eat or drink, and eventually they die."

Taro felt sick. He looked at the face of the girl he loved, so fragile and beautiful. "She won't die. I—I won't allow it."

The monk put a gentle hand on Taro's arm. "That may not be for you to decide."

Hiro, too, reached out to touch Taro, but Taro pulled away from them. "Wait," he said. He turned to the abbot. "Just now you were about to say something, when I interrupted. About the voyage to death being reversed *only once*. What did you mean?"

The abbot sighed, but it was a compassionate sigh—the sigh of one who doesn't want to give false hope. "That was a long time ago," he said. "When the last Buddha was still alive. It's said that after he achieved enlightenment, but before he ascended into nothingness, he had a ball, which represented all of *dharma* and samsara, too, and that with it he could order the world as he chose. Once, a demon attacked one of his best-loved disciples and stole away his soul to Enma's hell. The Buddha used the ball to get him back."

Taro smiled. "Then that's what I'll do."

"But the ball is just a story!" said the abbot. "It is never mentioned in the Sanskrit sutras, apart from that single time when the Buddha rescued his disciple. No one has heard of it, or seen it, in a thousand years. There's a folk tale of the amas, which says that it was thrown off a treasure ship from China, off the coast of Japan. But that's just a legend! People are easily seduced by the idea that something so powerful might be so close, yet so hidden."

Taro looked at Hiro, who raised his eyebrows. Both of them had reason to think the story was true—if only because Lord Oda believed it, and so did the prophetess. It was also true, though, what the abbot said about the seduction of power. Taro had never understood why people wanted it—why they wanted control over the world and the doings of men, and were willing to kill to get it.

But now he saw. Even if mountains and tides were raised against him, he was going to get the Buddha ball. And when he had it in his hands, he would destroy those who had hurt him. And then he would summon Hana's soul from death itself, and look her in the eyes again. She might hate him, perhaps. She might remember that it was Hayao, and Hiro, who came after her—that Taro had abandoned her.

And that was all right. Taro hated himself, after all. What was important was that he bring her back. Let her marry Hayao—at least she would *live*.

"Nevertheless," said Taro. He touched Hana's cheek again. "What will you do with her?"

"We can't move her," said the abbot. "We've tried. It's as if she is part of this place now. My idea was to build a new temple around her, and the scrolls in her hands. Already the story of her sacrifice is spreading. People will want to pay their respects."

"She looks like she might wake at any moment," Hayao said. He had come to stand next to Taro.

"Maybe one day, when she's needed, she will," said the abbot.

One of the monks gathering the bones of the nameless man who had died in the fire, an old one with white stubble, shuffled past, bent over. As he passed by Hana's head, he touched his own forehead, in respect.

"See?" said the abbot. "She is already a symbol, and an object of worship. She is like the monastery—it may burn, but it can never be destroyed."

"What about food?" said Taro. "Water?"

"I'm sorry?" said the abbot.

"You talked about men who had injured their heads. You said they starved. What will you do for Hana?"

The abbot looked confused. "I don't—I mean—"

Taro took a step forward, feeling a new momentum pulse through him, a fierce compulsion that he knew would agitate his limbs and his mind until he had found the ball and returned to this spot with it. "She is not just a statue, or the centerpiece of a temple. Do you understand? She is my friend, and I will wake her up again—I will return her soul to her body. Until then, I want you to keep her alive."

"You've tried to move her fingers," said the abbot. "You've seen how hard it is."

"Then you will have to think of something," said Taro. "Drip water onto her lips, if you must."

Hayao put a hand on Taro's shoulder. "I will make sure she lives," he said.

Taro smiled thinly. "Thank you." As if he needed Hana to be even more grateful to the samurai! But he kept the smile on his lips. "Just don't let her body die before my mother's cremation. I hope to be back before then."

"Back?" said the abbot. "But you helped to save the monastery—you and Hiro are our honored guests. And anyway, the sutras must be chanted. . . ."

"There are plenty of monks for that," said Taro. "I'm sorry. I have to leave. If it wasn't for me, none of this would have happened in the first place."

"But you fought bravely!" said the monk. "You couldn't have kept her from the flames."

"That's not what I meant," said Taro. "I meant that if I hadn't been here, the samurai would never have attacked. All I have done is bring destruction to your door—you should be glad to see the back of me."

"Nonsense," said the abbot. "The samurai have wanted to crush us for decades."

"But it was only when I arrived that they finally tried—it was *me* they wanted. Wherever I go, I bring danger. I am cursed." He thought of his father, of Shusaku, of Heiko and the prophetess. All dead because of him.

"No one is cursed," said the abbot. "Everyone is blessed equally by—"

"Not if they have bad karma," said Taro. "Believe me. It's better if I go."

"You cannot believe that army attacked the monastery just because of you!" exclaimed the abbot.

"I *do* believe it," said Taro. "It has happened before. And besides, Kenji Kira told me."

"Kenji Kira?"

"The man Yukiko killed. He is a *hatamoto* of Lord Oda's. He attacked the monastery to kill me."

"But why?"

"There is . . . something I have inherited, which makes me important to the daimyo." He didn't want to reveal too much. He couldn't tell the abbot either that he was Lord Tokugawa's son, or that his mother, a simple ama diver, might have received from her ancestors the ball of the last Buddha himself, a world in miniature, and with it the power to command the elements. Especially since the abbot seemed to think it was all a story for children. "Hiro—tell him."

Hiro shifted on his feet. "It's true that people are always hunting him," he said eventually, also being careful with his words.

"But an army!" said the abbot. "You're saying all those monks died on your account?"

Taro hung his head. "I'm sorry."

The abbot sighed. "Do not apologize. I am sure your burdens are heavy, but you cannot be responsible for this. The daimyo have wanted us out of the way for a long time. Even if this had anything to do with you—which I am very far from believing—it was only an excuse to finally act." He smiled at Taro. "There is no need for you to leave. Please, stay here with us. Perhaps you could even take orders. . . ."

"No," said Taro. "I apologize, but I must go. It is not only the samurai. There is . . . something I need to find." *And when I have it, I will bring Hana back to life,* he thought. And, further down in the darkness of his mind, there was another thought, one he could not admit even to himself, not completely. *Perhaps she was* not *spared,* said that thought. *Perhaps she was kept here by our karma, because she is the only woman I will ever love. As long as I live, she cannot leave me, and so she is kept in this realm till I die, or till I can make her live.*

"Very well," said the abbot. "When you are ready, an escort will take you down the mountain, in case the samurai are lying in wait."

Taro put his hands on Hiro's shoulders. "*You* can stay, if you like," he said. "You've done enough for me."

"Nice try," said Hiro. "I go where you go."

"I thought you might say that," said Taro. He turned to the abbot. "You *will* keep her alive?"

The abbot sighed. "We will try."

"Good," said Taro. "Then when I return, I will see her again." He bent down and kissed Hana's eyelids—the first time his lips had ever touched her skin. He felt as if he had been hollowed out, and filled with sharp things. His mother, who had survived an attack by ninjas, and traveled all the way to this mountain, was dead. Hana, who had abandoned her own father for him, was lost to him too, and it felt even crueler because she seemed to be sleeping, and only a call of her name away. He did not know how he could continue in this world, and he wished fervently that Yukiko had killed him, too.

But then, it had been her intention to keep him alive, to suffer all of this.

Focusing on revenge, he forced himself to turn away from Hana's peaceful body, and face the slope that led through cedar trees to the stone path, and farther, once he struck out north, to the sea and Shirahama.

From this moment, he would not rest.

He would get the ball. He would avenge these deaths. And then he would stand once again in this spot and hold the ball over Hana's body, and make her open her eyes and sit up.

She would hate him, he was sure. She would consider him a coward and a traitor, for leaving her alone to die. He didn't care.

She would live, and then he could die.

Taro had known that Hiro would want to go with him, of course, but he couldn't bear the thought of his friend having to suffer his company, or risk his life again on his behalf. What lay ahead could be more dangerous than anything they had faced before, such was the power and lure of the Buddha ball. That was why the next morning Taro rose earlier than the sun and snuck out of the monastery on his own. He left a note, assuming that Hiro would have one of the monks read it out to him.

Dear Hiro,

I'm returning to the ninja mountain. Please don't follow me. I have done enough to place you in danger this past year.

Your friend,

Taro

He knew that Hiro would follow him to the ninja mountain—but he also knew that his friend would be safe there, with the ninjas to protect him.

And anyway, it didn't matter if Hiro followed him to the ninja mountain, because he wasn't going there. He was going straight to Shirahama.

*Lord Oda no Nobunaga rode south. He had taken his swiftest horse—a stallion given to him by Father Valignano, the priest and spokesperson of the Portuguese. He wore no armor; just a heavy cloak and a* katana *strapped under it. Only two men accompanied him. He had sent a pigeon to his home province, the Kanto, and accordingly there would be samurai waiting for Taro in Shirahama, ready to take the ball and then kill him. Or just kill him, if that seemed necessary.*

*On Yukiko's suggestion, he had posted spies on the east flank of Mount Hiei. They had seen the boy leave, alone, and Yukiko was certain Shirahama was where he would go, to try to recover the Buddha ball.*

*Lord Oda wished to be present, physically, for the boy's demise. He had sent Yukiko to the ninja mountain. It was the only other place the boy might go—if he did choose that path, which was unlikely, then Yukiko would meet him there, and seize him. He smiled to himself. Taro had stolen his daughter from him, broken his body, turned him*

*into a dark spirit. He enjoyed his vampire strength, but it was unde-
niable that he was now a tainted thing, his dignity as a nobleman
corrupted. He had lost his only child, his posterity, and he had lost his
humanity, too.*

*So he rode. Shirahama was east, but there was a ship at anchor
only five* ri *to the south, which with a fair wind could carry him to
Shirahama before Taro got there. His country was an island—it
always paid to remember that. Lord Oda had no navy, at least not
yet. The Portuguese had told him that if and when he became shogun,
they would help him create one. For now, he used what was available.
The ship he intended to commandeer was a pirate ship. The captain
was in Lord Oda's pay and had lent his ship several times before
when Lord Oda needed a vessel whose provenance he could easily
deny, whose nefarious deeds he could vehemently denounce, even if he
had ordered them. Pirates, ninjas, bandits—they were all useful to a
daimyo with an open mind.*

*He pressed his heels into the horse's flank, steam blowing from
the creature's nostrils as it pounded down the wooded track. They had
crossed a stream a moment ago, then left behind the rice paddies that
stretched over much of this land, and entered a forest. Lord Oda glanced
around suspiciously. This was the kind of place, even in these civilized
times, where a* kami *might lurk—some ancient spirit of the woods,
housed and worshipped at a quiet shrine, dripping in moss. Lord Oda
couldn't stand that kind of thing. When he was shogun, he would burn
the Shinto temples, make everyone follow the way of Buddha instead.*

*Everyone apart from himself, naturally.*

*"What was that?" said one of the men behind him.*

*Lord Oda turned without slowing. He saw nervous expressions on
the faces of the two samurai. They were glancing around them rest-
lessly, allowing their horses to drop to a canter. He pulled on his reins.*

*"My apologies," he said. "I appear to have made a mistake. I
asked for two men to accompany me. I seem to have been given girls."*

*One of the men coughed; the other flushed red. "Come," said Lord
Oda, a little more gently. In truth he was not comfortable himself.
For many months his and Lord Tokugawa's troops had been stationed*

*below the mountain belonging to those troublesome monks. He had heard reports that parts of the country, in his absence, had become unruly—like unsupervised children. This was good land for a* kami; *but it was good land for an ambush, too.*

*"Ride harder," he said. "We will see the ocean by nightfall." Right now the spring sun was bright in the sky, riding high above the trees. Lord Oda didn't know how it was that he could be a* kyuuketsuki *and yet able to go unharmed in daylight. He had asked priests and wise men, and none of them could answer him. Certainly, though, it was useful. In fact, very few of his men, except some of the more highly placed generals—and that nuisance girl Yukiko, of course—even knew how he had changed, that night in his castle.*

*He spurred his horse again and heard the men behind him do the same, the beat of hooves growing faster, stronger.*

*And then, suddenly, he was riding the air instead, as the horse buckled and fell beneath him. For one moment he was thrown forward, stomach trying to drop out of his body, then his feet caught in the stirrups and he was snapped back, viciously. He was aware of nothing but a spinning maelstrom of leaves and ground and limbs—he thought it was how the world must look to a* taifun, *or a tsunami. He and the horse, tied together, went crashing to the earth. He heard things breaking, and he thought one of those things was himself. Then the world slammed into him all at once, stopping him, and all the breath was knocked out of him.*

*With a kind of detached curiosity, he looked around. He was lying under the horse, and the horse's dead eye was gazing right at him, white and huge. Blood trickled from its mouth. Broken neck, he thought. He couldn't feel his left leg—as he peered down, he saw that it was trapped under the horse's massive chest. He felt the ground beside and behind him. It seemed he had fetched up against a rock: that was what had smashed into him, unstoppable.*

*Something about the experience, he reflected, was humbling. There was a koan in it, if you wanted to look for it—some lesson about the ephemeral nature of life as measured against the immoveable. But Lord Oda wasn't one for learning humbling lessons.*

*Suddenly the pain hit him. He hissed out air through his teeth. If he'd thought pain would be less as a vampire, he'd been wrong. He could feel the shattered bones in his leg—they were pushing against his skin, shards of broken pottery in a leather bag. There was a thudding ache in his head, too, and he became conscious of blood oozing past his ear. His wrist and several ribs were broken as well, he thought.*

*"Oh, gods," said a voice.*

*Lord Oda looked up. One of his men stood over him—he wasn't sure of the samurai's name.*

*"Are you hurt?" said the samurai.*

*"Of course I'm hurt, you cretin," said Lord Oda. "Where's . . . the other one? Your companion."*

*"His horse fell too. He— His head hit a rock."*

*Lord Oda grimaced. "Can you move this horse?"*

*To his credit, the samurai tried—but the stallion had been a magnificent beast in life, and in death it was a heavy piece of meat and bone, something no man could hope to lift.*

*Lord Oda sank back against the rock, involuntary tears of pain running down his cheeks. The world had taken on a washing, maritime sort of rhythm, as if he and the whole forest were caught on a rocking tide. Darkness crept into his vision; crept out again. Everything swam murkily. His pain was absolute, and everything. It was the most important thing in the world; indeed, it seemed to have slipped out of him, past the barrier of his skin, and into the world at large—so that the whole universe was one throbbing ocean of pain, and he was just bobbing on it, carried by it.*

*Just then there came a shout from somewhere out there in the forest. Moments later two men appeared—peasants, by the look of them. They took one look at Lord Oda and then rushed to help his samurai lever the horse's deadweight off him. One of them turned to a boy, who had appeared beside them, and told him to run home, to fetch a sheet that they could use for a stretcher.*

*When they lifted the horse enough, Lord Oda dragged himself free, screaming. He promised himself that if he lived through this, he would kill his samurai and all these men—no one should hear Lord*

*Oda scream. But he must have fainted for a while, the tide of blackness streaming in, because when he next opened his eyes he was moving over the forest floor, suspended on a taut sheet, and at least the rocking motion was real now, not some illusion projected by his pain.*

*He reached down to touch his leg. He was afraid—afraid of the ruination he would feel. His fingers probed the flesh—he gasped with pain—and then he frowned. Earlier it had been broken pottery in a bag; now he felt tender tissue, yes, but the bone underneath seemed different. Not mended, but more suggestive of skeletal structure. He raised his hand to his face. The bleeding from his head had stopped, and it was then that he realized he was using the hand with the snapped wrist.*

*His wrist, evidently, was no longer snapped.*

*Gradually he started to smile. Pain still ebbed and flowed, but it wasn't something that belonged to the world anymore—it wasn't a feature of existence, like weather; it was something inside him. Something he could control. He took hold of it, and he wrestled it down. If there was something he knew, it was how to subdue an enemy.*

*His remaining samurai walked beside him, leading his horse. Lord Oda guessed that the third horse, like his, was dead. The samurai was talking to the peasants in a low voice—talking about crops and war. Lord Oda got the distinct impression that the peasants disliked his siege of the monks, that they resented the taxes to pay for it, and the levies of men for the army. Dimly, he reminded himself to kill them later.*

*Soon they came to some kind of inn, deep in the forest. Lord Oda could hear voices from inside—his hearing had grown ever more acute since he became a vampire. There was also a smell of cooking rice.* Disgusting, *Lord Oda thought. But there was another smell too—the smell of blood. He wondered if it was his own blood he was smelling, but he thought not. He thought it was the blood still moving in the men's veins, his own samurai's veins. Now that he thought of it, he could perceive it, something in between hearing and smelling. He was aware of red branching things around him, treelike structures, and he knew that what he was seeing was a different kind of skeleton—it was all the blood that was in these people, these peasants. It flickered and moved deliciously.*

*And now that he was aware of it the hunger rose up, snarling, and pounced on his stomach. He took in a sharp breath. He needed that blood; he needed it hot and iron-tangy in his mouth, pouring down his throat.*

*The inn door opened, and the men carried him in. The hubbub of voices stopped instantly. Lord Oda could see smoke from a hibachi, and he could smell it too, though he couldn't see where the brazier was. The makeshift stretcher was laid on the ground. From the number of feet he could see, and the murmuring voices that had preceded their entry, Lord Oda guessed there were at least ten men in the room.*

*Some of them might be women, of course. Not that it made any difference to him.*

*"Chika," said one of the peasants who had been carrying him, apparently to a woman out of Lord Oda's sight line.*

*So, at least one woman.*

*"See what you can do about his injuries," the man continued to the unseen Chika. "Get him some food, too." Then he crouched beside Lord Oda. "We don't kill, if we don't have to," he said in a low voice. A slow, disappointed awareness was growing in Lord Oda's chest. Bandits. Of course, they had to be bandits.*

*"You just hand over everything you're carrying," said the man. "Money, weapons, and the like. When your bones are mended a little, we'll send you on your way."*

*"What—," began Lord Oda's samurai, but he bit his tongue when a knife appeared at his throat, as if by magic.*

*"It's only fair," said the peasant. "We are helping you. Only right you should help us, too."*

*Lord Oda sighed. "You had a wire across the path, didn't you?" he said. He was surprised by how strong his voice sounded, by how little it trembled and wheezed. The peasant didn't seem to notice, though.*

*"'Fraid so," he said.*

*"Why didn't you just kill us there? I was trapped. I couldn't fight."*

*The man was crouching by Lord Oda's side—his lined face was right there beside him, his crinkled brown eyes, and Lord Oda saw the unfeigned indignation written on his face by eyebrow and mouth.*

*"We're not monsters," he said. "We just want to eat. To feed our children." He put a hand on Lord Oda's cloak. "Now come on, let's see what you've got." Out of the corner of his eye, Lord Oda saw other men searching his remaining samurai, the knife still at his throat.*

*His cloak parted under the peasant's touch. At the same time he flexed the fingers of his left hand experimentally. A little pain, but no indication that until half an incense stick ago the wrist had been snapped like a green branch. As he did so, the peasant examining him gave a small gasp. He stood and staggered back. Lord Oda wondered for one moment whether the man had guessed that he was a vampire, but then he saw the man's gaze fall to his side, where his sword was strapped. At the same time he was aware of its reassuring hardness, pressing into him.*

*Foolish of him, really. He'd not worn armor or helmet—he hadn't wanted anyone identifying him too easily as Lord Oda no Nobunaga, one of the most powerful daimyo in the land. But his katana was a stunning piece, made by a master craftsman—Lord Oda remembered decapitating the man after receiving it. He'd done it out of impatience, partly—the man just stood there stammering when Lord Oda asked his price. But partly, too, he'd done it to stop the craftsman making any more swords like it. It was a sword of violence, and one of the finest ever made. Of course no ordinary samurai would carry it.*

*It also, Lord Oda realized, carried the Oda mon on its pommel. All this flashed through his mind in an instant, and he knew that this was the decisive moment, when all the room was like the inside of a struck bell, all shimmering and shivering and full of latent energy.*

*"Y-y-you're—," stammered the peasant. Gods, but Lord Oda hated stammerers.*

*"Lord Oda no Nobunaga," he said. "And you are a dead man."*

*Panic seized the man. "Kill them," he shouted. "Kill them now. Hide the bodies—and someone go and get the—"*

*He broke off when Lord Oda sprang from the stretcher and landed, with only a dim shaft of pain through his leg, on the wooden floor. The peasant who'd been speaking to him moved toward him—he'd got a short-sword from somewhere, a wakizashi. Lord Oda didn't bother drawing his own sword; the movement would cost him too much time. He sidestepped, another bolt of pain shooting through him, and caught the man as he passed, one arm bracing the sword hand so that the sword dangled, useless, the other snaking around the man's head, hooking him in the mouth and snapping his neck.*

*Even as the others came for him, he held the dead man's weight, which wanted only to rejoin the earth it had come from, and his recently broken wrist screamed—but didn't yield. He sank his teeth into the man's neck, and the heart must still have been pumping—just— because a spurt of blood hit the roof of his mouth and gushed, hot and iron-tangy, down his throat. His eyes widened, and he saw the grain of the wooden floor, every knot and eye and scratch. He heard everyone moving toward him, heard their hearts beating in their chests and the whisper of the blood in their veins. He could almost believe the blood was saying something as it coursed around them, and another part of him knew that the special thing said by each person's blood was their soul.*

Their souls are whispering, *he thought madly.* I will take them inside me and they will nourish me. *He drank down as much blood as he could swallow, and then he dropped the corpse, and it rushed to be one with the ground—though he finessed the short-sword from the man's hand in the same movement. His eyes took in the whole space, the position of each body and the distribution of the weapons. He read the room, as if it were a kanji character only he could understand, and the most remarkable thing was that he had the time to do so.*

*He had all the time in the world, he discovered.*

*It was a single-roomed wooden structure, the brazier he had smelled stood at the rear, and there were several tables arranged in a haphazard placement on the floor. A tavern, of sorts.*

*He saw his samurai lying on the ground, his throat slit. He saw a very fat man behind a wooden table, a wood-splitting axe in his hand. There was a tattoo of a dragon on his arm, which marked him as a criminal. He saw another man with a scraggly beard, bran- dishing a* katana. *Yet another stood in the shadows to his right, a crossbow in his hand, slowly raising it to aim at Lord Oda's chest.*

*There were too many of them, that was sure. But they were going to be much, much too slow. Lord Oda could hear his own heartbeat, whoosh-thump, whoosh-thump, whoosh-thump, only it wasn't only his blood that was rushing around his body; he could see every-thing, every eyeblink, every pore on every vein-covered nose. He'd drunk before, of course, from animals and volunteers in the ranks, but never all the blood at once, never draining the very life from someone in one feeding. It was as if he'd been shown something essential about the universe, as if he had achieved some long-looked-for nirvana, only he'd never bothered to meditate for it, or go through suffering for it. All he'd done had been to drink.*

*He grinned, as the peasant with the crossbow—he could see a faint pockmarked scar on the man's face, perhaps from a burn—continued ever so slowly to lift it. Gravity was against his enemies, he realized. It was like with the corpse—the ground was in love with them and it wanted to own them, to drag them down to rot into it. But he wasn't subject to the ground; he wasn't subject to gravity.*

*He was his own master.*

*In one elegant motion, without looking, he thrust the dead peas-ant's short-sword behind him, spearing the man who had been about to stab him in the back. He didn't need to look—he heard the man's heart stop, and he left the short-sword where it was and darted for-ward. He hadn't heard the man hit the ground yet, of course. That would come much later, or in a fraction of an instant, which was how it might appear to anyone else and was the same thing anyway.*

*He jumped a table and landed in front of the scarred man with the crossbow. Ever so gently, he twisted the haft of the weapon, pausing only momentarily to aim it—the man was pulling the trigger already, as Lord Oda had known he would. At the same time he reached up with his crippled right arm, the one that had been useless until Taro bit him, and tore the man's throat out with his fingers. He danced left, and the crossbow bolt moved with him. As it plunged into the eye of the one with the* katana, *he snapped the man's fingers, twisting the* katana *to plunge it into the stomach of axe-man. He ripped up, for* once moving as quickly and forcefully as he was able, and was shocked when the blade tore the man all the way up, exiting through his head, causing him to cleave in two.

Letting go of the sword, he caught the axe as the corpse dropped it, turned in a tight pirouette, and let it fly. As he did so, he experienced another glimpse of the room as a totality, saw blood hovering in midair like a terrible red constellation against the darkness of the room. The second man he'd killed—the one who'd been behind him—was still falling, and the wielder of the crossbow was only just sinking to his knees.

There was a thump, as the first of the bodies hit the ground, and at the same time the axe blade buried itself in the forehead of a man who had been starting to run at him, a rice-working tool of some kind clutched in his hand. The sound of the axe crushing his skull was awful, a crunching boom to Lord Oda's sensitive ears. The force of it threw the peasant backward, and to Lord Oda it seemed like his trajectory, sailing back in a curve to finally hit the wall and slide down it, bloodily, was something as gradual and delicate as a swan coming to land on a body of water.

Slowly he became aware of screaming. There were others still alive, but they began to back away, spilling out of the door, leaving their companions dead on the ground. Colors still snapped and fizzled, the odor of the smoking brazier still filled his nostrils, and his eyes still twitched as he noticed, compulsively, each spot and drop of the raining blood. But it was fading, he knew—even as he looked, the slowness and oneness and elegance of things began to dissolve into random, syncopated chaos. His crippled arm slumped at his side; he felt a traitorous weakness creeping into it.

He took in a deep breath, smiling. No matter that the moment had gone—the moment of enlightenment, of satori. He could achieve it again, any time he liked. All he had to do was kill, and drink.

On his way out to retrieve his samurai's horse, he paused by the body of the first peasant, the one who had spoken to him, who had known who he was. He observed how it hugged the ground, how totally the pull of the earth had claimed it.

"You might not be monsters," he said. "But I am."

By the time Taro reached the mountainous region of Atami, near Shirahama, it was the height of summer. His feet were blistered and sore, his soul heavy with the loss of his mother and Hana. He missed Hiro, too—and though he had wanted to be alone, he found himself wishing often that his friend was there to make a joke, or tease him about something, to distract him from his worries. His mind was turning with the death of his mother, but there were more immediate concerns too—he was in Oda territory here, and every day that he moved in it he was placing himself in mortal danger. He was careful to travel as much as possible by night, and to avoid dwelling places, so that it seemed all he saw of the countryside was trees, and rivers, and cold rocky places.

He had survived by hunting rabbits and birds, sucking them dry of their blood. Twice he had even overpowered travelers, when they were on their own—though he had taken only enough blood to keep him from starvation. He was careful to leave them unconscious, but not fatally wounded. He told himself he was not like Little Kawabata, that he *had* to feed on these people, in order to survive.

But he knew, deep down, that he was exactly like Little Kawabata. He was a vampire, and nothing was ever going to change that. He told himself that it was only because he didn't want the ball to fall into the wrong hands that he was doing this, but that wasn't really true. He was doing it because he wanted to bring back the dead, and take his vengeance.

The air hung in a haze over the hills and the sea, as if the fabric of reality were thinned by the heat. At dusk, which was when he began to walk each night, the pine-covered slopes were great purple masses, looming over the endless darkness of the sea.

Though this region was only a handful of *ri* from home, Taro had never traveled through it before, and found it both familiar and strange. Torii gates and Shinto shrines dotted the hills and bays, as in Shirahama, but they were dedicated to gods he had never heard of, with evocative names such as the Dragon of the Pearl Lake.

As the days and weeks had passed, Taro was not aware that he was gradually losing his faith—his faith in the Buddha, his faith in the essential goodness of the world, his faith in others. But one morning, as he drew within two days' walk of Shirahama, he felt it break for good.

It was when he was resting for the day in the shade of a small forest, just inland from a long inlet. Taro saw a group of children catching dragonflies by the stream. From their excited exclamations, he understood that they believed these insects to be the reincarnated souls of ancient samurai, who had died in a great battle between the Minamoto and the Taira.

As he watched, Taro felt something inside him wither and die. He and Hiro had been just like those children once—only it was crabs they caught, the special ones with the horned shells, that people from Shirahama said were the souls of the Heike, killed in the great sea battle just off the coast. The same Heike, in fact, that had stolen away the *biwa* player Hoichi, and made him sing to them the ballad of their destruction.

*It's just a superstition,* he realized. *These children catch dragon-flies; we scoured the beach for crabs. Probably somewhere in the west or north they hunt for butterflies.* In that moment, it all became clear to him, and he thought with a horrified shudder that he would never have understood the truth if he had not traveled so far from home. He would have believed in the same *kami* gods; he would have taught his children that crabs were samurai. But he had seen other villages now, with different gods and different samurai, and he knew in his heart it was not possible for all these things to be true and real. The only constant thing was that people told the same kind of stories, *believed* the same kind of stories.

*Buddha and samsara and reincarnation—these are just stories we've told ourselves.*

Of course, if they were just stories, then the Buddha ball was a story too. But maybe it was. He knew that there were bad things in the world—ghosts and vampires and demons. But he had seen no evidence, ever, that there might be good things too. Maybe he was chasing after nothing. He thrust this thought away. At least, while he was looking for the ball, he had something to do.

No, he had to find the ball, and had to believe that it would work—and perhaps the force of his belief would make it true.

These thoughts turned in his mind every day and night, as he trudged alone through the woods and rice paddies, alternately dismissing religion and magic, then deciding once again that the ball *must* be real, and that the world *must* be ordered for the best, in the final reckoning, and if he could only find the ball, then he could solve everything, just like that.

Then the cycle would begin again and he would lose all hope and conclude he was a fool. Only children believed the means were available to change the world, just like that, and to obtain what they desired.

In this way, he passed through the landscape without seeing it. And then, finally, he stood near dawn at the top of the cliffs to the south of Shirahama, and could see the lights of the village twinkling on the steep slopes, like fireflies. On the warm breeze he

could smell pine oil and the sea, and while he had smelled these
things the last several days, the scent now seemed special to this
place. From various points in between the houses, steam rose into
the night air from the hot *onsen* springs, which the people used for
baths.

All he wanted was to get to the bay, to the taboo place where
the wreck was, and dive for the ball. But it was a cloudy night,
without even moonlight to guide him. The site of the wreck was
unsafe as it was—no ama would dive there, for fear of the spirits
that lay in wait among the coral and the seaweed-covered spars of
the broken ship. With no visibility, it would be suicide.

Not that suicide was something Taro ruled out. He just wanted
to get the ball first—to avenge his mother, and to try to bring Hana
back. Only if he failed would he contemplate that other option.

He traced the thin path that ran along the cliff top, heading
toward the village. He passed the torii gate that led to the shrine
of Susanoo, *kami* of storms and the god in whose hands lay the
lives of all fishermen. Men like Taro's father—when he had been
alive—worshipped at the shrine almost every day, giving gifts and
obeisance to this terrible entity, who could choose to sink their
boats if he so wished, or dash them against the rocks. On the other
side of the bay, beyond the houses, Taro could just make out the
other torii gate—the one that announced the shrine of Benten,
the Princess of the Hidden Waters, who protected the amas. In
both of these shrines, the very bodies of the gods were kept, in
a sort of mirror called a *shintai*. These mirrors—which reflected
the essence of the *kami*—were held in ornate wooden boxes called
*mikoshi*, and none but the priests could open them. It was said that
if you looked at the *shintai* of Susanoo, you would see a terrible
creature made of thunderclouds, and that the Princess of the Hidden Waters was a beautiful woman riding a great purple dragon.

Now, though, Taro suspected you would only see yourself,
staring back from the glass.

Just then, as he glanced at that far-off red gate, looming over
the pine trees, Taro saw lights moving in single file toward it. They

were leaving the village and winding through the trees, up the hill toward the shrine of the Princess.

*It must be* obon *already,* he thought.

He couldn't believe so much time had passed. He remembered last year's *obon*. Then, as now, he had largely missed the Festival of the Dead. But he had seen the little blue lanterns in windows as they passed, under cover of darkness, with Shusaku—on their way to safety in the ninja mountain. It was that night that he had first seen Yukiko and her sister Heiko. The two girls had been setting down candlelit lanterns in the stream outside their house, marking the end of the festival by sending the spirits of their dead ancestors back to the land of the dead.

It seemed impossible that only a year later Shusaku was dead, and Yukiko, who had been in Taro's eyes little more than a somewhat bad-tempered girl, had killed Taro's mother.

If the procession was only now wending its way to the Princess's shrine, then the festival was still at its height, and the dead were everywhere. During *obon*, the shades of one's ancestors—the *shoryo*, or shadows—were everywhere on earth, doing the things they had done in life. It was proper to welcome them, with joy in your heart and food on your table. If the person had been a painter, you laid out paint and brushes. If the ancestor had been a fisherman, you mended and put out their net, for their use. They stayed for three days, sating their hunger for rice and wine and the companionship of their living descendants. Then they left again in lanterns that floated down streams, or up to the sky—or, as was done in Shirahama, on gaily painted and lit boats, which drifted out to sea.

This procession, though, marked the end of the *ohaka mairi*, the Honorable Visit. The spirits of the dead were still here, and in their honor the villagers were going to the shrine of the Princess. For the last two days, her *shintai* mirror had been in the village, carefully protected from prying eyes by the priest, and by the wooden box it was kept in. For those two days, the people of the village—mostly the women, for the amas were particularly loved by Benten—were able to play host to their goddess and honor her with gifts of food and prayer. Hopefully, in doing so, they would raise the merit of their dead ancestors, so that they could pass smoothly to a new plane of existence and be reborn in glory.

Now, though, it was time for the goddess to return to her shrine by the sea, where she would spend the rest of the year watching over the bay and keeping its women from drowning. They said it was only because she was watching that no ama had ever been taken by a *mako* shark.

Taro quickened his pace, wanting to catch up with the train of people. He didn't believe in these things anymore, but he wasn't a gambler, either. If his mother's soul was anywhere, during *obon*, it would be in Shirahama, where she had lived and worked. His father's, too, perhaps.

Taking the quick way down to the village, then running across the soft sand of the beach, Taro came upon the children at the back of the procession as they entered the cedar woods. He ignored their gasps when they recognized him. They wore their new summer kimonos, the *yukata*, and he was painfully aware that he was still in winter garb, and sweating because of it. Some of the children carried lanterns, their flames representing the fourteen *kami* of the district.

Ahead of them were the men and the women of the village, and they, too, gasped when they saw him. He nodded to them and explained nothing, just hurried so that he could reach the front, where the *kannushi* priest walked. Finally, his breath coming in ragged gulps, he reached the head of the file. Here four strong fishermen walked behind the priest, carrying the *mikoshi*, which had been fitted with two long bars, making it a kind of palanquin. The heavy box was carved with elaborate designs, and gilded and jeweled all over.

When the priest saw Taro, he stopped, clutching Taro's arms. "Are you here, boy?" he asked. "Or are you a spirit?"

"I'm not a spirit," said Taro.

The priest had stopped, and half the procession, too—the

other half were bumping into the people in front, everyone murmuring, surprised to see Taro.

"But . . . you have been gone so long! Your mother and Hiro, too. What happened? We found your father's body, and there was talk of ninjas. Old man Michi swears he saw them chasing you on the beach. . . ."

Taro nodded. "There were ninjas. They came for— Well, they killed my father. We had to run. But now I'm back. I came because . . ." He tried to complete his sentence but found himself choking on the words, as if they meant him harm.

The priest put a gentle arm around his shoulders. "You are troubled, boy," he said. "What is wrong?"

"My mother died this spring," said Taro eventually. "I had hoped, with it being *obon* . . ." He didn't want to speak of his desire to find the Buddha ball, and really he was speaking of his mother to avoid the necessity—but as he said it he realized that was why he was here, at least partly. The dead return home at *obon*, and this was his mother's home. He found himself crying, and the priest held him for a long moment.

"I am sorry," said the priest. "She was a good woman. What happened?"

"It's a long story," said Taro. "We were attacked, and she was killed."

"Attacked? Again? But why?"

Taro shrugged. He couldn't tell the priest any of what had happened. "I wish I knew," he said, in a tone that did not invite further questions.

"Well," said the priest. "You are back. And in *obon*, too! It is auspicious. Come, walk with me, and tell me what you can about where you have been."

They walked together for a further half an incense stick, the terrain gradually becoming rougher and steeper as they approached the sea's territory. The rocks became larger and sharper, the air tangier with brine. The shrine of the Princess of the Hidden Waters was on a cliff directly above the sea—and not the calm sea of the bay, but the wild, unbridled sea, where it was not held and soothed by the arms of the twin headlands. As they walked, Taro told the priest about some of the places he had seen—Lord Oda's capital city; the lands between here and the ninja mountain. He left out all mention of the rival lords, or ninjas, or battle. But it soon became apparent anyway that the priest had never left Shirahama, and would not have batted an eye if Taro had told him he'd been riding a dragon over the three islands of Japan this last year.

Taro had forgotten, too, how quickly time passed in Shirahama, and conversely, how slowly it passed too. He'd been gone a year—a year in which he'd trained with ninjas, fought and killed a daimyo who was a sword saint, and participated in a battle at Japan's most famous monastery. In the same time, these people had fished and harvested abalone—day after day. His disappearance had surprised them, he could tell, but for them it was as if he had only been gone a day, because all their days were the same.

At long last, as a few drops of rain began to fall, they arrived at the red gate, and from there covered the short distance to the shrine quickly. The four men put down the palanquin, just outside the door to the shrine. Rain spattered on the rocks, mingling with the spray from the sea. The priest took from his sleeve a small silver flute, and without announcement or further ceremony, began to play a thin, melancholy tune, accompanied only by the roar of the waves, far below. It was a tune that hung at the edge of things, clearly present but impossible to grasp, like running water or moonlight. The atmosphere—falling rain, guttering candles, unearthly music—was almost unbearably moving. Taro felt moisture on his cheeks and was not sure if it was rain, or seawater, or tears—or all three combined.

Taro turned to look at the people of Shirahama, and saw that the lanterns held by the children were failing in the rain, falling apart into paper mulch and wood. The flames were dying out. He turned once again to the priest, and the man suddenly stopped playing, putting away his flute with as little flourish and drama as he had withdrawn it. Taking from the other sleeve an *onosa*—a stick covered in paper decorations that were meant to ward off evil—he waved it in the air, before allowing sake to be distributed by the men who had carried the *mikoshi*.

There were no words, no chants, and Taro was struck by the contrast between this simple ceremony and the all-night vigil at his mother's side, when the monks had recited the sutras over and over, seeking to ease their passage into death. He supposed, though, that whether there were words or not was not important. The ceremony was not about the Buddha, or the goddess, or even the dead. It was about bringing the living together, making them remember, for one three-day period, all those they had lost.

Taro needed no reminding. And he did not need to be brought together with people. He didn't know why he'd come along with the procession, really. He had thought he'd pay his respects to the Princess of the Hidden Waters, ask for her intercession in his mother's and Hana's cases, ask her to help them. He had thought he might pray, and in doing so increase his mother's good karma.

But he could not pray. He could only listen to the sea and the rain, whose song was harsher than that of people, and more true to the reality of existence.

There were no gods. There were no Buddhas or bodhisattvas, and no ghosts, either. Taro was not sure what he had seen on the mountain, with that samurai, but it had not been the spirit of his dead lover. Such things were impossible. It must have been something Taro conjured from his imagination, a being of air, which he had seen because he wanted to see it, or felt it right that he should see it. The samurai had been staring intently at nothingness, and so Taro had built a thing for him to see.

Because nothingness was all there was. There was no death, even—only nothingness. All of this was for nothing.

Through the open gate of the shrine he could just make out the demon they kept in there. It was a desiccated thing—the people of the village said that the Princess had killed it, when it threatened to drown an ama. It was meant to be a Kappa. It had the large shell of a turtle, but with hairy legs like a dog's. And its head, which ended in sharp teeth, was that of a snake. The demon was kept in the shrine as a reminder of the real threats the Princess guarded against, something to keep the children afraid. He almost smiled when he saw it. It was clear to him now that someone had made this thing—a resourceful person who had stitched it together out of bits of dead animal. It was no demon.

Taro wiped water from his brow and turned his back on the box that held the meaningless mirror dedicated to the Princess. He scanned his fellow villagers, seeing the faith in their weather-beaten faces, seeing their belief in this ritual, and he wished he could go back in time to when he had been one of them, and the biggest concern in his life had been what would happen when his mother could no longer dive.

And that was when he saw the ghost of his mother, standing among them.

*Yukiko glanced up at the night sky, which was torn and burning.*

*A great rip ran down the middle of the enormous canvas that covered the top of the ninja mountain crater. Swathes of star-filled blackness hung in tatters from the hole, through which the sun blazed fiercely, in the all-blue, heat-hazy sky of the Month of Leaves.*

*Below, a couple of the ninjas were still screaming, writhing in agony as the sunlight burned the flesh from their bones. A foul stench filled the air—something like the smell of rotten meat roasting, or leather being soaked in charcoal and piss. Yukiko wrinkled her nose and sighed. She had been enjoying this, until they started to blabber and cry. She didn't like that—it made her feel guilty.*

*"Put them out of their misery," she said to one of the samurai beside her. He bowed, stepped forward, and began to slit their throats with his sword.*

*Another samurai hurried toward her, the antlers on his helmet wet with blood. "There are several boys among the dead," he said. "We'll line them up, and you can see if you spot him."*

*Yukiko nodded. She knew that Taro would not be here—he had gone toward Shirahama, as she knew he would, with two of Lord Oda's best and most silent spies behind him. But her men had told her that another boy left Mount Hiei that morning, traveling in this direction. A large boy, who carried himself like a fighter.*

*Hiro.*

*Yukiko almost hoped that Lord Oda would keep Taro alive long enough for her to see him again, and read in his face the poetry of his grief—though she knew it was unlikely. The next time she saw Taro, he would be dead. In the meantime she hoped he was suffering, as she had suffered when her sister died. In the meantime, she would have some small measure of satisfaction, seeing Hiro's corpse among the dead ninjas.*

*She ran her fingers along the rock wall of the main cave, seeing the tunnels that led to the living quarters. She didn't want to go in there. The memories would be too strong—of her sister, laughing. Of herself, her sister, Taro, and Hiro sparring together, thinking that life was going to be only training and fun. But she knew now why the ninjas trained so hard with their swords and their* shuriken. *It was because people were always going to be trying to kill them.*

*People like her.*

*A flash of movement from her left, and she registered the grimacing face of a young woman, before a sword blade swished down past her eyes, where her head had been a moment before. She stepped back, startled but retaining her composure, keeping her movements smooth as she had been taught. The girl came at her again, the heavy sword moving lightly in her grasp. She'd been trained well, but had not yet been made a ninja—that much was obvious from the fact that she had all her skin on, and her muscles, too. Like Yukiko, this girl had been made to work, but had not yet been given the rewards—the heightened senses of smell and vision, the ability to move with animal grace, that came from being a vampire.*

*Yukiko could almost feel sorry for her.*

*But then she had been trained as a ninja too.*

*Ducking a sword-strike to the shoulder, she reached into her left sleeve and when her hand came out again, there was a shuriken throwing star flying from it. The star hit the girl in the cheek, and she stumbled, dropping her sword for one fatal moment. Yukiko stepped nimbly forward and opened her throat for her.*

*For the first time that day, the vague nausea she had felt since the morning faded. That had been a clean kill. An honorable kill. Not like the sky above—even though it had been she who had told the samurai about it, and conceived the plan to destroy it with burning arrows. That had been the logical strategy, for the canvas sky protected the ninjas from the light. But it had made her feel queasy, all the same.*

*The only thing that made the guilt worthwhile was the thought of Taro's utter destruction. She had received a pigeon from Lord Oda only this morning. It seemed he'd followed the boy to the coast. He'd hired a group of pirates, planning to intercept Taro at Shirahama. They'd take the ball from him, if he had it, and then they'd kill him. Yukiko was sorry she wouldn't be there to see it, but she also knew the value of loyalty. Lord Oda wanted her here, killing ninjas.*

*So killing ninjas was what she was doing.*

*From the tunnels there still came the occasional ringing of sword against sword, and the odd scream. She'd sent the lowest-ranking samurai in first, knowing that any ninjas who had fled into the darkness of the caves, or had been there anyway when the sky came down, would fight tooth and claw to survive. Nevertheless they numbered in the dozens, some of them barely out of childhood. She had hundreds and hundreds of heavily armed samurai at her disposal.*

*As she watched, one of the older samurai came out of the nearest tunnel, dragging a cowering figure. He stopped in front of her and gestured with his thumb to the sorry-looking specimen behind him.*

*"This one says he wants to speak to you," he said.*

*Yukiko nodded to the man, staying silent for the moment. She wore a steel mask, an armored body plate, and a horned helmet. It would be impossible for anyone to recognize her.*

*"My name is Kawabata," said the man ingratiatingly. "I see you wear the mon of Lord Oda, may the Amida Buddha preserve his spirit for noble rebirth. I wish to tell you that when Shusaku and the*

*children left to go and kill your lord, I sent a messenger to warn Lord Oda. I failed, I know—but I did try to prevent his death."*

*Yukiko raised her mask. "I know who you are, Kawabata," she said.*

*"Yukiko," he breathed, stunned. Then he smiled with relief. "So you know me! You know that I am not loyal to Lord Tokugawa, like the rest of these ninjas."*

*Yukiko smiled back. "Unfortunately, Kawabata, you make two mistakes."*

*"Mistakes?" he stammered.*

*"Your first mistake," said Yukiko, "is to believe that Lord Oda is dead. Nothing could be further from the truth." She leaned forward. "Lord Oda is a vampire now," she added.*

*Kawabata's mouth dropped open and for once, he was rendered speechless. Yukiko savored the moment.*

*"Your second mistake is more grave," she said. She saw him tremble. "You say you are not loyal to Lord Tokugawa. But the ninjas of this mountain are sworn to serve him, are they not? Certainly they were when Shusaku was in charge."*

*He didn't reply.*

*She impaled his heart with her sword. "Really, Kawabata," she said indulgently. "What use could I possibly have for disloyalty?"*

The ghost of Taro's mother raised her arm to point at him, then shook her head slowly. Taro blinked. What did she mean? He wanted to ask her, but when he rushed forward to where she stood, she was no longer there. Ama women and children looked at him strangely as he turned around quickly, trying to spot her. She *was* gone—but it had been her, he was sure of it.

The *obon* festival had brought her back, and rather than returning to the hut, she had followed him here to the cliff. As soon as he had seen her, though, she had disappeared, as if her existence were so delicate that the weight of his attention—like the touch of a hand to a spider's web—had made her unravel into nothingness. Even when she had been standing there, she had been as insubstantial as smoke, the leaves of the trees visible through her flesh.

Ignoring the stares and questions of the others, he hurried back down to the village, hoping that she might have gone there instead. But when he came to the hut, he found it empty and cold.

Only moments ago he had been dismissing everything he had once believed in, and the world had seemed devoid of gods and ghosts. But now he had seen his mother standing before him, even though her body had burned weeks ago.

*She looked sad*, he thought. *Sad, and hungry.*

He shivered. If his mother had returned at *obon*, it was because she was in the realm of hungry ghosts, and had not been reincarnated. That meant either that she had accumulated bad karma in life, or that something was tying her to this realm. He was suddenly filled with horror at the thought that she was somewhere cold and unfriendly, doomed to never be satisfied, either by food or warmth.

*She can't find the place*, he realized suddenly. Spirits were no longer used to the geography of the physical world, and had to be guided to their homes. People placed blue lanterns in their windows, to light the way back for their relatives. Hurrying to the store cupboards against the wall, he rummaged among the dusty items there until he found two small lanterns. Taking a flint from by the fire, he lit them and placed them within the paper windows.

*Now if she comes to look for me, she will find me.*

Looking around the small space of the hut, he was powerless to prevent memories of the last time he had been here from swimming to the surface of his mind. He looked at the open curtain that led to the sleeping area, and saw the mat on which his father had been lying when the ninja killed him. The blood was gone from the floor, but he could see it as if it were still there, staining the house forever. The fire he had built flickered and crackled just like the fire he had warmed his mother by, when she returned from the wreck.

Until he'd found her again at Mount Hiei, that had been the last time he'd seen her—a frail woman, huddling by the fire for warmth. He remembered their conversation, how she'd reminded him that *ame futte ji katamaru*—ground that is rained on hardens—to stop him worrying about his father. So much had changed since then, though, and Taro was no longer convinced that hard events hardened a person in turn. There came a time when rain and gravity only wore the ground down, and caused it to slide downhill, bearing everything with it.

But that was a trick to make himself feel better, wasn't it—to blame it on the rain, or fate, which is outside human power?

The truth was, it was *his* fault. If it wasn't for him, Yukiko would never have come to the mountain, and his mother would never have been killed. Her very death was an act of revenge against him. Tears blurred his vision. Grief seemed to expand inside him like a great balloon. He missed Hana, but he didn't feel about her this colossal, all-encompassing ache—he felt, he realized, as if she wasn't really dead, but would wake up again. Her body had to have been saved for a reason. But his mother was different. He just wanted to speak to her again, to say sorry, to tell her he loved her.

He wanted also to talk to her about the things that had remained unsaid—the prophecy that he himself would one day be shogun; what she knew about the ball. Ever since he had been aware of the world around him, he had looked to her for advice. It was she who had taught him to swim, she who had told him the stories of samurai heroism that had filled him with such a yearning for adventure, until he had found himself in the middle of one, and learned the obvious but unteachable lesson that blades, like noble actions, might be beautiful—but above all they are hard, sharp, and can cause great pain. He would give anything to hear his mother's stories again, the way she told them, rather than be in one.

But maybe he could.

When his father had died, he had been struck—and it literally felt as if he had been hit by something heavy and hard—by the sudden realization that he would never ever see him again, and it had physically buckled him. But this time he had *seen* his mother, standing in the rain. And it was *obon*. He might see her again. . . .

Brushing away his tears, he checked that the lanterns were still burning in the shoji windows, then went over to the corner of the room devoted to the *kami* and put his hands together. *Princess of the Hidden Waters,* he said under his breath. *If my mother is a ghost, let her come and speak to me.*

*Amida Buddha, let my mother come and speak to me.*

Taro spent most of the next day sitting on the beach, watching the boats going in and out, and the amas diving from their platforms. He couldn't dive for the ball until night, when no one would see what he was doing. The people of Shirahama feared the wreck, and they were kind and compassionate and meant well.

That meant they would try to stop him.

His eyes on the boats, he tried to contain his impatience. He was itching to get out there over the water, shining now in the afternoon sun, and dive down. He had loaded the offering shelf in the hut—the *shoryodana*—with rice and rice wine, so that Taro's mother could eat, as if she were at home again, and among her own things. He had laid out her diving belt for her, and the bag in which she used to collect abalone, for the dead liked to enjoy their old pursuits while they were back on earth. Taro wondered if even now her ghost was flitting among the mountains and valleys of the reef, frightening the fish.

As always, the fishermen and diver-women avoided the north

side of the bay, where long ago a ship had gone down, its drowned passengers contaminating the waters. There was only one way for the ghost of a drowned person to find release, and that was to drown someone else in the same place.

Taro knew now, though, that the wreck was no ordinary ship. The prophetess had told him that it had been a Chinese imperial ship, carrying three treasures from China, priceless gifts from the Japanese princess who had married the emperor of China. Just as they reached the coast of Japan, though, the ship was beset by storms—it was said that Susanoo himself, the *kami* of storms, desired the Buddha ball, one of the three treasures. Fearing that all aboard would drown, the captain had flung the Buddha ball into the sea, and the sharks of the sea *kami*, who was in league with Susanoo, had taken it into their guard, and thus it had been lost.

One day some years later, the prince, named heir of the emperor, brother to the princess who had sent the ball, had come to Shirahama and fallen in love with an ama diver. They were married and had a son together. Then one day, the prince told his wife the story of the ball, and how it was meant for his family, and seeing how much it meant to him, she dived down to recover it. Except that the sharks and demons still guarded it for the jealous *kami* of the sea, and she was wounded by them, her chest bitten open. Using her last reserves of strength, she placed the ball inside the hole in her chest and rose to the surface, where her husband plucked his prize from her dying body.

For years, once the prince acceded to the throne (and with the Buddha ball in his grasp, that had not taken long), he ruled Japan with inflexible authority, the ball giving him control over all of nature.

But there are greater powers even than the Buddha ball. The prophetess had told a story about a curse placed on the imperial family by the ama who had died in the process of recovering the ball—for her husband, blinded by his infatuation with his new-found power, had forgotten to perform any of the funeral rites that would have given her soul rest, and had passed over her son, making another woman's offspring his heir.

Her ghost remained by the seashore a long time, until one day her son—the one she had borne with the prince—came to Shirahama, to see the place his mother had come from. Revealing herself to him, she learned from him that he had been disinherited, his father the emperor choosing as his heir the son of one of his concubines. Her fury was like the sea in a storm—deep, violent, and implacable. When her son at last performed the *nenbutsu* rites and gave her peace, she used her moment of enlightenment—her melting into all of *dharma*—to gather the force required for a final, unbreakable curse.

She declared that the emperors would no longer rule Japan, and that one day the country would be governed by the son of a simple ama diver like herself, that this boy would be the rightful holder of the Buddha ball.

According to the prophetess, that son was Taro.

Now Taro watched the restless, silvery waters above the wreck. If he were to make his way there, the amas and the fishermen would try to stop him. The superstition surrounding that part of the bay was so strong, they would never let him dive there. Anyway, he didn't have a boat, and the site was too far to swim to and dive as well. The wreck was deep, and diving was exhausting. He'd make it out there and down to the ship—but he'd be drained of energy on rising again to the surface, and then he'd be stuck out there, prey to the currents that would eventually carry his flagging limbs, and his body with them, far out to sea.

Yet his mother had risked it and gone there on the day they were attacked by ninjas, when this whole nightmare had begun. She had been prepared to die when she approached the wreck. At the time, Taro had not understood it—but now he knew she had been hiding the ball. She had heard rumors of vampires in the vicinity, and she was willing to sacrifice herself so that it would not fall into the hands of evil men. Why she had it in the first place, Taro didn't know—but that ancient ama's curse must have worked in some strange way to bring it into her possession, when everyone else thought it was lost, or only a myth.

Taro himself had not believed it was real, until he saw that a man like Lord Oda no Nobunaga was willing to kill for it.

A voice broke into Taro's thoughts.

"Your mother dived the wreck the day you both disappeared," said the priest, sitting down beside him.

Taro stared at him, surprised.

"And now you want to go there yourself," the man continued, running his fingers over his gray stubble.

"No, I—," Taro stammered, but he wasn't sure what he could say.

"It's all right," said the priest. "You don't have to explain. I could tell you the wreck was dangerous, but I think you know that anyway, and I doubt it would do much good to discourage you. I could see, yesterday, that you had experienced much more than you were telling me. When you lived here, you didn't carry a sword beneath your clothing."

Taro's hand went to his side, where a *katana* was strapped beneath his kimono.

"Yes, I see more than I say," said the priest. "And one thing I can see is that karma wants me to help you, even if I don't know why." He pointed to a boat that lay bobbing in the water just off-shore, close to where they sat. "That's mine," he said. Then, apparently following another train of thought, he jerked his thumb back toward the village. "I'm leading a service this evening, before we send the ghosts back to Enma's realm in their little boats. There will be a lot of *o-sake*, and the service is likely to go on for a long time." He turned again to the sea. "If my boat were to go missing in that time, I would be highly unlikely to notice."

Taro couldn't believe what he was hearing. "I . . . thank you," he mumbled.

"You are welcome," said the priest. "You know," he added, "I was there the day your father brought you in his arms from the beach, after you rescued Hiro from the shark that killed his parents.

You were bleeding from a terrible wound, yet you had killed the shark, and when you opened your eyes and spoke, it was only to ask if Hiro was all right."

Taro glanced down, embarrassed.

"And you haven't changed since then," said the priest. "You're still brave, but also unswerving, which can be bad for one's karma, and one's health. Not many people would take a knife to a *mako*, let alone a boy." He looked at Taro, and his gaze was serious now. "I know you will go to the wreck, and that there's nothing I can do to stop you. But be careful, do you understand? There are things on this earth that you cannot even imagine."

*Like vampires and ghosts?* thought Taro. But he just nodded. "I'll be careful," he said.

"Good. Just don't get yourself killed. We have enough ghosts to be contending with, this *obon* season."

Taro sighed, thinking of his mother's ghost. "Why are you helping me?" he asked.

The priest gave Taro a keen look. "Do you believe your mother is at rest?" he asked, answering Taro's question with another.

"No," said Taro. "No, I don't."

"You've seen her? When we were at the shrine, you went as pale as a ghost. I thought perhaps . . ."

"Yes," said Taro. "Yes, I've seen."

"That is what I thought. It seems to me that whatever is keeping her on this plane might have something to do with the wreck. I am just a foolish old priest, but I see a woman dive there on the day she disappears and her husband is killed, and I wonder if there's a connection."

Taro nodded. "I think there might be," he said.

"You must be careful, though," said the priest. "There is a reason why people avoid the wreck, much as you may not believe it."

"Demons?" said Taro, with a weak smile. "Kappas?"

"Yes, and worse," said the priest, with no trace of humor.

Oars raised, the little boat rocked on the waves. Taro had rowed out to the far north side of the bay, taking the priest's fishing boat. The moon was bright, uncovered by clouds, and illuminated the scene before him as if it were daylight, only leached of color. Everything—the sea, the wood of the boat, the mountains—was silvery blue. Taro glanced back at the lights of Shirahama, seeing no movement. The people were inside the gathering hall, beginning the closing ceremony of obon. He had perhaps three incense sticks before they would move to the beach and place in the sea the boats in which their relatives' shades would return to the land of the dead.

Reaching out with one hand, he touched the water. It was cold, even though it was the Month of Leaves and the land was warm. But the sea was a different kingdom, and everything was different here. Still, he could not let the cold stop him. He had to hurry—not only so that he could return to the village before the congregation reached the beach, but also because he could feel the wind rising.

Already the sea all around him was becoming choppy, the waves standing up in points, like the teeth that encase a pinecone. Taro had never come close to this part of the bay. Now he felt a physically palpable animosity from the place, as if the wreck below him were a spidery monster, squatting malevolently on the sand. The air felt gelatinous and resistant—it wanted him gone too.

He sent a silent prayer to the Princess of the Hidden Waters, hoping that the *kami* would protect any diver, not only the exclusively female amas. Then, quickly so that he couldn't change his mind, he dropped backward into the water.

Immediately he had the old sensation of breaking through a membrane and into another realm. The water was clear in the moonlight, and even from so high up, he could see the first spars of the wreck, perhaps the depth of three men standing on their shoulders. Curving out of the sand, these glistening wooden staves resembled the bones of a whale. Farther to the north they disappeared, as the sand of the bay gave way to rocky reef, a landscape of the Kanto in miniature, with coral for hills and fronds of anemone for trees.

Taro felt that greasy resistance again, but he pushed downward, feeling the pressure in his ears. He was glad he was a vampire and did not need to breathe as much as an ordinary person. The wreck was deep. By the time he had forced himself through the water to the white sand below, his ears were ringing and his eyes stinging with the salt. He kicked forward and grasped the nearest rib of the ship, wanting some purchase in this shifting, contingent world. A cold current snaked around him and out to sea, ruffling his hair, as if wanting to take him with it.

Carefully Taro swam farther into the wreck, between the ribs of the ship. He could see other things now, sticking out from the seabed. A rusting anchor, a teacup, what looked like a bone. He tried to put himself in his mother's position. Where would she have hidden the ball? She could have buried it anywhere, in the sand, and it would take him days to find it. He stared hopelessly at the sea bottom.

Suddenly an enormous octopus detached itself from the reef

before him and moved quickly over the sand, its color—which had blended with the greens and grays of the reef—changing to an angry, pulsing red. Taro backed away, alarmed. He had been willing to dismiss dragonflies and crabs, but this was a giant octopus, and it was coming toward him. He grabbed another rib, pulling himself behind it. The octopus curled its legs around the same piece of wood and began to climb upward.

Taro knew that the amas feared octopuses more than sharks. It was said that no shark had ever attacked an ama, knowing that they were protected by the Princess. But octopuses were different—they were low creatures, and didn't answer to the *kami*, or to any bodhisattva. Once an octopus had caught an ama as she dived, and made her his wife. Some of the women said that they had seen her, a skeleton clothed in tattered flesh, floating out of a cave in the reef, tiny fish floating in and out of her eye sockets, crabs scuttling in her hair.

Taro felt panic taking him over. Forcing himself to be calm, he let go of the rib and kicked out, knowing that there was one direction he could move in quicker than the octopus—straight up. Moments later he broke the surface, gasping for breath. The wind was howling now, and his boat had drifted farther out to sea. He cursed. There had been nowhere to tether it, and he had not thought of what to do if he lost it. Now it was being carried farther away by the moment.

To the south, a large ship plied the coast, no doubt taking cargo from Osaka or Kyoto to the territory of one of the northern daimyo. It would pass him, but not close enough for him to wave for help. He'd just have to hope he could swim back to shore when he was finished.

Already, though, clouds were massing overhead. He didn't have much time. He treaded water for a while, then dived once again, heading closer to the reef this time, hoping that the octopus would have stayed where the ribs of the ship met the sand. A small voice at the back of his mind said that he was wasting his time, but he ignored it. Swimming strongly, he glided through the water toward the reef. Here the ribs no longer rose in mocking echo of their original shape, making a ghost ship that sailed on sand. There was only broken wood and debris, scattered all over the rocks.

Taro swam right down to the reef and then moved slowly along it, picking his way over splintered pieces of plank, so old that they were more barnacle and coral than wood. Fish moved serenely around him, unworried by his presence. Some of the bolder ones even nipped his fingers, as he pulled himself along the reef. In a crevice, he spotted an eel, seeming to glare at him. The coral was all the colors of bone and rust and wood, so that it was hard to see what was detritus from the wreck, and what had grown in this place. He wondered how he would ever find the ball in this underwater realm. There were countless cracks in the reef, and between them and the sand, it could be hidden anywhere.

But that was when he saw it.

Just ahead of him, cradled in the soft purple fronds of an anemone, was a golden orb, shining in the moonlit water.

Relief surging through him, Taro swam toward the ball. His lungs were burning and his limbs aching, but he didn't want to go back up, for fear he wouldn't find this spot again. As he came closer, he could see the etchings on the surface of the ball, which he was sure had been cast from a single lump of gold. What he thought were Sanskrit characters covered its surface, gleaming dully in the dim light. *This is it*, he thought. *I've actually found it.*

He reached out to touch it, and something gripped his wrist. He saw a head like a snake's, teeth sunk into his flesh. Fear struck him like a rearing horse, knocking his body backward in a convulsing effort to get free. Blood pounded in his ears and his eyes opened wide, and he saw before him an enormous turtle, its furry legs paddling the water as it worried at his arm, biting him.

*A Kappa. It's a Kappa.*

Taro struck out with his other hand, trying to free his wrist. The ball shimmered before him, seeming at once close by and far out of reach. *This is why my mother shook her head*, he thought. *She*

*wasn't pointing at me, she was pointing at this place. . . . She didn't*
*want me to come here. Oh, gods, I'm going to drown.*

Desperately he clawed at the head that had seized on his wrist,
but it had clamped on with the force of a barnacle. He looked
around him, trying to find something—anything—that might help
him. A length of wood, perhaps.

And that was when he saw them.

Swimming toward him over the reef, like grotesque shelled
dogs, was a school of grinning Kappa demons.

Taro nearly breathed in water as he twisted his arm, trying desperately to free himself. Salt sting burned his throat. Already he'd been under too long, and dark stars burst in front of his eyes. His forearm burned with pain, from the tight grip of the Kappa and his own attempts to tear his limb free.

All the while, the other Kappas swam toward him.

Taro knew that Kappas were notorious for drowning the unwary, latching onto them and dragging them down into the depths, to feast on their flesh and pick their bones clean. His heart was pounding, his legs and arms thrashing, while a detached and horrible part of his mind contemplated the idea that he might be about to die.

*At least I'll see them all again*, he thought. *Shusaku. Mother . . .*

A Kappa swam into him, bashing his head with its shell, and stars exploded in front of his eyes again. He scrabbled for purchase on the reef, and thought he'd seized a piece of coral, but it turned out to be a Kappa's head. The thing twisted, making a sort of watery snarl, and tore at his hand with its teeth.

Then, just as he thought his fear could not reach a higher pitch, the water went dark. A cloud must have covered the moon, cutting off its light, and in the gloom he could barely make out the demons intent on drowning him. The Kappas were so many that their shells brushed against one another, and the scraping and clicking of the ivory came at him now from all sides, out of an unknowable world of blackness.

And then something hard and sharp seized his leg.

Taro opened his mouth to scream and water rushed into his mouth. His lungs flared with agony, doubling him over, as his leg and arm were pulled closer to the sharp coral. He thought, *This is it—*

—and then there was an ama coming toward him out of the murk, trailing a wake of phosphorescence. The woman was lithe, dark-haired, and beautiful, and she glowed as if a private moon were shining on her alone. She was dressed in the traditional ama loincloth, her body smooth and strong. Taro had never seen her before, but he knew who she was—the woman from the prophetess's story; the one who had first dived for the ball and who had cursed the line of the emperors.

She was also, he realized suddenly, the Princess of the Hidden Waters. She and that long-ago ama were one and the same . . .

The glowing ama drifted to him and then stopped, gracefully hovering over the reef. She smiled, and Taro had never seen anything so pure or so perfect.

*She has come to take me to Enma's realm*, he thought. *So this is what death is like. . . .*

But the woman didn't come closer. Instead her face twisted into a fierce mask of anger, and she swooped, powerful as a dolphin, at the Kappa that clutched Taro's arm. She rushed through the demon, as if it wasn't there, and indeed when Taro looked down the mouth was no longer gripping his arm, and the terrifying vision of the dog-limbed turtle was gone.

Moonlight reappeared, and the scene was bathed again in

deep blue. Taro saw flashing white, all around him, a figure racing through the water in a protective circle. It dived on a Kappa, and the grotesque turtle became only water and bubbles. *She's saving me*, he thought with wonder.

His lungs fit to burst, Taro lunged forward to seize the ball, then pushed off the reef—he felt it tear the bottom of his foot, but that didn't matter now—and began to rise toward the surface. He knew he should not go up too quickly, but he could feel the pressure on him to let air into his lungs, and also knew that if he didn't get to the air above, he would gulp despite himself, and it wouldn't be air, it would be water flowing into his body. The golden ball was heavy in his hands, but he clung to it, holding it tight to his chest.

*I have the ball I have the ball I have the ball*, he thought, over and over like a mantra. He would command vast armies, and drive them against the samurai of Lord Oda, crushing them like dragonflies between his hands. He would summon his mother to speak to him, and raise Hana from her deathlike sleep.

But first he had to live, and right now the water was pressing against him, searching with cold fingers at his eyes and his mouth and his nose, trying to force its way into him and make him one with the sea.

Panicked but glad to be free of the demons, he saw the lightness of the surface as a rapidly nearing wall of white, and he prayed that he would reach it in time.

*One heartbeat . . .*

*Two heartbeats . . .*

*Three heartbeats . . .*

And then he broke the surface and air rushed into him like an invading spirit, angrily tearing his windpipe, as if to punish him for having absconded from the kingdom of air. His eyes stung, and he saw the night sky, twinkling with stars, through vision blurred by sea or tears or both, it was impossible to tell.

He was alive.

He was safe.

Shusaku steadied himself by gripping the ship's rail. He could feel the sting of salt spray against his face, yet he could smell pine trees, and knew that they were close to land.

"Is this the right place?" said Lord Tokugawa.

"You've been here before," said Shusaku. "It's where your son comes from."

"Yes," said Lord Tokugawa. "But I only ever saw it from the shore. You escaped by boat, you said. So tell me, are we there?"

Shusaku sighed. "I can't see. How would I know?"

"Come now," said Lord Tokugawa. "You snuck into the fortress of Hongan-ji, and you couldn't see then, either."

Shusaku shrugged. It was true. He'd completed the daimyo's insane mission and had delivered one of the new guns to the war-like monks on the mountain. It had been complicated by the fact that Lord Oda's troops were readying themselves, and the monks believed an attack was imminent. Yet with the help of Jun, he had scaled the walls—considered impossible to climb—and gained access to the *inner sanctum of the Pure Land sect, the Ikko-ikki. But nothing was over yet.*

*Back on the pirate boat, after the mission with the gun, the daimyo had greeted Shusaku warmly.*

*"You succeeded?" he'd asked.*

*"Yes."*

*"And the boy? He died?"*

*"No. I left him at the monastery, with the Ikko-ikki. As you instructed."*

*"Good," said Lord Tokugawa. "He will prove useful there, I'm sure." There had been a lot of commotion on the ship, and Shusaku had asked why.*

*"Mount Hiei is burning," said Lord Tokugawa. "The pirates take it for an evil omen."*

*"The sacred mountain?" Shusaku had asked. "I heard gunfire from there. What is happening?"*

*"I believe Lord Oda is making his move," said the daimyo. "Foolish of him, of course. One should never begin play before knowing where all the pieces are." With that, he had left Shusaku and retired belowdecks.*

*Then, with the rest of the guns distributed to the pirates, Lord Tokugawa had rendezvoused with his own ship, and now they were sailing up the eastern coast of Japan, heading for the place where Shusaku believed the Buddha ball to be, assuming he was correct in thinking that the amas must have kept it hidden in Shirahama bay, where the princess first threw it. Lord Tokugawa was determined to recover it, and with it the assurance that he would be shogun.*

*"Describe the place to me," Shusaku said.*

*"We're toward the north of a wide, shallow bay," said Lord Tokugawa. "There are lights on the coast, clinging to a steep mountainside. It looks familiar to me, but these coastal villages are so similar."*

*"Is there a torii gate ahead, on the promontory?"*

*A pause. "Yes."*

*"Then we're here. I'm not sure where the ball would be, if indeed it is here." He hoped that Taro was far from here—still safe on the*

*ninja mountain, preferably, if he was not dead. Shusaku wouldn't put it past the boy to try to recover the ball himself.*

*"No matter," said Lord Tokugawa. "We'll lower anchor here. In the morning we'll have one of the local divers tell us where it is, and recover the ball for us." None of the samurai could swim, or the sailors, either.*

*Shusaku could swim, of course—Lord Tokugawa knew that. All ninjas could swim. It was often the only way to get across a moat, and to the assassination within. But Shusaku was blind, and there was no one to guide. There had to be* some *things he couldn't do.*

*"They might not know where it is," he said to the daimyo. "And they might not go after it anyway. They're very superstitious. They believe certain parts of the bay to be cursed, or haunted, or both. They think it is fatal to dive there."*

*Lord Tokugawa chuckled. "I'm sure they do. But they'll learn that it's fatal to refuse me too."*

*Shusaku nodded, keeping his opinion to himself. Lord Tokugawa had become harder than he remembered him, more like the other daimyo than ever before. Shusaku remembered when he had been compassionate and quick to defend the weak. Shusaku himself had benefited from those traits, for he had once been a high-ranking samurai in Lord Tokugawa's army, and a minor lord himself. After he was made a vampire by a ninja who had fallen in love with him, Lord Tokugawa was appalled but did not cast him out as he might have, merely kept him in his employ, and Shusaku had been loyal to him ever since.*

*And yet Lord Tokugawa had been clever then, too, and his superior skills in strategy often depended on surprise, treachery, and deceit. The man was utterly ruthless in his pursuit of power. Shusaku had seen him put innocent men to death without a backward glance, simply because they knew too much, or had associated with the wrong people. He was also unflinching in his imposition of what the samurai called honor, and had made people commit seppuku for the mildest offense.*

*Deep down, in fact, Shusaku had always sensed that the daimyo had kept him close not out of compassion—but out of strategy.*

*That was why Shusaku had kept Taro's survival from him. It was one thing for one of your samurai to be made a vampire, especially if that gave you a valuable connection to the ninjas. But the son of a daimyo? It was unthinkable. Taro would have been killed immediately.*

Lord Tokugawa clapped Shusaku on the back. "Soon I'll have the ball," he said. "And then nothing can stop me being shogun."

"You have to get hold of it first," said Shusaku. "I'm not even sure that it's here. And even if it is, and you can convince the villagers to help you . . . Well, these are dangerous waters. You know what they say: Kappa mo oboré-shini." *The expression meant "Even Kappas drown." Kappas were the water spirits that abounded in these parts, a sort of supernatural turtle that sometimes caught swimmers unaware and drowned them for fun. But even Kappas could drown, just as monkeys could fall from trees, and amas could get their foot caught in the coral and die. Shusaku didn't want Lord Tokugawa to blame him if he was thwarted—Shusaku had seen the daimyo kill too many of his followers who had failed him. And anyway, what if the villagers didn't help? Even the threat of death might not induce them to dive the wreck. . . .*

"Oh no," said Lord Tokugawa. "I have every faith in you, and the good people of Shirahama. I believe I will have the ball in moments."

"Moments?" said Shusaku, confused.

"Yes indeed," said Lord Tokugawa, and Shusaku could hear mirth and triumph in his voice. "You see, a boy has just come to the surface by the ship, spluttering like a baby in a bath, and he's holding a golden ball in his hand."

There was a loud creak from behind him and Taro turned in the water, just as rough hands seized him under the arms and hauled him upward. The ball was snatched away from him. He thought for a moment that the Kappa had followed him to the surface, but then he landed hard on a wooden surface and looked up into the smiling faces of a group of samurai. At least, they looked like samurai—but none of them wore a mon to identify their family allegiance.

*Almost as if they don't want to be recognized,* thought Taro.

The armed men were clustered around a big man with startlingly sharp eyes—obviously the leader.

"Thank you," said this man. He weighed the Buddha ball in his hand. "You have saved me a lot of trouble."

Taro wiped the salt water from his eyes, looking around him. He was on a small ship, with a covered sleeping area at the back. He spotted a couple of suntanned men who had to be sailors, but otherwise everyone on board was a samurai.

Behind the samurai stood a figure dressed in a dark robe

that covered his face entirely. He was the only man on the ship not dressed in samurai garb, and he carried himself differently. Almost like a ninja. But that was absurd—why would these samurai be consorting openly with a ninja? Such men served private purposes, carrying out assassinations under cover of night. They didn't travel with warriors.

The big samurai bore down on Taro, and he pulled himself backward, wanting to get away from this colossal man with his hard eyes.

The big samurai chuckled. "It's as if he's seen a ghost," he said. Some of the other men laughed.

"Maybe he's never seen a samurai before."

"He is a peasant, after all."

Taro stood up, trembling. He didn't understand what was happening. One moment he had been in the sea, and now he was on this ship. Someone had stolen his ball.

But he was still a trained fighter, and he had his pride. He drew himself up and took a step toward the big samurai holding the ball.

"That's mine," he said.

The man laughed louder this time. "He has spirit!" he said. "I like that." But he didn't make any move to hand over the ball.

"Give it back," said Taro.

The man sighed. "He has spirit, but he grows wearisome." He gestured to someone behind Taro. "Seize him."

Several things happened at once. Taro heard someone behind him reach out to grab him, and ducked. At that same moment, there was a *whhhhhip* sound, and one of the samurai spun, then crashed to the deck, blood trickling from his ear. An arrow shaft stuck out of his eye. Taro dived away and rushed to the other side of the deck, dodging one of the samurai as he tried to slash at him with his *katana*.

There was another *whhhhip*, and Taro saw some of the samurai crouch. Following the sound, he looked to the west. There another ship sat heavily in the water, no lanterns lighting its rigging or deck.

"Pirates!" said one of the samurai. "They're firing at us." For a moment no one paid any attention to Taro as he backed toward the railing.

The leader grimaced angrily. "Stay standing!" he said to his men. "You're wearing armor, aren't you? They're only pirates with bows! Nothing for a samurai to fear." At his feet, the dead man with the wooden shaft for an eye silently disagreed.

"Just common pirates!" repeated the leader, and Taro felt the power of the man's authority, because even he felt somehow reassured. He sensed the other samurai becoming bolder too. One of them started to move toward him, only half ducking, even as another arrow whined overhead and buried itself in the deck.

But then Taro saw a flag unfurl, halfway down the other ship's mast, before being winched to the top. On it was a symbol Taro would recognize anywhere.

The *mon* of Lord Oda.

The leader gave a hiss of anger. "They will *not* have the ball," he shouted. Clutching it in his hands, he raised it to the sky. Addressing the ball, he said, "Strike them down with lightning! Sink their ship."

Taro held his breath.

Nothing happened.

Frowning, the leader shook the ball. "Destroy them! Raise up the sea to dash them to pieces!"

Again, nothing happened.

The other samurai were all down on their knees, as arrows continued to fly overhead, tearing the rigging and slamming into the mast. Taro felt one pass over his left shoulder and bent his knees to lower himself below the rail.

Only one samurai remained standing—the big one who was so obviously in charge. The hooded figure had gone down on one knee and was moving its head from side to side, as if listening to the arrows.

As arrows whirred around him, the big samurai stood screaming at the golden ball in his hands, ordering it to wreck the other ship, even asking it to stop the arrows in the air and send them back where they had come from.

But still, nothing happened.

Then there was a lull in the firing, as the other ship drew closer, and Taro saw the gleam of swords from its decks. *They're going to board,* he thought.

*Smack!*

A blow caught him on the temple, and his head snapped round, hitting the rail, as if the ship itself were turning against him and beating him for his insolence. Dazed, he looked up at the leader, who glared down at him furiously.

"You tricked me!" he said. "It doesn't work. Tell me where the real ball is."

Taro stared at him. "B-b-but that is the real ball," he said, stammering not out of fear but out of the ringing in his skull. "I recovered it f-from the wreck." But then he fell silent. He'd seen this man holding the ball in his hands, directing it to do his bidding. And it hadn't worked.

*It's nothing,* he thought. *It's a golden toy. I wasted my time looking for that thing, and now I have nothing to take back to Mount Hiei. . . .* He closed his eyes, a tear running down his cheek. He had failed. He was, suddenly, glad that this man was about to kill him.

"You are beginning to irritate me, boy," said the man. He turned to the samurai and roared, "Get up! We have a few moments before the pirates arrive. Anyone can fly an Oda flag—do not let it scare the wits out of you! Let's see if the boy will talk with his guts pooled around his feet." He reached into his kimono and withdrew a beautiful *katana,* chased with a gray wave along its edge.

The samurai seemed wary, keeping their heads low as they advanced, but they were advancing all the same. And they all carried swords. But the leader was closer, and it was he who struck first, aiming a stroke at Taro's belly that opened up his insides to the—

No.

Just as the blade was about to bite into his skin, the hooded man stepped out from behind the leader and raised a sword that was suddenly in his hand, blocking the strike with a ringing *clang*. Taro was briefly surprised at the speed of the man's action and the way he had produced that sword from nowhere, but he didn't have long to think about it, because in a continuation of his blocking movement the man in the dark hood brought his shoulder heavily forward and rammed into him, knocking Taro off balance.

He fell backward against the rail, his heavier top half pivoted over it, and then he was falling into the sea, the side of the ship catching him a glancing blow on the thigh. He spluttered, momentarily furious that he was still alive, in a world that didn't contain his mother or Hana.

From above, he heard a voice call down to him.

"Go," it said. "None of them can swim."

He would know that voice anywhere. It belonged to Shusaku.

Shusaku smiled to himself, then lowered his sword to the deck. Very slowly, he knelt on the hard wood, inclining his head. He waited for the blow that would end his life.

But no blade severed his neck. Instead there was a shocking, sudden impact that shivered through the whole fabric of the ship, and up through the bones of his legs. A crashing, splintering sound filled the air. He was reminded of the earthquakes of his youth, when he had lived on the western coast of Japan, but this was no earthquake—they'd been rammed.

Shusaku heard men screaming in the way they do when they attack, to give themselves courage, and the ringing of metal on metal. Above him, Lord Tokugawa made a tut sound of annoyance. "Kill them all," he said, and then there was the sound of men rushing toward where the pirates had boarded.

Shusaku held his breath, waiting again for the final blow—Lord Tokugawa could never bear betrayal, and Shusaku knew he would mete out punishment even as pirates swarmed his ship. It was a point *of honor. No doubt even if his men were overcome by the* wako, *and the pirates surrounded him with their swords drawn, he would ask them to wait while he beheaded the man who had embarrassed him.*

*Instead he felt something hard and round being pressed into his hands.*

*"You realize," said Lord Tokugawa, in a dangerously calm voice, "that I have no choice but to kill you now? You stopped my blow, in front of my men."*

*"Yes," said Shusaku. He could have said,* But the boy didn't know the ball wouldn't work—he wasn't lying to you. He didn't deserve to die. *But what would be the point?*

*"You can take that piece of shiny junk with you," said the daimyo, and Shusaku felt the weight and heft of the ball in his hands.*

*Only it wasn't the Buddha ball. It was a just a ball.*

*He lowered his head again but instead of a blow, what he felt was hands under his armpits, and then he was being hauled up and against the railing. In an angry whisper, Lord Tokugawa said, "I wasn't really going to kill him, you fool."*

*Then he thrust his sword into Shusaku's stomach, withdrew it again in a swift, economical movement that opened the wound upward, and shoved Shusaku over the side.*

Lights that could have been stars or sea creatures or just the pounding of the blood in his temples danced on the water around him, as Taro pulled himself exhaustedly through the water toward the shore. A moment later he felt the scrape of the shallow bay floor against his legs, and then he was able to haul himself up. He stood in the shallows, gradually regaining consciousness, after the long and terrible trance of swimming for his life.

He turned. Far out, beyond the farthest embrace of the land, was a dark shape that could have been two ships locked together in battle. He stared down at the glimmering lights around him. He was among miniature glowing boats, and the people gathered on the beach stared at him as if he were an apparition.

The *o-shoryo-bune*—the boats of the honorable shades—drifted past him and out to the deep ocean.

Taro felt as if he were in a dream. Water dripped from him onto the glowing surface of the sea. The little boats, each one painted and hung with bunting, bobbed on the lapping waves,

lit from within by whale-fat candles. As they floated out to sea,
they took the souls of the dead with them, back to Enma's realm.
Inland, Taro had seen it done by Yukiko and Heiko with lanterns,
on the surface of a stream. But the people of Shirahama were of
the sea, and their dead, who had spent their lives on boats, sailed
into death on them too.

So captivated was he by their beauty, that it was a moment
before he realized what this meant. *Mother!* She would be leaving
too, drifting ever farther from him as the tide took the boats out.
Then, as he walked up out of the shallow water on gently shelving
sand, his eyes swept to the north. He saw something that made
him stop suddenly and stare in disbelief.

Dead men were walking out of the water beside him, seaweed
dripping from their rusted armor, starfish in their hair and barna-
cles on their swords. They wore a *mon* that Taro didn't recognize,
but by their numbers and the weapons in their hands, he knew
what they were—they were the Heike, who had been destroyed
in the bay, and to whose ghosts Hoichi had sung his song of their
defeat. And their ghosts were coming up out of the water in the
thousands, passing through Taro, some of them. They didn't see
him—fish had eaten their eyes, and anyway they stared only ahead
of them, fixed on the land, their features skeletal under their armor,
skulls looking out blankly from helmets. Then, slowly, they began
to fade downward, shrinking almost, as if melting into the sand.

No, not melting. Taro gasped as he saw a ghost gradually dim
to a dark shadow, then grow claws and a shell, and go walking
sideways—*clickety-click*—down the beach. On the giant crab's
back was a skull. These were the crabs that were seen only in
Shirahama, the ones people said were the spirits of the Heike.
Taro felt something wet on his cheeks, and it took him a moment
to realize that it was not sea water, it was tears.

*They are real,* he thought. *They are real and the dragonflies
must be real as well, and they were free to take human form again for*
obon, *but now they must be crabs once more.* Suddenly he felt a pang
of fear. The Heike were crabs again—all along the beach they were

morphing into the creatures—and that meant his mother's ghost would be disappearing too.

He staggered up to the beach, and then to where the priest stood in front of the village people, declaiming a monotone mantra to the departing souls. Some of the children stood off to the side, laughing and singing one of the little *obon* songs.

> *O, lantern, bye bye bye,*
> *Throw a stone at it,*
> *You'll die, die, die.*

Taro had been one of those children once—singing as the dead went on their way. The thought nauseated him.

"Shut up!" he roared at the children, and the adults whirled to stare at him. The priest faltered in his recitation.

"My mother is going, and I can't speak to her now!" he screamed. One of the women stepped toward him, her face radiant with sympathy, and he could bear that least of all so he turned on his heel and ran toward his hut, and his shelf of offerings. Perhaps his mother would be there—he could tell her how he hadn't heeded her warning, but the Princess had saved him anyway. He could tell her how he had lost the ball, which was his only chance of saving Hana, and how he wasn't sure it was truly magical anyway, how it had failed to work when the samurai on the ship used it. He would tell her all this, and maybe she would take him into her ghostly arms.

But when he reached the hut, it was empty. He sank down onto the floor. It was all real, all of it—ghosts, demons, goddesses. But if all that was real, then what about the ball? He needed it to save Hana, he *needed* it—and it had turned out to be a useless lump of gold.

He drew in great sobbing gasps as he cried.

Then, from the door, came a soft tapping. Taro looked up, confused. Was this his mother? If so, would she knock so politely? He jumped to his feet.

"Come in," he said.

It wasn't his mother. It was the priest, and there was a look of sad kindness in his eyes. "She's gone," he said.

Taro nodded. "Yes. I know."

The priest brushed away one of Taro's tears. "I am sorry," he said. "Did you find what you were looking for, out there in the bay?"

"No."

"Then I am doubly sorry." The priest sat down on the ground of the hut, and after a moment Taro sat beside him. "You love your mother very much, don't you?" he asked.

"Yes."

"And she loved you, of course. It is no wonder she returned, to see you again."

Taro smiled. "She was a good mother."

"What do you think she wanted?" said the priest.

"I don't know. I think, maybe, to warn me. To tell me the bay was dangerous."

"I could have told you that. I did, I think."

"Yes."

The priest closed his eyes as if thinking. "I wish I could help you," he said. "To lose a mother is a terrible thing. Of course, that's what *obon* is all about—the death of a mother. It is meant for us to help the dead, but it seems to me that for many people it is merely painful."

"The death of a mother?" said Taro. "*Obon* is when all the dead return. Not just mothers."

The priest gave an indulgent smile. "Yes, yes. But originally it was something rather different. People don't seem to tell their children about the first *obon* anymore," he said wistfully.

"The first *obon*?" said Taro. He didn't know much about anything, it seemed.

"Yes, when Mokuren went to hell and spoke to his mother, and saved her soul."

Taro sat up straighter. "He saw his mother again? After she'd died?" He dimly remembered the abbot saying something similar, about someone conquering death.

"Yes, and not as a ghost, either. He actually entered the land of the dead."

Taro's thoughts raced. If it was possible that crabs and dragonflies were ghosts, and that demons existed, then might it not be possible that this story—like the story of the Buddha ball—was in some sense true? If it was, then perhaps he could speak to his mother again. He could ask her about the ball—he was sure she'd hidden it in the wreck, so why had it not worked for the samurai? Did it require special words; the touch of a special person? Her shaking of her head had seemed to him a warning not to dive for it—what did that mean?

He *needed* that ball. He had to save Hana's life. Otherwise he was just a curse that brought death to people.

"Tell me," said Taro. "Tell me everything."

*Mokuren was the son of one of the emperor's many consorts, and because he was not a true heir, he could never hope to be emperor himself. Mokuren's mother, knowing that in her son lay her only remaining chance of social advancement, encouraged him day and night to devote himself to his studies. And when he came of age, at twelve, she indicated her desire for him to enter monastic service. Many years before, a serving girl had whispered to her during a Noh performance, "Flattering the emperor with your beauty will get you somewhere, but not everywhere. Better to have a son who reaches enlightenment. As a woman, you are barred from the Pure Land of paradise as firmly as you are barred from the most elevated positions. However, your son is not subject to these restrictions. Maybe, if he achieved enlightenment, he could even save you from whatever lowly realm you are reincarnated into."*

*Soon after, a visiting monk had told her that the greatest merit lay in sending one's son into the order—and it seemed to her that these two pieces of advice constituted more than a coincidence.*

*Mokuren was not sure he wanted to be a monk—he was a boy of naughty inclinations, who loved to play pranks on the guards and pinch serving girls' bottoms. Nevertheless, to his dismay, the abbot from the great Tendai monastery at Mount Hiei had already been sent for.*

*Mokuren loved his mother more than anything. More, even, than poetry and dancing and young women, all of which he loved very much indeed. As a result, when his mother told him she wished for him to be a monk, he accepted it with a glad heart. So it was that when the abbot arrived, Mokuren prepared for his departure. There was not a dry eye in the palace—all the serving girls loved Mokuren, though they looked forward to being able to turn their backs without fear of him pinching their bottoms.*

*As Mokuren walked out the door, his mother came running out after him in tears. Until now, he had never once left the confines of the palace's jeweled doors; he had never once been seen by anyone of importance except through his mother's screens. Mokuren didn't want to leave either, but he knew that any show of weakness might dissolve his mother's resolve. "Although I shall be far away on Mount Hiei," he said, "in the end I will come back and show myself to you, wearing the robe of liberation. Since it is my fate to follow the path of Buddhist practice, let it at least be a blessing for my future and my family."*

*All the guards and serving girls admired Mokuren's composure, but his mother was not impressed. "Mokuren," she chided, "please hear me. Although the pain of parting is hard to bear, you must not show weakness of the heart. Once you have left this place with the abbot, you must forget about the palace entirely and work to sever any attachment you feel to me. Throw your heart into your scholarship as you have always done, and accumulate merit for yourself through an ascetic life. Become a monk and then come back and show yourself to me, wearing your* gedatsu no koromo, *your robe of liberation. To become a monk in name alone, while remaining illiterate and ignorant, is a grave sin, as you know. If this is what happens to you, never return here again. I will consider us mother and son no more. But if you apply yourself and attain enlightenment, come back and visit your mother who will miss you so. I say all this not to hurt you but to strengthen your ties to*

Buddha's teaching and to weaken the apron strings that tie you to me."

With that, she presented Mokuren with a simple under-robe. "Let this robe, with its lack of ostentation, guide you in your studies."

At Mount Hiei, Mokuren showed himself quickly to be a true prodigy, becoming famous at court for the depth of his learning. One day he was invited to participate in a *hokke hakkō*, a series of lectures on the Lotus Sutra to be held at the Imperial Palace. The Empress Mother herself requested his presence. When it came time for Mokuren to return to the monastery, the Empress Mother piled gifts on his horse. Ever the loving son, Mokuren sent a portion of the gifts to his mother. However, a disapproving letter soon arrived:

Son, I received the gifts you sent. But while I am boundlessly happy with the gift you have shown for scholarship, I am displeased with the worldly gifts you have attained as a result. When I sent you off to the temple, I had no intention that you should participate in such lectures at the court, which are no better than theatrical productions. When I sent you off, I thought, "I have no daughters, only a son. I will send my son to become a great monk, so that he might be revered as a saint and save me in the hereafter." It was not my intention that you should become one of those monks who is tantamount to a lord, and who travels around in grand style to the palace and back.

At the end of the letter was a sort of religious poem:

In this revolving triple world
there is no end of loving indebtedness to parents.
to cast away indebtedness and enter the unconditioned,
that is true devotion.

Mokuren understood that he should cut off his attachment to his mother if he wished to attain enlightenment. He wrote her an apologetic letter, and then remained isolated on the mountain for many *years, atoning for his sin through solitude and meditation. Always he read the sutras, remembering his mother's admonition about ignorance and illiteracy. In winter he piled up snow next to his bed so that it would reflect the moonlight and enable him to read late into the night; in summer he captured fireflies and hung them from the eaves.*

*Meanwhile, Mokuren's mother did her own part for his success: She prayed nightly that the other monks at the temple would die, so that there would be no one to eclipse her own son's reputation.*

*One day, many years later, Mokuren had a premonition that his mother was going to die, and so he set off immediately for the capital to read the nenbutsu rites with her. But when he arrived she had already died. "For what purpose, now, was all my studying?" he asked. "The one person in this world I love has gone." After holding the appropriate ceremonies and burying his mother, he returned to the mountain. From then on, he wore only the robe she had given him— calling it his* katami no koromo, *his memento robe. Even when he achieved enlightenment, in the eyes of the other monks, and was given the robe of liberation, he continued to wear the robe his mother had given him underneath it, to remind him of her. She was constantly in his thoughts—he heard from people that it was right to let the dead go, but he found that he could not accept his mother's death.*

*Soon after, Mokuren's mother began to appear to him when he was alone in his cabin, reading the sutras or meditating. She spoke to him, but the shape of her lips as she spoke did not fit to any words he knew, and he found himself going slowly mad, as he tried to understand what she wanted to tell him.*

*But he never could learn what she was saying. Meanwhile, he was growing weaker and weaker, his skin paler and paler. When he looked in the mirror, he saw that he himself was beginning to resemble a ghost.*

*Mokuren was dying, but he knew too that his mother was suffering, and he couldn't bear it. Soon, though he didn't know it, his enlightenment had fallen away from him as the leaves fall from trees at the first hint of winter's hard frost. He thought only of his love for his mother, and how he could not bear for her to be in pain. He was not* detached and at one with dharma—he was linked to his dead mother, as if by an umbilical cord that stretched from this world to hell.

Mokuren felt that the only way to help his mother was to go after her to hell and discover what was troubling her. He found a way to follow his mother to Enma's realm, and from there to the realm of samsara dedicated to the gaki, the hungry ghosts. His teacher from the temple, who had died the previous winter, met him there, and warned him to be careful of the flames. Mokuren laughed. "Do not worry, old man," he said, "my robe of enlightenment will protect me." But when he looked down, he saw that he was not wearing the robe of liberation, but the faded old robe that his mother had given him, so many years before. He understood truly at that moment that he had turned his back on nirvana and through his love for his mother, condemned himself to reincarnation in this world, or worse.

Through the holes in his robe, his skin was red raw with the heat, scarred and burnt. He was a walking wound, in agony, but he pressed on behind his teacher, farther into the realm of hungry ghosts, which was just the same as this world, only there was no grass and no leaves and no food of any kind, and everything was always on fire.

Mokuren's teacher led him into the depths of the realm, showing him the poor sinners who were being tortured. As they walked, they passed a pot, which a demon was stirring with a spiked pole. Suddenly Mokuren's mother raised her head from the boiling liquid. "That is my son!" she cried, and now Mokuren could understand what she was saying, because he was in the land of the dead and all in the land of dead can speak the tongue of death. "Because you will not forget me," she said to Mokuren, "I am bound to you, unable to leave this plane of hell. I suffer helplessly, consumed by hunger that I cannot feed and thirst that I cannot slake. Help me!" Mokuren's teacher tried to hurry Mokuren along, telling him that this was not really his mother. But Mokuren would have known her voice anywhere, even in hell.

"That is my mother," he said.

"And that certainly is my son," she said. "I may not have seen him for many years, but he is the spitting image of his father, the emperor."

"Show me my mother!" Mokuren commanded the demon, who

*fished her out of the pot with his spiked pole. Mokuren recognized the Sanskrit letters that he had written on her body to prepare her for her funeral, and asked her what he could do to relieve her suffering.*

*"You must go back to the world and do the following things," she said. "On the fifteenth day of the seventh month you must copy the Lotus Sutra in one day. Then you must prepare an offering of clean basins full of rice and spices and the five fruits, and other offerings of incense, oil, lamps, candles, beds, and bedding, all the best of the world, to the* sangha *of the ten directions. On that day, all the holy assembly of Mount Hiei, whether in the mountains practicing meditation, or obtaining the four fruits of the way, or walking beneath trees, should gather in a great congregation and all of like mind receive the* pravarana *food, accept its gift in spirit. Then, in offering the food and the readings of the sutra, you must truly let go of your love for me, and accept that I am gone. Only then will you and I be saved."*

*Finally understanding why he had been met here by his great teacher, Mokuren returned to the world and did the things his mother had asked. Grateful, she appeared before him, telling him that she had—alone among women—been promoted to the Pure Land. He was so full of joy that he danced for an entire night.*

"And ever since then," said the priest, "people have followed Mokuren's example, leaving food and drink for their dead relatives on the days of *obon*. People forget about Mokuren himself, but they remember the ritual."

Taro sat on the floor of the hut, feeling empty.

"So . . . For my mother to be at peace, I must forget her?"

"Not forget," said the priest. "Let go."

Taro stood, frustrated. "But what about when Mokuren went to hell? How did he do it? You didn't say."

The priest spread his hands. "I do not know. It is a story—it is meant to illustrate a point about attachment, and the way to enlightenment. It's not something that happened."

"How do you know?" said Taro.

"Well . . . I don't, I suppose," said the priest.

Taro shrugged. He would like to speak to his mother again, but he was not sure he was prepared to go to hell for it. Besides, his mother would not *be* in hell, he was almost sure of it. She had returned for *obon*, but so did so many of the dead. It only meant that she had not yet entered the Pure Land, that her soul had remained in limbo, perhaps still being judged by Enma. She was gone now, and would return next year if she was still in the planes of existence. He cursed himself. He wished he had spoken to her about the ball when they were both on Mount Hiei, about what it was and how it worked—it would have saved so much effort, and so much heartache.

He went to the door. "Thank you," he said. "For helping me."

"You're going already?"

"Yes. There are things I have to do." He had to go to Hiro at the ninja mountain, make sure his friend was safe, and then he had to decide what to do about the ball. Was it worth trying to recover it from the samurai who had taken it? He would need to learn who it was—the man had worn no *mon*. Or, if it wasn't the true ball, he would have to look for it. But where to start?

He stilled his thoughts. The first thing was to return to Hiro. He could worry about the rest later. He opened the door and turned to the priest.

"Good-bye," he said.

"Good-bye," said the priest. "May the *kami* keep you from evil spirits."

Taro laughed. "Too late for that," he said. And then he closed the door on the man and left.

As he started up the path that led away from the village into the hills, and from there to anywhere he wanted to go, he turned one last time and looked out to sea. The dark boats far away, laden with men who wanted him dead, and the small boats in the bay, laden with the dead themselves, were both the same size from this vantage point.

Both tiny, and frail.

He was sure that it had been Shusaku's ghost on the ship. His spirit must have returned for *obon* and been drawn to Taro. In one night, Taro had been saved not once but twice: by the spirit of the ancient ama who had first dived for the ball, and by Shusaku, who had died in the courtyard of Lord Oda's castle.

He sent out a silent thank-you to both of them, and a good-bye to his mother. Both of them, now, would be far from this shore and on their way back to hell, or limbo. But he would be back next year at the same time, to see them again. For now, he would go to the ninja mountain, to meet Hiro. Then, before making any decision about the Buddha ball, he would return with his friend to Mount Hiei. He might not be able to bring Hana back, but at least he could see her again, and witness his mother's cremation.

He set off up the path, but stopped dead at a fork where the shadow of a tree fell over the stones.

His mother stood there, shimmering in the darkness, holding out her hands to him. She was speaking, but the words made no sense, and the shapes of her mouth corresponded to no language he knew.

*Shusaku lay panting on the sand. The water lapped insistently at his feet, as if wanting to pull him into the sea again, as if angry with him for escaping its clutches.*

*He ignored it.*

*Over the mountains behind him, the glow of sunrise was beginning to pale the sky. He knew that he would have to find shelter soon, or experience the pain of burning again, as his scar tissue was roasted once more by the sun's rays.*

*He ran his fingers over his stomach, feeling the flesh and bone already knitting itself together. It was agony, but Shusaku was used to agony. He had been a vampire a long time, and this was not the first wound he had endured. If it was, he wouldn't have been able to pull himself through the water, wave after wave, bleeding all the while, just to reach the shore.*

*The strange thing was that he was not dead. Not because the wound had been a fatal one—it hadn't.*

*But that was just the problem. Lord Tokugawa knew how to kill a vampire—he had dealt with ninjas before and was aware that only a direct blow to the heart, or a decapitation, would destroy them.*

*Yet he had not aimed for Shusaku's heart. He had cut his stomach instead.*

*And there was something else. Lord Tokugawa knew he could swim.*

*The more Shusaku thought about it, the clearer it seemed—Lord Tokugawa had deliberately kept him alive. And he had given him the ball before he kicked him over the side. Why?*

*Shusaku couldn't work it out. There was one, impossible explanation—that Lord Tokugawa had somehow recognized Taro as his son, had known who he was, and had preserved Shusaku's life so that he could preserve Taro's. It was said that Lord Tokugawa didn't plan in days or even in months, but in years—that he wasn't just several moves ahead on the chessboard, but playing an entirely different game. Could he have planned this—all of this?*

*But it couldn't be. How would the daimyo have known? So far as Shusaku knew, the man had never laid eyes on Taro since he was a baby.*

*For now at least, it wasn't important. What was important was that he still lived, and that Taro did too. Now he could go after the boy and help him. It had been months since he had last seen him. He had so much he wanted to say, so many things he wanted to teach. What had happened—his brush with death at Lord Oda's castle—had made him realize how much he wanted to impart the knowledge and skills he had learned over the years. Taro had been a good pupil—the best. Shusaku almost thought of him as a son.*

*In a way, too, he considered the boy his redemption. He had killed so many men, and as on that night in Nagasaki, he sometimes felt them crowding around him, an entourage of the dead. There was a saying the Tendai Buddhists had—akuji mi ni tomaru. All evil done clings to the body. Occasionally Shusaku felt that this was literally true, that the ghosts of those he had killed were clinging to him. But when Taro was around, he'd felt something different—a possibility that he might redeem himself, if only he could teach Taro to make the most of his natural gifts.*

*Perhaps all those killings would even be worth it, if they put a good and just man on the throne of the country. A man with Taro's instincts of kindness, protection, and compassion.*

*His fingers brushed against the raw edge of his wound, where it was still open and ragged to the touch.*

When I move, it's going to hurt very badly, *he thought. However, the stars were starting to fade now, as the light in the east brightened. He had to get to shelter, and very quickly. He stretched out his hand to pull the ball, which he had placed on the beach beside him, against his side.*

Stupid thing, *he thought.* It doesn't even work. *And yet Lord Tokugawa had pushed it into his hands, and Lord Tokugawa didn't do anything without having a good reason. So although every fiber of every muscle in his body had screamed in fury at the pain of swimming with a heavy metal ball in one hand, he had kept it with him as he swam. And even though he himself was screaming inside with fury at the fact that Lord Tokugawa had wounded him, he knew he would pick up the ball and carry it with him, keeping it safe for whatever future moment Lord Tokugawa had foreseen. Because long before Lord Tokugawa had hurt him, he had saved his life—and Shusaku owed him still. And even if Shusaku didn't understand* why, *it seemed the daimyo had saved his life again. Lord Tokugawa could have killed him on that ship. He hadn't.*

*Sighing, Shusaku hauled himself to his knees.*

*He had been right. It hurt very badly indeed.*

Taro rushed to his mother, but she evaporated in front of his eyes, turned to hazy mist. He looked up the hill and there she was again, farther away from the village, still speaking to him in that nonsense language.

*The language of the dead,* he thought with a shiver.

Again and again she appeared, disappeared, and then shimmered into being again farther along the path. It was as if she were leading him away from Shirahama, and that was all right with him. He did not understand how it could be that she had not returned with the other spirits at the end of *obon*, and a chill went through him when he thought of it. *What if it is my fault?* he thought. *What if I'm keeping her here because of my love for her, as Mokuren did?* He had never felt such a mixture of emotions—to see his mother, even as a pale ghost, filled him with gladness, and yet he was afraid, too, and worried for her soul.

As he neared the Kyoto road, she appeared right in front of

him, speaking more urgently this time. He felt a great weariness settle on him.

"I can't understand you," he said.

His mother's face fell, sadness settling soft on her features. She spoke again, and again he distinguished no words he knew. He stepped forward, to try to touch her, and she was gone.

*Oh, gods,* he thought. *I am being haunted, like Hayao, and I don't know whether to be happy or sad.*

A moment later he saw men ahead of him, blocking the path and standing among the cedar trees. Had his mother been trying to warn him again? The place was close to where he'd killed the rabbit, the day when his life changed forever, when ninjas sent by Lord Oda arrived in Shirahama and killed his father.

*This is Oda's territory, his province,* thought Taro. *I was arrogant to think that wouldn't matter.*

He could turn and run, but there would be no point. Besides, he'd seen the ghosts turn to crabs before his eyes—he knew that there was more to the world than most people saw, and that made him think that just possibly prophecies were real too, and he might not die on this anonymous path. Or if he did die, then just as well. He would rejoin his mother—maybe Hana, too.

That wasn't all of it, though. There was also the anger that burned in his chest when he drew closer and saw that the men wore the Oda *mon* on their breastplates, and on the tusked and horned helmets on their heads. The need for revenge was like something trying to force its way out of him by charring his flesh, some fire-breathing demon living within his flesh, beneath the cage of his ribs. He understood now how Yukiko must have felt about those she considered guilty of her sister Heiko's death.

Taro kept walking, but slowed. He scanned the path ahead, counting the men, checking where they stood. He had only a sword to defend him, and there were at least eight of them. Some of them had bows, he could see. Well, he could send some of them to hell, at least. Even as he thought all this he was gauging the distance to the nearest bow, wondering if he could get to it in time to nock an arrow to the string—he had always been good with bows.

"Stop, boy," said the biggest man. His helmet was a demon's face, leering and pulling its tongue.

Taro stopped.

"You must be Taro. We've been waiting for you." The man drew his *katana*. "Hand over the ball."

"I don't have it," said Taro.

"You expect me to believe that?"

"I don't expect you to do anything. I'm just telling you I don't have it."

The samurai sighed. "Where is it, then?"

"The last I saw of it, a samurai had it. He wasn't wearing the Oda *mon*."

A ripple of unease ran through the men at that. Taro heard several of them draw in breath, heard it whistle over their lips and tongues. His senses turned more acute, he had noticed, when a fight was brewing. His hand twitched at his side, wanting to go to the sword.

"Liar," said the big man, evidently a *hatamoto*, judging by the spear he carried with the Oda *mon* on a small pennant—and so a prominent member of the Oda hierarchy. "There are only Oda samurai in these parts."

"That's strange," said Taro. "Because the men who took the ball were being fired on by a ship flying the Oda flag. It seems to me your enemies must have the ball. Maybe even Lord Tokugawa." As he said it, a thought flashed through his mind. The big man on the ship—it couldn't have been Lord Tokugawa, could it?

No, it was impossible. The daimyo would not be on a ship in Shirahama bay, deep in Oda territory. It would be tactical madness.

The leader took a step toward Taro. "Give us the ball or die, ninja scum," he said.

"Not much of a choice," said Taro, "when I don't have the ball." But he moved forward anyway, his hand outstretched, fingers closed, as if clutching something. The *hatamoto* took the bait—leaned toward him, looking down at his hand. Taro flicked his hand and the sand he'd put in his pocket sprayed out, hitting the man in the eyes. He followed with a right-hand strike to the neck, his large ring striking a pressure point on the *hatamoto*'s neck and causing his legs to give way, as if the tendons at the back of his knees had been severed.

Taro used the man's bulk as a shield to take the first three arrows that flew toward him. Then he pushed the corpse to the ground and rushed at the last man to fire—the one who'd be slowest to reload. He still hadn't drawn his sword—instead he jumped at the man, clung to his shoulders, and flipped over him, turning in the air. He landed behind the man, hugged him tight, and dragged him, twisting, to the ground. An arrow whooshed over his head as they fell. He bit deep into the man's neck, tearing open the windpipe. Limbs flailed. He registered in some deep part of him the iron beauty of blood on his tongue, but he didn't drink— he didn't have time. Still, some of the life force trickled down his throat, a warm blessing.

With one hand, he snapped the quiver from the dying man's back, and with the other he tore the bow from his loose fingers. He came up on his knees, aimed, fired. A samurai staggered, clutching at the feathers suddenly protruding from his throat, gagging on blood.

Taro nocked, drew, fired—a smooth rhythm, and his arrows took one archer in the heart, one in the stomach, and another, who had turned to run, in the back. The one who had been hit in the stomach went down on his knees beside the tree he had been using for cover, but still started to arm his bow once more. Taro put another arrow in his eye.

The world had shrunk to this moment, this scene before him. He could hear nothing but his own heartbeat, *whoosh-boom, whoosh-boom, whoosh-boom*. He wasn't aware of the sunlight falling through the leaves, the distant smell of the sea, the crying of birds. He was aware only of the other men, and him, and the work that would have to be done to put them in the grave. He wasn't even thinking about revenge, not really. He was just conscious of

a consuming imperative, which was to kill these Oda samurai, to
give them a taste of what they had done to the monks of Mount
Hiei, to his mother, to Hana.

A lithe samurai with bushy eyebrows beneath his mask came
at Taro, sword swinging wildly. It was no kata Taro had ever
seen—he thought it was pure fear and desperation turned into
movement. Taro didn't even bother deflecting the blow, just let it
swing harmlessly past, and brought his sword up into the unde-
fended side of the man, splitting him from his armpit to his opposite shoulder. There might have been a gurgling sound, though
Taro may have imagined it because he saw the blood bubble from
the man's mouth.

Two more samurai crept toward him—he was surprised to see
that they appeared to be the only ones still living. He bounced
his sword in his hand, a sort of invitation and a sort of taunt. He
suddenly became aware that he was screaming, though he hadn't
heard that either.

A horrible thought went through his head, almost as if someone else was thinking it. *They're already dead,* said the thought.
*They just don't know it yet.*

There must have been a *clang* that rang out through the trees
when his blade met the onrushing sword of the first man—but
he didn't hear it. He focused on the eyes of his enemies, watching for their next moves. He blocked, parried, slashed. These two
were good, he realized. They were driving him back, cramping his
movements, keeping his sword so busy defending that he wasn't
able to draw blood. He glanced down, to avoid a stone or a corpse
at his feet—it could have been either—and a line of fire traced
itself down his arm.

Blood dripped from the wound. It wasn't deep but it was bad,
anyway, it meant he was losing. He saw one of the samurai—
blankly, he noted that the man was missing most of his teeth—grin
at him. Swords flashed, spun, danced. He was growing weaker.

Then, an opening. The man on his right stepped awkwardly,
catching his foot on the armor of a downed archer. He recovered

quickly, getting his sword up in a block—but Taro wasn't concerned with that. What the pause from the right-hand man had enabled him to see was that the samurai on the left was coming at him with a classic kata, and he raised his sword, deflected, took off the man's jaw with a devastating blow that continued in a blood-spattered right-hand arc, finished by biting into the other man's shoulder.

Shaking and convulsing, the left-hand man went down—though again, his companion was stronger. He twisted away from Taro's sword, the blood running down his arm forming an almost exact counterpoint to Taro's own wound, as if Taro were facing himself across a mirror, a nightmare version of himself in Oda armor.

The samurai spat. "Now we're equal," he said, as if this were some kind of stupid childhood game.

"No," said Taro. "We're not. You're a samurai and I'm a fisherman."

"So?" said the man.

"So I don't bother with things like honor," said Taro. He brought his hands together as if to grip his sword with both, then flicked his left wrist. A throwing star embedded itself in the man's cheek, or rather it was there so quickly and suddenly it was as if it had started out within him, and grown outward through the flesh. Observing Shusaku's actions had taught Taro always to carry such things; somewhere in the folds of his cloak were also gold coins, explosives, daggers disguised as quills.

The man grinned again—it seemed a fixation with him—and leaped forward, pressing Taro back with a flurry of strikes. Taro met them easily, though he gave ground anyway, to give the man a good death, if nothing else.

"You missed," said the man.

"No," said Taro. "I didn't." Just then the man's leg gave way beneath him and he crashed heavily to the ground—Taro heard a crunch as his knee hit a rock and broke. He clutched at his windpipe, his eyes going big and bulging.

"Poison," said Taro. "Just the thing for ninja scum like me."

The samurai was starting to turn an alarming purple color. Taro decapitated him with a single blow, to put him out of his misery. Then he limped over to the leader's body. He must have pulled something in his leg during the fight, though he couldn't think when. He looked down into the proud, arrogant, stupid eyes that looked out blankly through the mask. The Oda *mon* was set in the middle of the section of steel that covered the man's forehead. Then, as he looked into the dead eyes, it wasn't the *hatamoto* he saw anymore but Hana, lying with the scrolls clasped to her chest, not moving, and then it was his mother, too still in her white clothes.

Without warning, a tsunami of fury washed away any trace of Taro for a moment, any trace of a human being, and left him a demon of revenge. He screamed and this time he knew he was screaming. He brought his sword down, brought it down again, again. He felt blood hot against his face, like hell's rain, and he kept stabbing down, butchering the already dead body.

Then there were great racking sobs going through him, and as he shook the sword fell from his fingers and struck the ground wetly. He was crying, he realized, and his tears mingled with the blood on his face, and there was a sound coming out of him that was like a broken bellows, a terrible, sad, lonely sound.

He gazed around him, at the broken bodies and the blood. He gazed inside him, and saw that his mother was still dead and Hana might be too, and it still hurt. None of their deaths had done anything to help him; his revenge was a hollow thing—a rice bowl with nothing in it but chopsticks.

Feeling sick, he dragged himself to his feet and lurched from that place. *If I kill Yukiko, and Lord Oda—will it feel this empty?* he wondered. He couldn't think about that now—it made his head hurt. He *had* to kill them—they had killed his mother, had taken Hana from him. It was because of Lord Oda that all of this had happened, that his father had died—the man he'd thought was his father—and his mother, too.

There was something else, too. If he didn't cling to revenge, to the desire to hurt those who had hurt him, then what was there? The Buddha ball was nothing—a golden trinket. Perhaps there was a real ball somewhere, and he would look for it, of course he would. He wasn't going to give up on reviving Hana. But in his mind that quest was shapeless, amorphous. He didn't know how he was even going to begin to find the real Buddha ball, even if it existed.

A small, quiet voice inside him—a voice he didn't like, a sniveling voice—also told him that Hana might not wake as he wanted her to, might not wake to embrace him and take him for her husband but to stand by Hayao's side, to marry the samurai she clearly deserved. He told that voice to shut up; it made his skin crawl.

As he took the path, he turned and saw his mother's ghost following him. It didn't even surprise him anymore—he accepted it, with a weary horror. His mother was gray against the green of the grass, she was shaking her head, over and over, and she was weeping. She had seen him kill those men, he realized—had seen him lose control of his anger, anoint himself with blood.

He turned, so that he couldn't see her anymore. His shame was a heavy enough burden—he didn't need to see it reflected in her eyes.

*I'm doomed now,* he thought. *I'm lost.*

The man turned around, and Taro crouched behind a tree. It had been four days since he left Shirahama, or had it been three? He was finding it hard to keep track anymore. He seemed to be walking so slowly, too—every footstep a painful effort. He needed blood, that was it.

Well, soon he would have it.

He slowed his breathing right down, until he could hear the susurrus of the wind in the trees, and the song of a faraway bird. He waited for the sound of footsteps, but none came. Eventually he eased himself onto his feet and peered around the tree. The old peasant was continuing on his way, his bony back now a fair distance down the path.

Taro cursed. Now he'd have to get close again, and he was so weak he couldn't move with his customary grace or silence. He didn't even want this old man's blood—not really.

But he did need it.

It had started with the outstretched hands, the beseeching

expression. But every time he went toward his mother, she scattered on the air like a dandelion clock, and he was left embracing a column of nothingness. More and more often she had appeared to him, until she was almost a constant companion on his journey to the ninja mountain. Always, now, she was trying to tell him something, but though her mouth opened and closed, no sound came out, her lips speaking the silent language of the dead. Perhaps he should have been returning to Mount Hiei, to see her body again before it was cremated. But he had time, he thought, before the last rites. And besides, he had been wrong to send Hiro off on his own. His friend had always been loyal. It was time to repay him in kind.

Did she understand, when he asked her what she wanted? It was impossible to tell. She only went on speaking to him in her incomprehensible, soundless speech, and sometimes shaking her head. If he tried to approach her, she turned back into air.

The day before, he'd looked down at the surface of a stream as he was crossing it, and caught sight of his face. At first he'd recoiled, thinking someone desperately ill was standing behind him. But then he'd realized that the haggard, pallid features were his own. His skin was stretched taut over his cheekbones, as if his skull had grown tired of being hidden away beneath his flesh and was pushing through to show itself to the world.

His eyes were the worst. They gazed blankly out from within sunken bruises, the eyes of a dying person. Horrified, he thought of Mokuren, and how he had grown pale and thin when his mother's ghost was visiting him—he saw Hayao, sitting in the inn, a wasted, skeletal vestige of his former self.

*My mother is a gaki,* he realized. A hungry ghost.

There was a ghost killing him, and it was his own mother.

So it was that the need for blood grew stronger and stronger. He'd hunted two peasants already in this valley, and if he wasn't careful there would be men all over the woods, holding burning torches and makeshift weapons, looking for the *kyuuketsuki.* Still, it would be what he deserved, wouldn't it? He felt sick with shame as he moved as quietly as he could between the trees, stalking the old man.

Still, it wasn't enough to stop him.

The old man paused by a tree and took some tools out of his bag. He began tapping something into the wood with a hammer. *No doubt taking the sap for glue or something,* thought Taro. Now was the time, while the man's hands were occupied. Ordinarily Taro could have chased down any man—any deer, too—and over-powered it easily.

(*Him,* he corrected himself.)

But now he was weak, and no amount of blood seemed to keep him going for long.

Stepping closer, he snapped a twig, and the man turned just as Taro reached out for his neck. Reacting instinctively, Taro lashed out with his heel, stamping on the sensitive spot between the man's ankle and the top of his foot. The man went down on one knee and Taro caught his neck, his fingers jabbing into the peasant's pressure points. The body went limp in his hands and he lowered it to the ground

(*him*)

before sinking his teeth into the neck and drinking deeply. He felt that surge of power, like a deep breath after a long dive, and then his limbs were no longer heavy wooden appurtenances, seemingly attached to him with the sole purpose of weighing him down, but light, lithe, and essential components of his being, the parts of him that touched the ground and allowed him to shape the things he could hold. He gripped the man with fingers of iron.

For a long moment he was conscious of nothing but the unbelievable sensation, warm and comforting, of satiety, but then there was a flicker of movement and he looked up to see his mother, standing a little to the side, a shadow cutting across her body. She was looking at him with disappointment in her eyes, her mouth opening and closing uselessly as always.

He pulled away, feeling blood trickling down his chin. He looked down and saw that the man was very pale indeed, his pulse only a faint irregular vibration of the skin on his neck. Usually Taro could sense a person's heartbeat from strides away, a drumbeat that encoded their state of health, their age, their level of excitement. But this man's heart was barely beating.

*You nearly killed him,* he thought—and for once, when he looked at his mother's mouth, he thought that was what she was saying too.

It may have been a day after that, or it may have been a week, when he came finally to the little hut at the top of the meadow. It was near dusk, or near dawn, Taro wasn't entirely sure. Small flowers dotted the high grass, nature bombarded his senses with the rich smell of its healthiness, its vigor, the vivid colors of the new life. He couldn't wait to get inside and see Hiro again. Hiro would know what to do.

No, Hiro probably wouldn't know what to do. But he would help, that much was certain.

Taro dragged himself up the slope. Then he saw that something was wrong.

The door to the hut was open.

Taro stared. The door was *never* open. Nobody knew that the ninjas used this summit's crater as their base, and the ninjas had every intention of keeping it that way. Then he saw something even worse.

The trapdoor inside was open too.

His hand on his sword's grip, Taro stepped slowly into the main hall. Reddish light flooded in, making a bright shaft in the middle of the cave, something that seemed to Taro as though, were he to step into it, he might dissolve into light himself. His eyes went up, and he saw the great tear in the canvas that had once held the night sky, and its charred edges.

*They burned the sky,* he thought.

He took a step forward, then stopped. He stood very still, look- ing around him. Piles of clothes lay on the ground, evocative of splayed and agonized bodies, though there were no bodies to fill them.

Only ash.

He fought back a wave of nausea. *They're all dead,* he thought. *All the vampires . . .*

At first he wanted to turn on his heel and leave. Then he remembered Hiro. His friend was not a vampire—that meant his body would be here, if he'd died too. Something had already torn in Taro's mind, that night on the top of Mount Hiei, when he lost everything—so he assumed that there was no more of him left to break.

He was wrong.

Taro got down on his knees, began to crawl around the floor of the great hall, checking the clothes, turning over pieces of black and gray fabric, but he found only bones and dust. Tears stinging his eyes, he began to crawl faster, stirring up the burnt remains, mingling the dead with one another in his haste to find his friend. A distant part of his mind remembered the Tendai monks in the ruins of the Hokke-do, prizing up the pieces of their fellow monk with chopsticks, putting them so carefully into the urn, in order from toe to top. Familiar shame rose hotly in him, as he thought of these dead ninjas waking up in whatever new plane they found themselves in, their reborn bodies a jumble of different parts, as if Enma had assigned them new heads and feet and hands as a final, humiliating prank.

Ignoring these thoughts that raced around his mind like rats, he moved quicker and quicker still, wasting the energy from the old man. There was a larger pile than the rest, but it turned out to be a girl, one who had been at the wrong end of a sword. Taro thought he recognized her. She was the daughter of one of the older ninjas—she'd have been made a vampire soon, if she'd lived.

There was a scraping sound behind him, and he was turning on his knees before he even registered alarm, his sword jumping up from his side as if suddenly animate, and he was moving up onto the balls of his feet, snarling.

Just before his sword bit into the body before him, he stopped it, gasping with the effort.

"*Taro?*" said Hiro.

Hiro stepped aside and Little Kawabata appeared beside him, both of them seeming to emerge from the rock itself.

*The hidden passage,* thought Taro. He'd had so many occasions to curse it, when Kawabata Senior would suddenly appear to put him off his concentration while sparring. But now he blessed it with all his heart.

Hiro threw his arms around Taro and hugged him tight, cutting off Taro's breathing, but that was all right.

"What happened?" Taro asked, when Hiro finally released him. "Did you see?"

Hiro nodded. "The sky started to burn first. Nearly everyone was here, for a ceremony. One of the boys was going to be turned."

"It was as if they knew," said Little Kawabata.

"The light came bursting through," said Hiro. "Arrows, too. People were screaming . . . running around . . . Then they were falling. I was just . . ." He turned his head from side to side, as if to mime his incomprehension, his inability to *do* anything.

"I was the only one who could bear the sunlight," said Kawabata. "I grabbed Hiro and pulled him in here. After that we only heard."

"The screaming," said Hiro, "went on for a long time."

"Who did it?" said Taro. But a horrible suspicion was forming in his mind.

"Yukiko," said Little Kawabata. "We heard her . . ." Now it was his turn to raise his hands, in silent mime of his inability to describe what he had witnessed.

"We heard her kill Little Kawabata's father," said Hiro.

"Gods," said Taro. "I'm sorry. I mean, I know your father tried to kill me. But he was still your father."

Little Kawabata bowed. "But that's not the worst thing."

"What?"

"Yukiko said Lord Oda was still alive."

Taro swayed on his feet. "Kenji Kira said that too. How is it possible?"

"It gets worse," said Little Kawabata.

"Worse?"

"Yukiko said Lord Oda was a vampire."

Taro's jaw dropped open. "A vampire?"

"That's what she said."

Taro shook his head. "No—he can't—I mean—" Everything that had happened, the people who had died . . . if Lord Oda was alive, then that was one thing—he could always be killed. But if he was a vampire, then it would be infinitely more difficult. Taro felt himself swaying.

"You don't look so good, Taro," said Hiro worriedly, and his voice seemed to come from a long way away. "As a matter of fact, you look terrible."

"Just . . . a shock . . . that's all," said Taro. He hadn't even killed the man who killed his father. He hadn't succeeded in anything. The ball didn't work. His father and his mother and perhaps Hana had died for *nothing*.

"No," said Hiro. "You haven't looked well from the start. It's like you're wasting away." He was examining Taro closely, and his eyes were full of concern.

Taro smiled at him. He was glad to see his friend again, even if everything was falling apart. "It's my mother's ghost," said Taro. "I think I'm being haunted."

Little Kawabata looked at him as if he were mad, but Hiro had seen the haunted man on Mount Hiei too, and he gasped with horror. "Are you sure? But you could die!"

"I'm sure. She comes to me all the time, trying to tell me something."

"Trying to tell you what?"

"I don't know," said Taro. "Her mouth moves, and there is a sound of sorts, but I don't understand the words."

"Is it about the ball?" said Hiro. "Is she telling you where it is? Is she trying to help you?"

Taro shrugged. "I don't know. I went to Shirahama. I dived the wreck, and I brought up the ball. It didn't work. It's just a ball of gold."

"But a ball of *gold*?" said Little Kawabata, unable to conceal the greed in his voice. "You could do a lot with—"

Hiro shot him a look, and he shut up. "What will you do?" he asked Taro.

Taro looked down at his emaciated arms, the tendons and bone visible through the paperlike skin. "My mother's ghost . . . it's consuming me. I need help."

"Help?" said Hiro. "What help? Just tell me."

"I need to go back to Mount Hiei," said Taro. "The priest in Shirahama . . . He told me a story about a man who went to hell, to speak to his mother who was haunting him. Maybe the abbot can help me do the same. My mother's body will not have been burnt yet . . . I don't think . . . Are we still in the Month of Leaves?"

"You want to go to hell?" said Little Kawabata incredulously.

"Taro," said Hiro. "This is madness."

"Just take me to the abbot," said Taro. "Do you promise?"

Hiro sighed. "Yes, of course I promise."

"I want to know what my mother is trying to tell me," said Taro. "Otherwise I'll die."

Hiro put a hand out to steady Taro, as he swayed again. "I won't let you die," he said.

Taro shrugged. He sat down on the ash-strewn ground. "If I die, at least I'll know what she's saying," he said.

*Little Kawabata supported Taro's weight with his arm as they climbed the stone steps. The stumps of burned trees lined the sides of the path, and Little Kawabata wondered whether trees knew they were burning, and felt the pain of their loss.*

*Little Kawabata had to admit the place was beautiful. He could see why the monks would choose it for their meditation. The land spread out below them like tatami mats laden with seeds and bowls of water, which were lakes. The perfect dome of the mountaintop loomed above them.*

*Someone, though, had gone to a lot of effort to erase the mountain from the map. Everywhere, the ground was burnt, and Little Kawabata saw what looked like bloodstains on the rocks.*

*At one point they had passed the ruins of a building, and Taro had groaned as they walked past it. A small wooden structure was being erected in the middle of the destruction, as if the temple had the ability to regenerate, like a worm's head, and was rebuilding itself from the inside out.*

"That's where Hana is," said Hiro, who was carrying Taro on the other side.

Little Kawabata looked at the monks working, and felt a sense of wonder. In that great oblong of ash, gray and long as an enormous grave, the unburnt body of Hana lay hidden from view.

He shuddered. There was something unnatural about it. But then, thought Little Kawabata, there was something unnatural about all of this. Sometimes, when he was sleeping, he would hear noises and wake up, and Taro would be staring into the shadows of the forest, talking softly.

"Tell me," Taro would say. "Tell me what you're trying to say."

The empty forest never answered.

The last few days, Hiro had been giving Taro his own blood. Taro had protested at first, but Hiro had insisted. Anyway, Taro was so weak he could barely refuse. Occasionally he would become lucid and talk about Lord Oda and the ball and Shusaku, whose ghost he seemed to have seen on a ship somewhere. Little Kawabata wondered whether something had torn in the boy's mind, and now he saw the ghosts of his dead all around him.

Must have lost his mind, *he thought,* to let that ball of gold get away from him.

Most of the time, though, Taro seemed to be moving through another country altogether, peopled with different personages. He addressed trees, rocks, temples. He asked them what they wanted to tell him, sounding increasingly distressed, as if angry with these objects for not giving up their secrets.

Sometimes he called them Mother.

The world was moving back and forth gently, and Taro thought, *I'm back on that ship. I knocked my head and imagined everything after that.*

*I'm not haunted after all!*

Then he opened his eyes and the abbot was before him, sitting cross-legged in front of him on the floor of the training hall, and his own hands in his lap were so thin they were like the hands of birds. It was all real, and he was still dying. Hayao stood beside the abbot. He looked at Taro with eyes full of infinite sadness.

"Is that what I looked like?" the samurai asked the abbot.

"Yes," said the abbot. "But you had Taro to save you. He has no one. I fear for him."

"Can't you do anything? Give him spells . . . sutras . . ."

"I have tried everything, when he was sleeping. I have given him the charms. I have read him the texts. Nothing has helped. With you, he saw your ghost. None of us can see his."

"He mustn't die," said Hayao. "He's . . . I don't know. He's necessary, I think." This was an odd thing for Hayao to say, and Taro wondered if he was hallucinating, if this was all a dream.

"I agree," said the abbot. "But I don't know what I can do."

"Help . . . me," said Taro softly, and he was shocked by how weak his voice was.

The abbot looked at him, startled. "You hear us?" he said.

"Yes," said Taro.

"Hiro and your other friend tell me you see your mother," said the abbot.

Taro managed a nod. The whole world was gray and colorless, and it was an effort just to keep his eyes open. He was not aware of how he had come to be on Mount Hiei. He had a vague memory of being carried by Hiro.

"Hmm," said the abbot pensively. "Does she grow more solid?"

Taro thought. Yes, it seemed to him that the light no longer shone through her when she appeared to him. "I . . . think so," he said.

The abbot frowned. "And you are weak. I can see that for myself."

Taro croaked a "yes."

The abbot sighed. "This *gaki* will kill you, if we don't do something."

"I know," said Taro. "I want . . . go to hell."

"I'm sorry?" said the abbot.

"My mother . . . she speaks. But I can't understand."

"She is speaking in the language of the dead."

Taro nodded—the movement caused his neck to ache, and he wanted to close his eyes and go to sleep, but he knew it was important to get the abbot's help.

"Need . . . to know . . . what she's saying."

The abbot's face fell. "It's impossible. Only the dead know that language."

"Send me . . . to hell."

The abbot blanched. "I don't know what you are talking about," he said.

Taro sat up, gasping with the pain of straining his muscles. His mother was standing behind the abbot—she was always there now—and she was nodding at him, encouraging, and he knew this was what he had to do.

"Mokuren . . . went to hell," he said. "I need . . . also. Tell me how he did it."

The abbot was staring at him in horror. "You don't understand," he said. "Here at the monastery, it's said that Mokuren sat on the mountainside, and didn't eat or drink for weeks. You want to know how he went to hell, Taro? He *died*."

"Died?"

"The monks said he stopped breathing. They began to prepare him for his funeral, but then he opened his eyes again. And he said that he had been to hell, and had spoken with his mother."

"Good," said Taro. "Then I . . .will die . . . too."

A bird landed on his shoulder. He was glad, because it meant he was still, and the bird did not recognize him as a threat.

At first Hiro had tried to bring him blood, to sustain him, but he had pushed it away.

He sat on a rock, overlooking a ravine that stretched down and into the far valleys below, though he didn't look at anything but the blankness inside his head. The abbot had told him that Mokuren, when he wanted to find his mother, had sat in this exact place. His fellow monks visited him every day, and one day they found that his heart had stopped—just for a moment. When it began beating again, he opened his eyes, and that was when he told them what he must do, in order to save his mother.

Taro didn't know how to make his heart stop, but he believed that if he could only *feel* every part of his body, and its joins with the world, he might be able to learn. He knew the abbot was angry with him—or disappointed, anyway. He said that Taro was suffering from *kokoro no yami*—darkness of the heart. He said that if Taro could only let go of his mother, stop loving her so much, everything would be all right again.

But Taro couldn't stop loving anyone, and he knew that even if he could, not everything would be all right. Not for his mother. And of course that was the problem, that this idea bothered him, and so he was back at the start again, and could not do what the abbot wanted of him. He had seen in the abbot's eyes that the man thought he would fail, that he would die on this rock, bled dry by his mother's ghost.

*Nevertheless,* he thought, *he's curious. If I step from his mountain into hell, then he will have seen two miracles in his lifetime.*

The hardest thing was ignoring his mother, who floated all night and every day now in the ravine, mouthing all the time in her nonsense tongue, before melting away in the dawn light, slowly receding until she was just a dot, and then nothing. He had learned to focus on a point just in front of him, a point of nothingness, that nevertheless felt like it might just be the center of his being.

To describe the thoughts that passed through him, or say how long he sat there, would be impossible. The only way to know would be to experience it for yourself, and even if you had, you would not be able to describe it to others.

All Taro knew was that for a long time there was blackness, and then suddenly there was a great searing pain in his chest and he clutched feebly at it, with his weak hands, and then the mountain seemed to drop away beneath him.

Taro opened his eyes. Light was beginning to glow on the horizon, and his mother's ghost was beginning to fade backward, as if she and the sun were somehow the same thing, and so could not manifest at the same time in this realm.

As she floated backward, growing ever smaller, he saw that she was leaving a trail behind her, a sort of glowing mist like a thread, and he couldn't believe he'd never seen it before.

Standing up—though he couldn't be sure it was *him* standing up, and anyway the notion of what was and wasn't him had become very blurred in his mind—he stepped off the rock and into the ravine.

He walked across the air and took up the shining thread, then followed it. He crossed landscapes that were either not of this world, or were in countries far away, and were illuminated by other suns and moons. He seemed to walk for a long time on the bottom of the sea, climbing its mountains, which are much like the mountains of the earth, only life accumulates at their tops, rather than their bottoms, and the water streams *up* their flanks. A great fish swam past him, bigger than a ship, and it sang a plangent note of grief.

Then, after he had walked for three lifetimes, he stepped up to the edge of a wide river and found that he was holding coins in his hand. He seemed to have conjured them up, just by thinking of them, and at the same time he understood that the coins were just a symbol. They didn't *matter*, really. Before him was a bridge, glittering.

He walked over death's bridge, which was inlaid with jewels, and which was exactly as it had always been described, even though it was completely different. He would not be able to explain how this was, if he was asked. He would not be able to explain how it felt, to be in this place—the closest thing he could think of was a dream, that strange state of being where it is logical to be one moment on a mountaintop surrounded by white peaks and then the next in the sea, and yet having the sense of following a path. He was aware of the souls of evil men, struggling below him in the dark waters, and yet he was not afraid. His body was numb—he didn't even know if it was his body, or if it was just an image projected by his mind. When he touched his skin his fingers didn't pass through it; but he didn't feel them either.

On the other side of the river, he passed by a great throne made of bones, and on it sat a man with long horns who could only be Enma.

Enma was the judge, the one who decided which realm of Samsara each deceased person would be consigned to. In this way it could be said that he was a god presiding over death—for he and he alone could choose, after weighing a person's deeds, to send that person to be reborn as an ox, or to languish in hell, or to pass into the light of the Pure Land.

But Enma was not a god, not truly. The priests and monks taught that he was always a man, chosen from among men, to judge his own kind. The name Enma, in fact, was a title, a crown—many had worn it. Taro peered at the current incarnation. He seemed a smallish sort of man, a thin mustache joining a long white beard. His eyes were bright and black, though veiled by boredom. At his sides were Horse-face and Ox-head, his retainers, and in his hands were the scroll and pen with which he recorded the names of all the dead.

Enma looked at Taro, then down at the scroll in his hand. "You are not dead," he said.

Taro shook his head.

A smile twitched at the corners of Enma's mouth. "Interesting," he said slowly. Then he waved Taro past, already turning to the next shade to cross the bridge.

Taro steadied himself, and proceeded into death. He should have been terrified to see Enma, he knew, but instead he felt nothing—it was no worse than facing a tax collector. Enma was not Death, he was human, and one day he too would die—his own name would be written in that scroll, by Enma-taka, the Death of Death, and then another person would be chosen to be Enma for a while.

Once, the priest in Shirahama had explained to Taro how death could die. There was a story, he said, of a monk in Tibet who knew that if he meditated for fifty years without pause he would achieve nirvana. Yet on the forty-ninth year, and the eleventh month, and the twenty-ninth day, he was disturbed by bandits, who wished to steal his robe and jewels. "Please, wait until tomorrow and I will give you all the gold you wish," he told them. He was a footstep away from eternity. But the bandits would not wait, and they hauled him out of his cave and killed him.

Furious, the monk felt himself changing. A sort of satori, a moment of enlightenment, seized him, and in an instant he realized that the old Enma was gone and he was the new one. He grew tall and terrible. He tore the two bandits into small pieces, scattering them on the mountainside. Then he descended into the valley, and began slaughtering its inhabitants, such was his anger. He had the power not just to judge the dead but to kill, too, and he wasted no time in using it.

But the abbot of his monastery, seeing this, also felt a change come over him—and suddenly he was Enma-taka, the Death of Death, and his stride encompassed mountains. He walked to his old disciple, his countenance appalling to behold, and he reached down and touched Enma, the gatekeeper of death, and Enma looked up and realized that his own death had come for him. He sank down and was a monk again, lying still on the ground. And after that the abbot shifted again, changed, and was himself Enma.

Taro wondered if this was still the same Enma that he had just passed—if it was still the abbot who had been forced to bring death to his own monk. He wasn't sure if he believed the story anyway, though he did like the idea that death could die—he would kill death himself if he could, for one more day with his mother. He turned, but already he couldn't see Enma anymore. He saw only mist behind him.

The thread led him onward, and soon he was walking through a landscape made of heartbreak, in which ran rivers of tears. He crossed a vale of devastation, and then he was in the realm of the hungry ghosts. This was as the priest had described—although at one and the same time it was completely different.

For one thing, it didn't burn—and it didn't burn in such a way that it made Taro understand it was his own world that was always burning. He lived in a realm that was on fire everywhere you looked, being destroyed at every moment, and the name of that fire was time.

Here there was no time, and so nothing was on fire. Instead everything was still. That was why there was no food, because nothing could grow, thrust itself out, become fat, be eaten, and in being eaten, die. There was nothing to eat or drink because nothing changed, ever.

Taro walked through this landscape—or it would be more accurate to say that he remained entirely static, and the landscape did too, but somehow he arrived at last at his destination.

The demon was not a demon and the pot was not a pot, but otherwise everything was exactly as the priest described in the story of Mokuren, and his mother was there with hunger in her eyes and in the emaciation of her frame.

"At last," she said.

Taro bowed. "Mother," he said. "I am so happy to see you again. I love you so much."

His mother nodded. "I know," she said. "But after this, you must let me go. *Ko wa sangai no kubikase.*"

Taro felt a sadness the exact same size and shape as his body settle itself over him, and knew he'd have to bear it the rest of his life. What his mother had said was this: *A child is the yoke that ties us to this world.* The abbot had used the expression too, the day that Taro sat down on the rock and asked to be left alone.

Taro understood, finally, that it really was his love for his mother, and her love for him, that was keeping her in this terrible place.

"You were trying to tell me something," he said.

"Yes," said his mother. "I tried to tell you before I died, but that girl cut me off."

Taro smiled. It was precisely like his mother to make a joke at this moment.

"But what was it?" he said. "What did you want to tell me?"

"You were looking in the wrong place," she said. "I dived the wreck the day the ninjas came, but not to hide the ball. I only wanted anyone watching to think so."

"So . . . there's another one? A real one?"

"Yes."

"Then where is it?"

Taro's mother smiled. "Have you heard the story of the ama and the prince?"

"Yes," said Taro. "The prophetess told me."

Taro's mother nodded, as if the prophetess were known to her, and not a complete stranger, but Taro thought that perhaps all the dead knew one another. "And where did the ama put the ball, when she recovered it from the wreck?"

Taro's eyes widened. "In her chest."

"There you have it," said his mother. "I'm sorry for haunting you, and stealing your strength. But perhaps now you can see why I needed to tell you, before you went ahead with my cremation."

"But . . . if it's in you . . ."

"Then it's smaller than the fake I put on the reef. Yes. A thing doesn't have to be big, or made of gold, in order to be precious." Joy burst in Taro's chest; the sensation was of his heart starting again. The ball was real. He could take it, and he could make Hana wake.

Taro had a hundred more questions, but just then his mother started to shine—it was the only word for it—and then it was as if she were wearing a robe of light. She looked down at herself. "Ah," she said, as if her appearance explained something.

And then she was dazzling—again, there was no other word for it—and it seemed like she couldn't possibly belong to this still world with its lack of movement and growth and nourishment, and then—just like that—she didn't belong to it anymore.

She was gone, and only an impression of light, fading fast, remained.

Taro then felt a similar light enveloping him, and he looked down at himself. He had seen his mother disappear from this spot. Now he saw the mountains that were not mountains and the clouds that were not clouds dimming, and he knew that he was returning to life; that really had been his heart starting, and now he was going to leave this place. His own body was growing faint, indistinct. As everything faded, so something exploded in his mind, bright as a sunburst, and suddenly he found that he understood . . . everything.

He thought, dimly, *So that's what it means.*

And then he didn't know what "it" was anymore, and soon he didn't know what the word "means" meant, and then finally he didn't know what a word was.

And then there was nothing.

*Hiro was holding Taro's wrist, and so he felt it the moment the pulse stopped. He seized the abbot's hand and said, "Do something!" but the abbot held his hand up in a soothing gesture.*

*"Wait," he said.*

*Hiro opened his mouth to speak, but then he felt a twitch beneath his fingers, and it came from Taro's wrist—he felt as if he had lifted a dead chick from a broken nest after a storm, and it had come back to life in his hand.*

*Taro opened his eyes and smiled at him with something like the old light in his expression. "Am I alive?" he said.*

*"Yes," said Hiro. "But you scared me, you idiot."*

*"Sorry," said Taro. He turned to Hayao, who was sitting to one side. "I'm glad to see you again," he said. "Hana . . . did you keep her alive as you promised?"*

*"Yes," said Hayao. "I fed her with water and honey."*

*"Good," said Taro. "Good."*

*"Where did you go?" asked the abbot.*

"I don't know," said Taro. "I can't remember. But I remember what to do." He put his hands on the rock, palm down, and pushed himself up into a position roughly approximating standing, and then he accepted Hiro's arm under his as he staggered off the rock. "Take me to my mother," he said. "And someone get me some blood."

"As an offering?" said the abbot.

"No," said Taro. "The blood is for me."

Tattoos had been etched into the skin of her arms and her face, Sanskrit symbols meant to help her on her journey.

*And they worked,* thought Taro bitterly. *They sped her on her way to the realm of hungry ghosts. . . .*

But she was at peace now. He kissed his mother's forehead and then untied her white kimono at the neck. The abbot was standing to one side, seemingly uncomfortable with this desecration of the dead, but Taro had *been* to death. He was aware that his mother's body was nothing now but sinews, meat, and bone. The essential part of her had dissipated into brightly glowing light. He remembered that part at least.

With the intricate ties undone, he parted the kimono so that he could see the middle of her chest, where the ribs met. There was an old scar there, a silvery line that ran down her collarbone, a hand-span long. His mother had always told him that she was wounded in childhood, falling onto a sharp agricultural tool.

Taro wondered why he had never questioned this dubious story before.

He traced his finger along the scar. Then, taking a deep breath, he raised his other hand—the hand that was holding a very sharp knife.

Holding the air in his lungs, he pressed down with the blade, and was surprised when no blood welled up. But he supposed the body had been drying here on the mountaintop for nearly a month, turning slowly from living flesh into earth. He was glad there was no blood, anyway. It made what he was doing seem less an act of violence, and more a ritual performed on the corpse—or at least that was one of the advantages.

It also removed any temptation. She was his mother, but he was still a vampire, and a weak one too, his *qi* depleted by days of haunting and near starvation. He wasn't sure he could resist the smell of blood at full strength, let alone now.

Drawing the knife toward him, he expected to have to cut through the ribs, but met with almost no resistance. The skin opened up smoothly, like earth behind the blade of a plough. Suddenly Taro's fingers trembled, and he dropped the knife. It bounced off her chest and clattered on the ground.

"Sorry . . . ," he said. "I can't do it."

He felt more than saw the abbot move up beside him, stooping to pick up the knife. He turned away. Hiro clapped him on the shoulder. "You did well to even start it," he said.

The abbot was far too old and wise to gasp as he withdrew what lay inside Taro's mother's chest. But he did suck in air through his teeth, making a whistling noise. Taro turned to see, and the abbot handed over what he had found.

It was small—much smaller than the golden, false ball. But it felt heavy in his hands.

"It's not even gold!" said Little Kawabata.

Taro frowned at him. "No," he said. "It's not."

The object he was holding was a tiny, perfect sphere. The outer layer seemed to be a kind of glass. Beneath this was a layer of air, which in places—he was turning it in his hands to examine it—was white and opaque with what seemed to be clouds. Inside, beneath the air, was a smaller sphere. Mostly blue, it was also covered with strange, warped shapes of green, and at the top and bottom were circular coverings of white.

"It's a representation of the world," said the abbot. "As it would look from up there." He pointed up at the sky.

"Don't be silly!" said Hiro. "That can't be the world! If it was round like that we'd all slide off."

"Idiot!" said Little Kawabata. "Have you never seen a globe? My father saw one when he had to kill a Portuguese merchant."

They entered into a loud discussion, but Taro was still looking at the ball. "I'm not sure it's a *representation*," he said. "Look." The others leaned over and peered into the ball, as Taro held his finger over the clouds.

"What am I looking at?" asked Little Kawabata.

"Wait," said Taro.

It was the abbot who saw it first. "Oh, my," he said.

The clouds were *moving*.

At first Taro thought an earthquake was coming. But he could see that the others didn't feel it, this thrumming, vibrating feeling. It was the ball that was doing it, he realized. It was humming to itself, and the noise and movement were tiny, but the impression was of unbelievable, enormous power, which just happened to be contained in something small.

Taro looked closer, and then he was falling through clouds, air rushing at him, whipping his hair, forcing itself into his nostrils, a hollow whooshing in his stomach. He broke through the clouds and then he was in blue sky, in freefall, the sensation of speed thrilling and terrifying at once—he passed a gull and it squealed, wheeling away from him. And then his breath stopped with terror when he saw that there was ocean below him, the sharp waves rising to meet him, very fast, getting bigger and bigger, and soon he was going to crash into the water. He leaned back and—

He was standing with his friends again.

He twisted the ball, peered in close to the green. Instantly he was falling through clear air, unobscured by clouds, only the moon was out on this side of the world, and glowing fatly in the evening sky. Rushing toward him was a landscape like nothing he had ever seen, a whole country, it seemed, made entirely of beach sand. This great beach stretched out thousands of *ri* in every direction, scattered with a sparse covering of tough-looking trees, and uninterrupted by rivers or lakes of any kind.

Taro leaned his head to try to work out where the sea was, but the ground was moving toward him so quickly that he finally pulled back, and found himself on the mountain again, his mother's body before him.

"Are you all right?" asked Hiro.

Taro grinned. "Yes. Yes, I'm all right."

"What does it do? Is it . . . real?"

"Yes," said Taro. "I think it is."

"Make something happen," said Little Kawabata.

"I plan to," said Taro. He turned to Hayao, and the abbot. "Take me to Hana," he said.

He wasn't sure what he was doing as he descended the stone steps, or even as he stood in the wooden structure that had been erected around her body. She looked the same as when he had left her—hair dark and glossy, eyes closed, skin almost luminous in its paleness. Her chest rose and fell gently with her slow breathing. The abbot and Hayao had kept her alive, as they had promised. Now the two of them, as well as Hiro and Little Kawabata, waited anxiously outside the shrine.

Taro wanted to be alone for this, and not least because he didn't know how it was going to work—or if it was going to work, even. The sutras did not record how the Buddha had saved his disciple, and Taro was hoping, perhaps naively, that the ball would somehow show him the way.

He held the ball over Hana's sleeping form and gazed into it. Shadows chased one another over the sea; tiny stars covered half the earth, blanketed in darkness. He concentrated on the tiny sun, which rotated gradually around the bright side of the miniature earth in his hands. If death was darkness, then the sun was its opposite. Holding it in his sight, he felt gravity let go of him, and then he was plunging down toward the ball of fire, his skin burning up with the heat.

In the past he had always pulled back, before the ground crushed him or the sea closed itself around him. But this time he closed his eyes and fell. His stomach slid down and backward, seemingly into his legs, as if trying to abandon his plummeting body. The glow from the sun grew brighter and brighter, even through his eyelids, until he might as well have had his eyes open.

The pain grew more and more intense, until he couldn't bear it anymore, and he felt blackness overtake him. The last thing he was aware of thinking was, *Please let Hana wake up.*

He fell into the sun, and he didn't burn. When he was conscious again of anything, he was crossing that jeweled bridge that was not jeweled, and he was once again in death, though he had entered it another way. This time his body was shining, and he knew that last time he had entered death as a dead man; this time it was the ball that had brought him, and he was under the Buddha's protection. He would not know the speech of the dead, and if they talked to him he would understand nothing.

He walked past Enma's throne, and the *kami* of death cowered from him, covering his eyes. Taro smiled. He continued, over the mountains and seas, and finally he came to the place where the dead were. Shades pressed at him from all sides, shadows looking for a sun to cast them. He thought of Hana, and then the dead before him parted, and he passed through them. He climbed a thousand mountains and then the quality of the light changed, and he knew he was no longer in hell. In fact there was no longer any ground beneath his feet—he was standing in darkness, surrounded by stars.

*Hana,* he thought. *Hana.*

*Kenji Kira was screaming. He had been screaming since he came to Enma's realm. There were no demons poking at him with swords, no pots for boiling. Instead he was in a field of dead men, surrounded by the stench of decay, and there were no spirits around him and no demons either, and yet he knew he was in hell.*

*He was trapped again, among the rotting bodies. His leg was once again shattered beneath a horse—was it his horse? He thought perhaps it was—and the low things were feasting on his fallen comrades. He saw the maggots crawl from their mouths, he saw the rats gnawing at their entrails.*

*He had known from the beginning that one day the rats would finish their meals, and they would turn on him, and eat him, too. Even on the first day he had felt things crawling on his flesh, and he had tried to brush them away, screaming, always screaming.*

*Now, though, he had been here for some time, and the creatures were in his body. He felt them—he felt every agonizing incision as the larvae and the vermin attacked his flesh with their tiny mouths. He felt them fluttering, like painful emotions. He heard them, consuming. He heard them even over his own screaming, and he thought at first that the pain would lessen, that he could not bear it and he would pass out, but there was no passing out in death.*

*Yukiko.*

*It was Yukiko who had sent him here—who had come up behind him and ended his life. As he watched a fly settle on the swollen purple lips of a dead samurai to his right, he dreamed of her death. Certainly on dying she would come to hell, and he would be waiting for her here. Maybe he would be her hell—maybe instead of a battlefield of corpses she would see him, killing her, for all eternity. . . .*

*He was picturing her face as he tortured her, when there came the sound of footsteps. He thought that was odd—he heard only the calls of crows, usually, as they fought over scraps of human meat; or the munching of worms on flesh, or the chewing of rats. There was no other sound in this place—there was no sky, only a gray nothingness above.*

*Yet here came footsteps.*

*He struggled up on one elbow and was stunned to see Taro, walking through the dead men and horses as if they were not even there. His knee burst through a stallion's head, and in its passing it allowed Kenji Kira to see beyond the illusion, and for a just a moment he saw that underneath all this decomposition was just blankness, which was somehow more terrifying.*

*Following behind Taro was Hana, and Kenji Kira recognized her for a soul like himself, lost from life. Taro was alive—that much was obvious. He shone so bright it hurt Kira's eyes. But Hana was a shade; she was like a beautiful female shadow behind the boy. He narrowed his eyes.*

Taro is taking her back to life, *he thought.*

*He had stopped screaming, he realized, for the first time since he came here. He was aware of the things inside him, eating him, but he ignored them.* They are not there, *he told himself, just like the dead men and the horses—and to his surprise it helped. The pain was still an enormity—it was a cloak he wore, it was the bones inside his body—but it was manageable, conquerable.*

*He got his hands under the cold corpse of the horse on top of him and he heaved, all the while watching Taro's slow progress across the battlefield that was somehow also a blank place among impossible mountains. He bit into his tongue and was surprised, and horrified, to find a maggot in there—he sawed it in half with his teeth, and he swallowed it, and he wasn't sure if it was just his imagination or not but it seemed to give him strength.*

*Cursing, his forearms threatening to snap, he managed to lift the horse enough to pull his leg free. He stood. He noticed, in passing, that his leg seemed fine. He turned his back on the awful place and he scrambled, slipping in blood, toward Taro and Hana. He found that a sort of wake flowed behind Taro, a slipstream of brightness, and in it there were no dead things. He touched himself—his own body was unharmed, the holes made by the rats and crows had gone.*

*He smiled.*

*And he followed Taro out of death.*

When Taro opened his eyes, he was standing over Hana again, the ball in his hands. Once again it was just quietly turning, a patchwork of clouds and brightness, smooth and efficient as a well-oiled machine.

Hana's chest rose and fell slowly, but her eyes were closed.

*It hasn't worked,* thought Taro. He had dived into the sun and walked into death for her, and it had done nothing. He let out a deep sigh.

From outside, Hiro's voice. "Taro!"

"Are you all right?" called Hayao.

Taro wondered how long he'd been in here. A moment? An incense stick? More? "I'm coming out," he said.

Before leaving, he bent down to place a last kiss on Hana's forehead, and that was when her eyes opened.

He took a step backward, and he must have gasped or screamed, because suddenly Hiro and Hayao were in the small room, and they were gazing at Hana in astonishment.

Hana looked up at them, as Taro shrank back into the shadows. He was afraid of her, he realized suddenly. He was afraid of what she would say.

"Is this . . . heaven?" she asked.

"No," said Hayao. "No, you're alive."

"I had the strangest dream," said Hana.

"Yes," said Hiro. He turned to beckon Taro forward, but Taro's feet would not move. "Yes, but it's over now."

"Hayao . . . ," said Hana softly. "You came after me. I saw you running down the hill. You entered the building; you were not afraid of the flames. You were so brave." She sat up, then raised a hand to touch his face, still scarred from the fire. "And you, Hiro—I saw you running too."

Taro felt a sob escape his chest—it was as he'd feared; he had abandoned her, and she would never forgive him.

He glared at Hayao. "You're welcome to her," he said.

Hayao stared at him, said nothing.

He staggered from the room, and he only half heard voices behind him, telling him to stop. He walked to the cliffs on the east side of the mountain, the world around him a blur, and sat down. He put his face in his hands. Hana would marry Hayao, he was sure of it, and he would . . . he did not know what he would do. The only thing he was good at was killing people.

Time passed.

Later someone came up behind him, and their step was soft on the grass. "Go away, Hiro," he said.

"It is not Hiro," said Hana.

Taro looked up at her. Her cheeks were streaked with tears, but she was smiling. "They told me about your mother," she said. "I'm sorry."

Taro nodded. "I'm sorry I—" His voice broke off. "You will never forgive me, I know. But Hayao is a better choice anyway."

Hana sat down beside him, frowning. She was as beautiful as ever, that was what hurt the most. "What are you talking about?"

He looked down, so as not to meet her eye. "I chose my mother. When you were running to the burning temple—I went back to save my mother instead. Hayao went to save you. I've seen . . . I've seen how you look at him. I won't stand in your way."

Hana laughed, a sound like bells. "Of course you went to your mother," she said. "I didn't want to be saved anyway. I wanted to rescue the scrolls."

"And you did," said Taro. "While my mother still died." He moved a little farther from her. "I bring death everywhere I go."

"That's not true," said Hana. "Hayao said you would not let me die. He said you searched for the ball, so you could use it to save me. And then you did."

Taro was obscurely surprised. He had thought that Hayao would take this opportunity to claim Hana as his own.

"I *did* want to save you," said Taro. "But I wanted to kill Yukiko and all of Oda's men. Lord Oda, too, when I learned he was alive."

"My father's alive?" asked Hana.

"Yes. It's complicated. I'm sorry."

"Don't be. I'm just sorry he isn't dead."

Taro felt something untether inside him, some great weight. "After my mother died and you . . . after you went to sleep, I wanted revenge. I would be a liar if I said I just wanted the ball to bring you back from the dead." He took the small globe from his cloak and held it in his hand.

Hana put out her hand, palm up. "Can I see it?" she asked. Taro handed her the ball, and she twisted it in her fingers.

"Such a small thing," she said absently. Then she looked into Taro's eyes. "Did you kill her, then?" she asked. "Yukiko? And all of Lord Oda's men?"

He shook his head.

"Did you kill anyone?"

"Some of Lord Oda's samurai. And not with the ball—it was before. But when they were dead, I just felt sick. It didn't bring my mother back. It didn't bring you back."

"Well, then," said Hana. "But you *did* save me." She moved over to sit closer to him, and put her hand on his.

"Do you remember anything?" he asked.

"It seems to me I was in the burning temple," she replied, "and then I woke up to see Hayao and Hiro. I don't remember much in between."

"Nothing at all?"

A dreamy expression overtook her. "It seemed that I was crossing a bridge, and it was all sparkling as if it were covered with jewels, only there weren't any jewels. And then I was in a strange place, where nothing ever moved, and there was only black sky and stars. That was when I thought I saw you, but it's all so confused. Sorry," she said, seeing his expression. "It's very vague."

Taro smiled. "No," he said. "I know exactly what you mean. I think I remember the stars too. I looked into the Buddha ball, and then I was with you in starlight, and then I was back in the room, and you were waking up."

She sighed. "I can't believe my soul died. The abbot said he thinks my body was preserved because I rescued the scrolls."

"Yes. He says it's a miracle."

"That's nice," said Hana, with a smile. "I like the idea of being a miracle."

Taro swallowed painfully. "It suits you," he said. Then he cleared his throat. "I meant what I said. I would not . . . I mean, I like Hayao. I think he would make you a very good husband."

This time Hana laughed so hard she began to hiccup. "Not very ladylike," she said.

"You never were," said Taro. He was looking at her quizzically. What did she find so funny?

Hana squeezed his hand. "I don't want a husband," she said. "I don't want any husband."

Taro blinked. "Oh," he said, happy and disappointed in equal measure.

"But . . . ," said Hana slowly. "If I did want a husband, it would not be Hayao. It would be you."

Taro stared at her. "Really? But I'm just . . . I mean, I'm not high-born like you. I'm a peasant, and a killer."

"Your father is Lord Tokugawa."

"Yes. But not really. I mean, not in the way that counts. I was raised by peasants. I'm not good enough for you."

Hana held up her hands. "I'm not burned," she said. "But . . . I was in the fire . . . it was so hot . . . And then I thought I was floating among stars, and I saw you there—and after that I opened my eyes and the scrolls were undamaged, and I was unhurt. And do you know what, Taro? It didn't surprise me. It didn't surprise me that you saved me, that you brought me back from the dead. You're good enough risk everything because you wanted to save me so much. You're good enough to come after me into death itself and bring me out." She paused. "You're good enough for anyone, Taro."

"I—," he began.

"No," said Hana. She put a finger on his lips. "Don't talk."

She leaned toward him and closed her eyes, and his heart leaped in his chest, and when their lips met everything fell away from around him, and he was one with her, and it was as if they were floating in the stars again.

Someone screamed, from higher up the mountain. Taro heard yelling, the sound of people running. He broke away from Hana, jumped to his feet. Together they ran up the steps, breathing hard. Was it another attack on the mountain? When they reached the top, though, Taro saw no soldiers, no samurai anywhere. There were only monks, standing around in confusion. Then he saw a body, lying near the biers on which the dead had been laid. He began to rush down the other side, toward the main hall, Hana behind him.

His first thought was for his mother, but as he neared, he saw that she still lay peacefully in her white clothes, the abbot having covered her ruined chest. Near her lay the other monks who had died, awaiting the moment—as prescribed by the traditional obsequies—when their bodies could be burned.

He came to the body on the ground—monks surrounded it, muttering. *They sound scared,* Taro thought. The idea sent a frisson down his spine.

He pushed through the monks and saw the body up close. It

was one of their own order, lying dead on the ground, his eyes open and white. His neck was bent at an unnatural angle, as if someone had snapped it, but it would take force no human could possess to break it so fully. The head seemed attached to the body by little more than a flap of skin.

"Gods," said Hana. "What did that to him?"

One of the monks turned to them. He pointed to the bier behind that of Taro's mother. Taro hadn't noticed it, because he had been thinking only of his mother, but now he saw it was empty. He stared at it.

*That's where Kenji Kira's body was,* he thought. A sickness had taken root in his stomach and was growing, spreading branches through his limbs.

"The b-b-b-body got up," said the monk. "It got up!" He burst into tears.

Another monk put a hand on his shoulder and looked at Taro, terrified. "He saw it—it's quite unhinged him."

"Saw what?" said Hana. She still didn't understand—she hadn't known where Kenji Kira's body was laid.

"The dead man got up," said the second monk. "That's what Yamada says. He got up and he killed that monk because he was in the way, and then he went down the mountainside. He was shouting something, apparently."

"Shouting what?" said Taro.

"It doesn't make sense."

"Shouting what?"

"Yamada says he was saying, 'Yukiko.' Over and over."

Taro shivered.

"*What* dead man?" said Hana. "What are you talking about?"

Taro was looking at the broken neck of the man on the ground, and at the empty bier, and that sickness was everywhere in him now.

He pointed at the bier. "It was Kenji Kira," he said. "Yukiko killed him, and we laid him down there."

"But . . . he was dead," said Hana. She had gone very pale.

"So was my mother," said Taro. "I still saw her again."

As much as it could, the world returned to normal.

Kenji Kira's dead body was abroad somewhere, if the hysterical monk was to be believed—the man spent a lot of time in a darkened room, these days—but what was there to do? The abbot and his monks had surrounded the mountain with charms and Buddhas, to ward off evil. If Kenji Kira came back, he would want Taro, no doubt—but for now he seemed to be after Yukiko. And anyway, lots of people wanted Taro dead. He was getting used to it.

Often, Taro practiced the sword with the abbot. He still couldn't move as fast as the other man, couldn't see how to manipulate the sword with the same dexterity.

"Do you still have the scroll?" the abbot had asked, on the first day of their training.

"Yes," Taro had said. "I still don't understand it."

"Well," said the abbot, "keep reading it. One day you might."

This evening, though, Taro was working with the Buddha ball. The trick was to be inside the ball and in the earthly realm at one and the same time, seeing the same thing from two angles; one part of you floating above the surface of the miniature world, the other standing in your own skin on the solid, undeniable ground.

The oak tree, then, was both below and before him.

He reached out with his mind, inside the ball, and pulled. As one, the leaves dropped from the tree, and he caught them with the wind, swirling them up into a spinning column that gleamed green and gold in moonlight. He'd been working all day, and now, in the dead of night, he had started to get the hang of it.

He concentrated. Slowly the turning leaves began to take on a shape, round at the top. He fashioned arms, then legs. A man of leaves opened his arms in an embrace and stepped toward Little Kawabata.

Startled, Taro's friend drew his sword in a quick, lithe movement and slashed through the leaves and air that were approaching him.

Taro let the leaves fall to the ground, then grinned at Little Kawabata.

"Yes, very good," said Little Kawabata. "But it's just leaves. Go on—make *me* take a step forward."

Taro's sense of achievement faded. He couldn't move people—just air and water, fire and earth, the four elements. He had not *tried* fire yet, but he sensed it would work. Yet try to command a person to do something—to do anything they didn't want to do—and the ball became useless. It seemed it was one thing to control nature and another thing to control people. What use was power, if it didn't extend to individuals? He couldn't hope to defeat Lord Oda with leaves; he couldn't hope to stand up against the reincarnated body of Kenji Kira with nothing but air.

At first he hadn't wanted to think about Lord Oda, or about violence of any kind. He remembered those men he'd killed in Shirahama, the emptiness he'd felt afterward. He didn't want revenge anymore, he knew. But Hana had reminded him of how desperately Lord Oda wanted the ball.

"He won't stop until he's got it," she'd said. "He'll kill us all—

me, Hiro, Hayao. You, if he gets the chance. The only way to stop him is to kill him first."

Taro had argued, but in the end he had seen it was true. Now he had only to master the ball, so he could do it. He'd help the monks destroy Lord Oda's remaining army, and then he would go somewhere else. He was thinking of a fishing village, perhaps. He'd mentioned it to Hana, and she had smiled.

"I will go anywhere with you," she'd said.

Peering into the ball, he brought himself again to the spot on which he stood, until he was hovering over his own self, a floating consciousness without form. He reached out with his mind and plucked at Little Kawabata's legs, as if he were a puppet.

Nothing happened.

Hana was practicing sword katas under the trees, and she laughed at Taro's expression of frustration. "Forget the ball for a moment," she said. "You should focus on your own skills." She beckoned with her sword. "Come and spar—you look like you've gotten slower since I've been sleeping. Slower, and fatter."

Taro snorted. "Look who's talking! A month curled up asleep hasn't done your forms any good—or your form, either. . . ."

"Nonsense," said Hana. "It was beauty sleep." She dropped into the sword stance again and whipped out at a tree with a perfect high strike—if anything, Taro thought, she was quicker and more centered than she had been before, almost as if she had carried something of Enma's realm back to this one, some lingering knowledge of the true nature of things, clinging to her like smoke.

Turning away from her, Taro again concentrated on the ball, trying to make Little Kawabata trip himself up and fall to the ground.

Absolutely nothing happened. He cursed angrily.

The abbot, who was sitting under the tree meditating, looked up. "She's right, you know," he said. "You would do better to practice the sword. I don't think the ball will work—at least not for your purposes."

"Why not?"

"The ball belonged to Buddha. Do you think it is in the nature of his conception of *dharma* to control others?"

Taro thought about the teachings of Buddha, which he had been discussing often with the abbot over the last few days. "No," he said eventually. The Buddhist way was one of compassion, calm, and freedom from bonds. For one man to be enslaved to another was a violation of the Eightfold Path.

"It's one thing to have power over leaves, the wind, the weather even," continued the abbot. "We already have such power, in fact, when we farm, and when we build boats whose sails catch the air. But people are different."

Taro sat down. "So the ball is useless."

"No," said the abbot. "*Nothing* is useless. The ball is merely an instrument of *dharma*, but that doesn't make it any less powerful. I believe that it will help to further the true way—it just won't *interfere* with the way."

"I don't understand," said Taro.

The abbot stood up. He drew a *katana* from beneath his robe and held it out in front of him. "Pick it up," he said. Taro stepped forward. "No. With the ball."

Taro focused, then slowly raised the sword into the air. It was made of metal, and he could feel the true name of metal, and was able to command it. He let the sword hover in the air.

"Now run me through," said the abbot.

"What?"

"I said, run me through. Strike."

"But—"

"But nothing. I'm older and wiser than you, and I have quick reflexes, which is more important. Just do it."

Taro had no intention of hurting the man, but he sensed it would be foolish to disobey, so he compromised—he sent the sword slowly forward, tip pointing at the abbot's chest. But then he grunted, surprised. The sword stopped in midair, as if pressing against a solid barrier of rock, or steel. He pushed. It didn't move.

The abbot smiled. "You can't do it, can you?"

Taro was really trying now. He felt the muscle of his mind strain as he attempted to force the sword forward. Eventually he gasped, and the sword fell from his invisible grasp and landed with a thud on the ground. He sank back into the grass, looking up at the sky.

"Useless," he said. "How can I do *anything* with this thing?"

"You can do *good* things with it," said the abbot. "I think that's rather the point."

Taro laughed hollowly. Actually, there was one positive thing about this—the ball would be completely useless to Lord Oda, too. The daimyo had expended so much time and effort—killed people even—in order to possess it, and it was nothing like he had imagined. It didn't grant power over the world, not even close. It only allowed the holder to bring about, perhaps more quickly, the good and right progression of events. It was almost funny.

The murderous Lord Oda had killed Taro's father—at least, the man Taro had thought was his father—and Shusaku, and all the ninjas of the mountain, just to try to get hold of a ball that was a pure instrument of goodness, and would be as helpful as a rock in his hands.

Still, it wasn't that funny. Because Taro was now stuck on the mountaintop, close to Lord Oda's encampment, with nothing but a vampire who had once tried to kill him, a stocky friend, and a girl—even if she was good with a sword. There was Hayao, too, of course, though Taro had seen little of him since Hana had woken. He thought maybe Hiro had said something to him, about Taro's stupid jealousy, and the man was giving him and Hana some space. He was grateful; and he was grateful still to the samurai for coming over to the cause of the monks. But that didn't improve their odds much, did it? Some few monks, the meager survivors of the battle on the mountainside, Little Kawabata, Hiro, Hana, and a traitor who was still weakened by his long haunting.

That was all that stood against Lord Oda.

And Lord Oda didn't know the ball was useless. He still wanted it.

*We're all going to die,* thought Taro.

Just then, as he was thinking about death, a man in a hooded cloak stepped out from among the pine trees. He pushed the hood back from his head and it fell to his shoulders, leaving nothing but empty air where the face should have been. Taro stared in horror at this invisible newcomer, and was just remembering when he had last seen something like it when—

"Taro, Hiro," said the man. "It is good to see you. I have had a very long walk."

Taro stared. He'd seen this figure before. *Gods,* he thought. *Was it not enough with my mother—must they follow me always, these dead people?*

It was the ghost of Shusaku.

Taro stepped backward, holding the ball tight in his hands. His mother hadn't returned on the shade-boats at the end of obon, and it seemed Shusaku hadn't either—somehow their spirits had remained in the earthly realm. And now, just as Taro had saved himself from his mother's ghost and given her peace, his old mentor had come to haunt him too.

He was about to turn and run when he saw that Hiro was walking toward the ghost. "Shusaku!" his friend said. "Shusaku, what happened to your skin? I can't believe you're alive!"

"Wait," Taro said. "You see him too?" His friends had never seen his mother, he knew, and neither had Hiro or Hana seen the ghost that had been haunting Hayao, the samurai.

"What?" said Hiro. "Of course. He's right there. I just can't believe it!" Uncharacteristically, Hiro seemed to be crying. "We thought you were dead, Shusaku!"

"I can see him as well," said Hana, walking over to stand with Taro. She bowed to the man in the hood, the terribly burned man who spoke in Shusaku's voice. The ground seemed unsteady beneath Taro's feet; he felt as he had when he fell into the ball for the first time, leaving the world behind. "We met in the woods," said Hana. "When you saved me from the bandits."

"I remember," said Shusaku. "Well met, Lady Hana."

Shusaku came closer. "I'm not a ghost," he said, and when his mouth moved, the terrible scars on his face creased and folded. "The sun burned me, but it couldn't kill me."

Hana reached out a hand and touched Shusaku's face. "Those scars . . . ," she whispered. "It must have been terrible."

He shrugged. "It was. Lots of things are."

Taro's heart seemed about to grow wings and fly out of his throat. "Is it really you?" he asked.

"Yes. It's me. I'm sorry I didn't find you sooner."

Taro shrugged away the apology and ran forward to throw his arms around the old ninja. Even the odd, disconcerting feeling of talking to a man whose face you couldn't see was still welcome. He closed his eyes and wished this moment would go on forever, and Shusaku lifted him from the ground and spun him around.

Shusaku gave an embarrassed laugh. "It's good to see you, too," he said. "I have thought of you every day." He coughed. "Those I train do not usually occupy my thoughts so much."

"But how did the sun not kill you?" Taro asked.

The abbot spoke from behind him. "The Heart Sutra," he said. "Interesting. Does it make you invisible to other vampires?"

Shusaku nodded.

"Ah," said the abbot. "So the sun . . . Well, the sun is a spirit too. She is Amaterasu, in the Shinto faith. Your tattoos hid you from the sun itself."

"That was my conclusion also," said Shusaku. "She couldn't see me properly to burn me." He pointed to his eyes. "Unfortunately, I lost my sight. That is why it has taken me so long to find Taro again."

Taro realized then that he couldn't see Shusaku's eyes—always before he'd been able to see them floating in the air. They were the one part of his body he'd been unable to tattoo, and thus the only part that vampires and other spirits could see. They had been his downfall at Lord Oda's castle—giving away his whereabouts to the ninja called Namae, who had struck out and cut him down.

"You lost your *eyes*," said Taro, remembering when Namae cut them out. "I'm so sorry."

"Why?" said Shusaku. "You didn't do it."

Taro swallowed. "No, but you were helping me when—"

Shusaku raised a hand to cut him off. "No. Anything I do is my own choice. You may blame yourself for what you choose, but not for this." He looked around, then coughed discreetly. "Abbot," he said. "Could I have a moment alone with Taro and his friends?"

The abbot bowed. "Of course. You are welcome here, as you know." Taro remembered that the abbot and Shusaku knew each other, though the abbot had never said how. He didn't think it likely that Buddhist monks had many dealings with vampires. But then he also knew that Shusaku had been a samurai before he was turned, so it was possible he had spent time at the monastery, attending sutra readings and the like. Anyway, there were far more pressing questions on Taro's mind.

When the abbot had disappeared into the shadows, heading toward the ruins of the Hokke-do, Shusaku gestured to them to sit down, then crossed his own legs on the grass. Taro sat down beside him and took his hand, so the blind man would know where he was. Shusaku smiled at him. "Taro," he said. "After I threw you off the ship—"

"That *was* you!" said Taro.

"Yes. After that, I was wounded by Lord Tokugawa, and I—"

"By Lord Tokugawa? But I thought he was your sponsor?"

"He was. But I did stop him killing you on that boat. That's enough to make any man—"

Taro's legs almost gave way. "On the—you mean—that was *him*? The big samurai on the boat?" He'd been standing in front of his *father*, that night in Shirahama bay, and he hadn't even known it. His father had almost cut him open, in fact. And Shusaku had saved him. Taro couldn't imagine the consequences of such an act—it was bad enough that Shusaku was known to Lord Oda as the ninja who had infiltrated his castle, but now he'd made an enemy of Lord Tokugawa, the other of the two most powerful daimyo, and the man who had protected and hired him even after he was turned.

"Yes," said Shusaku. "But that's not our biggest problem. What really worries me is that Lord Oda's troops are gathering at the base of the mountain. I sensed them as I climbed the steps. I believe they're readying another attack on the monastery."

Taro closed his eyes wearily. "Gods. How did he find me?"

"He must have had you followed. Were you aware of anyone behind you, as you came here from Shirahama?"

"I didn't come here from Shirahama," said Taro. He explained about the trip to the ninja mountain, the carnage they had found there—and his haunting by his mother, which had required Hiro and Little Kawabata to practically carry him here to the monastery.

Shusaku nodded slowly. "Perhaps you were followed, and perhaps not. It is possible that Yukiko merely suspected you would return here, when she didn't find Hiro at the mountain."

Taro sighed. "Lord Oda's never going to stop, is he?" He looked at Shusaku. "But why did *you* come, when you knew the army was there? You could have stayed safe. If you're here with me, you could get yourself killed. I'm not worth that."

"You are," said Shusaku. "But that's beside the point. Remember the prophecy? You will be shogun one day. I don't think sticking by you can possibly be a bad plan."

Hiro laughed. "He's not too bad, once you get used to him," he said.

"Anyway," said Shusaku, "we haven't lost everything yet. I believe Lord Tokugawa has a plan. He could have killed me on that ship, but he didn't—and I don't believe he does anything by accident." He unslung the bag from his shoulder. "Lord Tokugawa pressed this into my hands," he said, "before he threw me overboard with a hole in my belly." From the bag he withdrew the large, gaudy golden ball that Taro had found on the reef.

Little Kawabata gasped. "Now *that's* real treasure!" he said.

"But it doesn't work," said Taro. "Not like the real one." He held up the Buddha ball, much smaller and less prepossessing than the gold fake in Shusaku's hands.

Now it was Shusaku's turn to take in a sharp breath. "You found it? The genuine Buddha ball? Why didn't you tell me immediately?"

"I *have* it," said Taro. "But it's not what you think. It can't hurt anyone, or make anyone do anything they don't want to do." He told Shusaku about his journey to hell, his meeting with his mother, and his failed attempts to use the ball to subvert the right way of things, or make people perform actions against their will. "It lets me pick up weapons with my mind," said Taro. "But it won't let me use them."

"Interesting. But unsurprising, I suppose. It belonged to the Buddha, after all. Does it do *anything*?"

"It can control the four elements," said Taro. "The wind, the earth, leaves—things like that. Weather."

"Hmm," said Shusaku. "That's not quite what I had hoped." He leaned forward over his knees, as if thinking. There was silence for a long time, and Taro met Hana's eye and saw that she was concerned too. It seemed that even Shusaku didn't know what to do, and he was *always* the one who knew what was best.

Just then a monk came running into the clearing. "The abbot sent me," he said, as he neared them. "He says there's a single samurai riding up the east slope of the mountain, bearing Lord Oda's *mon* on a flag."

What seemed like only moments later, Taro stood beside Hiro and Hana in silence as they waited. Shusaku had gone with the abbot to meet the messenger. It had been decided that Taro and his friends should stay hidden in the shadows of the hall—it was better to assume that Lord Oda didn't know Taro was here. No point in endangering themselves if they didn't have to.

Of course, Taro knew that there was little hope Lord Oda didn't already know everything. He'd known where the ninja mountain was, thanks to Yukiko, and he'd even seemed to know where the fake ball was hidden in Shirahama bay, given that his ship full of pirates had turned up just after Lord Tokugawa's. But Taro was willing to stand in the shadows, if it meant there was the slightest chance of protecting his friends from violence.

After what seemed an interminable delay, Shusaku and the abbot entered the hall. They walked close together, and Taro wondered again what shared history they had—though he could think of no way of asking that would not be too direct. He'd learned over the months with Shusaku that the ninja did not respond well to direct questions.

"Lord Oda has given an ultimatum," said the abbot without preamble. "We hand over Taro by dawn, or they attack. This time they will destroy us completely." He turned to Taro, and hesitated.

Hana leaped to her feet. "No! You can't just *sacrifice* him."

The abbot looked pained. "We wouldn't do that," he said hurriedly. "Of course not. But the monks . . . there are still dozens left. And the scrolls. If we resist Lord Oda, he will crush everything. It will be as if the monastery was never here."

"I should go to them," said Taro, his shoulders slumped. "I should let Lord Oda have me."

"No!" said Hana. "Stop it! There must be some other way."

Hana turned to Shusaku, an imploring expression on her face, but the ninja seemed to be still deep in thought. Finally he raised his head to the abbot. "He didn't mention the ball," he said.

"I'm sorry?"

"The ball. The messenger didn't say anything about it. So Lord Oda doesn't know whether Taro has it or not. By the time his pirates reached Lord Tokugawa's ship, the *fake* ball was gone, and he can't know anything about Taro's journey to hell."

"I don't see what difference it makes," said the abbot.

"It explains their caution," said Shusaku. "They could have attacked straightaway, but instead they gave us a deadline. It means they're on edge, and likely to make mistakes." He hung his head in thought a moment longer, and this time when he looked up he was facing Taro, though Taro could not, of course, see his face.

"You say that thing can control the weather?" he asked.

"Yes," said Taro.

"In that case," said Shusaku, "I think I finally understand what Lord Tokugawa has been planning."

They had until dawn.

Smoke rose into the sky behind them, and it was as if the samurai had burned the mountain again. But it was only the funeral pyres of the dead, disintegrating into their constituent atoms and blowing away in the wind. Hiro had once again supported Taro as the abbot lit the kindling, his hand under his arm, but Taro had not needed it so much this time. He knew better than anyone that his mother had gone on to a better place, and what was burned by the flames was nothing but a husk.

He was glad, actually, that it was all over. And with Hana by his side, he knew that death was not the end. He had brought her back from the edge, and he had spoken to his mother after she was taken from him. He felt lucky, as the flames grew in heat and fury. Now he had only one more thing to do—rid the world of Lord Oda and Yukiko, before they did any more damage in their insatiable quest for the ball and its power.

Of course, Taro was meant to remain with the bodies of his

mother and the monks as they burned—that would be the respectful thing to do. And it was precisely on this point of etiquette that they were relying. Lord Oda, seeing the smoke from the cremation, would with any luck assume that everyone on the mountain was occupied with the rituals and the chanting.

So he *wouldn't* be watching the steep gorge on the east flank of the mountain, down which Taro, Shusaku, Hiro, and Hana were creeping, keeping their bodies in shadow. Little Kawabata had stayed behind with the monks, to help them fight if the plan failed.

In conception, the plan was very, very simple. Shusaku had explained that, some time before, he had on Lord Tokugawa's order smuggled a special new gun to the Ikko-ikki monks of the Hongan-ji—the mountain that lay only a couple of *ri* away, on the other side of Lord Oda's army. These guns, he said, came from the land of the barbarians, far away to the west over the sea, and they were designed to work with a spark, not fire, which meant they would work in the rain. Lord Tokugawa had wanted the Ikko-ikki to copy the design.

"I didn't understand the significance, at the time," Shusaku had said. "I wondered to myself why it was so important to Lord Tokugawa to have these guns—for the Ikko-ikki had pledged to his side in the battle for the shogunate. I thought it was strange, to go to such lengths to have them copied—what's the use of a gun that can work in the rain, unless you can control the weather? I remember asking myself that question when I was coming down from the Ikko-ikki's stronghold."

Taro had looked at the Buddha ball. "You think . . ."

"I think Lord Tokugawa must have known that the Buddha ball could make it rain. It's the only thing that makes sense. The Ikko-ikki, armed with guns that work in any weather . . . and a ball that can make the weather do what he wants? That is a plan of the kind Lord Tokugawa likes."

"But . . . so many things could have gone wrong. And how could he have known about the ball? He would have had to plan everything. . . ."

"Lord Tokugawa plans in years," said Shusaku. "Everyone else plans in months. I say we go to the Ikko-ikki and convince them to attack Lord Oda's army. If you can make it rain with that ball, Oda's guns will be useless. Providing we take them by surprise, it could be a rout."

Taro had looked at the ball in his hands. "It's worth a try," he'd said. "It's the only plan we have."

The simple idea, then, was this: They would go to the Ikko-ikki, who had their own forges, and who had been tasked by Lord Tokugawa with copying the new barbarian gun. Then they would recruit the monks to their cause, Taro would make it rain, and all together they would attack Lord Oda's army from behind, using the advantage not only of surprise, but also of weapons that actually worked in the wet.

There were just a couple of minor problems in the execution.

First problem: To get to the Ikko-ikki's fortress, they had to get past Lord Oda's army.

Second problem: They also had to get past Lord Tokugawa's army.

Shusaku had explained that the surface alliance between the two daimyo was still in effect, and nowhere was it more apparent than in the fact that they had joined together to destroy the Ikko-ikki. And even though Lord Tokugawa was secretly supplying the monks with these improved guns for them to copy in their forges, the generals of his army didn't know that.

If it came to battle with the monks, Lord Tokugawa's army would almost certainly join the fray alongside Lord Oda's. Lord Tokugawa's force occupied the left-hand side of the valley below them, camped on one side of the stream that served as the border between the two armies. Hundreds of tents filled the valley floor, all flying the Tokugawa *mon*. On the other side of the river the scene was reflected—only there the tents flew the Oda *mon*. Samurai milled around in both camps, while smiths honed blades, and cooks prepared food at great fires. Smoke and the hubbub of voices filled the air. Taro counted at least five hundred horses still on the Oda side, despite the losses on Mount Hiei, and countless guns leaning on racks.

And that was just Oda's army. Lord Tokugawa's was just as big, and just as likely to crush them like ants beneath a rolling buffalo's back if they were caught.

The friends' only hope was that the pigeon Shusaku had sent would reach Lord Tokugawa in time. Attached to the pigeon was a brief message. It didn't explain the plan, because that would give too much away, about Taro *and* the ball, but it did ask one thing: If Lord Oda attacked, then Lord Tokugawa's army was to leave the field of battle, instead of joining the assault.

And that was without even mentioning the other problems—like whether or not they would even be able to convince the Ikko-ikki to fight by their side. Though Taro did think that the possibility of ridding themselves of Lord Oda forever would swing the decision.

Nevertheless, the plan was clearly madness, and no one knew it better than Hiro. As they skirted a boulder, giving them a wide vista over the plain in which both armies were laid out before them, in gleaming, serried ranks, Taro's oldest friend stopped and whistled. "Let me get this straight," he said. "We've got to get past them, climb the cliffs that lead to the Hongan-ji temple, convince the Ikko-ikki to join us, create a thunderstorm, and then win a battle against Lord Oda's undefeated army. Does that about cover it? Oh, and we've also got to hope that the pigeon message we just sent is going to reach Lord Tokugawa and persuade him to remove his army from the field of battle."

Shusaku shrugged. "That's about it, yes. As for Lord Tokugawa—I'm hopeful. He knows I would not ask such a thing lightly. And he has reason to trust the abbot, too."

Taro sensed that there was something they were not being told, but he held his tongue, knowing from experience that Shusaku would answer no questions he didn't want to.

"What about the other parts?" Hiro said. "Sneaking past Oda's army, climbing the unclimbable mountain?"

"I've climbed it once," said Shusaku. "And I'm blind. It's not so unclimbable as all that. Anyway, do you have any better ideas?"

Hiro fell silent.

Hiro was trying to lighten their moods, Taro knew, but he was also scared. Taro didn't blame him. He, too, could see the sea of men that was Lord Oda's army, the rows and rows of horses, and the moonshine on the barrels of thousands of guns—and that wasn't counting Lord Tokugawa's army, just as big, on the other side of the river.

"What if the Ikko-ikki just kill us?" he said to Shusaku.

"They won't. They know me already. They may not have met *you*, but once they learn what that ball can do, they'll welcome you with open arms. They want nothing more than to be rid of the army besieging them."

"Then what if they just kill me and take the ball?"

Shusaku paused. "I'll tell them you're under Lord Tokugawa's protection. They won't dare to touch you then."

"Are you sure?"

Shusaku hesitated again. "No."

"Wonderful."

Shusaku stopped, as a cloud passed away from the moon, revealing even more clearly the layout of the camp below, showing the group of friends the little avenues that led between the tents. It was late at night, and if fortune was on their side, all but the watchmen would be asleep.

Of course, it was the watchmen they were worried about.

The scale of it was breathtaking—a veritable sea of tents and men and horses, filling the entire flat valley between the two mountains.

"It's impossible," said Taro.

Shusaku protested weakly. "No, it's just . . . difficult." But Taro could tell by the tone of his voice that he was afraid.

Just then, though, there was a scraping noise behind them, as of someone clambering along the rocks, and a samurai appeared on the path.

"Hayao!" said Taro. The man looked so much healthier now. He was hale and rosy, even slightly overweight, but still immediately recognizable. He wore the armor of a samurai, his epaulets bearing the Oda *mon*. All that was missing was the helmet.

"I said I would repay what you did for me if I could," said the man. "And now I think I can. The abbot told me what you're planning—to get past Lord Oda's army and climb up the Hongan-ji."

Taro nodded.

"The problem is, it's nigh-on impossible," said Hayao.

Shusaku visibly slumped, as if the strings holding him up had been cut. Hayao grinned. "It's *nigh-on* impossible," he said. "But not *completely*. You see, I was stationed down there, before I had my . . . troubles." He pointed to the west side of the encampment, and Taro saw a line of trees. "Those trees run alongside a river. In places they are thick, and the undergrowth is heavy with thorns. Also, it's said that Shinto spirits live in the river and on its banks. The watchmen don't venture too far into the thicket." He looked at the friends. "But I don't suppose thorns and spirits hold much fear for you, eh?"

Taro stepped forward and clapped Hayao on the back. "Thank you!" he said.

"Yes," said Shusaku. "This gives us a chance. A small chance— but a chance nonetheless."

Hiro glared at him. "You mean we didn't have one before?"

"Not really, no," said Shusaku. "But better to die hopefully than to die in despair, don't you think?"

Hiro raised his eyebrows, but offered no other answer.

Hayao edged past Taro to take the head of the procession. "You're coming?" said Taro.

"Of course," said the samurai, turning his head. "I owe you my life, don't I? I'll see you as far as the other mountain."

Taro flushed. "I'm sorry for what I thought . . . I mean, about you and Hana . . . I was an idiot. I shouldn't have been so childish."

"I don't know what you're talking about," said Hayao.

Taro smiled.

Shusaku spread his hand in the general direction of the valley, indicating the army. "If this works," he said, "Lord Oda will be neutralized. Lord Tokugawa would be free to take up the shogunate."

Taro shrugged. "Perhaps."

"You wouldn't rather be shogun yourself?" asked Shusaku. "With the ball, you could—

"No," said Taro. He'd seen enough of the way the daimyo operated to know that he was not interested in that kind of power.

"But the prophetess said it would be you," said Shusaku. "And the things she says have a way of coming about."

"I'm not interested in being shogun," said Taro. "I just want to be left alone."

Shusaku laughed. "That," he said, "is why you would be so good at it."

The watchman froze.

Taro cursed silently. He and Shusaku could move without noise, almost without disturbing the leaves of the trees, or the air that stirred them. But the others were not vampires—they broke twigs, and they twisted their ankles in holes, and gasped, and bumped into trees.

Just now, even worse, Hana had cried out when a thorn tore her cheek.

They were close enough to the river that they could hear it, babbling its incomprehensible song. The watchman before them was deep into the undergrowth, farther than he should be, his bearing that of a young man anxious to please his superiors. He began to pick his way toward them, suspicion darkening his features, looking from left to right, trying to identify the source of the sound.

Taro looked behind him, but they had inched through thick vegetation, and they would not be able to retreat quickly enough.

To their left, the river formed a fast, cold, treacherous barrier.

To their right lay the vast army of their greatest enemy.

Taro saw the others crouching low, as the watchman came inevitably, unstoppably toward them. He held his breath.

That was when Hayao pushed loudly forward through the brush, putting a hand over his mouth as he yawned deep and long. He hailed the watchman heartily. "Gods, I hate this camp," he said. "Get the call of nature and you have to force your way through thorns to relieve yourself!"

The watchman laughed. "True," he said. "Still, could be worse. You almost got a bullet in the gut for your trouble!"

"Now that," said Hayao, "would not pass so easily."

The watchman frowned—he was close enough that Taro could see the wrinkles on his forehead, through the leaves. Then, after a moment, he guffawed. "Ha!" he said. "That was a good one."

Taro still hadn't breathed out. He couldn't believe that Hayao had done this—put himself in danger like this to save them. Nevertheless, the samurai did still wear Lord Oda's *mon*. The army might just assume he belonged there—as he had, until his lover's ghost began to kill him. He would have to hope that no one recognized him from the battle of Mount Hiei.

There had been no time to say good-bye—it had all happened so quickly. Taro sent a farewell with his mind, and at that moment Hayao turned and winked at him, and he was sure his message had got through. He smiled, as he listened to the two samurai chuckling and sharing anecdotes about camp life, their voices getting quieter as Hayao led the watchman skillfully away from the friends.

"Someday," said Shusaku, under his breath, "you'll have to explain exactly what you did for that man. It must have been pretty special."

*When Yukiko could no longer ignore the fullness of her bladder, she rolled off her sleeping mat and picked up her sword. She never went anywhere without her sword. There would always come times when you needed a sword, and if you didn't have one at one of those times— well, you only got to make that mistake once.*

*She went outside, then threaded her way through the tents to get to the river, and the clump of trees that stood beside it.*

*As she entered the copse, she heard a rustle of leaves—and as the air was completely still, she ducked behind a bush, holding her breath. Deeper into the trees, a wood pigeon flew from its branch in a sudden clatter of wings.*

Someone is here, *she thought.*

*Very slowly, no longer conscious of her bladder but only the steady pounding of her heart, she leaned forward and craned her neck to peer through the leaves.*

*She couldn't believe what she was seeing.*

*Creeping through the undergrowth, their footsteps almost silent, were*

Taro, Shusaku, Hiro, and Hana. She was stunned that they had made it this far, without alerting one of the watchmen—they had already crossed half the encampment! Where were they going? she wondered.

But then she remembered Lord Oda's insistence on sleeping in humble quarters, far from the grand tent that bore his flag. The daimyo feared assassination more than anything, and it seemed he was right to do so. Wouldn't it be simplest for Taro if Lord Oda was dead? She had to admire his courage, really. Rather than waiting on the mountaintop for the battle to begin, he had decided to come down into the very embrace of the army, a nest of serpents, and kill the big snake in its middle.

As they passed, Yukiko eased herself up and followed at a safe distance. What she needed to do was warn Lord Oda, but how could she manage it? If she lost sight of her prey, they might get away from her—she had been lucky to stumble upon them, and might not have the same luck again. They made no noise now at all, after their mistake with those loose leaves.

It seemed impossible. It was all she could do to keep them in her sights, while following far enough behind that they couldn't hear her. How could she warn her lord?

Then, suddenly, she came face-to-face with a watchman in light armor. He was relieving himself into the bushes—for a moment she was uncomfortably reminded of her original purpose in coming out here, and felt a twinge in her belly—and he opened his mouth in surprise when he saw her.

She moved like a snake, clamping her hand over his mouth. They must have walked right past him, she thought. Hopeless. He was holding a lantern in one hand, its weak light illuminating the area immediately around him, but robbing him of the night vision he would need to see anything significant.

Fool.

She held a finger to her lips, then raised her eyebrows in an unspoken question: Will you be silent?

He nodded, and she gently withdrew her hand. She glanced over his shoulder. She couldn't see the little group, but she thought she could catch up with them again. The river cut them off to the south, after all, and on the other side were only tents and battle-ready samurai. Taro and his friends would have to stick to the shelter of the trees.

"Go to Lord Oda," she whispered to the watchman. "Tell him the boy is here, in the camp. Tell him—" She stopped. How would Lord Oda know where she was? She could follow Taro, but that didn't mean Lord Oda would be able to follow her.

Then she saw the gun in the watchman's other hand. Perfect—she would fire it when she was ready, and Lord Oda would have only to follow the sound, assuming of course that no battle began between now and then, ruining her plan by filling the night with gunfire.

She might even fire the gun at Hiro, if she had the chance—the shot could serve as more than just a signal to Lord Oda. Why not deprive Taro of another person he loved? It would be worth it just to see the expression on his face.

"Give me that," she said, putting her hand on the gun. "Tell Lord Oda to follow the gunshot—it will lead him to the boy."

At this, the watchman seemed to come back to his senses. He pulled the gun away from her. "Wait," he said, his gaze turning steely. "You're just a girl!" He grabbed her wrist. "I think you'd better come with me and explain what you're—"

Yukiko moved like the falling rain, twisting from his grip, bringing her sword up to rest against the bulge of his throat. She angled the grip of the sword toward his startled, wide eyes, showing him the petals of Lord Oda's mon. "See that?" she hissed.

He swallowed, and her sword was so tight against his skin that the bobbing of his larynx against the steel made a shallow cut, which beaded with blood.

"If you don't do as I say," she hissed, "I will tear out your windpipe. Do you understand?"

This time he didn't dare move a single muscle, for nodding would have been fatal. He just blinked his eyes. Satisfied, she withdrew the blade.

"Now," she said. "Did you get all that, or do I have to repeat myself?"

The man whimpered. She raised her eyes to the heavens. Gods, the things she had to work with. And all this time Taro was getting farther away.

"Go to Lord Oda," she said, as if speaking to an idiot. "Tell him Yukiko says the boy is here." The watchman opened his mouth to ask a question, but Yukiko cut him off. "Yes, he will know who I mean. Tell him to follow the gunshot—it will lead him to me." She tore the gun from his grip.

She turned to follow Taro again, then paused, seeing that the watchman hadn't moved. She sighed. "You needn't tell him that I caught you urinating while intruders crept through the camp. But believe me, if you don't do as I ask—I will."

The watchman turned on his heels and ran, toward Lord Oda's tent.

"That's not a path," said Hiro. "That's a cliff."

They were standing in a clearing at the far end of Lord Oda's encampment, looking up the almost sheer slope of the mountain on which sat the Hongan-ji monastery. Behind them another steep slope, heavily wooded, led down to the army's tents and the fluttering pennants. Trees had anchored themselves in thin soil, their roots a twisting labyrinth underfoot, and it had been a struggle for Taro and the others to climb through this near-vertical forest and reach the bowl-shaped clearing in which they now found themselves.

The cliff above them was curved, extending its arms around them on either side, so that it was as if they stood in a natural theater, or in the dubious embrace of the mountain.

"It can't be any steeper than the seaward side," said Shusaku. "I climbed that easily—and I'm blind."

Hiro sighed. "Yes, and you're a lot harder to kill than me. You really think this is going to work?"

"I have no idea," said Shusaku. "But it's better than just wait-ing to die, isn't it?"

Hiro shrugged as if he wasn't convinced. Actually, Taro was worried too. He had a surer sense of poise, and a firmer grip, since he'd been made a vampire, but that didn't mean he was infallible. Where he came from, there was an expression: *Even Kappas can drown.* Hadn't he seen for himself how the sea demons were pow-erless against some greater forces? He thought that went for climb-ing vampires, too. And even though a fall probably wouldn't kill him, it would definitely hurt.

He turned to look back where they had come from. Down there, smoke rose in wreaths from the tents, and it was just pos-sible to see the horses and gunners arrayed on the lower slopes of Mount Hiei. It was an awesome sight. The biggest army Taro had ever seen, and it was all assembled to kill *him*. They had been lucky to get past it once—to try to return would be suicide.

And yet, on the other side of the grassy theater in which they waited, the rock face loomed over them, almost mocking their intention to climb up to the Hongan-ji.

In the end it was Hana who stepped up to the cliff first, brush-ing her hands together to dry them. Hiro had no choice, then, but to follow.

Shusaku pushed his bag over his shoulder, putting the weight of the golden, false ball on his back. Taro followed suit, though his bag was smaller and lighter, for it carried the real ball. Taro had asked Shusaku why he was bothering to carry the big lump of use-less gold, and Shusaku had shrugged. "It might come in handy," he'd said simply.

Now Shusaku chose a section of cliff next to Hana and reached up to seize a thick root. Taro was climbing behind them when there was a loud *bang* from the trees at his back, and he whirled round, startled. Shusaku dropped to the ground and spun, crouch-ing. But there was nothing there that Taro could see—just the hint of a shadow, flitting between the trees, and a thin trail of smoke that lingered in the night air.

*A gunshot,* thought Taro.

Shusaku's hand went to his sword, and Taro followed suit. Hana pulled back her own blade, which she had slung over her shoulder as she approached the cliff.

Nothing happened.

Taro looked around for shelter, but the clearing was bare— and anyway, no further shot followed.

"It could be a watchman's signal," said Shusaku, sounding nervous. That was what scared Taro most of all. He'd never seen Shusaku unsure of himself before. "We should get moving," continued Shusaku. He turned again to the cliff, holding his sword in his teeth.

"Stop," said a voice that Taro knew all too well. He turned to see Yukiko standing by a cedar tree. She threw a spent gun to the ground and pointed her sword at Taro. "You were careless," she said. She was smiling, and Taro felt a rush of anger that literally stopped the breath in his lungs. She'd killed his mother, and now she was standing there smiling at him.

But wait.

He peered at her. Though she was smiling, her skin was sallow and creased, as if she was already developing wrinkles. There were dark patches of skin under her eyes. *She looks sick,* he thought. But then she smiled even wider and he didn't see her illness anymore, he saw only the person who had taken a sword to his mother.

Taro was moving before he was really aware of it, as if his sword were dragging him forward across the grass. Yukiko raised her blade and read his first slash, blocking him easily. But she had only one sword this time and was not in full armor, as if she had readied herself quickly. Taro guessed that she'd been sleeping when she heard them, or sensed them, or whatever it was she'd done to find them.

She was fast, but something seemed to be weakening Yukiko, and he was faster. Their blades flashed in the moonlight as he danced around her, looking for the opening that would see his blade dart in and cut her down. She panted for breath, her lips no longer ruby red but drained, pinched and white, as if she herself were the passive and helpless victim of a *kyuuketsuki*. She spat in his face, and at that moment all his peace left him, and he was no longer content that his mother had melted into oneness.

He just wanted Yukiko dead.

He was dimly aware of Hana saying something behind him, expressing some kind of concern, but he was not in that world anymore, he was in the circle of steel. He noted that Yukiko, too, was twisting the katas to her own devices, using moves he'd never seen before. At one point she ducked under one of his strikes, then slashed open his forearm. He barely glanced at the wound before landing her a cut right across the scalp.

Then came the moment he'd been waiting for.

Taro feinted to the left and for some reason, though she had seen through all his previous deceits, Yukiko went to block his sword. Twisting his blade in mid-movement, he brought it down toward her side.

Then something hot and hard struck him in the right shoulder, knocking him back and causing his blade to drop to the ground from his suddenly numb fingers. He stumbled, pressing his hand to the wound and taking it away wet with blood. Before him, a samurai emerged from the woods, holding a gun.

Behind the samurai, walking casually, came the unmistakable figure—lopsided, its right arm withered; a beautiful *katana* in its stronger left arm—of Lord Oda Nobunaga.

"Kill the old one," said Lord Oda. "He's dangerous."

Obeying his daimyo's orders, the samurai rushed past Taro to attack Shusaku.

Lord Oda winked at Taro. "You," he said, "are going to die." He turned to Hana. "And you are coming home with me. I haven't decided yet what your punishment will be. Probably I'll lock you up in the tower for good this time, after I've cut you up a bit. I wouldn't want any noblemen—*or peasant boys*—getting any ideas."

She stared at him. "Father . . . ," she said, and Taro wasn't sure if it was a plea, or a statement, or an expression of horror.

"Oh, don't worry," said Lord Oda. "Your wounds will only be superficial, if painful. I wouldn't want to . . . ruin you." He paused, cocking his head to one side. "You know, you look more like your mother than ever."

Hana let out a scream and ran at him, her sword high. But Yukiko came forward to meet her, blocking Hana and then dropping back, keeping up a quick succession of parries that did little more than ward off Hana's blows.

Taro bent down to pick up his sword in his left hand. The world had taken on a greater brightness and detail, as if his wound had opened him to reality and let more of it in. He could hear Shusaku behind him, muttering to himself as he fought the samurai. Taro wasn't sure if Shusaku knew that he did this. Probably not—it was like he went into a trance when he was fighting.

It was almost funny, or would have been, under different circumstances. Taro knew that Shusaku would kill the samurai—that wasn't a concern. What was a concern was Hana's safety, and Hiro's. Other samurai were bursting into the clearing now, and one of them ran toward Taro's large friend.

*He doesn't even have a sword,* thought Taro.

But he needn't have worried—Hiro went down on one knee, knocked aside the man's sword, and rammed his shoulder up and forward into his chest, sending him flying. There was a time when Hiro had challenged passing *ronin* to wrestling matches, pocketing the money that their overconfident friends bet against him. His instincts had obviously not left him.

Taro turned away from Hiro, worried for him, but knowing that he had to kill Lord Oda if this was ever going to stop. He moved forward, glancing occasionally at Hana, who was still fighting Yukiko. It was odd—Yukiko had fought free-form with him, but now she was meeting Hana's competent but unimaginative kata forms with predictable blocks and simple moves.

*Why isn't she fighting properly?*

But he didn't have time to think about it, because at that moment Lord Oda was on him, his sword nothing but a silvery streak in the air, coming at Taro from the wrong side, which would confuse and distract a swordsman educated according to the conventions.

Yet Taro was not a conventional swordsman.

Taro met Lord Oda in the center of the clearing, keeping his hand loose on the pommel of his sword. Neither he nor Lord Oda said anything—it wasn't necessary. When they'd last fought, Taro had left the daimyo for dead. He wasn't going to rest until Taro paid for it.

*I might as well have signed my death warrant,* he thought, as he was pressed irresistibly backward, toward the cliff. A strike from Lord Oda came within a finger-span of his chest—would have speared his heart if he hadn't turned, letting the blade go past. For a moment there was an opportunity—he lunged at the opening in Oda's side, but the sword saint was too quick. Leaping back, Lord Oda got his sword up and twisted Taro's blade aside, raked his blade along Taro's arm as its point pressed toward his chest again. Only by giving up more ground, his back almost against the rock now, was Taro able to avoid the blow. Taro was slower than the daimyo—as he parried the blows, he knew that the fight couldn't go on for much longer. Terror was a hand gripping his heart, squeezing it. He was finding it more and more difficult to breathe.

But Lord Oda was too arrogant in his strength. He lowered his guard for a fraction of a moment to attempt a clever strike, and Taro put his blade through the man's sword arm, rather than the heart he had been aiming for, feeling the scrape as it filleted the daimyo's bicep from the bone. He was pleased for a heartbeat, but then he yanked back on the sword and felt it resist his pull—he'd stuck himself to Lord Oda now, and left himself open to a sword tip in the guts.

His sword came free, but not before Lord Oda dealt him a deep cut through his side. Pain was a bright flash in Taro's vision, making the forest scene in front of him pale and luminous. He clutched at the cut with his left hand, feeling how deep it was, biting his tongue at the agony of it. It had missed his organs, at least. As he explored the wound with his fingers, he realized that he was lucky—the daimyo's injury had taken the force out of his strike, which could otherwise have gone right through him. Without thinking, he raised his bloody fingers to his face and wiped streaks of red on his cheek.

"You'll have to do better than that," Taro spat, the pain of the cut in his side making his voice tremble more than he liked.

Lord Oda screamed, as much in frustration as rage, and

stepped back into the fighting stance. Taro saw Yukiko look over to see what had happened to the daimyo, then return her attention to Hana as she redoubled her attack.

Lord Oda's wounded left arm hung awkwardly. He glanced at it, then tossed his sword into his withered right arm, the one that had been wounded so many years ago, forcing him to adapt his technique. He came at Taro with a flurry of blows.

"At first," said the daimyo as he fought, "I learned to fight with my remaining good arm. I made myself a sword saint again, learned every move backward."

He turned aside one of Taro's strikes and got his blade inside Taro's, his sword tip plunging into Taro's bullet wound before it was pulled back, as Lord Oda leaned away from Taro's counter-strike. Over Lord Oda's shoulder, Taro saw a group of samurai wearing the Oda *mon* run into the clearing.

*Oh, gods, we're outnumbered,* he thought. *Badly outnumbered.*

Lord Oda must have heard them, because he raised his bloody, wounded arm and shouted, without turning, "Keep back! The boy is mine. Seize my daughter if you can."

Then he focused on Taro again, his sword still leaping and slashing, and began to talk once more, as if this were a polite conversation, not a fight to the death.

"But then I saw my small-mindedness," Lord Oda continued. "Why should a *weak* arm be a *bad* arm? I began to teach myself to fight with this arm too. The sword is not just about strength. It's about speed and agility."

As if to demonstrate, he let loose a succession of lightning-fast moves, forcing Taro to block ever more quickly. Taro was beginning to tire. Lord Oda was a *kensei*, a sword saint, and Lord Oda was going to kill him.

Then Taro heard Shusaku's voice. "Drop your sword, Nobunaga."

Lord Oda held Taro's sword down and turned to see what Shusaku was doing. And then, to Taro's surprise, he backed away.

And dropped his sword.

*At first, and as always, Shusaku felt the dead pressing in on him. Shadowy forms, they filled the clearing, and all of them had been opened up or shortened by his sword—he could see its mark on them like a trace of silver.*

*This is my karma, he thought. It surrounded him, crowded him, threatened to drown him. He'd never had a child. All he had done was to send people back, into the darkness, and their souls as they passed into hell were like a great counterweight, dragging Shusaku farther and farther down into his own hell, from which only death would be an escape, and even that would lead to nothing but suffering.*

*At first, and as always, he didn't want to kill the samurai before him. But really, what was the choice? It was either the other man or him, Shusaku knew. And one thing was for sure.*

*It wasn't going to be him.*

*Gathering his qi for one final time—I promise it's the final time—he saw the samurai in his mind's eye, a skeleton of pulsing red, smelling strongly of sweat and horse dung and leather. He blocked the childish, almost insulting attack, and sighed inwardly. Once he had woken a man he was supposed to assassinate, just to see what it was like when they fought back.*

*The answer was that it didn't really make any difference.*

*Shusaku had long since come to the conclusion that the sword loved him, for some reason. It was nothing to do with being a vampire—it was a deeper romance than that, between every fiber of his being and the hammered steel. He saw the same thing in Taro, and much as he loved the boy, he felt sorry for him.*

*Almost of its own accord—almost as if it was cursed, or he was— his sword flew forward and slashed the samurai's throat.*

*He gathered himself. A little in front of him were Hana and Yukiko—he knew because their blood ran colder than the men's; that and they didn't smell so much of sweat. He could sense which one was Hana, too, because her blood was strong and pure. Yukiko's, though, was not.*

*Yukiko was sick.*

*Shusaku wondered how long she had been wasting away. He had known people like that before, had smelled their blood. They were eaten away from inside, their own sins and their own guilt feeding on their souls. It hadn't happened to him—maybe because he didn't, deep down, feel guilty enough.*

*But it was happening to Yukiko. Her guilt had got ahold of her, and it was killing her. Akuji mi ni tomaru, thought Shusaku. All evil done clings to the body. It was one of the precepts of the Tendai monks, including his friend the abbot. They maintained that the fruits of evil actions clung to people like plums to a tree, weighing them down. Shusaku had never told the abbot about the dead he saw at the start of battles, but he thought the abbot would not be surprised.*

*Then, as he was sensing the movements of the girls, he noticed it.*

Yukiko's sick, but there's more to it than that. She isn't fighting.

*Hana was much weaker, it was obvious. Her movements, while quick, were uninspired. She was not a person loved by the blade. But Yukiko was dangerous. And yet, as Shusaku sensed the moving bodies, it seemed she neglected several opportunities to kill Hana.*

*Shusaku raced forward, seeing a way out of this mess.* She's been ordered to leave Hana alive, *he thought.* That means Lord Oda doesn't want her dead. . . .

*He was past Hana in a flash, and with nothing more than a twitch of his sword he dealt with Yukiko's guard, sending her sword spinning away over the grass. He pressed his own blade against her neck, feeling her pulse as it thrummed weakly through the steel.*

*It was not in his nature to do so, but he hesitated. Few of the ghosts that had attached themselves to him were female—and he wasn't sure he wanted to add to their number.*

*"Please," said Yukiko, trembling, and he was afraid that she might beg, sapping the last of his resolve, but then she seemed to push toward the blade, not away from it. "Please, end me," she said.*

*Shusaku heard Hana gasp. To Yukiko, though, he nodded gravely. "You are suffering?" he asked.*

*A tear rolled down her cheek—he could smell its salt tang against her skin. "Yes," she said. "The ghosts . . . they surround me. I feel them feeding. Not my sister, she only watches, in sadness. But the ones I have killed."*

*"I understand," said Shusaku.*

*"You cannot," she replied.*

*"Yes," he said gently. "Yes, I can. And that is why I cannot kill you. Don't you see?"*

*The tears ran down her cheeks.*

*"Go, girl," he said. "I can't help you."*

*Her eyes narrowed, and she spat at his feet. "Next time I see you, I'll kill you," she said, and then she ran from the clearing.*

*Shusaku shrugged. He turned and saw that Hana was beside him—she looked grateful to him for intervening, for saving her from Yukiko. She would not be so grateful in a moment.*

*Spinning on his foot, he threw his sword up to stop, trembling, just below Hana's throat. He couldn't see the expression on his face, but he sensed her pulse quicken with fear.*

*"Trust me," he whispered, and he hoped that was enough.*

*Then he reached back with his other hand, pulled his bag over to hang on his chest, and pulled out the golden ball, the one that wasn't real. He held it up as his blade rested against the throat of Lady Oda no Hana, the daughter of the second most powerful daimyo in the land. Then he called out, because he could hear Lord Oda talking menacingly to Taro as they fought.*

*"Drop your sword, Nobunaga," he said.*

Lowering his sword, Taro edged toward his mentor and his love.
Hana was shaking, her eyes wide with surprise, as Shusaku held
her tight, the blade against her throat. Hiro had just wrestled one
of the samurai to the ground, and as silence settled on the clearing
like ash, he slowly got to his feet. He sent to Taro one of those
looks that only people who have been friends for many years can
use—this one said, *Are you hurt?*

Taro shook his head. *No.*

Lord Oda stood like a rabbit hearing the pad of a wolf.

"Remove that sword from my daughter's throat," he said to
Shusaku, trying to inject his voice with authority, but managing
only shrillness. "My samurai are practically infinite. This cannot
end well for you." He gestured to the forest. Ranks upon ranks of
armed men stood under the trees, like a ghost army in the mist.
They wore full armor and held swords in their hands. There were
hundreds of them.

"That depends," said Shusaku.

"On what?"

"On whether you let us go."

Lord Oda laughed, a harsh, barking sound. "Why would I do that?"

Shusaku hummed noncommittally to himself, as if consider-ing his options. "If you do," he said finally, weighing the fake ball in his hand, "I will give you *this*." He turned his head a fraction toward Taro, and Taro understood what was wanted of him.

"No!" he said. "Not the ball!"

Lord Oda smiled at him. "Ah, how we are betrayed by our teachers," he said. He turned again to Shusaku. "You will give me the ball? Just like that?"

"Not just like that. In return for you allowing us to climb up to the Hongan-ji."

Lord Oda ran his fingers through his beard. "Why shouldn't I just kill you, and *take* the ball?" he said.

"If you let us go," said Shusaku, his tone taking on a new, implacable hardness, "I will allow your daughter to live. If you don't, she dies." He pressed his blade to her, and blood beaded on the shining steel.

This time Taro shouted out "No!" without feigning of any kind. He knew Shusaku—he knew the ninja was strong and ruth-less and capable of great sacrifice in the name of the greater good. Shusaku had decided that Taro's life was worth giving anything to save, and so Taro feared that he might kill Hana, if it came to it.

Taro rushed forward, his thoughts swirling opaquely, not sure how this standoff could possibly be resolved, but wanting to get Hana away from Shusaku, who would open her throat if he had to. But Shusaku only increased his pressure, and Taro was forced to stop—there was nothing he could do to save Hana. It would take Shusaku less than a heartbeat—less than a step over the grass from Taro—to kill her.

"It would appear," said Lord Oda, "that you would be making two deadly enemies if you killed her. The boy is in love, I see." He said this in the same contemptuous way that he might say, *The boy is a coward*, or, *The boy entertains intimate relations with cattle*.

Shusaku shrugged. "If he kills me, he kills me. But he *will* be shogun."

Lord Oda still hadn't moved, and his sword lay on the ground beside him. He lowered his shoulders, resigned. "Very well," he said. "Give me the ball."

"No," said Shusaku. "First you send your men away. *Then* I give you the ball. Only when you have returned to your camp will I take my blade from her throat." He jerked his head toward Hiro. "And give that boy your sword, so you're not tempted to do something stupid."

Lord Oda didn't hesitate for long—Shusaku could tell that he was in no position to negotiate. "Agreed," he said. Then he turned to his samurai and ordered them back. Quickly they melted away, downward, into the trees that covered the slope leading to the encampment. Then he picked up his sword and walked slowly in Hiro's direction, before, on Shusaku's instruction, throwing the sword to Taro's friend, grip first.

Shusaku beckoned Taro and Hiro forward. Keeping his sword on Hana, he rolled the ball toward Lord Oda, who seized it triumphantly, grinning widely as he turned it in his hands, the Sanskrit engravings flashing in the moonlight. "It's mine!" he said. "Mine!" He turned and walked quickly back toward his camp, as if forgetting all about his enemies, or as if someone might take his prize from him if he wasn't careful. He held it in his arms like a baby.

Only when he reached the tree line did he turn. "You realize," he said, "that when you arrive on top of that mountain, you will be surrounded? We have held this siege for months. And now that I have the ball, the Ikko-ikki will be powerless to resist me." He held up the ball, a ghastly expression of delight on his face, then pointed to Taro. "Next time you see me," he said, "I'll be coming at you with an army of thousands. I give you till dawn, before I launch the attack."

"Good," said Taro. "We look forward to it."

And then, cackling and murmuring to himself, or to the ball, it was difficult to tell, Lord Oda disappeared. Taro was almost shocked at how quickly he turned his back on his daughter when he had the instrument of power in his hands—but then he had encountered Lord Oda before, and knew his capabilities. The man was obsessed with power and with winning—the cost in human lives was not important. In a way, his drive was almost admirable, almost monk-like, in its abandonment of earthly ties—though the impulse that underlaid his actions was evil.

*The ball is like a curse that has got hold of him,* thought Taro. *The idea of being shogun, too.* He could almost feel sorry for the daimyo, as he pictured the expression on the man's face when he got back to his tent, jealously guarding the ball all the while, to discover that it didn't work.

Almost, but not quite.

"You two go first," said Shusaku to Taro and Hiro, gesturing upward. "I'll follow with Hana, once it's safe."

Taro put his hands on the rock and began to pull himself up. Craning his head back, he could see the walls of the Hongan-ji, far above, and the guns that bristled on its ramparts. He half expected a shot from below, or an arrow, but none came.

On a ledge, he rested until Shusaku and Hana caught up. The color was returning to Hana's cheeks, though a thin cut on her neck was trickling blood. Taro was disturbed, but not surprised, to note that it stirred in him a mixture of pity and hunger. But the hunger he could deal with. He was *used* to it. And anyway, soon they'd be fighting Lord Oda's army, and he would have all the blood he could desire, flying around him, leaping from wounds, as if it wanted nothing more than to abandon the enemy samurai's bodies and become part of him instead.

He was almost looking forward to the attack, to the battle.

Almost, but not quite.

Lord Oda would attack before dawn, with his thousands of gunners, ranked in threes to keep the bullets coming. But if everything went according to plan, then Taro would have not only the warrior monks of the Ikko-ikki on his side, with their superior weapons, but also the true ball, and with it the control of the rain. Lord Oda would find himself on the steep slopes of a mountain, leading an army effectively disarmed by the weather.

It *could be a bloodbath,* thought Taro, feeling a queasy mixture of sickness and excitement. *But sometimes a bloodbath is necessary.*

The sun's glow was just creeping over the fields from the east, setting alight the helmets, armor, and weapons of Lord Oda's army. The sea of samurai was no longer facing Mount Hiei, but was gathered at the foot of the mountain on which Taro sat, a great tsunami wave about to break itself on the rocks.

Taro dangled his legs over the side, looking down at the vast ranks of Oda's men and Tokugawa's men, at the barrels of their thousands of guns, which from this height were visible as little pine needles in the hands of dolls. He took a deep breath. The Ikko-ikki had better guns, it was true, of the improved flintlock variety, but they were not as numerous as the Tendai monks. Perhaps two hundred of the Pure Land sect waited with Taro, along the crenellations and at the foot of the wall. As he watched, some of them looked to him—a couple murmuring words that might have been prayers, and others with black looks in their eyes.

*They blame me for Oda's coming,* he thought. *They thought they could weather a siege, but they are not sure about a direct attack. I can see why.* He was looking at those tens of thousands of samurai and thinking this was madness, and he was seeing his thoughts reflected in the faces of those Ikko-ikki beside and below him. But if *he* didn't believe he could turn the battle with the Buddha ball's help, then why should the Ikko-ikki? Faith. He had to have faith. He patted the bulge in his black ninja's trousers where the ball was, and he hoped.

The Ikko-ikki might be outnumbered, but they had something else on their side. They had knowledge, and they had preparation.

Taro and his friends had not slept at all. Shusaku had introduced Taro, Hiro, and Hana to Jun. The boy seemed nice—kind and helpful, in a slightly simple way. Taro could see why Shusaku had chosen him to be his eyes.

Right now, Jun was sitting on the parapet next to him, with Hiro between them.

"What is that you're reading?" said Jun.

Taro looked down at the scroll in his hand. "It's a story," he said. "Someone gave it to me. They said it would help me with my swordplay."

"I don't see how a story could help with that," said Jun.

"No," said Taro. "No, nor do I."

He glanced again at the massing army—it had been organizing itself for what seemed like ages now, the ranks forming and then re-forming, the horses going to one side, then the other. It was interminable, and it was frustrating. Taro wasn't anxious to die, but he hated waiting. If this was going to be his last battle, he wanted to get on with it.

Trying to distract himself, he looked down at the scroll again, and for the dozenth time he read the abbot's story.

In the dark ages, in the cold ages, there was a ravine—and in that ravine was the most ancient kiri tree in Japan, a crooked-branched king in a kingdom of rock and wood. Its upper leaves were one with the sky, trembling with the joy of their privilege as they conversed, at night, with the stars. Its roots plunged deep into the earth, around hard rocks, becoming confused in the blackness of the earth with the scales of the dragon that slept underneath.

One day a powerful wizard cut a branch from the tree—which would have resisted such an attempt by anyone less powerful than he—and made from it a remarkable harp, of which it was said that it shone in the day like the sun and glowed in the night like the moon. For many years, this harp was the most treasured possession of the emperor, but in vain did his musicians try to play it—no one could draw a melody from its strings. And if ever someone tried, all that would come from the harp were harsh, discordant noises, as if the instrument hated and disdained its player.

At last, the prince of musicians, Peiwoh, came to the imperial court. On being presented with the harp, he stroked it gently, as if taming a wolf, and drew from it a wondrous sound. He sang of nature and the seasons, of mountains and the sea, of soft-glowing stars and the soft earth. And as he sang, the memories of the tree from which the harp was made were awoken, and the people of the court were stunned to find themselves surrounded by the scents of spring, by the murmuring of a summer breeze, by the chirring of insects, the pattering of rain, the call of the cuckoo. Then Peiwoh switched key, and the room echoed with the sharp, clean sound of falling snow, the ringing stillness of ice, the beat of a swan's wings, and the rhythm of falling hail.

Peiwoh sang of love, causing the air in the room to grow sweet with expectation. Clouds scudded across the ceiling, white and beautiful against a summer sky—but trailing black shadows of despair across the floor. He sang of war, and everywhere resounded the clash of iron and the screams of dying men. The dragon that slept under the tree flashed, quick and lithe, in the corners of the ceiling.

Enraptured, the emperor asked Peiwoh his secret.

Peiwoh said, "The others failed, Emperor, because they asked the harp to accompany them as they sang of themselves. I have let the harp choose its own songs, and I did not know as I played whether I was the harp, or the harp was me."

♦ ♦ ♦

Taro cursed, and threw the scroll off the parapet, to bounce on the grass below. He was starting to think that the abbot was having a joke at his expense.

"Nothing?" said Jun, with a smile.

"Nothing," said Taro.

"Well," said Jun. "At least you have the Buddha ball. That's better than any sword anyway."

"I hope so," said Taro. And he did hope.

He looked down at the army again, to see if it had changed since he last looked. If anything, it seemed to have swelled, and then he saw why—Lord Tokugawa's flag was flying over a second enormous army, this one ranged on the other side of the stream that ran down the mountain, flinging itself over rocks in glittering waterfalls, before crashing into the plain as a meandering silver river, all its energy expended.

*Oh, no,* he thought. *The message didn't make it.*

In all the excitement, he had forgotten that *two* armies were laying siege to the Hongan-ji, not one. Lord Tokugawa was still Lord Oda's ostensible ally, and now that Lord Oda had determined it was time to attack, Lord Tokugawa's generals, or Lord Tokugawa himself, must have agreed to stand by him.

Taro turned to the monks, saw the eagerness on their faces as they clutched their new and improved guns, forged in their own subterranean workshops from the Portuguese pattern smuggled in by Shusaku. He didn't have the heart to tell them that their stand was threatened, that they faced not just the wrath of Lord Oda, but the wrath of Lord Tokugawa, too, which brought with it many more thousands of heavily armed men.

Below, a bugle sounded, and the army began to stream up the slope. Taro bit his lip, and the blood that flooded his mouth was delicious. His heart pounded in his chest as he watched death coming up the mountain toward him. But then he turned to his left and saw Hiro, a gun in his hands, and Hana to his right, also standing bravely in the face of the onslaught. He smiled. He was lucky, really. It was just a shame Shusaku wouldn't see the battle, hiding as he was below, so as not to be burned by the sunlight.

*But if I live,* he thought, *I'll tell him about it.*

Then he noticed something curious. Lord Tokugawa's men were not joining the charge. Instead it looked like . . . yes . . . they were turning away, and departing over the plain, away from the river and from their allies.

They were abandoning the field of battle.

Taro turned back to the monks, a surge of joy flowing through him.

"Today," he said, and though he was speaking quietly, he had the sense they could all hear him, "we destroy Lord Oda." It was all he needed to say.

A great cheer went up from the monks, as they took their positions along the wall, some standing behind to reload, or pass forward fresh weapons, because Taro had learned from that terrible night on Mount Hiei, and though he was still appalled by what Lord Oda's gunners had achieved, with their organized ranks, he wasn't so naive as to not adopt the practice for his own troops.

*My troops?* he thought. *Since when do I think of them as my troops?* But then he looked again at the monks, and saw the way they regarded him, reverentially almost, their eyes on the ball in his hand, and he thought, *Yes. They are my troops.*

The samurai below were getting closer—he could hear their curses, the jangle of their armor. A bullet whined by overhead, disconcertingly close. The samurai were moving with discipline, as they had on Mount Hiei—the first rank had fired, and now the second rank stepped forward, guns already primed, and let loose their shots. The range was not ideal, though, and the Ikko-ikki were able to shelter. For now. Soon, though, Oda's army would be upon them—that incomprehensible horde, many times bigger than any group of men Taro had ever seen, even the army that had attacked the monastery, and that had seemed to Taro so bafflingly huge. *They will sweep over us,* he thought. *As if they were a tsunami, and we a seaside hut made of wood and straw.*

"It's time," said Hiro.

"Yes," said Taro. He looked away from the terrifying hugeness of Oda's army and took the arrow at his feet, lowered it into the brazier beside him. The oil cloths wrapped around the end of the shaft caught light, and he nocked the arrow, then drew.

*"Now!"* he shouted. Other arrows flared beside him, and when he loosed his, a flock of burning birds followed it, arcing toward Oda's army. The arrows were few, though, and the samurai kept coming.

And then—

*Boom.* Taro's arrow had found its target, and a flower of flame bloomed in the middle of Oda's men, flinging bodies and armor into the air. The fireball was enormous, a sun in the darkness, and Taro narrowed his eyes, seeing the devastation it caused through a narrow pane of vision. Two more explosions followed, ripping through the great army of samurai, as the Ikko-ikki too hit the right spots, though several of the fire arrows simply disappeared into the dark mass of the advancing army.

Yet it was enough—Taro saw panic seize the samurai, as they witnessed the carnage wrought by the landing fire arrows. Bodies littered the ground, the ground itself torn into terrible petaled craters, black soot and earth still raining down where rain itself would soon fall. They had buried the barrels under cover of darkness, a thin layer of torn grass on top to hide them from eyes that would be fixed on the monastery above, not the ground below.

That was the thing about the Ikko-ikki. They might not be many, but they had plenty of guns. And plenty of gunpowder.

Taro leaned down and picked up another arrow. He lit it, then nodded to the archers near him, before sending it into the air. It flared as it flew, and some of the samurai scattered, all discipline lost. There were only a couple of barrels left, Taro knew, but Oda's men had no idea of that—they just saw fire arrows streaking toward them, and the bodies of their comrades beside them, where the earth had surged up in fiery explosion, or worse still the places Taro could see, close to the barrels, where there had been men and now was nothing but mangled armor and scorched earth.

*Boom. Boom.*

Two more barrels went up, and again samurai were hurled through the air, or dismembered where they stood, or simply wiped from the earth as drawings from sand. Taro looked to the Ikko-ikki, and he saw excitement in their eyes now, defiance. Lord Oda's army was not broken—there were many thousands behind the front ranks, who had suffered the worst of the gunpowder trick, but they were no longer advancing in such confident, perfect formation. Some of those who had turned to run had been impaled on the swords of their companions, and now Taro saw anger and fear in the men attacking this little mountain stronghold.

And yet, even now, the main bulk of the army continued to advance.

*Boom.*

And despite the hole torn in their ranks by the latest explosion, they continued to come, and now the fusiliers were arranging themselves in a row, lowering their guns to fire, and they were still as numerous as the pebbles on a beach.

"That's the last," said Hiro. "Time for the ball. Now, Taro. They're getting ready to fire. . . ."

"I know," said Taro. He turned to Hana, took her hand in his. "I love you," he said.

"Yes," she replied. "I love you, too."

Then he looked down into the ball and the mountainside was no longer important, or even *there*, in any real sense. He was both on it and above it, floating over the turrets and the walkways and the towers and the courtyards. He reached with his mind into the air before him, pulling water from the sea behind the mountain, massing it into clouds.

He took a deep breath, and he made it rain.

Oda, like Kenji Kira, had arranged his arquebusiers in rows of three, so that they could maintain a constant barrage of fire. As they alternated, they moved up the hill, the men at the back loading their rifles as they walked.

At least, that was the theory.

In fact, the men were not loading, they were not firing, and they were not moving, for the most part. Their guns were useless in the heavy rain, the water extinguishing the fuses that made them fire, and the matches that made the fuses burn. First the ground had exploded beneath their feet; now their rifles were useless as sticks in their hands.

Some had turned to run, only there were samurai with swords behind them, and some ran onto the swords while some were just cut down for their cowardice. Chaos reigned among Oda's troops. The arquebusiers, panicking, turned from their own samurai and attempted to run up the hill, only to be caught in a terrible squall of bullets, fired by the monks with their waterproof guns. The balls tore through their ranks, dropping them in the mud.

Rain fell heavily, blanketing the battlefield so that it seemed to Taro he was viewing it through a shoji window, imperfect and shifting. The ground, churned by boots and water, was a sucking bog.

Taro stumbled down the hillside, Hiro beside him. He had told Hana to stay on the battlements, and though usually she would have objected to being left out, to being treated like a girl, she had only nodded. She understood what he was doing—he was going to try to kill her father, and she might not stop him, but that didn't mean she would want to watch.

Ahead of Taro, the main line of the Ikko-ikki stretched across the top of the plain. Like the army below, they had formed into disciplined lines—but unlike the army below, their guns worked. They kept up a relentless pace, reloading and firing so that the volley of bullets was constant and inescapable. Even so, they had not had time to make more than a hundred guns, and the vastness of Oda's army was such that samurai were breaking through, running screaming up the hill, swords in their hands, cutting down some of the gunmen. Taro saw a wedge of armored men crash through the line, the Ikko-ikki stumbling and turning in confusion to try to shoot the attackers.

He flicked his eyes to the ball—he was its master now, could control it with the merest inflections of his thoughts. He drew the energy out of a dark cloud above, massed it into a pulsing orb, then sent it down to the ground as a searing bolt of lightning. It tore into the ground, raising a furrow of splattering mud, flinging the bodies of the samurai up and outward in a geyser of death. Hiro gasped.

"Did *you* do that?"

Taro nodded, as he continued to move.

They were surrounded by a small guard of the Ikko-ikki, armed not with guns but with *katanas*, for short-range fighting. Formed into the shape of an arrowhead, their aim was to fly into the heart of Oda's army, to seek out the daimyo in its center. Taro, like Hiro, wore a horned helmet—it bore no *mon*, for the Ikko-ikki had no respect for nobility, but it protected his head, while leaving a thin gap through which he could see.

The Ikko-ikki arquebusiers parted to let them past. Taro glanced at them, saw the concentration on their faces as they aimed their rifles and fired. It was terrifying, really, how easily the new guns loosed their bullets into the air—how the flintlock mechanism whipped round in a tight circle to ignite the spark that fired the ball. Taro had seen the older, matchlock guns in action on Mount Hiei, and he knew how long it took for the fuse to burn down, even when it wasn't raining. Seeing these new Portuguese models firing again and again, he could almost feel sorry for the dying men of Oda's army.

Almost, but not quite.

He squeezed the ball again, drawing more water from the sea into the clouds above. Somehow he was able to run down the hill while being in the clouds at the same time, a bird with no body, only eyes to see, floating up there in the heavens, a part of every raindrop and a presence in every bolt of lightning, a voice in the choir of thunder. In some sense, he *was* the weather. He was linked inextricably with the natural world around him; in fact, it was as if he could feel the beat of the men's feet on the ground, as if he was the mountain, too.

He was also, though, a young ninja, hurrying toward the most powerful sword saint in the land, praying under his breath that this time he would have the strength to kill Lord Oda, to put an end to the horror that had begun when his foster father had been killed.

Ahead, a samurai ran at the foremost of the Ikko-ikki, screaming and holding his sword ahead of him. He wore a tusked helmet, emblazoned with the Oda *mon*. Two of the Ikko-ikki sprang forward, cut him down.

"Hurry," one of them said. Taro looked up—somehow they had already closed the gap of the no-man's-land between the Ikko-ikki arquebusiers and Oda's army. Mere paces ahead of them was a phalanx of *hatamoto*, spears and swords in their hands, formed in an orderly, protective square.

*Lord Oda's retainers.*

Beside Taro, Hiro roared unintelligibly. Taro found himself roaring too.

Then, with a ringing crash, the two bodies of men met, and everything became madness. Taro staggered, swinging his sword indiscriminately, still screaming, and he saw a man's arm severed just in front of him, though he didn't know if it was his sword that had done it. He had never been in battle like this—on Mount Hiei, he had spent most of the time lying with the bodies, trembling with shock at the devastation wrought by Kenji Kira's guns. This time, he was in the thick of it.

He glanced to his right, saw Hiro bludgeon a samurai in the face with the pommel of his sword, then turn the blade to gut the man, ducking as a blow from another samurai behind him nearly took off the top of his head like the crown of an egg. *This is madness,* thought Taro. The greatest swordsman in the world—even a legend like Lord Oda—could die in a moment in a battle like this, stabbed by an ordinary dagger in the side, or tripping on a body and landing on a blade. There was no logic to it, no skill, no fairness.

Even as he thought it, he was fighting. The ball in his left hand and the sword in his right, he whirled and spun, always cutting, blocking, feinting. The Ikko-ikki were trying to maintain a cordon around him and Hiro, but it was impossible for men not to get through, and Taro buried his sword in one's man's stomach as the enemy samurai brought his blade down, two-handed, trying to split Taro in two.

The world shrank now—it reduced itself to what he could see, framed by the helmet; an oblong window onto hell, populated by sword-wielding demons and bloody corpses, carpeted with blood, rocks, and soggy earth. He felt something, a caress of air behind him, and turned to see a *hatamoto*'s sword coming down on his neck. Then, at the last moment, the man slumped forward, following his sword to the ground. The back of his head was a bloody mess, and Taro saw the Ikko-ikki arquebusier, a hundred paces back up the hill, kneeling, reloading.

*That would have killed me,* thought Taro. *It would have been just a sensation of a breeze, then death.*

He didn't dwell on it, brought his sword up to block a strike from his left, put all his strength into a counterstrike upward and sideways, saw the man's head spring into the air and fall. He thought he could hear someone saying his name but it was impossible to tell. The battle was a raucous chorus in his ears, a jangling, discordant music of gunfire, metal on metal, and screaming.

He backed into something and turned, sword spinning— stopped the blade an inch from Hiro's face. Hiro nodded, turned again, and Taro did the same—so that they were back to back, swords a blur as they defended, slashed, killed. The Ikko-ikki were pressing the *hatamoto* back—though Taro saw another band of samurai break off from the assault on the mountain and come running toward them, as fast as their heavy armor would allow. Taro flipped—one moment he was standing in the cold, wet mud, water trickling into his boots and the blood of others slick against his skin—the next he was clouds.

Drawing himself in, he paused, then expressed himself. Another bolt of lightning flashed down, tore into the samurai, and sent them—in pieces—in the four cardinal directions, a sickly, burning smell lingering after them.

For an instant the madness paused—it seemed some of the *hatamoto* had seen him look into the ball, then seen the lightning strike, and had connected the two. They backed away, swords lowering as if it was the blades that were nervous. In that moment of calm, Taro knelt and seized a man who was still alive, a terrible wound opening his belly. Taro whispered a request for forgiveness, then sank his teeth into the man's neck.

He closed his eyes and the noise and stink of the battle disappeared—there was only the hot blood on his tongue. He drank deeply, feeling the man's force enter him, taking on more life than his body should have been able to hold, feeling the man's spirit fill out his skin.

He stood, ignoring Hiro's stare, and looked around, trying to get some sense of the lay of the land. It was impossible—there was only flux, only a storm of swords and bullets. It seemed like there were more dead people on the ground than there were living people standing on it, but he couldn't tell who was winning.

Then Hiro let out a cry.

"There!" he shouted. "Lord Oda!"

Taro turned to follow Hiro's finger, saw Oda striding forward, dragging samurai in his wake, as if he were a great fish and they the minnows that swam in his slipstream. Oda was enormous, though not tall—it was something hard to explain. He seemed bigger than everyone else on the field, more alive—his armor seemed made to contain him, not to protect him; it was as if he were a monster temporarily encased in metal. A malevolence spread from him, like heat—it was as if he were invisibly on fire. Enormous horns rose from his helmet, spearing the sky.

Taro took an involuntary step backward. He had faced the man on the staircase of his own tower, had fought him hand to hand at the bottom of the cliff. But he hadn't seen Lord Oda in his element, on the battlefield, among his troops. The sight was terrible to behold. He noticed the Ikko-ikki, too, shrinking back; even Lord Oda's own samurai gave up ground, as if Lord Oda were projecting in front of him some wave of malefic energy that pushed bodies aside like driftwood.

Taro glanced down and shivered. Lord Oda held a sword in each hand, one long and one short. He'd tried to face two blades before, with Yukiko, and it had been a disaster. Taro flicked his eyes left and right, afraid.

Lord Oda's ruined right arm was held unflinching in front of him, a *wakizashi* clutched in the pale fingers.

Like Yukiko, he was going to fight with two swords.

Taro took a deep breath and willed his feet not to turn him round and run him back up the hill. He faced his enemy, the man who had ordered his foster father killed, who had ordered his own daughter to commit seppuku, who had sent Kenji Kira to kill his mother.

None of the Ikko-ikki attacked Lord Oda—they seemed to recognize that this fight was Taro's. Neither did any of the samurai continue to fight. They put up their swords, and soon there was a circle of men around Taro and the daimyo, a point of calm in the storm of the battle.

Taro looked up. Beyond, he could see Mount Hiei, and the distant Tendai monastery. The conical shape of the mountain was ringed by mist, haloed—and it shone in sunshine that didn't reach here, *couldn't* reach here, because Taro was making it rain. He glanced behind—the stronghold of the Ikko-ikki loomed gray and massive behind him. A good place to fight. He imagined his mother's grave, up there on Mount Hiei, and wondered if people would visit it, in time, if he won here.

Or if he lost.

He gripped his sword. Lord Oda stepped closer. The daimyo looked at the ball in Taro's hand, the simple glass ball with its simple globe in it, power housed in humility.

"So small and unimpressive," said Lord Oda. From a fold in his clothing he produced the gold ball, the fake one, and threw it down in the mud. "Yet I suppose there's a pleasing irony in that." He spread his hands, the twin swords stretched out on either side, like the gleaming wings of some awful insect. "Come on, then. Kill me with it. Show me its power." He pushed back his helmet, let it fall to the mud. "I am not afraid. After spending the night trying to make that golden trinket work, I'd practically welcome death right now, if I at least got to see the true ball in action."

"It doesn't work like that," said Taro. He thrust the ball into his cloak and edged forward, sword extended.

"Ah," said Lord Oda. "I suppose you think this is honorable. Well, so be it." He was standing there, and then he was in front of Taro—that was how quick it was. He brought his *katana* down, brutally fast, and followed it up with a downward strike of the *wakizashi*, almost slicing Taro's leg off at the knee.

Taro dodged and blocked, barely, grunting with effort. Lord Oda grinned, his lips drawing back so that Taro could see his pink gums, the sharp points of his canines. There was something appalling about the daimyo, a claimant to the position of shogun, smiling at him with the teeth of a vampire.

*And I did that,* thought Taro. *I made him like that.*

Just then Taro wished that Shusaku could be with him. But of course, it was Taro's fault that they were here, in the light, and Shusaku was hiding in the monastery—it was Taro's blood that had made Lord Oda like this, just as he had done for Little Kawabata, too. He had given Lord Oda this gift, this ability to transcend the limitations of his spirit nature.

At the same time, he fought. He caught a glancing blow on his helmet that would have opened his forehead if he hadn't been wearing it, and for a moment Lord Oda's blade lodged against one of the horns. He lunged forward, pushing the daimyo off balance, and slashed at his side, his blade ringing against armor. But Lord Oda recovered his equilibrium in a flash, danced back onto his heel, and then thrust with one blade, pushing Taro's sword out of the way with the other.

The point of Lord Oda's sword drove into Taro's shoulder, a flare of pain that stunned Taro into a moment of inaction. Lord Oda ripped the point out again and brought the blade glimmering down at Taro's neck—he only just got his sword up in time, blocked it with a scream as blood ran from his wound.

Taro gasped for breath. He was dimly aware of something large pushing past him, and then Hiro was throwing himself at Oda, his sword swinging.

"Die!" Hiro was shouting, over and over.

Lord Oda met the big boy's first, wild gambit and counterstruck viciously, raining down blows.

*No,* thought Taro. *No, no.*

He sprang forward, ignoring Lord Oda, and struck decisively at Hiro with his ring, aiming for the pressure point on his neck. Hiro crumpled to the ground and Taro vaulted over his body, pushing Lord Oda back, whipping his blade so fast back and forth that for the first time the daimyo struggled to meet his thrusts.

"Ruthless," said Lord Oda. "I like that."

Taro stared at him blankly, still trying to find a way to strike his heart, or take off his head.

"Didn't want your friend to have the glory of killing me. You know, if you weren't standing in my way to immortality, I could use someone like you."

Taro almost smiled at the depth of the daimyo's inability to understand. He hadn't minded Hiro stepping in—he just didn't want his friend to die, and so had knocked him out for a moment. Even now he was pushing forward, forcing Lord Oda ever farther from Hiro.

But Lord Oda was too strong. Taro misread one of his parries, got a *wakizashi* slash to the thigh as his reward. He nearly fell, but managed to stay on his feet. His shoulder and his leg were on fire. The worst thing was that he could smell his own blood, and his stomach snarled at the scent of it—even now, the monstrous side of him was threatening to take over. He saw it in Lord Oda's eyes too—saw the pupils cloud with red as the other vampire's nostrils flared, saw the bloodlust in those noble features.

He tried to get a grip on himself, to remind himself of his need for revenge, but part of him could see the dead samurais from Shirahama, and he could still feel the emptiness inside that had followed their deaths. Perhaps he shouldn't kill Oda. Perhaps it would be better to kneel down here, to lower his sword and wait for the final blow . . .

He was surprised when his sword arm snapped up of its own accord, blocking Lord Oda's strike, the clash so powerful that pain resonated down his arm, indistinguishable from sound.

"Will. You. Just. *Die*?" asked Oda, his voice a harsh whisper.

"No," said Taro.

He pulled off his helmet, widening his view, and let his sword take over. Just then he saw Hayao, behind Lord Oda. Could it be him? Or was it a ghost? Whatever it was, it was shouting at him, shouting something over and over. Taro frowned, watching the lips, his hearing ruined by the guns.

Hayao's whole posture and his expression screamed urgency; his mouth screamed something Taro couldn't understand—it seemed to be two syllables, repeated. He glanced away, to parry another strike from Lord Oda. He glanced back, and something about the movement of Hayao's lips touched something inside him, and suddenly he saw the word—

*Peiwoh.*

He thought of the story he had read for the last time on the parapet. He had thrown it away, as if it was useless. But now the whole story rushed back into his mind, and carried along on the rushing river of his memory was a thought, and the thought was that just then, his sword had blocked a strike of its own accord.

He tried to not feel his sword arm, to pretend it wasn't there. To his surprise, the speed of his strikes increased—he knocked the daimyo's sword aside and opened a small nick on his cheek. Oda bellowed furiously and rushed at him with both swords flashing.

In Taro's mind, Peiwoh's words echoed. *I have let the harp choose its own songs, and I did not know as I played whether I was the harp, or the harp was me.*

And just like that, Taro saw. It was better than when he had seen the hair clip on the ghost haunting Hayao, because that had been something that just happened, something he had no power over. It had been *sight*. This, though, was *insight*—it was understanding.

Of course.

It was so utterly simple. The abbot had said, *There is no sword.* But that wasn't quite it, was it? It was more a case of realizing that the sword did not belong in his hand, or anyone's—that it was there by a conjunction of chances, that its swordness continued nevertheless, unchanged by the hand that held it. And its sword- was at once everything and nothing, because it was only a of the universe, and all the universe was one.

not, there is no sword.

nstead—the sword and me, we are the same. We are one. the same as being nothing.

*There is no sword. There is no me. There is nothing.*

He looked down at the sword and allowed it to flash forward, then move back to his side. It was easy, because his arm did not exist, and nor did the sword. His sword wasn't even a blur, it was as if it hadn't moved at all. Lord Oda didn't even see the strike— his sword made no move to block it, and it pierced the gap in his armor at his arm pit, cut through his muscle and tendon, ruined his right arm again. The sword dropped from it, and Taro could swear that even over the thunder of battle he heard it hit the ground.

Lord Oda was staring at him with something like horror. Taro danced back, danced forward. It was like he was moving through something less viscous than air, or like Lord Oda had to fight in thick mud that just looked like clear air, while he was free to move. He saw Lord Oda's blade rise, impossibly slowly, and he could almost laugh; he had all the time in the world to step around it, to push it uselessly away, to slash again at the man's armor.

This was it, he was going to win.

He was focusing on his sword hand, or rather not focusing on it, which amounted to the same—and so for the first instant he didn't register as Lord Oda backed away from him, reached for the samurai closest to him. Then he saw the daimyo embrace the man, put his mouth to his neck, and tear out his throat. Blood fountained from the wound; Taro reeled, shocked. Lord Oda drank deep, then cast aside the corpse.

He faced Taro again, and his eyes now were black pinpricks. His sword struck out, quick as a snake, moving now in the same plane, the same medium, as Taro's.

"I'm a sword saint," said Lord Oda. "Did you forget that?" He came forward like a whirlwind, single sword matching Taro's, every blow, every strike, every thrust. The people around them had disappeared into a blurry fog—Taro thought maybe he and Lord Oda were moving so quickly the ordinary world had faded into nothingness.

He cursed. He had understood the secret of the sword, and it didn't matter—he was fighting the one enemy, apart from the abbot, who knew it too, or knew a shortcut to it. Vaguely he wondered if killing his own samurai had given Lord Oda some extra measure of strength, had been for him the equivalent of Taro's moment of enlightenment—vaguely he wondered if it depended on the nourishment of the samurai's blood and so would pass and dim, allowing Taro to take control.

It didn't matter. Lord Oda was pressing him back again, and unless his strength failed in moments, it would be too late.

Taro yanked his sword arm up to block a strike, and he was in the wrong place entirely. The other man's blade leaped at him, he barely even saw it moving, and then his chest was open, gouting blood. He went down on one knee, felt something tear inside his leg.

Lord Oda smashed him in the face with the pommel of his sword. He felt something break, sharply. He spat and teeth flew from his mouth—he ran his tongue along his gums and felt the spaces where the teeth had been, gaping and pulsing holes.

Just as he perceived a booted foot, it struck him in the chest, drove him backward. He felt his ribs splinter, cut their way into him, his own body turned into treacherous knives in his flesh. The only way he knew they hadn't pierced his heart was because he could still feel the pain, or rather he was dressed in the pain, it was like an outfit encapsulating his whole being. His jaw throbbed, his chest seemed full of broken glass.

He heard someone screaming, and he thought maybe it was Hiro. He supposed his friend must have woken up. He saw Hayao's face floating somewhere in front of him, was still not sure if the man was real or a ghost. His hand shaking, his vision blurred by tears, he raised his sword. With a shuddering impact, it was knocked from his hand—he just saw it spinning and landing in the mud.

*Don't . . . give . . . up,* he thought. He conjured a vision of his mother, to strengthen him. Of Hana, waiting for him. He let himself fall to the ground, began to crawl toward the sword. Every movement cost him dear in pain—every movement ground broken bone into flesh, severed nerves. He felt as though he were already in hell.

His vision, now, had shrunk even further. Instead of the window of the helmet, he looked out at a circle of pale light, an image of mud, darkness encroaching all around, the sole object in all the world his sword, shining in the wet mess ahead of him. He could not tell if it was near or far—he thought maybe one of his eyes had been ruined by the pommel blow, and it could have been just in reach or many *ri* away and he wouldn't know the difference.

Still, he crawled toward it—he was a low thing, a slug or a snail, crawling over broken glass.

He reached out, and his fingers brushed something. He saw them, in the tiny circle of his vision—strange, foreign white fingers, touching the pommel of his sword. If he could just grip it, try to stand . . . only his fingers didn't seem to belong to him anymore, they didn't want to grip.

Then the boot came down—*crunch*—and Lord Oda's foot was on his hand. He felt the delicate bones in it break, felt his hand turn to a mushy bag full of shards.

Lord Oda kicked him in the chest again. More ribs broke and he was on his back now, the clouds above, rain falling in his eyes and blurring his vision even further. He felt rough hands on him, searching him, saw the ball in Lord Oda's hands.

"Ahh." Lord Oda sighed —the sound of bliss.

Taro blinked, trying to clear the water from his vision. Hiro had stopped screaming, and certainly he was nowhere to be seen. Taro didn't know if that meant he was dead, or if he was just being restrained by the Ikko-ikki. The gunfire, too, seemed to have stopped. Perhaps they'd won, and the Ikko-ikki were simply allowing Taro his final battle with Lord Oda, before they slaughtered the remaining samurai. Or perhaps the opposite had happened.

Lord Oda loomed above him, a giant in the limited frame of Taro's vision. He had the ball in one hand, his sword in the other. He addressed the ball.

"Make him die. Kill him."

Nothing happened.

Lord Oda frowned down at the little globe in his hand. "Why doesn't it work?" he asked softly, and Taro wasn't sure if he was speaking to him or to the ball.

"I told you," he said, in the voice of an old man—all shaky and sibilant where his breath ran over his missing teeth.

Lord Oda roared, and cast the ball down in the mud. He brought his sword up high. "In that case, I'll just cut off your head," he said. He brought the blade whistling down.

At the same time, Taro's hand—the one that wasn't shattered—was scrabbling through the mud, almost entirely of its own accord, clutching for something. He wasn't surprised when his fingers closed on a smooth shape and he had the ball in his hand again. Well, it seemed he'd die holding it.

He closed his eyes. His last thought was, *Please stop the blade. Please don't let it hit my neck....*

Silence. Then, distant, a scream of rage.

Odd.

He was dead, clearly. Except that death smelled strangely of mud and blood, also a bitter scent, richly organic and decaying— perhaps the smell of a man whose guts had been opened.

He opened his eyes. Quivering, just above his head, was the blade of Lord Oda's sword. Lord Oda himself stood straining, his face red with effort, a bottomless fury in his eyes. It was as if he were trying to move the sword, and it wasn't letting him.

Taro frowned, then dropped himself into the ball, leaving his agonized body on the mud, sighed with relief as he left the pain behind.

He was outside himself, now, he was just weather and atmosphere; and he turned his entire focus on Lord Oda, trying to understand what was happening. He looked down on the scene from above, and saw that the Ikko-ikki had won; the arquebusiers were standing in silent triumph over the bodies of the dead samurai. Only those in his immediate vicinity still lived—and as soon as his fight with Lord Oda was over, they would die too. Even as he watched, he saw that Lord Tokugawa's army was taking to the field now, coming up on the straggling remnants of Lord Oda's troops from behind, catching them in a pincer that would crush them utterly. He understood that Lord Tokugawa and the Ikko-ikki intended to make sure that every single one of Lord Oda's samurai was dead.

There would be no prisoners.

*He's going to die, whatever happens,* thought Taro. *His army is destroyed. His only chance was the ball, and he doesn't know how to use it. Now it's only a question of whether I kill him, or they do.*

He contemplated, for a moment, whether it mattered to him how Lord Oda died—certainly he was no longer motivated by revenge, no longer thought in any way that by killing Lord Oda he could cause his foster father or his mother to rise from the dead.

But then he saw Hiro—his friend was standing, held back by three of the Ikko-ikki, as if he had been trying to reach Taro, to save him. There were tears on his cheeks and his eyes were red, but his mouth was open in an expression of wonder, and indeed everyone seemed frozen, staring intently at the sword that trembled, unmoving, above Taro's head.

The temptation was there, of course, to leave himself forever. To melt into the rain and the clouds, and let his husk of a body die. But there were those tears on Hiro's face, and there was Hana, leaning over the parapet of the monastery, trying to see what was happening—distance was nothing to him now, and he was beside her as soon as he thought it, was the rain in her hair and on her neck. He could see the love in her eyes.

He was the love in her eyes; it was for him and from him—he could see that now.

And he would not leave her.

Purposeful now, he turned his gaze—and his gaze encompassed everything, so it wasn't so much a case of turning as of adjusting what he was looking at, the level of granularity, and he was looking down on Lord Oda, *into* Lord Oda. He was interested in how he, Taro, had managed to stop the sword only by wishing for it to stop. Before, at the Tendai monastery, when he had tried to control anyone else he had found it impossible.

There was a flicker inside Lord Oda, like a candle flame in darkness, or a lick of fire inside a brazier. He narrowed his gaze. Then the flicker came again and it was beating, he realized, with his own heart.

*Whoosh-boom, whoosh-boom, whoosh-boom.*

*Oh, gods,* he thought.

He extended his spirit to the flicker and felt it pulse back, leaning, as if to rejoin him.

*It's me. The flicker is me.*

He understood then. He had turned Lord Oda into a vampire; it was *his* blood that had changed the daimyo and given him his power—so there was a part of Lord Oda that was forever Taro.

In that moment, it was like a shoji window was torn down, and light came pouring in. Taro saw other flickers inside Lord Oda, candle flames, other spirits—for that was what they were—and these ones did not beat in rhythm with Taro's heart. They were victims, people killed and drunk by Lord Oda, and there were many of them, their blood coursing through Lord Oda's body along with his own, imprisoned, unhappy.

He'd known he could see ghosts, of course—he'd saved Hayao that way, he'd been haunted by his own mother. But he'd never thought to look *inside* a person for them, to delve into their being. Lord Oda carried the men he'd killed in his own blood—Taro had just seen him do it, take the whole life force of a person, kill him and drink his fill. It must have given him great strength, but it had made him a vessel, too, for the spirits of others.

It was a weakness.

Taro didn't know why, but he shifted his focus again and took himself under the monastery, and into the cells. He had an idea that when he was in the ball, ordinary time stopped, and so he had no concern for his neck. He peered down at Shusaku, the ninja sitting anxiously on a cushion, awaiting news of the battle.

Yes—there. Inside the man's heart he felt the same flicker—not all around the body, for Shusaku did not drain to kill, he attempted to feed without murder. But there were ghosts in the ninja's heart, yes. Taro reached out to them and shivered, as he understood something. They were *not* ghosts, not in a certain sense, anyway.

Shusaku kept them there, Taro realized. He thought the ninja had held the men he'd killed tight to him, drawn them into him, making his heart a tomb for his ghosts, feeding his own guilt.

*All evil done clings to the body,* Taro thought. It was something Shusaku had told him. But now it seemed to Taro that it was Shusaku who was clinging onto his evil, or what he thought was his evil—that Shusaku was inviting the dead to share his body, was killing himself with shame and guilt, wadding it into his heart as powder is wadded into a gun, with consequences that would be just as lethal, if slower. They were not haunting him. He was keeping them in him.

Taro reflected that if he survived this, he would need to tell Shusaku. To encourage him to let go of what he had done, and to set himself and his ghosts free.

Then, he allowed himself to rise again, and he gazed down once more at the field of blood and at Lord Oda, a small figure now in the center of it, frozen in an attitude of anger. He knew what to do now. He couldn't use the ball to command another's body, but he could move his own body, that was something even a child could do; and he didn't need the ball to see ghosts, that was an ability that he had possessed all along.

*I never needed the ball to defeat him,* he thought with wonder. He could have killed Lord Oda from the other side of the battlefield, if only he'd been able to see how simple it was.

He prepared to re-enter his body, not wanting to because of the pain, but knowing that he would eventually have to, or be lost to the rain and the sea and the drifting clouds.

Before he did so, though, he let something click in his head and took control of his blood that was circulating in Lord Oda's body—it was his, and so it was in his power to command. Momentarily he wondered whether Shusaku knew he had this power over *him*, over Taro—whether Shusaku had ever sensed his own life force in Taro and known it would still obey him. He wondered if *any* of the vampires knew. The consequences, the ramifications, were terrifying. . . . He could tell Little Kawabata to jump off a cliff, because he had turned him, and his blood beat in the other boy's heart.

Later he would ask Shusaku, and find out if he knew. If he did, then Taro was grateful—grateful that the older ninja had never used this ability to control him, even when he was behaving hot-headedly and stupidly.

Calmly he asked the flickering spirits within Lord Oda a question, and they answered him silently. He wondered why they had never rebelled before now, but he thought maybe Lord Oda's spirit was too strong, was subduing them in there, and it took the spirit of the boy who had made their jailer a vampire to help them overcome their bounds.

He slid back into his body.

And then he asked his blood, and the blood of Lord Oda's victims, to leave Lord Oda.

There was a moment of tense compression, a hollow moment, as when the diaphragm has expanded and air is just about to fill the lungs—then blood sprang from Lord Oda's eyes and his ears and his mouth, and then a heartbeat later he exploded; blood was flung into the air with the force of a fountain, and it was pattering down, soft percussion on the ground and a gentle hiss on armor and blade, and it was one with the rain that Taro had called down with the ball, clear water and red blood mingling in the air, running together in the soft mud and coursing away in twisting rivulets, snakes of liquid that carried Lord Oda's life away in all directions, in tiny particles, to end one day in the sea.

Lord Oda's sword fell, and it would have struck Taro's neck, only somehow Hiro had gotten away from the men holding him and he caught it, by the blade, the cutting edge sinking into his flesh, so that some of his blood joined Taro's, and Lord Oda's, and that of the men whom Lord Oda had killed.

For just a moment, Taro thought he heard voices, only they

weren't voices, they were people speaking somehow in his mind, only they weren't speaking, they were simply conveying something of their essence as they left this plane of existence. He was aware, somehow, that one of the men who had helped him kill Lord Oda had been a peasant and a bandit, and that Lord Oda had torn out his windpipe with his teeth, in a wooden building in a forest—and that was just one of the stories he knew.

Holding tight to the ball, he closed his eyes. He heard Hiro shouting to the Ikko-ikki, telling them to help lift him, and he heard the clang and scrape of fighting, too—presumably the monks dispatching the last of the samurai.

Well, let them. Right now he just needed to sleep, and mend. There'd be plenty of time for looking at things later, and moving, and doing all the things that people do.

He'd hug Hiro. He'd go to Shusaku and tell him what he'd seen, tell Shusaku to forgive himself. He'd kiss Hana.

But all that would come later.

Later.

*Kenji Kira could not believe his luck when he saw the girl run past him, through the trees. She hadn't even seen him—she'd been so busy crying, which he thought was pathetic. She wasn't even armed, and a small part of him regretted that he would have to do it like this. He would have liked some resistance.*

*Of course, she didn't fail to see him just because she was crying. She wouldn't* expect *to see him, would she? He was dead, after all. She'd killed him herself.*

*No. He would be the last person she would expect to see.*

*He would be the last person she would see.*

*Kenji Kira moved quietly through the trees. He had no sense of smell, now he was dead, and so he did not know if his clothes were giving off a foul odor. He thought they probably were. He had rotted, after all. His body had lain on the mountaintop for a month, he supposed—he'd seen the smoke from the biers the day after he escaped, and bodies were usually burned one month after death, on the first auspicious date.*

*One month of rot. His flesh when he'd returned to his body was loose, bruised-looking. After he'd gotten far enough from the monastery—leaving a monk dead on the ground behind him—he had stopped to examine himself. He had pressed his fingers into his left arm, and he had been surprised and horrified when the nails broke through the skin, and pushed through to the bone beneath—the consistency of his body was that of boiled rice.*

*At first he'd screamed. A deer had gone leaping off into the woods before him, and he had sunk to his knees. He'd escaped the battlefield in hell, he'd followed Taro out of death. But he had not escaped the corruption. Something inside his arm burrowed away from his probing fingers, something white and squirming, and he screamed and screamed and screamed.*

*He'd wanted to be stone, he'd wanted to last forever. He'd always feared this stinking mess that was death.*

*But then, as he kneeled on the forest floor, a thought had come to him.*

*He'd pressed his fingers into his flesh—right into his flesh—and it hadn't hurt. Surely it should have hurt? But then, he was a living thing in a dead body. He wasn't sure if any of the usual rules applied.*

*Experimentally he pushed his fingers in farther, seized a handful of muscle and fat and skin.*

*And he pulled.*

*There was no pain.*

*Now he stalked through the woods in his funeral clothing, but only the white garments covered his bone. He had flayed himself—had torn the stinking soft stuff from his skeleton, leaving the hard smoothness beneath. He'd started with a leg, pulling all the wet and soft stuff from it, to leave only bone. He'd wanted to see if it would still move, with no muscle to animate it. And, to his surprise, it had. It had moved just fine. Concentrating, he had applied himself to the rest of his body. It had taken a long time.*

*The organs, in particular, were tricky.*

*He'd kept the clothes—had put them on in case anyone saw him. At a glance, from a distance, he would appear an eccentric in white, flowing robes. Only closer up would the observer see that he had no skin on his face, that he was nothing but a skeleton walking. He hadn't finished the job yet, of course. He'd torn off what he could, scraped with stones and sticks found in the woods. But to clean himself properly of his body he would have to rub himself with sand, bathe in the salt water of the sea.*

*That was all right. He had all the time in the world.*

*He saw a flash of Yukiko's clothes ahead—she was moving quickly, but she was no match for him. That had been another surprise. He'd only meant to strangle that monk, back on the mountain, and he'd near taken the man's head off with his bare hands. Being in hell had made him strong.*

*He pressed the pace, flashed through the trees, a nightmare in white clothing. Idly he wondered why Yukiko was alone, where she had left her sword. He didn't really care, though. She'd killed him, and now she was going to pay. He may have gotten what he'd always wanted, but revenge had to come first. He saw Yukiko stumble; recognized the moment at last.*

I am stone, *he thought.* I am bone and I am incorruptible. I have sloughed off my covering of vile flesh. I am reborn, and I am beyond the betrayal of living things, the weakness of the flesh, the depredations of low creatures. Nothing will ever feed on me.

*He lunged forward and caught Yukiko's ankle in his hard fingers. She went sprawling. To her credit, there was still some of the fighter in her—she sprang up, and though she didn't have a sword, a branch seemed to appear in her hand, so quickly did she pick it up.*

*She stared at him, and then she screamed.*

*"What—what—what—?" she stammered.*

*"Don't you recognize me?" he said. "This is how I always looked . . . underneath."*

*She was backing away. It wouldn't do her any good. "Ken . . . ji . . . Kira?" she said.*

*He bowed. "At your service. You know, when you put that sword through my heart, it hurt. It hurt a lot."*

*He was looking into her eyes, and so he saw the exact moment her mind snapped—it was like the darkness in her pupils suddenly became not just a darkness but an emptiness. He recognized that emptiness. It was the true face of hell, under the illusions it conjured to torture you.*

She knows she's dead, *he thought.*

*He leaped forward and caught her, and his bony fingers closed on her throat. He wished he could smell, because he was sure he would smell pure fear, in this instant. He pressed hard, and as when he had squeezed his arm, his fingers broke through the skin, scraping on tendon, brushing against her spine with a noise like heaven as he shook her, shook her, shook her.*

*Her eyelids fluttered. Her legs kicked—he was holding her right off the ground, and he wasn't even aware of the weight. Then, the strangest thing. He could swear that, just before she died, she smiled.*

*He saw her lips move, though no sound came out—he had crushed her voice box and her airway, had felt them break brittle beneath his fingers, as if they were the bones of a small, delicate creature, a rabbit perhaps.*

*"Heiko," she seemed to say. He remembered that was the name of her sister, whom he had killed.*

*Well, perhaps they were together now. It seemed unlikely—he was fairly sure Yukiko was going to hell. But if it had helped her in her final moment, then so be it. He had no power to enter her mind and remove any comfort she might find there, as he had scooped out his own innards.*

*More was the pity.*

*He had heard people say that they felt empty after taking revenge, but that wasn't the case for him. He looked down at her dead body in his hands, and he laughed and laughed, and then he dropped her like a child's doll to the ground and he capered around her, dancing in his glee.*

*He didn't smell her blood, exactly—but he was aware of it; keenly aware of it, as he imagined a wolf must be, when it came to the spoor of prey. He hadn't known until now what was required of him, what was needed to maintain his hardness of stone, his beauteous absence of useless flesh.*

*But it seemed right, all the same, and he made no conscious deci-sion, he just crouched by her side. He tore open her ribs, reached inside, and ripped out her heart. All his life he had been afraid of things feed-ing on him when he was dead. Then he had died and things had eaten him in hell, and he had followed Taro back to the living world.*

*Now he was dead but alive, and it seemed like to stay that way, he had to eat the living; he had to become the thing he most feared, to become a maggot or a rat or a crow. He appreciated the irony—he appreciated it almost as much as the joy of Yukiko's death.*

*He raised her heart to his lipless mouth and squeezed it, and blood ran down his throat and through it and soaked into his bone, and he laughed as he fed.*

*Lord Tokugawa was enjoying a cup of steaming sencha tea when a messenger appeared in the doorway of his private teahouse, a charmingly rustic structure on the beautifully tended grounds of his castle, its shadowy interior a cool and calm retreat from the phenomenal world, with its rivalries and battles and deaths.*

*He raised his head and sighed. "Yes?" he asked.*

*"Two pigeons for you, sire," said the messenger. He approached, bowed deeply, then kneeled, the two rolled-up pieces of paper on his hand, his head held low so as not to meet Lord Tokugawa's eyes.*

*Lord Tokugawa lowered his cup and took the messages. "Go," he said.*

*When the irritant footsteps had retreated, he finished the cup of tea. It was, like everything else, an exercise in patience and control. Drink the tea, and then read what the messages had to say. It was thanks to these moments, these constant challenges to his own self, that he had been able to secure the position in which he found himself. Slip up for just one moment, allow emotions to cloud his actions, and he could be destroyed.*

*He could end up like that fool Oda, who by now—Lord Tokugawa hoped—was dead. He anticipated that one of these messages would bring him news of that death, but he was in no hurry. He wanted to savor the moment.*

*Finally he set the teacup—a gorgeous and ancient Chinese object, chased with golden dragons, which had been presented to him by the Portuguese merchants—aside. He slowly unrolled the first message.*

The boy has the ball, *it said, and it was signed by the abbot of the Tendai monastery on Mount Hiei.*

*Lord Tokugawa smiled. Everything was going according to plan.*

*Then he unrolled the second message, and smiled even wider. It was from Jun, and it said that Oda had attacked the Hongan-ji, as Lord Tokugawa had known he would. The monks had slaughtered the samurai with their swords, and Lord Oda himself had died in some fantastical manner—Jun reported that some witnesses claimed to have seen him burst into pieces in front of their eyes, spraying blood everywhere.*

*The ball, no doubt.*

*He made a mental note to send a reply to Jun, to thank him for the news, and to ask him to stay with Shusaku and his son, to await further instructions. He was pleased with the boy's performance. Ever since he had contrived to have Shusaku take him on, Jun had kept him faithfully informed. He would reward him one day, when this was all over.*

*He called out for someone—it didn't matter who, there would always be someone, waiting just outside, impassively, for the time when they would be called to do their duty—that was one of the advantages of being a daimyo.*

*When a head appeared at the door, he said, "Bring me the generals." The head nodded, bowed, then disappeared.*

*He leaned back on the cushion, granting his spine an unaccustomed break from erect rigidity, and allowed himself to feel one moment of pure peace and happiness.*

*Everything had fallen into place, and the prophecy was unfurling as he wished it to do, like a bolt of silk rolled across a smooth wooden floor.*

*He allowed himself a moment of self-congratulation. He had read the signs and researched the legends, and gone to Shirahama one day in search of the woman who would give him this son, this shining vampire son—and now it was all coming together as he had hoped.*

*The boy, Taro, had the ball.*

*Lord Oda was dead.*

*The end had begun.*

## ACKNOWLEDGMENTS

Thanks, as always, to the fabulous team at AP Watt literary agency—Caradoc, Elinor, and Louise. Thanks are also due to Alex Cooper at Simon & Schuster and Sarah Norman at Atlantic for their brilliant and insightful comments on the earlier drafts of this book. It would be a far, far poorer novel without them. Finally, thanks to Valerie Shea for doing such an extraordinary job of checking through the manuscript, picking up on all the things I had written that flatly contradicted my statements in Book 1, and pointing out the many errors and inconsistencies. By the time the book arrives in your hands, dear reader, it is (one hopes) relatively free of mistakes and satisfying in its structure—so you will have to take my word for it as to what a sterling job these editors do. I'm extraordinarily grateful.